The
Hum

The
Hum

An Extraordinary Journey of Awakening

Lee Mothes

The Hum
An Extraordinary Journey of Awakening

ISBN: 978-0-9765804-4-7
Library of Congress Control Number: 2014904434
First edition: June 2025
First revised edition: May 2026

Oceans and Dreams Publishing
425 Dixon Street Kaukauna, WI   54130 USA

www.oceansanddreams.com
www.newisland.net
Instagram: @leemothes

Other books by Lee Mothes:

The Hum – Episode One, Gordy
Oceans and Dreams, 2024

The New Island Guidebook, Third Edition.
Oceans and Dreams, 2023

Lee Mothes, An Artist's Journey to Nevermore.
Oceans and Dreams, 2014

To my family

**Vicki, Katie, Ali, Maddy
and
Brother Dave**

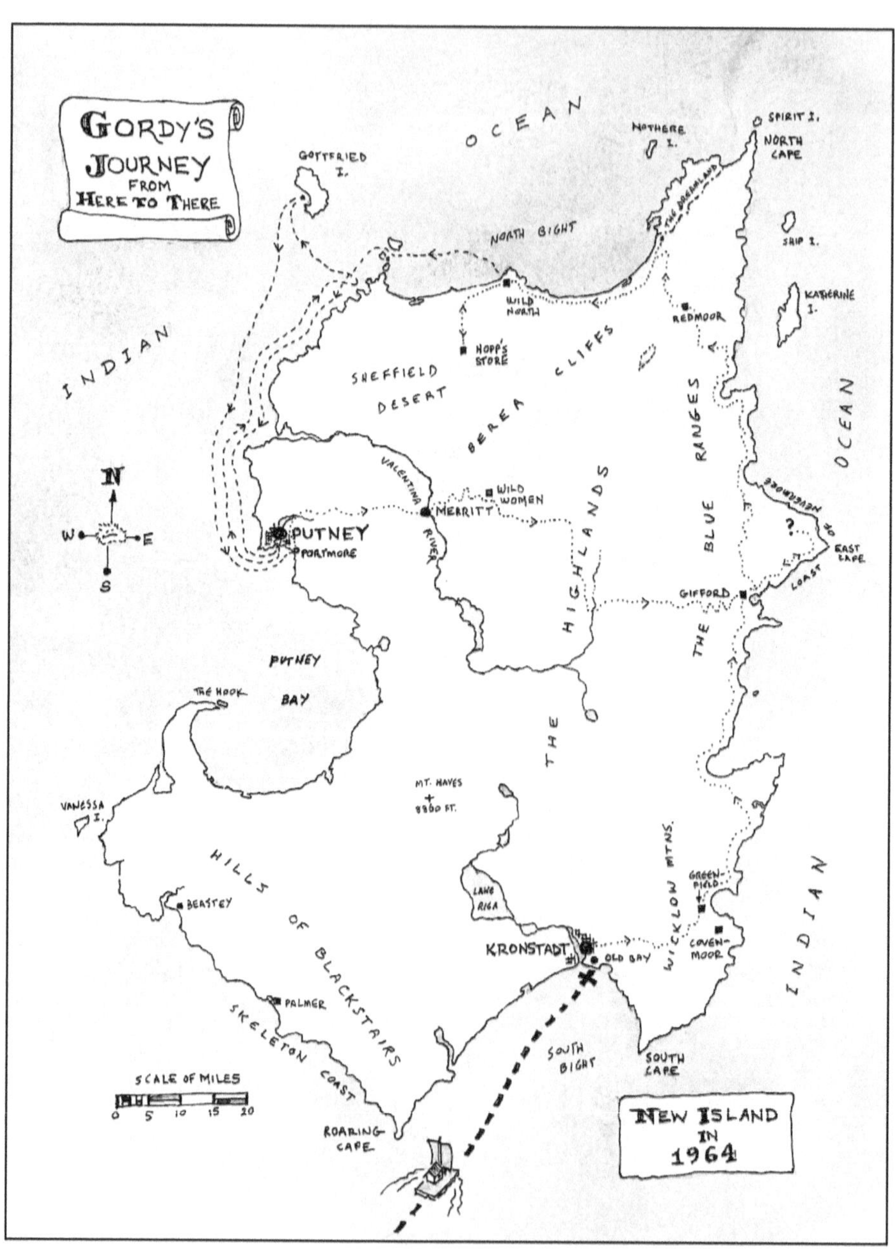

It all began as a dream.

Contents

Hmmmmmmmm…

PART I

GORDY

Earth Shocks May Send High Water to California Coast

SAN FRANCISCO, May 22 (AP)—The Coast Guard tonight said a tidal wave may hit the California coast as a result of tides generated by the Chilean earthquake.

A spokesman said it should reach the Coast possibly late Monday. But since the tide will be going out at the same time, water may only rise 2 or 3 ft.

In May of 1964, this warning of a tidal wave appeared in the morning paper.

Most of the kids in our neighborhood, including me, couldn't wait to get out of school, run out to the beach, and watch it. Luckily, our impulse wasn't fatal, because the wave was quite disappointing. It was more like a fast tide coming in, hardly noticeable in the choppy surf.

*

A week later, a very real nightmare plunged me into a dream that still might be happening. I'll never know for sure. In the dream, a much bigger tidal wave, now called a tsunami, was about to crash over our entire town.

But my friend Mr. Barnes had built a raft that would save me.

And I *really* needed his help.

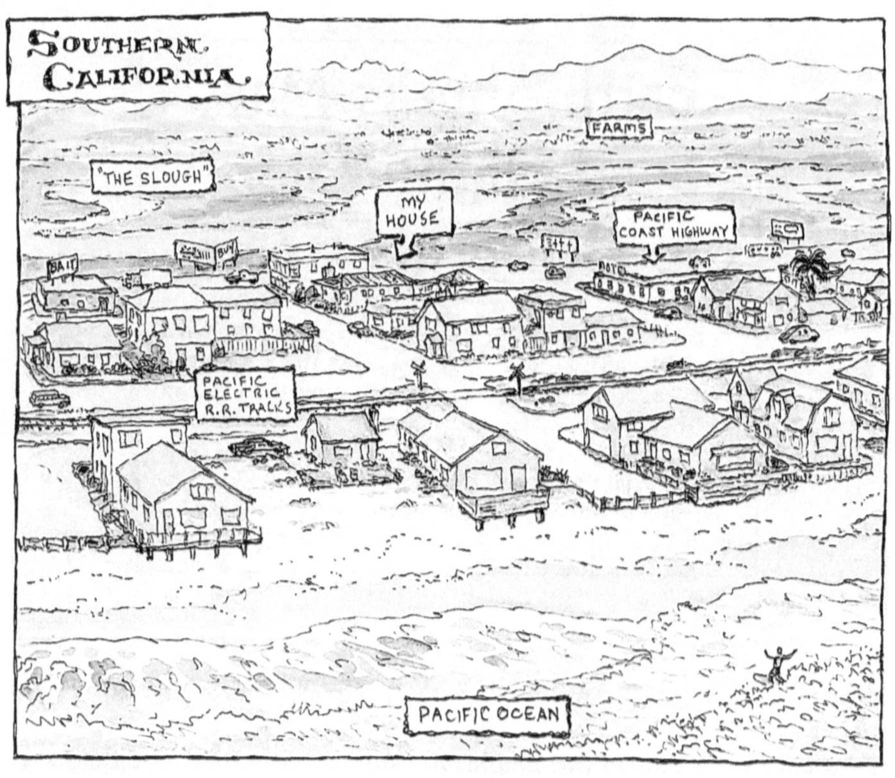

This is where I grew up.

SHOCK DREAM

"Hey, twerp!"

I was in another world, reading one of my comic books. Scrooge McDuck had just triggered an ancient Incan booby trap deep in the Andes.

"Hey, twerphead, listen up!"

Thwick!

My brother Ricky liked to get my attention by thwicking his finger at my head. It kinda stung.

"I have to go out," he said. "There's hamburger and stuff in the fridge, so make your supper just like I showed you, okay? And you know what to say if Mom asks anything, right?"

"Okay, Ricky. Jeez."

After he left, I rubbed my head at the irritation. Ricky's mention of hamburger, however, inspired thoughts of supper. Stiff from sitting for two hours, I got up, pulled some ground beef from the fridge, shaped up a fat patty then fried it over a high gas flame, sending greasy smoke through the kitchen. I opened a can of sliced peaches, put the blackened patty on a plate, grabbed a fork, and took the plate and the can with a spoon in it to the dining table. This time I opened a *Superman* comic book.

So began another long evening when Mom was at work and Ricky was supposed to 'babysit,' even though I was fifteen. Watching after me was still Mom's rule, and *no one* argued with Mom.

Ricky had graduated from high school last year, and his social life was everything. The last thing he wanted to do was hang around with his little brother, so he let me watch TV in his room if I promised not to tell. Though he was annoying sometimes, he didn't hit me or yell at me like my dad, Leon, used to do. Ricky was okay.

I lived in my own world by reading comic books or drawing pictures of imagined disasters. I sometimes read other books, too. I often hung out with my neighborhood friends, but I avoided most of the kids at school, which was a six-mile bus ride away. All I really wanted to do was wander along the beach and be left alone. I was sometimes bored, but it felt safe that way.

I was in my head a lot, but I was *not* 'slow'.

Sometimes when I was alone, this strange sound happened. It was a soft humming, like the buzzing of a million bees or that soft echoing sound of a choir in a cathedral. It would swirl around me, in stereo, sometimes soft and sometimes loud. During its visits, I felt comforted in a way I still can't explain.

I began to call it The Hum.

*

Mom has been raising us on her own since Leon left us several years ago. She worked nights in restaurants, leaving just after we came home from school, and not returning until around two a.m. the next morning. She seemed to enjoy her waitress jobs, and sometimes threw all-night parties for her friends at work, which I heard were pretty wild.

She also loved to 'express her creativity' as she said it, and had built a side business decorating handbags. When demand grew, she opened a gift shop for a while, but her profits rarely exceeded her expenses, so she closed her shop and returned to her old waitress job.

She seemed to shut down after that, and when I look back, I should have paid more attention to her, tried to cheer her up or something. After closing the gift shop, she became quiet and moody, spending her free evenings in front of the TV drinking a smelly wine called Thunderbird. She made us supper, but didn't say much beyond asking me, "How was school?" She hardly spoke to Ricky at all.

Once, when I saw tears that she couldn't quite hide, I asked her what was wrong, and she gave me a level look. "It's my business, Gordy, and I need to deal with this on my own." She said this in a low voice that also warned, *Don't push it!* Though self-absorbed in my own world, I could tell something was very wrong. I should have helped her more, tried to get her to talk.

*

A week after that tidal-wave-that-didn't-happen, Mom snapped.

She had somehow found out that Ricky was skipping out instead of watching after me. She was off from work that night, and by the time she had supper ready, she was red-faced and slamming plates. The room was buzzing with her fury, and I knew not to say a word. I also saw the empty bottle of Thunderbird in the trash.

Ricky ambled into the kitchen, probably following his nose.

"Siddown!" she said.

He stopped, looked at us, then slowly sat at the table.

"Now tell me exactly what you were doing last night when you were supposed to be watching your brother."

Ricky glared at me as if I'd told on him, then looked down and stammered, "I, uh, had things to do, and I made sure he was okay…"

She was breathing heavily as she fumbled to light a cigarette. "You went out to the Rendezvous Ballroom with Cindy, didn't you? And don't deny it because someone I know saw you there."

"Well, yeah Mom, but…"

She cut him off. "I'm sick and tired of you leaving Gordy alone while I have to work. I know this has been going on, so don't look at me like I'm stupid."

"But Mom, I was…"

"Don't you say another word! If you're not going to help out, then *get* out. You're nineteen now, so find your own place to live, get a job, do *something!*"

Visibly trembling with anger and hurt, Ricky sat a moment, then stormed out, slamming the front door.

Mom took one long breath, stubbed out her cigarette, and without looking at me whispered so quietly I could barely hear it… "I'm going to bed."

I sat there holding my fork, stunned—feeling only a soft buzz tickling the back of my consciousness.

*

Despite his calling me Twerp and his thwicking thing, I liked Ricky. He was funny sometimes, and on slow evenings when he 'babysat', we would go to the beach and build things in the sand. I felt bad for him getting yelled at, but Mom was probably right—Ricky didn't seem to be doing much other than surfing, drinking beer with his friends, or seeing his girlfriend.

But why did Mom have to be so *mad* at him all the time?

Trying to forget what happened, I turned on the television and stared at whatever shows came on. Hours later, toward midnight, my numbness was overcome by that strange buzzing again, that something wasn't right. Why did she go to bed so early?

On my way to my bedroom, I decided to look in on her. As soon as I nudged her door open, something smelled weird. I saw her lying face down on her bed, then the pills, and then our names on an envelope and I began reeling. The world was tilting fest, and my whole body began to shiver, then buzz with something like the hum-sound I'd heard.

Stumbling across the hall to my bedroom I went into a free-fall with all the alarms going off. My buzzing body turned into rubber as I crashed onto my bed.

*

The next thing I knew I was calmly standing in front of our house, in the dark, like nothing had happened. Then out of nowhere my friend Mr. Barnes appeared, carpenter tools and all. In a breathless voice, he said, "Gordy! A tidal wave, a big one this time, is on its way! I built this raft to protect you. It will take you to the other side. Now move!!"

Once he said that, the raft appeared out of the darkness. It was complete with a big square sail and a tiny hut, and was almost blocking the street. A lawn chair bolted to the deck seemed to say, *sit here!*

This was all happening so fast!

I climbed aboard, sat in the chair, and gripped the flimsy armrests. This was beyond my comprehension. Was I actually going somewhere? I looked back on the street for Mr. Barnes, but he was gone.

Then I heard more hum-sounds almost like movie-theme music at the beginning of a long journey. That seemed like too much! But Mr. Barnes was right, water from the ocean began surging onto our street.

But as it began to move, the raft seemed to know something. I held on tight to the chair while it easily carried me over the roiling water. I only looked straight ahead—I didn't want to think what was happening to our neighborhood!

Once out at sea, the raft veered south, as if powered by more than the wind. It also sped along quite smoothly, as if it was floating slightly above the swells and chop. I just sat there, shivering and stunned.

The ocean had calmed, but I stayed in the chair just in case. The star-filled sky was clear, with a half-moon shining over the shadowy coastal hills. Luckily, the night was warm enough and I stopped shivering, but I was exhausted and somehow dozed off.

The next morning I was still in the chair, still on the raft. *This dream isn't over!* As soon as I awoke to a glorious warm sunrise, a terrible sense of loss immediately grabbed me. What drove Mom to do what she did? And why did Mr. Barnes, a neighbor that I visited sometimes, build this raft for me?

And why is this happening?

I cautiously stood up, feeling stiff and wobbly. The raft's deck was still heaving and when I tried to stretch I almost fell over. Suddenly thirsty, I turned to the little hut. Inside it was a built-in bunk next to a tiny kitchen and a storage locker. Inside the locker I found fresh water in jugs, bottles of juice, a pile of fresh bananas, and cases of cans and packets marked "US Army."

Water! Food!

After downing some water and a banana, I also noticed a stack of brand-new comic books and several issues of *National Geographic Magazine*. On top was a folded map of a large island. A note attached to it said: **STUDY THIS!**

Okaaay…

*

I'd been riding the raft for about five days when I found a weird sort-of TV screen the size of an Etch-a-Sketch. Why hadn't I spotted it before? When I pushed a little slider switch on its edge, I was startled when a map of the Pacific, Atlantic, and Indian oceans instantly appeared, lit up like a color TV. A blinking red light seemed to be telling me the raft's progress, with an odometer-thing adding up the miles. Right now I was, let's see, already off the coast of Ecuador…

Ecuador? *Whoa!*

All I could do was accept this journey, or whatever it was. Sitting in the tied-down chair, I continued to marvel at the mysterious power of this raft as it gracefully slid over the broad swells. When the ocean was calmer I could read my comic books, though I spent a lot of time, as if mesmerized, looking at the hazy South American coastline slowly passing by.

And I wasn't alone. Sometimes curious fish and breaching whales passed close by, and birds often perched on the hut to check out this strange craft, or maybe just rest. At night I often stayed up to watch frequent fiery displays of stars, the Milky Way, and distant fuzzy galaxies I'd never seen before.

Galaxies? Without a telescope? I had to rub my eyes and look again, just to make sure.

In the following days, those coastal hills became huge hazy mountains—the Andes! Sometimes the raft moved in close, and I could see buildings, towns, and occasionally traffic moving along a coastal highway. Once the raft passed very close to a big fishing boat. I waved, but they didn't seem to see me.

So maybe this isn't real?

About a half-hour later though, a very fast naval patrol boat flying a big flag appeared out of nowhere and began chasing the raft! Someone shouted through a bullhorn in Spanish, then English, "Heave to and prepare for boarding!" Afraid they might try to shoot at me, I dove into the hut. But the raft was fast, and they soon gave up. I later wondered if the fishing boat had alerted them, and I didn't answer their radio calls – no radio! I also realized I couldn't stop this raft even if I wanted to.

This _must_ be real…yes?

Further south, and several days later, bitter winds began to blow in off those mountains to my left. The raft was now off the coast of Chile, according to my TV map. Luckily, I found extra pants and sweaters neatly folded in the locker. Remembering an old geography lesson, I realized it was almost winter here—snow was thick on the distant peaks. I huddled in the hut to stay warm, but boredom pulled me outside just as the raft entered the icy Strait of Magellan—the blinking light had moved that far.

Though the air was freezing, the wind had calmed as the raft turned east through the winding Strait, then northeast, and away from any more coastlines. A few islands named 'Falkland' and 'Gough' slipped by in the distance. I was in the Atlantic!

Day after day the raft skimmed over the open ocean. The weather slowly warmed again. The wildlife visits tapered off, and I fell into a delirium of loneliness and boredom. But then, more comic books and a few new *National Geographic* magazines mysteriously appeared in the locker, along with more canned goods and water!

While sitting on my lawn chair and reading a *National Geographic*, I spotted a cloud-capped coastline that was apparently the southern end of Africa. But the raft didn't stop. I was amazed at how determined this thing was to get to wherever it was going.

I sat through more long days, but they were slightly less boring thanks to the new magazines and comic books. By now I was back in my tattered sweatshirt and old shorts, stiff from salt-spray. My hair had become shaggy and salt-crusty as well. The TV map said I was now crossing the southern Indian Ocean, almost in a straight line toward Australia.

How was this accomplished?

A few days later I was in a panic—the screen had begun flickering, and the last time I looked at it, the odometer-thing said I had already traveled over 16,000 miles!

When the TV map failed, I felt lost, *really* lost, especially when I couldn't find any batteries or whatever to keep it going. But the raft kept up its steady course toward the east—by now I'd learned to read the sun and the stars. *Maybe I'll see Australia soon...*

Then came a change. After all those breezy, sunny days, a chilly, blustery wind blew up from the south, and quickly turned into a violent storm. The rain, salt-spray and the pitching deck forced me into the hut. While I huddled and braced myself on the bunk, canned goods crashed and clattered inside the locker. What a racket!

After an hour or more of this, the raft began to lift and drop, bobbing over what felt like huge swells. An ominous and frightening roar grew louder—the thunder of crashing surf. I was approaching a beach!

Then the raft was tumbled by a huge wave. The hut caved in and everything went black.

WASHED UP

I woke up feeling sticky, hot, and disoriented, and something told me this wasn't Australia. My mouth and hair were full of sand, and something was crawling on my head. When I opened my eyes, all I saw were big red crabs, pincers aloft!

I jumped up to shake them off, and immediately barfed up a ton of seawater. Yuck! I stumbled further from the reach of the waves and flopped down once more, but I couldn't ignore the sun burning my skin. Though dazed and terribly thirsty, I forced myself to sit up.

Where am I? Did I actually sail here all the way from California? Or just dream it? Then I tried very hard *not* to think of how all this started.

I looked out on a broad sandy beach under a blue sky—the storm was long gone. Behind some sand dunes were a few blocky houses backed up by green bushy hills—but no people anywhere.

The rolling surf and screeching seagulls made this feel like the beaches back home. But nothing else made sense, and maybe this was why my head was throbbing.

But I was alive! And weird dream or not, this all felt quite real.

A few yards away I spotted the remains of the raft, its sail tangled among its broken planks, and what was left of the tiny hut. What a mess. But the sturdy food locker was still intact and firmly latched. I managed to pry it open and dig around for something to drink. *Ahhh,* there was a single unbroken bottle of orange juice under some soggy comic books. Gulping it down, I sat on the sand again, trying to comprehend it all…

Okay, I'm on solid ground, but where?

The orange juice tasted wonderfully of home. As I finished it off, six tall, furry ring-tails seemed to float behind some beach grass. Several heads popped up. Lemurs! A whole family of them sauntered past me, then settled down about ten feet away, grooming each other and chattering, as if I wasn't there. I'd read an article about lemurs in one of the *National Geographic* issues on the raft. This was all too crazy—their antics were delightful and made me snort my orange juice.

I was still admiring their wide-eyed faces when a growling engine-noise grew louder from the direction of the houses. The lemurs were gone in an instant! A green jeep-truck roared up and abruptly stopped.

Two men in uniform jumped out—soldiers! One of them barked, "*Stoyat!*" or something like that. He then shouted more strange words while his partner pulled out a wallet and pointed to his I.D. card.

In the rush to get on the raft, I'd left my wallet at home. I hunched my shoulders—*Sorry*! They looked at each other, then one of them pulled a black pistol from his holster and waved it at me with a kind of up-and-down motion. I figured he meant either "Stand up!" or "Hands up!"

Uh-oh…

I slowly set my juice bottle down, fumbled again to my feet, and raised my hands. My mind went blank—nothing happening except what was happening. The fellow with the pistol nodded to his partner, who approached me slowly, like I was an alien or something—maybe I was! He patted me all over, just like cops frisking a bad guy on TV. He looked back, shaking his head.

The other fellow kept his gun on me as he motioned to his partner to poke through the nearby junk. From the locker the guy soon held up my damp comics and magazines, and the folded paper map, which flopped open in the breeze. Luckily, the ocean-map-screen was nowhere to be seen.

The two men looked over the big road map, then at me, chatting excitedly.

Who are these guys? Why are they doing this? What did I do?

As they marched me to their truck, my legs felt wobbly from weeks of just sitting on the raft. When I tried to ask them what was happening, the gun-wielding soldier angrily said, *"Molchat!"* His partner was already speaking rapidly into the truck's radio.

When he finished, they wedged me between them on the long front seat and ignored me, except for that pistol pointed at my side. The truck made quite a racket, like it had no muffler.

From the beach, we bounced over some railroad tracks, then pulled onto a road that led us past those blocky houses. Minutes later we were roaring into a big town, a city almost, beside a broad harbor. I was amazed to see so many cargo ships and what looked like navy ships with their big guns. The streets were busy with carts on bicycle wheels, pedaled by skinny-but-muscular men and women, dressed in shorts and colorful sleeveless t-shirts. We passed more green military trucks and a few buses, but I saw only one car, a big black thing with 'fifties fins and little red flags mounted on the front fenders. I was nearly frozen with terror, but these things *were* pretty cool.

At the edge of town the truck approached a guarded gate. After a brief talk with the sentry, who studied me closely, we made our way up a broad, landscaped hill.

We finally stopped in front of a massive yellow building that looked out over the harbor. A big red flag flapped briskly atop a tall pole in front of the entrance. Then I remembered from my world history class—*That's a Soviet Union flag!*

Near the main entrance, food vendors were setting up their carts. The wonderful smells made me suddenly ravenous! "Hey, could I maybe get something to eat? I'm really hungry and…"

"*Nyet!*"

I guess that means *No!*

At the doors, three men dressed in snappy white shirts and dark blue pants were there to meet us. This must have been arranged from the talk on the truck's radio. I was guessing they were navy sailors. Without a word, one of them handcuffed my wrist to his in one smooth move. Pointing to the handcuff, he barked sternly at the patrol soldiers before sending them off. He and another sailor escorted me into the building and the third carried off my comic books and the map like they were precious gifts.

We took many turns through long hallways, getting looks from anyone passing by. With my raggy sweatshirt, no shoes, and wild sandy hair, I'd gawk too.

The sailors ushered me into a small windowless room, uncuffed me and quickly left, slamming the heavy door. While walking away, the two talked and laughed in rapid Russian, their voices slowly fading. Then it was eerily quiet, except for the ringing of a distant telephone.

I stood there stunned—no thoughts, no feelings, nothing.

I finally looked around. The room was painted a sickly green, and lit by a single naked bulb. It was furnished with a thin-mattress bunk, a table, and one chair. In a corner sat a large white pot with a lid on it. On the table I spotted a pitcher and a single tumbler made of thick rubbery plastic—water! While downing nearly all of it, I looked through the tiny door-window. Nothing moved in the empty hallway except someone's knee next to the door. A guard must have arrived and was likely sitting in a chair. All I could see was his jiggling knee.

I had to pee. I looked at the covered pot, but I didn't want to do something wrong and get into more trouble, so I held it and flopped on the bunk.

*

"*V stavat'!*"

I had fallen into a dead sleep. The guard was standing over me, motioning me to get up. The two sailors were behind him, and as I sat up, the same guy efficiently cuffed me to his wrist. Still only half-awake, I was marched back toward the front of the building.

We soon approached a glowering woman who was waiting beside an ornate open door. She ushered us into a large paneled room with a view of the harbor, and motioned me to stand in front of a stern-faced forty-something man, sitting at a big desk, his gaze fixed on me.

I stood before him trying hard not to flinch. His neatly trimmed beard and crisp uniform made me even more conscious of my bare feet and grungy shorts.

I looked down, shaking—I really had to pee.

"Vnimaniye! Smotret na menya!" The man said. *"Ya Zevnikov Sergei, komendant etoi bazy."* His booming voice reminded me of Leon's, but without that *you will soon be annihilated* edge.

The woman barked, "He is saying, 'Attention! Look at me! I am Sergei Zevnikov, Commander of this base.' I am his secretary. Do you not speak Russian?"

I looked at both of them and nervously shook my head. I was sweating now!

Sergei-the-Commander then fired off a string of questions in Russian, which the secretary quickly translated.

"What is your name and nationality, young mister? Are you American?

Who are you working for? Who sent you?

How did you get here? By what route?

Do you know where you are?

What is your name?"

"I, um…"

"Otvechat! Answer!" they both shouted at once.

"Uhh, Gordon Love."

"Louder!" barked the secretary.

"MY NAME IS GORDON LOVE. I live in California, I came on a raft across the ocean, and I don't know where I am!"

The secretary translated this, then she told me, "Do you know, Mister Love, that you were found in a, what is the word, *restricted zone?* We also found American literature and a forbidden map." She pointed to the map that another sailor was holding up. "Where did you get this?"

"It was, uh, on the raft."

Sergei said something more to the secretary, and she announced to me, "Under Soviet military law, you are to be detained in our guest-lodgings. You are under suspicion of espionage for the American government."

Whoa…a *spy?*

"Now, if you have anything more to say that would enlighten us, say it!"

I can't hold it!

Pee dribbled down my leg, creating a dark bloom of wet on the carpet. The sailor I was handcuffed to took one look and edged as far from me as he could. The secretary's eyes went wide, but the Commander didn't flinch. He looked at me without expression, then at the stain growing on his carpet. He shook his head and nodded to the waiting sailors.

Miserable in my chafing wet shorts, I was briskly escorted back to my 'guest lodging'. Nothing was offered to help me clean up. The guard-in-the-chair quickly opened the door, waited, just as quickly shut it, then sat down again. I could hear his keys jingling to the rhythm of his jiggling knee.

I fell onto the bunk and curled up into a ball.

I'd never felt so embarrassed.

Nor so alone.

I must have slept again, because the next thing I knew, I was hearing a very different female voice. She was talking to the guard in a mix of Russian and a strange melodic English. The English parts sounded wonderful!

The guard opened the door, and a young woman walked in carrying a steaming tray. I was stunned by her small stature and countless freckles. She might have been twelve except for a much-older look in her eyes, plus a hint of attitude. She knew things!

As soon as I smelled the food, I realized how hungry I was, but the guard stopped her. He slowly lifted the cover and looked closely at the tray, taking his time. He finally took the fork and the butter knife, leaving the spoon. *"Nyet, Nyet!"* he said, waving the confiscated items at her.

She nodded solemnly while looking at the floor, then rolled her eyes at me when she bent down to hand me the tray.

But when she looked *into* my eyes her expression changed to some kind of intense recognition. I couldn't look away.

"I'm Janie," she finally whispered. "And you smell like pee!"

When the guard barked *"Poshla von!"* she winced and snapped back, "Okay! I'm going."

The guard, a sour-faced fellow with a military buzz-cut, watched Janie as she walked out, his narrow eyes following her a little too long. He gave me a leering wink as he left. What a sleaze.

Once the door clunked shut, I dove into the meal—sausages, potatoes, and some kind of hot wilted greens, all of which were gone in no time, even the slimy greens.

Hours later, a taller, frizzy-haired woman brought in another tray. She stood by while a different guard, older and more easy-going, inspected my meal. This time it was a big bowl of soup smelling of cabbage, plus another chunk of bread, and a spoon on a rough paper napkin. He returned the tray without comment.

When the woman set down the tray, she looked at me like she was inspecting my eyeballs. This was quite unsettling, since her left eye seemed to wander on its own.

What is it with these eyeball stares?

She then left without a word.

*

As the light dimmed in the hallway, I realized it must be getting dark outside. At least I wasn't hungry anymore, and I decided I'd better use the covered pot for my business. A handy roll of toilet paper was hidden behind it. As I was finishing, the ceiling-light went out, leaving only a glimmer shining through the little door-window. All I could do now was sleep.

Next morning, the taller, wandering-eye woman returned with my breakfast tray. After the guard's inspection, she moved up close to hand it to me. Her brief smile turned serious as she quickly jabbed her finger at the napkin under the spoon. Then she was out the door, followed by the guard.

When I spread the napkin on my lap, I was surprised to find handwriting on the inside layers. So that explained the finger jabbing. I quickly refolded it and glanced at the door-window to see if anyone was looking in. No one. I ate my meal, all of it, then I sat on the covered pot where I wouldn't be seen.

The note said:

Hi -

I'm Louise. Janie and I want to help you. We think you are aware of the Hum. Do you hear it? It's a deep sound that sometimes swirls around you. It often sounds like singing, and sometimes it's loud.

We have known the Hum to be a gift only Islanders can possess, but we've both seen Hum energy in your eyes! My teacher, Roselin, studies Hum phenomena and will definitely want to meet you.

We have heard rumors that you are an American spy. We don't think you are a real spy, but they probably won't release you until the American and Soviet governments stop meddling with each other, and that might be a while.

I know certain procedures that will help get you out of here. Would you be willing to come with us? If <u>Yes</u>, leave your water cup upright. If <u>No</u>, put it upside down. We really want to see it upright!

PS: Keep your napkin but tear off this part and eat it.

Eat it? *Ick.* But I did.
The Hum!
So they hear it here!
And I like how they use the same word I use. No one I knew back home has ever heard it, and my friends at school laughed whenever I told them about it.
Now my brain was running everywhere at once and I began shaking with thoughts of what might happen. Would the Russians keep me here indefinitely? Would they torture me to make me say stuff, like in the spy movies? Or just 'eliminate' me? Would this stupid Cold War ever end?
Crap!
I'll definitely leave the cup up!
And who is Roselin?
I must have dozed again because I was startled when the heavy lock clunked open. The younger one, Janie, appeared with a tray of cabbage soup again, but at least it had some of that tasty sausage in it. She gave me a wide-eyed look, nodded to the napkin, then quickly left as the sleazy-guard's eyes followed her. Folded inside was another note...

Hi –

At the end of the day on Friday (this is Wednesday), Louise will deliver your supper. When she returns to collect your bowl, she will set off the alarm system on the entire base, so be ready! They will think it's an air-raid by the Americans. They drill for this all the time, so what will happen is this: All the military staff will go into the basement bunkers, and all the civilians, like us, will be ordered to leave the base as quickly as we can.

Louise will then distract the guard with her 'procedure'. If it works, she'll take you out a back door to my uncle's pedivan. He delivers the meat to the base cafeteria. He and I will be waiting there for both of you.

We don't know if this will work. Louise thinks it will, and I hope she has practiced enough! If the guard locks the door, it's all off.

Be sure to eat this!

-J

Yessss!

Janie and Louise continued to deliver my meals, but they ignored me—no eye contact, I suppose to not arouse suspicion. I still felt they would help me on Friday, but I became desperate for even a wink! The napkin-messages had also ceased.

The endless hours between meals were mind-numbing. The same distant telephone rang once in a while, and I sometimes heard people talking in Russian in the halls, but it was all soft muttering. Loudspeakers occasionally echoed announcements, in Russian and in a strange Russian-English, I suppose for the local civilian workers. By listening I learned a few Russian phrases, like *nyet* means "no," *da* means "yes," *Molchat!* means "Shut up!," and *Poshla von!* means "Get out!" because the guards said that a lot.

I was never summoned to answer any more questions, nor was I told what would, or might, happen to me.

On Thursday morning I looked through the little window and the jiggling knee was no longer there.

This was feeling creepy.

What did I do to be here? Was this all my fault? I must look like a hopeless dweeb, and I know I smell bad. What if Janie's plan doesn't work? What if they change their minds?

Aaack!

The door-lock clunked open, and the sleazy guard followed Janie in as she handed me my breakfast. He was ogling her behind again, and I think she knew it when she gave me a brief *we're-still-with-you* smile.

Aahh…a shred of hope.

She quickly left.

Smile or no smile, I had to do something to stay sane, so I began to think about stuff…

Leon.

It was hard for me to call him Dad.

Before he left for good he was rarely home, and he constantly intimidated me when he was. He fought with Mom a lot, and that scared me even more. Ricky described how, as he was going to sleep, he often heard Leon and Mom through the wall talking and laughing while drinking something called highballs. Sometimes the laughter would turn into loud arguments that we could both hear, and their yelling and screaming terrified me.

"You make me so GOD DAMN MAD," Leon would bellow with that deep bullying voice of his. Mom would shriek back at him in defiant response, but I could hear the fear in her voice.

On those nights I wanted to be gone.

Then there was the incident in the backyard when I was six. I was building stuff with wooden blocks when I heard Leon shouting at Mom in the house. Something crashed, and he stormed out the back door in a red-faced rage. He grabbed an old board meant for firewood and furiously swung it against our brick barbeque, sending pieces flying. Then he grabbed another…

I was sitting on the ground only a few feet away, frozen in place, hoping he wouldn't notice me. Luckily, my eyes were shut tight, because a sharp piece of a board smacked my head so hard I was stunned. I didn't feel much pain, but when I touched the place and saw the blood on my fingers, I screamed with the certainty Leon was finally going to kill me.

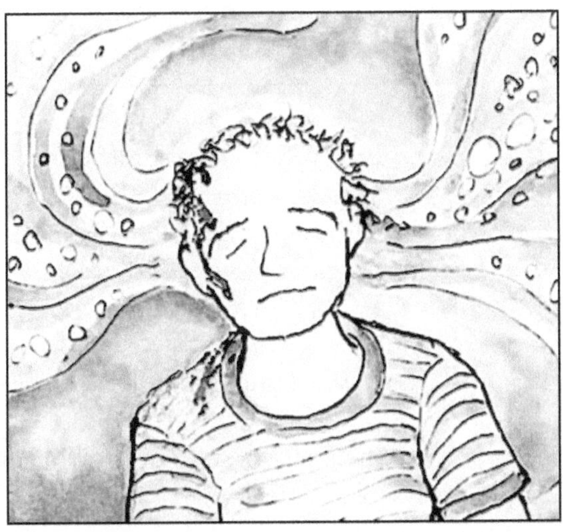

That was the first time I heard the Hum. The sound dissolved my panic, then seemed to carry me off to another place, a kind of different reality! I don't know how long it lasted, but when it was over, Ricky was sitting next to me on the back steps, looking very relieved when I focused on his face. I'd never seen him so worried. When I could stand up, he took me into the bathroom to clean up my bloody head.

Leon and Mom were nowhere in sight.

Ricky.

Ricky is Ricky—sometimes kind and caring, sometimes a brat, but he's usually okay. I didn't mind when he snuck out in the evenings, because then I could watch my favorite TV shows. He showed me how to make burgers or tacos for supper so he could get away earlier to be with his friends.

Ricky has his ways, though. When he's in a foul mood, he likes to call me 'the mistake'. He swears Leon said those very words once during an argument with Mom. My problem is that I've come to believe that's what I am to my family—a *mistake.*

Mr. Barnes.

He's just a neighbor, but sometimes I like him more than I do my family. Is that weird?

I first noticed him when he was building his house, all by himself! I was eleven then and fascinated that someone could do this, instead of merely buying a house. But because he was a man, like Leon, I was a little afraid of him, and I didn't want him to notice me. But I was so fascinated I had to stop and watch.

Of course, he *did* notice me, and one day he called out, "I'm Eddie Barnes, what's your name?"

"Gordy," I said, looking at the ground.

"Pleased to meet you, Gordy. Come on in if you'd like—just watch out for the wood scraps and nails everywhere."

When I looked up at him, he seemed friendly, and not in a creepy way. He moved with an easy sort of grace, and his dark hair was unusually long at a time when crew-cuts were the thing. He wore a special belt for his tools and nails, which clinked and rattled as he moved about, and I liked the red pencil he tucked above his left ear.

It became a habit to stop by his place after school. I probably asked him a thousand questions about how to build a house, and he patiently answered them. When I asked about his tools, he stopped and showed me how to measure a board, how to use his handsaw to cut it, and how to hammer nails. I was enthralled.

I finally told Mom about Mr. Barnes when she was talking about rebuilding our rotting back steps, a project even beyond Ricky's skills. At first, she looked at me hard. "You've been visiting this man at his *house*? You don't know him! Did he touch you anywhere? What if he tries something…" She and I had been through this before about men in general, but she never explained what the 'something' was.

I told Mr. Barnes about the steps, and he came by, introduced himself, and told Mom he would fix the steps for free if I would help him. She suddenly decided he wasn't a potential creep after all.

It took me a while to accept his friendship. Why would he want to hear anything *I* had to say? Yet his open look told me he was willing to listen, so I began telling him things I never talked about with anyone else.

One day he was nailing up plasterboard when I told him my dad had left without a trace. Mr. Barnes kept working, but I could tell he was upset. "That man was a damned fool to leave you. A kid needs a dad," he said.

Later, I felt brave enough to ask him, "Did you have any kids?" (No). "Were you married?" (Yes, once, but not anymore.) He stopped nailing and added, "I think I married too young, and I wasn't yet ready for kids. But my wife, Jen, really wanted a family so she eventually found someone else who wanted one. That ended our marriage, and now she has four kids, two dogs, and an overbearing husband I can't stand."

Then, pausing, he looked right at me and said, "You know, you're the kind of boy I'd be proud of to have as a son, and I mean it! I can see you have a lot on the ball, whether you realize it or not."

His words made the hair rise up on the back of my neck—a wonderful giddy feeling.

But why did he put me on that raft? Did he send me here?

Ricky again.

I've been growing fast. When the gym coach at school measured me recently, he announced, "Five feet, ten inches." With a quick glance he added "You're ahead in your growth, Love." In the mirror, I could see the changes…muscles! And new hair growing on my chin, legs, arms and…other places.

Ricky noticed this too.

Just last month he asked out of the blue if I had a girlfriend. (No!) He went wide-eyed, like he was shocked, then settled into the role of Wise Older Brother. He explained *The Look.* "Girls may look at you like you're a total spazz, or just ignore you, but down inside they really want to be *kissed.* They want to be *luuuved.* Do you get what I mean?"

I stared at him.

"Okay, here's how it works. If a girl is interested in you, she'll give you *The Look.* The Look tells you what she *really* wants, even if she doesn't know it yet! Your job, my man, is to recognize that look, then plant one on her, and she'll melt in your arms. If you don't, she'll just move on to the next guy."

"You mean *kiss* her?"

"Yeah," he grinned, "kiss her right on the mouth with all you've got."

"Is that, uh, how you got to know Cindy?"

He hesitated. "Well, she actually planted the first one on me at the beach last summer. It works both ways!"

Ricky's counseling only intensified my curiosity. So, what does The Look *look* like? One day at school Jody Jones looked at me in a funny way that triggered some weird feelings—was *that* it?

My own feelings of longing and loneliness, combined with Ricky's twisted wisdom, set me off on a whole new quest:

I wanted a girlfriend.

Okay, I've wanted a *friend* forever, but I've never trusted guys, nor even really liked them, so that leaves girls.

But how?

My first problem was that I looked like a dork. My pale freckly skin never tans, and my roundish eyes inside my roundish head earned me the term 'bubble-eyed fathead', though only from Ricky so far.

My second problem was that I couldn't imagine approaching a girl, even Jody Jones. What would I *say*? What would we *do*? I was also paralyzed with the certainty that any girl would laugh, walk off, and tell all her friends how weird I am.

And what is *luuuve* anyway? Is it what Ricky does with Cindy? Kissing and hugging a lot?

I had the feeling I was missing something essential here.

*

Voices in the hall brought me back to this ugly green room, and it was still Thursday! I obsessed (again) about what the Soviet Navy might do to me. For a while I played with the idea that they had other more important stuff going on, that I'm just a minor inconvenience, and they'd let me go.

Or, they'd just kill me to get rid of the inconvenience!

They can do anything they want!

Unh! Not good. My only thread of hope was with Janie and Louise. Would they be able to help me?

For some reason I didn't hate these Russian guys. I suppose I would have done the same thing to me if I was them. But I don't understand any of this—the Communist Bloc, the Domino Theory, the Iron Curtain, The Bomb. This stuff was always in the news, and my social-studies teacher talked about it constantly. It's scary, and all for what? I just didn't get it.

I was hungry again, and I stank.

I wish they would let me take a shower.

I wish I had my comic books, or something to draw with.

I wish I wish I wish...

Sand was still falling out of my hair…

ZAP!

*I*s this finally Friday?

My little row of bread crumbs on the table said it was. The cup was up. I was thinking about suppertime already, and Louise and Janie's 'event' was still several hours off. Worry and dread were getting so bad I was shaking again.

Will this even work?

Footsteps! Is that Louise? No, too early. Now I was sweating and shivering at the same time. I sat up and drank some water, then lay down again, got up, paced around the room, tried to bring up more memories, couldn't think of any, flopped down again.

Is this what *stir-crazy* means?

When the lock finally turned, I sat up so fast I was dizzy! Louise held out the tray for the guard's inspection—soup and bread again. She blinked at me with a straight face which I took for encouragement, then she left.

A half hour later she returned as usual to pick up my tray. She looked a little thick around her middle. Once she was inside the door, she turned fast and snapped her fingers at the guard to get him to look at her. Once he focused on her eyes, she shot him a stare that must have drilled straight through his brain.

He froze!

She then shut her eyes tight, creased her forehead in a funny way, and twiddled her fingers in every direction.

A brief, intense *squeeel* shot through my head followed by piercingly-loud alarm bells echoing through the building. The loudspeakers soon began to bark commands in Russian, then English:

This is not a drill! Report to your assigned shelter! All civilians must leave the base at once! Repeat, this is not...

Uniformed and civilian workers burst into the hallway, hurrying past my open door. Sailors carried heavy bundles of what looked like files, and one was struggling with a yapping terrier. This looked real!

The noise apparently awakened our guard, who looked wide-eyed at me, shoved Louise aside, and bolted from the room, slamming the door behind him.

"*Shite!*" hissed Louise.

"Uhh, maybe it's not locked..." I said.

She tried the handle—very slowly—and the door opened!

"*Eeee—yay!*" she squealed, then quietly pulled it almost shut.

As the commotion continued outside, Louise quickly unbuttoned her smock. She pulled out a pair of almost-new shorts, a large button-down shirt and a pair of sandals.

"Quick, change into these."

As I pulled my old clothes off (with no thought to modesty) she pulled a hairbrush from a hidden pocket and furiously attacked my shaggy hair. Though it hurt, I didn't complain, as yet more sand came out. She told me to stuff my old clothes inside my oversized shirt. Then she said, "You *really* need a bath!"

Before I could agree, she cracked opened the door enough to look up and down the now-quiet hallway. Then she said, *"Now!"*

I was so scared I could only follow her through endless empty hallways, my new sandals squeaking on the waxed floors. She led us through the now-empty dining room and the huge kitchen to a large exit door. "Okay," she said, "so far so good!"

She pushed the door open. Outside was a loading dock and the rosy evening sky. Sirens were wailing but I hardly heard them—I was so overcome by the sweet smell of eucalyptus and the lovely just-after-sunset glow.

Fresh air! Sky! Trees!

Louise hurried us to a boxy tricycle-truck similar to those I saw on the jeep-ride into town. Janie and an older guy hopped off to meet us.

"I thought ya'd never get 'ere," the man said. "Now, both a' ya climb in the back, an' no talkin'! Janie and I will take yer to me place o' business."

His melodious accent was appealing, though difficult to follow. He helped us climb into the cramped cargo-box and tied the flaps. It was a snug fit and the ripe smell of old meat assaulted us!

We were soon bumping over an uneven street. After a moment, we slowed to a crawl, heard a sharp voice off to the side that said, *"Idi! Idi!"* and we were moving again.

"Gate sentry, whispered Louise. "That meant 'Go! Go!' I think we made it!"

Through the back streets of Kronstadt

After jostling and bumping over more rough streets for what seemed an eternity, we finally stopped. Janie opened the flaps. "Welcome to the MacEvoy Meat Company," she said.

Her uncle unlocked his shop and led us beneath garlands of various sausages hanging everywhere. Large chunks of beef filled a long display case. It all looked kind of gross. We entered a bigger room crowded with cutting blocks, meat grinders, and knives in racks. All was silent at this hour. He led us into a small office in the back and switched on a desk lamp.

He looked me over.

Janie finally said, "Meet uncle Norbert. He agreed to help 'cause he doesn't really care for the Russians."

"To start, I'd like to know yer name," said Norbert.

"I'm Gordy, er, Gordon Love," I told them.

Norbert offered his hand, "Hullo, Gordon. My niece here told me about yer, ah, predicament. I'm going to trust her when she says you're not a spy. I'd say ya look a bit young fer that line o' work."

I stared at them. "I'm really, really glad you got me out of there, but I'm wondering why you did it…and where am I?"

Norbert looked at Janie and Louise, then at me again, closely. "I helped them because Janie told me she saw the Hum in yer eyes." Seeing it for himself, he then seemed to relax.

"You have a gift, Gordy!" said Janie. "We Islanders have heard the Hum since our ancestors first landed here over 150 years ago. We understand the sound has something to do with a kind of energy focused on our Island. We have a lot of questions about this, but so far our most brilliant minds have come up with very few answers."

"Okay, but I still don't get why you did it."

Louise almost shouted, *"You are the first non-Islander we know of who hears the Hum!"* Janie and Norbert nodded in agreement, and they all looked at me like I was some kind of weird specimen.

Finally, I said, "So I'm on an island…?"

"Yes," said Norbert. "You've arrived on the Commonwealth of New Island, located in the Southern Indian Ocean. We usually refer to it simply as 'the Island'."

Whoa! Such passion.

Norbert continued. "Now I'm very curious as to how you traveled here, given the apparent difficulties. Are you actually an American? Were there others with you? Did someone send you?"

I took a breath. "I'm from California, and I was alone. When I think about it, though, my friend Mr. Barnes *might* have sent me here, but I don't know why. He was there in the beginning of my dream."

Silence.

"You had a *dream* about being sent here?" Norbert said thoughtfully.

Then Janie gave me a wide-eyed impish look that I would see many times. "This is utterly fan—*tas*—tic," she said. "Do ya think yer still, ah, *dreamin'*?"

I took a deeper breath. "Something bad had happened to my mom, and I kind of blacked out—straight into this dream about being swept out to sea on a raft. The raft kept going for weeks and weeks, and it crashed on a beach near here in a storm. I know it sounds impossible!"

I felt like an idiot, but I had to add, "The raft seemed to know where it was going."

Norbert, Janie and Louise exchanged looks, then Norbert said, "Excuse us a moment." He motioned Janie and Louise out of the office, shutting the door behind him.

*

While I waited, a calendar titled *Islander Festivals* caught my eye. So it's June and I know it's Friday, but *which* Friday? Then, curious, I flipped back to January to see all the pictures…

I wonder what the Wave Festival is?

When they returned, Janie said, "We, ah, think it would be best if I took ya home to me parents' place. It's in Gifford Haven, about a six-day walk from here. We could catch an Islebus, but we don't know, um, how badly the Russians will wanna find ya."

"A six *day* walk?"

Norbert added, "We agreed it would be best if Janie took ya the back way, on the paths. They might be looking for her too."

Louise said, "Wouldn't you fancy a hike over some mountains and along some beautiful beaches?"

I looked at everyone. "Uhh, sure. But I might be slow 'cause I haven't walked in a while."

"And you need to eat something—you look skinny," said Louise.

"An' yer shakin'!" said Janie.

I *was* shaking, I guess from all the stress of escaping.

"Maybe we could all use some fish and chips," said Norbert. "There's a takeout shop down the street."

"Fish sounds fine!" said Janie, looking at me, but I only nodded—fish wasn't on my favorites list.

Louise, her wild eye dancing, suddenly announced, "I need your attention."

We all looked at her.

"I don't feel safe going back to my job at the base. I'm going to head down to Covenmoor to talk to my teacher, Roselin. She'll want to know all about my intervention. She'll also be very interested in hearing about you and this story of yours, Gordy."

"Who's Roselin?" I said.

"Ah," Louise beamed, "Roselin Bell is *the* sorcerer-witch-goddess of Hum energy. She knows her stuff."

A witch-goddess?

"And by the way, this was my first intervention, you guys, and *no one* is to know about what I did back there."

"So, what *did* you do?" said Janie.

"All I can say is it involved the Hum."

Janie rolled her eyes. "I got that part!"

"And Gordy, once you get to Gifford, stay put. I'll need to know where you are."

And with that, Louise was gone.

While Norbert went to order the food, Janie found an old quilted jacket and draped it over my shoulders. "I don't like that shakin'," she said.

"Ah, thanks."

Then she pinched my neck. "Ow! What was that for?"

"Just checkin'," she said, grinning. "I think yer *really* here, and not in some dream!"

Norbert soon returned with a fragrant cardboard box, which he opened with a flourish. "Freshly baked South-Cape salmon, chips, and fishdip," he said. He pulled a bottle from his coat pocket. "And wine from the Pinoak Hills."

"Those 'chips' look like fat french fries," I said.

"Never heard of 'french fries'," said Janie.

Norbert cleared his desk while Janie poured wine into some water glasses and put one in front of me. I had never tasted wine, and the very look of it reminded me of that Thunderbird stuff Mom drank.

Will this make me weird like it did to her?

Janie raised her glass, "Cheers! Now eat hearty, 'cause we need to be goin' soon!"

I took a slow, cautious sip and it tasted okay.

"It's riesling," she said. We ate quietly. The salmon, dipped in the buttery 'fishdip' was surprisingly good. Being hungry helped—I had been too restless to eat much of my soup back at the base.

After we finished, Janie said to me, "We'll stay at Norbert's place tonight."

*

A shorter ride in back of the pungent pedivan led us to a narrow stone house nestled among similar houses in a block-long row. Once inside, Norbert told me to make myself at home. I sensed a gentle though businesslike kindness about him. So different from Leon.

Janie dug around in a coat closet and pulled out a worn but usable backpack for our trip. From a kitchen cupboard Norbert piled up some cans of 'weenie-beanies', a tiny camp stove and a cook-kit. After rooting around in his bedroom, He added walking shoes, socks, underwear, a warm overshirt and a thick sweater.

I was astonished at his generosity. "This is, uh, wonderful. Thanks, Norbert."

Janie walked up and surprised him with a smooch on his cheek.

Norbert nodded with a shy smile, and then gave Janie a handful of coins he called rogers. "You'll need food on your way, and some rest at an inn or two." Then he pointed out his couch and said to me, "You can sleep here. I'm going to bed."

Janie smiled at me. "Me uncle's a man of few words, but he's a real gem, and I think he's warmin' up to ya. That was a long speech!"

"Ah," I said, feeling relieved. "I'll pay you guys back one of these days, somehow."

Janie waved it off and said, "Yer can 'av the bathroom first, and take a shower—ya really need one!"

She later brought in a long nightshirt and some blankets from Norbert's closet, said "G'night" and disappeared into what she said was her 'cubby.'

*

But we didn't leave the next morning.

Just before daylight I threw up in the toilet, and my whole body ached. Janie slept through it, but when she was up at seven, she took one look at me and then felt my forehead. "Yer runnin' a fever, an' ya look awful!" she said. "At least ya smell better."

Her cool hand on my sweaty forehead felt divine.

She went into their little kitchen and brought back a tall glass of water. "Ya need this, so drink as much as ya can."

Norbert soon came out of his bedroom and took one look. "Ah, I thought I heard retching last night. A bit blasted are ya?"

"Something like that," I said. "I don't feel very well."

Janie said, "Yer gonna need some good anti-virus herbs—from Miss Martell's over in Northside. Feel like getten' 'em for us, Uncle?"

"Aye, 'an I'll pick up some groceries on the way, since we'll have a guest for another day or so. Do ya know the right medicinals to get for 'im?"

"Of course! I studied herbal remedies at Covenmoor, remember?"

Norbert nodded patiently. "Then write me a list."

After he left, Janie made tea for us, with toast and fruit. I was able to get up on one elbow, but even looking at the food brought a dire warning from my stomach.

While Janie ate at the table, I lay back and tried some of her tea, which seemed to calm my grumbling belly. I tried *not* to listen to her toast-munching. For a while, she stared at nothing, but when she turned to look at me, her face changed. Her eyes warmed with a caring gaze.

This was *so* new. Even through my fever-fog, I could see she really cares!

She brought her tea over to the couch, perched on the arm and said, "So what 'appened to ya back home?"

I looked at her. " You want the whole story?" I squeaked.

"Well, it looks like we have some time, if yer up to it."

Jeez, where do I start? "Okay, I'm Gordon Love, and I'm almost sixteen, in case you needed that."

"Duly noted…I'm Janie MacEvoy and I'm nineteen," she said, trying to look serious.

"Got it." I was flattered, thrilled and flustered all at once.

Does she really care, or is she just bored-and-curious?

I took a deep breath.

I guess I'll have to trust her.

I told her my family story—of growing up with Leon, Ricky, and Mom. The hard part was recounting that last night after Mom went crazy at Ricky.

"Wait…ya mean he was supposed to be *babysittin'* ya?"

"Well, sort-of," I blushed. "But that's been the rule since I was about seven. Mom couldn't afford a real babysitter, so she had Ricky do it for his allowance. As I got older, she still insisted Ricky stay home with me when she was at work. I think she was really trying to keep him away from his girlfriend Cindy. I heard her name a lot when they argued."

Janie raised an eyebrow. "I'll bet yer mum was afraid Cindy might lure him away from her. I knew a boy in Upper School who had a mum like that—very jealous of girlfriends!"

"Ah, I never thought of that, but that's what the fight was about, and Janie, it was all *my* fault. If it wasn't for me, none of that stuff would've happened."

"Well, yer can hardly blame yerself fer *existing!* Ya have to know they made their own choices, and none of that was *your* fault."

"Yeah, but when I saw my mom lying there, I should have called someone instead of passing out!"

"Ah."

"And I still don't know what happened to her, and that was *weeks* ago."

Janie pushed my legs aside, sat down, and said, "Okay, put yer feet up here, and tell me more about yer friend Mr. Barnes."

I was relieved by the change-of-subject, and intrigued by her move-to-the-couch. I sipped more of the still-warm tea. Up close, her freckles were amazing, her smile enchanting.

"Mr. Barnes..." Janie reminded me.

"Oh, yeah! He's probably my best friend. I met him when he was building his own house a few blocks from where I lived, and he sometimes let me help him. And when the Hum came one time, he shut his eyes while it was happening. We never talked about it, but I think he knew I could hear it too."

"*What?* You mean this fella also knows the Hum? Are there others?"

"Uh, only Mr. Barnes as far as I know. Oh, and I just remembered this—at the beginning of my dream he said, 'I built this raft to protect you, and get you to *the other side*.' What do you think *that* means?"

"Humm, not sure, Gordy. Anyway, like Louise said, yer connected to the Hum, and that might be what brought ya here, to this 'other side'. I also think yer friend is connected too, and he might have actually helped ya get here. I'd like to meet 'im some time!"

Janie reached for my hand, and I melted a little just as my stomach felt calmer. She reached further and felt my forehead again.

"How are ya feeling now?"

"A little better."

"Hey, ya wanna hear *my* story?"

"Sure. Do you have more tea?"

After a few minutes Janie brought in another full mug.

I said, "You sound like our Irish neighbors back home—are you Irish?"

"You betcha," she said. "From Cork, on me mum's side, *waaay* back. Her ancestors were on the convict ship, *Lady Marie*."

"Convict ship?"

"Yeah. You've heard the British once shipped convicts to Australia, right?"

"Uhhh…"

"I'll fill you in on that later. Anyway, I grew up in Gifford, where we're goin'. It's one of the Elsinore Bay tribes on the eastern coast. Me mum's people settled there in the 1800s. Gifford's a berry-crop tribe, and I worked a few summers picking. It was hot, sticky work, I'll tell ya."

I looked at her. "What do you mean by a tribe?"

"Well, our tribes are like big families or clans, who sell their stuff to other tribes, and sometimes to the Russians. We have a Festival of the Tribes every year where the Island's tribes gather and make deals."

"So, the tribes are like little towns?"

"Yes…and no."

Janie thought a minute.

"Okay, it's like this. Me mum's convict-ancestors were blown off course in a storm, and they landed here, stuck on a beach, never reaching Australia. And on the *Lady Marie*, the convicts were all women! Fortunately, the crew opened the cages, and they managed to not only get ashore, but eventually salvage enough supplies to survive here on their own. The Island was uninhabited."

"So what does this have to do with tribes?"

"Be patient, Gordy! The women far outnumbered the sailors and guards, and with the help of our founder Cecelia, they were able to take command of the situation, as it was. They had no interest in marryin' any crew members, an' in fact, most of the women bitterly hated 'em. *Bu-utt*, there was still a lot of flirting and messin' around, so many women wound up bein' single mums. But Cecelia, with the help of the *Lady Marie's* captain, arranged marriages of a different sort, and started a whole new way of livin' together."

"Ahh…wow! So what kind of different sort?"

"I'll tell ya later. So instead of raisin' their kids on their own, they figured that one big common kitchen was better than many small ones, and everyone could take turns watchin' the kids. The idea caught on, and now there are tribes all over the Island."

"Oh."

Trying to spot *the look*, I stared at Janie maybe a bit too long.

"What," she said.

"Oh, nothing!"

"Well, quit lookin' at me like that. Yer bein' weird."

I blinked and glanced away.

"Okay, I think I get it about the tribes."

She rolled her eyes.

*

To make amends I said, "So, what was it like for *you* growing up?"

Janie sat back. "Well, me parents were okay, I guess. When they weren't makin' me pick berries, they pretty much let me do what I wanted, like roam the countryside 'til dark. They also let me wear boys' clothes at home, though I wore my colors at school."

"Colors?"

"Yeh, like a uniform. Dark blue shorts an' a yellow shirt with the school's crest on the pocket, plus the tie. All the schools have their own colors."

"Hey, I like that," I said. "The crest sounds classy."

"Anyway, as soon as I graduated from Upper School, I wanted to learn witchery."

"Witchery!?"

"Yeh. I'd heard I could learn witchcraft for free as an apprentice at Covenmoor—that place where Louise is heading. I went straight down there when I took the Walk."

"The Walk? What's that?"

"Yer sure full 'o questions! Okay, after graduation, nearly all the kids take a journey, on foot, stopping for a while at different settlements around the Island to help out in exchange for meals and lodging And to maybe learn a trade. We call it the Long Walk."

"So after high school everyone goes on a big hike? What about college, or getting a job?"

"Gordy, it's *The Walk*, not some bring-a-lunch hike! We see it as a kind of real-life school. We meet other people in different tribes, and see what we really want to do in this life. We might even find a mate if we're lucky."

I was wide-eyed. "I wish *we* had that. No one walks in California. Everyone just drives."

"Drives? As in a private car? Yer people must be awful rich to own one o' them!"

"Yeah, uh, I never thought of that. So how did you wind up working in a Soviet Navy cafeteria?"

"Ah, good question there, Sherlock.

"When I arrived at Covenmoor, I was full o' fantasies about puttin' spells on people and dancin' naked in the moonlight. But I found out it wasn't like that! The Covenmoor witches mostly made healing potions for anything from stomach aches to lunacy. So my job was to go into the bush to find all sorts of strange herbs, mushrooms, newts and creepy grubs from a picture-card they gave me. It was icky work and it always seemed to be raining.

"Then I met Estelle, a fellow apprentice with a *baaad* witchy look in her eye. Until then I thought I only liked boys, but she was the most enchanting creature I'd ever known. She woke up my soul, she did, and also that, uh, physical part of me. She was a wonderful, sweet companion, at least while it lasted."

I blushed, questions blooming everywhere.

"But the honeymoon was short! Our being together aroused some crazy jealousy in two other girls who were in love with Estelle as much as I was. They were nasty, and gave me hell by doing things like throwing out my hard-earned grubs or peeing in my bed an' then telling the master *I* did it. And Estelle didn't even stick by me! In hindsight, I think she got off watching us fight over her."

"Whoa, that must have been rough!"

"Yeh, I was a mess, and right at the end of all that I met Roselin. I'd seen her around Covenmoor, and I'd gotten the feeling she could see right through riddles and enigmas!"

"Ah, Roselin the mysterious."

"Yeh, she *is* mysterious, but also compelling. She asked me to sit at her table one time at dinner, and she got right to the point by sayin', 'You should train with me. I've been watching you and I think you

have the potential to know the Hum. I work with Hum energy—
something far beyond the sound we hear.'"

"Hum *energy*?" I said. "Like what Louise used at the navy base?"

"Yeh, something like that. You and I can hear the Hum, but Roselin
knows how to do things with it, and Louise has been training with
her."

Whoa!

"But I thought you said Covenmoor was all about herbal cures. So,
they also study the Hum?"

"Well, only Roselin does. She told me she was born there, and the
tribe invited her back after her big discovery." Janie glanced at my
questioning look, then went on. "When Roselin was a student at
Putney University, she made one of the biggest archeological
discoveries on the Island, or so she said."

"So, uh, what did she find?"

"She wouldn't tell me, but her intensity was scary-cool, and I liked
her right away. I almost said yes about the training, but I was too upset
over Estelle, so I left. Soon after that I heard the Russians were hiring
at the base."

"So, are you a witch now?"

"Not even close. I did learn a few herbal cures and remedies. By the
way, where's me uncle?"

She no sooner said that when Norbert sailed through the door.

"I was a bit held up," he said. "Had to have a pint with a fellow I
bumped into. I have your medicinals somewhere here…"

"Thanks, Uncle, an' yer lucky our Gordy didn't pass on! Anyway, I
think he's startin' to come around. Another day of rest and we can hit
the trail. Right, Gordy?"

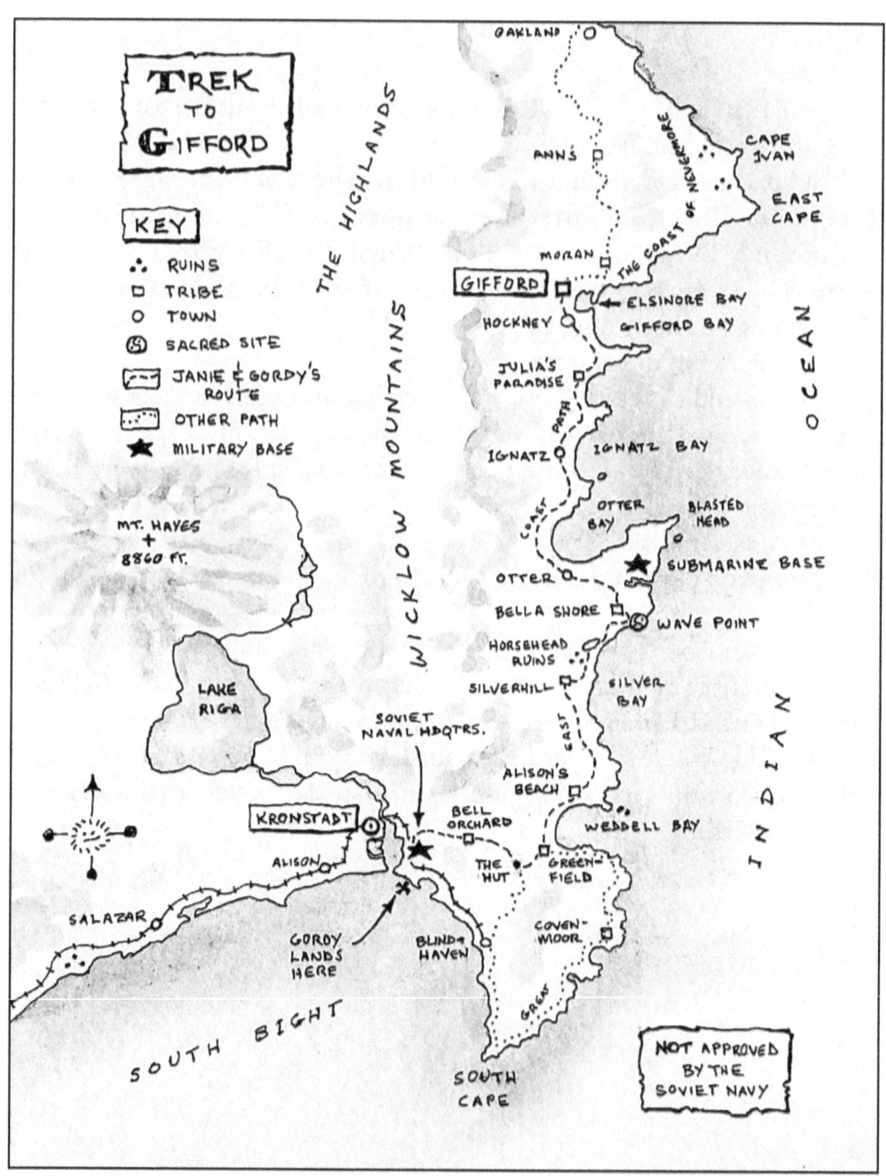

After another restful night of no television (unbelievable), Janie felt
my forehead and pronounced me fit to travel. At breakfast she served

me a mug of pungent eucalyptus tea into which I poured copious amounts of sugar and cream. I tasted it, added a little more of both, then tasted it again. I looked up at them, both staring at me. "I kinda like my tea just so, especially after you put those, uh, medicinals in it, Janie."

Norbert stared a bit longer, then said, "Well, Janes, give my love to Alan and yer mum. I'll get up there one of these days. You know this meat business keeps me tethered here."

We all stood up and he gave Janie a long hug.

"And Gordy, we stuck our necks out for ya, so I'm expecting to hear only good things about yer in the future."

I gulped down the last of my tea and said, "I'll do my best."

He gave me the quickest wink. "Well, goodonya then."

At the door, Norbert helped Janie hoist the heavy pack on her back. She let out a grunt and turned to me. "I'll take this today, but you'll get yer turn as soon as yer stronger!"

"Thanks, Janie, and thank you, Norbert, for all your help."

Outside, I felt a strange shiver of excitement as we stumbled into a chilly blue-sky morning—a whole new place, another world!

Am I really here?
And what is this place?
And how...?
And, why...?

*

Janie led the way out of town, wobbling a little as she adjusted to the pack's weight. The sun had just risen over the hills, blazing with an intensity I hadn't felt in a while.

As we steadily climbed, the view opened up. A wide bay spread out behind us, which Janie called the South Bight. A well-traveled path led us into some wild-looking hills. Someone passed us pushing the handle of a curious bicycle-wheeled cart, which Janie informed me was a felix-hauler. Just as I was thinking how much work that must be, a pedivan, smaller than Norbert's, lumbered up the hill pedaled by two sturdy women. They wore the same brightly-colored shorts and shirts I saw on my jeep-ride into town. The women were at once beautiful and terrifying, their arms and pumping legs glistening with sweat, leaving me feeling weirdly giddy. Both of them cheerfully waved. Janie waved back, and I just gawked, envious of their energy.

When Janie noticed me lagging behind, she found a gnarly branch near the path, whittled it smooth with her pocketknife and said, "Here. This can help ya pull yerself up the hills!"

Then she stretched out her arms. "I'm soooo glad we're on this walk. I didn't know how much I needed this. People do this all the time here, ya know. They'll walk for days to enjoy all the nature, see friends, or sometimes trek all the way to the Dreamland."

I looked at her. "The Dreamland?"

"Yeh, Roger's Dreamland. It's a place not even all Islanders can experience, but I have a feeling you might be able to. I'll tell ya more about it when I think yer, ah, ready."

My curiosity was running everywhere, including those cosmic questions regarding reality.

Janie was looking at me, guessing my thoughts, "Ya better believe this is real," she said. "Just as real as that cage you were in."

I wish I could forget that.

"Do you think they're looking for us?"

"Nah…don't think so. After all, that guard *did* leave the door unlocked, and all civilians were ordered to leave, so why wouldn't ya simply walk out?"

*

At mid-day, we spotted a farm village surrounded by vineyards. "This place is called Suring-Wigsthorpe," said Janie.

"Suring-Wig…? What a name."

"I see a pub up ahead…wanna get a sandwich or fish-an'-chips?"

"Okay, and maybe a cold drink?"

A refreshing coolness greeted us inside the Wig Tavern. "I'll buy," Janie said with a wink. "I grabbed me savings on Friday, plus we have Norbert's rogers."

"That's good, 'cause I'm quite penniless."

After lunch, we walked into more hills, some of them crowned with huge rocky outcrops. The path became narrower, with only a few pushcarts. The sun has been warm all day, but a rising breeze from the south began to chill the shadows. I had to keep in mind the seasons are reversed here—it's June so it's more or less winter!

We walked on in silence. I felt energized, my senses sharpened. These wild hills had a strange allure—I wanted to keep going deeper. My legs were still wobbly but so far, so good.

Lunch at the Wig.

Then the birds stopped chattering, and there was no wind. A weird tingle ran up my spine, my neck-hairs bristling.

From far off a faint buzz slowly intensified in volume, and soon deep waves of uplifting sound were swirling around us. Janie glanced at me, eyebrows raised. "Do ya hear that?"

"Yeah, I hear it!"

"Nice, eh?" Then her eyes went wide. "So ya *can* hear it! Louise and I were right. Welcome to the land o' the Hum!"

I grinned at her as I was overcome by a strange weightlessness, a sublime lightness.

Finally, I'm not alone with that sound.

The humming rose a few octaves, then dipped again as it danced around us in full stereo.

"At home, it seemed to come from the ocean," I said. "It's a lot louder here."

We stood there as the humming shifted into something like the singing of a full choir before echoing off into the hills.

"Gordy," she said, "I think it did that just to make us feel good."

"Yeah," I said. "I feel like I'm floating."

*

Later, we reached the top of a high hill from which real mountains revealed themselves in the hazy distance, some capped with patches of white.

"You get snow here…?"

"Yeh, those are the Wicklow Mountains. They get several feet up there some winters."

The afternoon wore on. We reached the top of another hill just as my wimpy leg muscles began to seriously complain. "Hey, I see rooftops down there."

"I think that's the Bell Orchard tribe," said Janie. "Uncle Norbert told me some of the residents rent rooms there for about 200 pence per night—not bad."

With a mischievous eye on me, she spread her arms out toward the settlement. "Behold, Gordy. A tribe!"

"Okay, Janie…I get it!"

We walked down to a cluster of smallish houses, all built of stone or sand-colored brick, many with tiled roofs. Colorful wood-framed windows and doors gave them all a delightful home-made look. Hens scuttled among flower beds in the yards, orchards covered an adjoining hill, and sheep dotted the more distant meadows.

I felt like I was walking into a movie.

Soon we were among the houses and heading into an open space Janie called the commons. A swim-pond and playground shared space with a closed-up shed in front of several long benches. The place looked almost deserted.

A girl of maybe thirteen sat by the pond watching over three lively toddlers splashing in the water. The girl's sun-bleached hair contrasted with a load of freckles on her face, arms, and legs—more than Janie can boast. The girl waved at us.

"Halloo," said Janie. "We're wonderin' if there's a place fer us to stay tonight?" The girl said something like *yes'm*, then ran to a nearby two-story house. She called out, "Muuuum? Some people wanna stay th' night!"

As the girl quickly trotted back to the pond, a stout woman emerged, gave us a brief look, and said, "I'm Mrs. Kemp. Needin' lodgin' are ya?"

After some discussion with Janie, Mrs. Kemp led us upstairs to a sunny room wallpapered with an old-fashioned floral design. A white knobby bedspread covered a double bed next to a nightstand with a kerosene lamp. A narrow cot piled with folded blankets occupied the far corner.

Janie nodded her approval to Mrs. Kemp, handed her some coins, and we all smiled as Mrs. Kemp left the room.

Janie dumped the heavy pack on the floor with a great sigh of relief. "This thing is yours tomorrow."

Then she asked, "So, do yer like this place?"

I looked at the cot. "Yeah, it's okay."

"We're expected to have dinner with the family in about an hour," she added.

"Okay. So, can I go out now and look around? I want to check out that sandy swimming-pond."

Janie looked at me.

"What?" I said.

She was smiling with a kind of appraising stare.

Is that *the look?*

"I'm realizin' yer still a boy-child…well, an *older* boy, yet yer actin' more like a man sometimes. I like ya both ways!"

I glanced at her with a growing appreciation. *Janie is taking such risks for me, and then she says* that!

"So, can I go?"

"Yeh, go. I need to change out of these clothes, an' I could use some quiet time. An' don't be late fer supper."

"Okay," I said from halfway down the stairs.

I stepped out and looked around at the houses and the commons. The sandy pond fascinated me. It wasn't lined with concrete, yet the water was clear. The whole place looked like pictures I'd seen of old European villages, and the bushy geraniums reminded me of Mom's flower beds back home.

Ahh, Mom…what happened?

The girl we met earlier waved to me. I wasn't sure I wanted to talk to her, so I approached warily, eyes to the ground.

"Halloo, I'm Alaine."

I looked up. "Hi. I'm Gordy."

She didn't smile. "Ya talk funny."

"So do you."

Still not smiling, she looked me over in a thoughtful way. "Yer from somer else, eh?"

"Yeah." I looked around at these home-made houses, the gardens, and no cars. "So, this is a tribe?"

She looked at me like I was one card short. "Uh, yeh, we call it that. So where might ye be from?"

For some reason I wanted to tell her all of it. "Well, I'm from California, in America. I had a dream about a raft that carried me over three oceans, and then a storm wrecked it and I woke up here on a beach…"

"Whoa there…so ya just floated all the way here? On a *raft?*"

"Uh, well, I *dreamed* about the raft. And Janie, who you met, got me out of, er, some trouble with the Russians, and now we're on our way north somewhere."

Alaine looked at me wide-eyed. "Oy-wow! I wish I was going somewhere. I *loooong* to see those big Russian gunboats down in Kronstadt, an' the ocean, an' the Dreamland."

"You've never seen the ocean?"

"Naw, only on the telly."

"Telly, like television?"

"Yeh. In the shed over there. We watch it most ev'ry evenin'." Then she abruptly called out to the kids, "Come on out, yer mums'll be home soon!".

And off they went.

*

I sat on the bench she was using to absorb all this, trying not to go on brain-overload. It's all *kind* of familiar but somehow very different.

My staring into space was soon interrupted by several women and men who appeared to be heading home from work. A few nodded when they saw me, but no one approached, which was fine with me.

Janie soon called out, "Hey, come and get yer supper!"

When I walked in, Mrs. Kemp had already begun serving peas and buttery potatoes alongside some slender fish fillets. The aroma put me on full hunger alert, but I knew I had to be patient. Not sure about table etiquette here.

Alaine waltzed in, freshly changed, her wild hair roughly tied. She took the last chair. This tribe-girl fascinated me, but I couldn't figure out why. Was it all those freckles?

Mrs. Kemp closed her eyes and uttered a long *Ommm* sound before softly saying, "Thank you for this day, and for this food. Amen."

"Amen," said Janie and Alaine, then I, with only a slight delay.

After some minutes of no sound but the clinking of forks on plates, Mrs. Kemp looked at me. "So, Mr. Gordy, I'm curious about you. I have a feeling you're from somewhere far from here."

Her sudden question put me off, and I stammered, "Uh, yeah."

Janie shot me a glance and quickly added, "He lost his memory so we're, uh, trying find out where he lives. Me uncle and I found him wandering around in Kronstadt, so we're helpin' him get home."

I looked at her, I *did?*

"That's not what he told *me*," said Alaine.

Surprised, Janie glared at her, then at me. I stared down at my plate and quietly took another bite.

Mrs. Kemp's knowing eyes didn't miss a thing. She got up and brought in an apple pie. "I had a feeling you'd been through quite a bit," she said. "Lost your memory you say?"

I concentrated on cleaning my plate. "Yeah. I, uh, got knocked out."

"Well, we've all been through experiences we sometimes find difficult to explain," she said to the table in general. "I trust you'll find your way soon, Mister Gordy." Janie and I both smiled at her, while Alaine glowered.

"Hey," Janie said to Alaine. "Could ya take us on a walk around this place? We'd like to see yer town, er, village."

Mrs. Kemp nodded her approval, and Alaine suddenly brightened.

"Arright. I'll show ya around."

Alaine led us past the houses to some long sheds by the orchards, talking a mile a minute. "We grow pears, peaches, apricots, and kiwi. We sort all the fruit here, an' the overripe stuff goes to the cannery over there."

We followed her into one of the orchards. "We've been growing some o' these trees fer over a hunnerd years, except these kiwis we just brought in from New Zillen. We export some of our fruit all th' way to th' So-vi-yet Union."

Then she stopped short. "And by the way, Mista Gordy, ya *did* tell me you had some trouble with Russians, didn't ya? And don't try t' tell me ya didn't, neither of ya!"

Janie, taken off guard, looked at her hard, then at me, and finally said, "Okay, Alaine, here's what's happening. Gordy *did* lose his memory, and we *are* on our way to find his home. He's confused an' he doesn't know what he's saying half the time. Right Gordy?"

"Uh, yeah, right!"

"Arright," said Alaine, "I'll tell ya what. Ya hand over a roger's worth o' coinage and I'll forget what Mista Gordy *actually* told me."

Janie's face reddened—she was livid. "Yoooou stinker!"

She hustled me aside and hissed, "*What—did—you—tell—her?*"

"Um… about my dream and waking up and getting caught by the Russians, then I stopped myself. I didn't say anything about *escaping*."

"Well, you apparently said enough. If she spews the story here, it could spread like a disease. *Shite!*"

Janie stomped back over to Alaine. "All right, I'll pay you, you robber, but if I *ever* hear one word of what you *think you heard* Gordy say, I'll come looking for you. This means even if *you* didn't say anything, I'll still come lookin' for ya. Do—you—unnerstand—me?"

Alaine paused, gave a tight-lipped nod, and said nothing.

Janie gave her the money and one more nasty look, then turned to me. "The tour is over, Gordy. Let's go."

Oh, jeez…I'm such a blockhead.

*

On our walk back to our room, we heard the noise of the television in the commons and we stopped to watch. Several families sat on the benches or in folding chairs in front of a news program given by a woman speaking Russian. On the stage next to the TV, a young man frantically wrote the newscaster's words in English on a chalkboard. It was the unfolding story of the "Kronstadt air-raid":

> ...This incident was a direct provocation upon our peaceful presence in the Indian Ocean. The Americans are again rattling their sabers and threatening our existence!

"Whoa," Janie whispered, "Is that what Louise set off? Do ya know this is coming all the way from Moscow?" She turned away. "Let's get to bed. If I see Alaine any more this evening, I might have to rip her head off. And you and I need to get our stories straight, *Mistah* Gordy."

I nodded, still feeling like a dork. To change the subject, I said, "So are all the TV shows from Russia?"

She gave me one more stern look, and sighed. "As a 'gesture of solidarity', the Russians gave a free telly to every village with electricity or a generator. But they really did it so they could feed us all their crap."

"Ah."

"But some of the programs are pretty good, especially the symphony and dance concerts. I *love* the Bolshoi ballet."

Tired from the long day, we quietly and politely got ready for bed. Janie helped me make up the cot without either of us saying a word.

Later, I could hear her tossing and fretting in the big bed. She finally whispered over to me, "Yer awake?"

"Yeah."

In the moonlit room I could barely make out her sleepy eyes. *Is this the look?*

"What, Janie?"

"Here's the thing, Gordy. We have to be careful because once someone finds out yer from some place off the Island, they'll be all over you with questions. And no matter what ya say, the rumors will fly. Islanders live in their own little bubbles here—real small-town! And *you* might as well be from the far side of Mars, and I can't afford any more blackmail!"

"Okay, Janie, I get it."

"Another thing is, I can tell yer still in pain, especially when I look into those big green eyes of yours, an' I still like you."

I immediately blushed and muttered into my pillow, "I like you too."

Now *should I try to kiss her?*

I fell asleep instead.

*

The aroma of sausages and coffee from Mrs. Kemp's kitchen woke me up. Janie was still snoring.

"Time to get u-u-u-p." I sang.

"Ummph, go away!"

"I smell saw-se-jezz."

One eye opened. "Okay, okay, gimme a minute. I'll see ya downstairs."

Breakfast was delicious but quiet, with no sign of Alaine. Mrs. Kemp looked only at her food. Finally, Janie put down her fork. "Nice breakfast, Mrs. Kemp. We'd best be on our way, then."

I got up fast, relieved to be getting out of there.

"I do hope you regain your memory, Mister Gordy."

"Ah, not to worry, Missus Kemp, he'll be just fine!" Janie was so flustered she almost forgot it was my turn with the backpack.

MOUNTAINS

Once outside of Bell Orchard, it was a steady uphill climb. My shoulders and legs were already complaining about the backpack, but so far, so good. Following a splashing creek, the path had narrowed to something like a cow-trail. A few travelers passed in the other direction, but there were no more pushcarts or pedivans. Many walkers seemed to be in some other zone, and didn't look at us at all.

In less than an hour, we came upon a newly-paved road. "Get down," hissed Janie, "and stay in the bushes while I check for traffic. I don't want anyone to see us."

"Why not?"

"Because, you idiot, the Russians use these roads, and they don't like being slowed down with our pushcarts and pedivans. They also don't like anyone watching them, an' I don't want them to see *you*!"

Just then two canvas-covered, military-green trucks, rounded a curve in the distance, approaching fast.
"They've been hauling a lot of stuff to their military bases lately, and the noise and stink are awful!"

After the trucks roared by, Janie listened for some minutes, then said, "Okay, go!" and we scuttled across the pavement.

Safely in the bushes again she said, "That's the only road for a while, and there's only wilderness from here to the coast. I'm glad it's cooler today, though I hope it doesn't get too cold. We'll be going up to 6,000 feet this afternoon."

I groaned. This pack will destroy me by then, but I was determined to show Janie I could do this, especially after the Alaine incident.

As we climbed, the creek alongside the path dwindled to a trickle. "So, we're going up there?"

Janie followed my gaze, "Yeh, somewhere in there we'll walk through a little valley between the peaks, a place me uncle calls a cwm.

"A coom?"

"Yeh, c-w-m. It's Welsh."

"Welsh?"

"Arrgh! Okay, Gordy, lesson time again. *Welsh* is one of the old languages some Islanders speak here. Once our people got settled, they revived many of the old traditions, including speaking Welsh and Irish-Gaelic. They've been mixing these in with our English, got it?"

"Aye."

"Are you mocking me?"

"Nay," I smiled.

"Yes you are, and those aren't Welsh words anyway!"

We stopped in a pine grove for a some cheese, apple slices and a bit of smoked fish, all from Norbert's pantry. While sitting, we felt a more ominous chill in the air. "I'm glad we brought some sweaters," said Janie.

The pines bent with the wind, their long needles sighing like a slow, meandering song. The once-pale sky had become an intense blue as we continued toward some patches of old snow.

We soon reached the "cwm" Janie described, and once over it, a wide vista ahead revealed massive clouds steadily advancing. The temperature dropped, the wind pushed harder, and the sunlight soon faded. Janie stopped and pulled out two thick pullovers.

"Now I wish we'd brought long pants!"

As we fumbled with our sweaters, the distant peaks ahead of us faded to a whitish gray, one by one.

"There's snow coming," she said. "See, it's already falling on Isabel Peak over there. We'll have to hustle to get down the other side. I don't wanna be stuck up here."

As soon as she said the word 'snow', big wet flakes began to fall around us.

"This is one of those sticky snows," said Janie. "It usually doesn't last long."

I was enchanted. Snow was rare back home, sometimes blanketing the distant mountains, never close. The wet flakes bit my face, yet the thrill of this sudden change made it feel not so cold.

Janie was getting worried. "We'll have to find some shelter before we sleep tonight—I don't like this!" I nodded as I leaned into the weather. "Keep yer eyes open for any kind of cave or a hole in a tree or somethin,' okay?"

"Aye."

"This is serious, ya know!"

"Okay, Janie, I know. It's just so wonderful to look at."

We had kept a steady pace and again found ourselves among trees. The snow worsened, obliterating everything around us. Janie almost stumbled trying to shield her eyes. It was then I happened to notice a shadowy wall between some bushy pines.

"Hey, what's that?"

We could barely make out a tiny stone hut, built into the hillside. "Goddam, Gordy, it's a path shelter!" said Janie, grinning. Then she smooched me on the cheek, leaving me thrilled and blushing.

The door's hasp was secured only by a tiny green pine branch, a sprig, as Janie called it. "This means someone was here, but no one is now." Inside, we found four narrow bunks, a rough wooden table with benches, and a big stone fireplace. A large bin was stocked with firewood, kindling, and old *Putney Times* newspapers. A nearby shelf held a kerosene lamp, candles, a tight-lidded jar of matches and a few somewhat moldy books.

"Pretty sweet, eh?" said Janie.

"Yeah!"

She studied a rough map tacked on the wall. Ah, this explains it. We've come upon the Isabel Traverse path," she said. "The local tribes maintain these huts for travelers, like us! Good eye there, Gordy."

Janie got to work building a fire, while I dug food out of our pack.

"Ahh, this'll be a fine evening," she said as the flames warmed the room. She selected some sausages, and pears from a "care package" Mrs. Kemp had sold to us. "We can have this tonight, and we can cook up these eggs in the morning."

Darkness arrived early, but the oil lamps we found gave off a warm glow.

After supper, Janie made a sort-of couch by arranging our blankets and sleeping bag on the floor in front of the fire, using one of the bunks as a backrest. She settled herself, patted the space next to her and said, "Here. Sit."

*

I was beginning to feel more at ease around Janie, but Ricky's kissing theory still niggled in my mind. Even though I got us in trouble with stinky Alaine, Janie hadn't treated me like an idiot. And no one, except maybe Mr. Barnes, had treated me with this much *kindness* before.

The fire slowly settled into a glowing mound of embers. Janie threw another blanket over us and scrunched her hip against mine.

She looked over at me.

This must *be the look!*

She put her arm over my shoulder and pulled me against her side. "Gordy, if there's anything else ya wanna tell…"

Okay, here goes!

I turned and mashed my lips against hers, and for one short second, she didn't move. Then she became as rigid as a stone.

Uh, oh…she's not melting!

She pushed me away, hard, and stood up fast. "What are you *doing?*"

I fumbled with the words. "I—I thought you wanted that."

In a wild-eyed fury, she grabbed my arm and the blanket, opened the door and shoved me outside with surprising force.

Slam!

Stunned, I tumbled onto the wet ground, thick snow flying around me.

Ohhhh, crap! What have I <u>done</u>?

I tried the door, but she had locked it. Then I knocked. Nothing. Then a little louder. Still nothing.

I went around and tapped on the little window, and yelled, "*I'm soorrrry!*"

No answer.

I blew it.

The blanket didn't help much as I hunkered down against the door. The wet, cold wind penetrated everything, and my feet were slowly going numb.

My mind fell into a hole.

No one is ever going to love me no matter what I do. So why is Janie being so nice to me, yet she won't let me kiss her?

Isn't that what girls <u>really</u> want?

Stupid Ricky!

I don't remember how long I sat there, but I was shaking violently when the door opened.

"Get in here."

I crawled back in and crouched close to the now-revived fire. I could feel Janie's eyes on me, but I could only stare at the flames, unable to face her.

Her voice was thin and distant. "Can I tell you something?"

I turned, and she was again leaning against the bunk, looking only at the fire. "You can sit by me again if you want."

I crawled over next to her.

"Something snapped inside me when you did that," she said. "Remember that creepy guard back at the base?"

I nodded.

She took a deep breath. "When I first started working there a year ago, I knew *nothing* about guys like that. My new job title was 'kitchen help' and my boss, Irena, assigned me to serve the cafeteria line alongside Louise, some other Islanders and a few Russian girls. I saw all types of men there, military and civilian, as I loaded their trays three times a day. Some were very polite, some openly flirted, and some just stared like they'd never seen a woman before—sailors just off the fleet, I suppose.

"I didn't know anything about *love* then, even after being with Estelle. But I was lonely, and one of the sailors, who was really cute, began to smile at me like he meant it. He would find me on my break, grin like it was Christmas, and start chatting. I knew squat Russian. He kept saying all this stuff that sounded like questions. I wanted to impress him, of course, so I nodded a lot. *Big* mistake!

"One night after work he convinced me to take a walk with him, and we 'accidentally' wound up among the trees in the back of the base. I should have suspected something was up when his questioning eyes lit up a little more with my every answering nod. How stupid! Before I knew it, he grabbed me and began slobbering all over my face, and he was strong! He slapped me hard for resisting, and then he raped me."

A long silence. We stared at the fire while I tried to absorb what she had said.

Wait'll I see Ricky again!

When I looked at her, her eyes were wet with tears. "I haven't told anyone about this before."

I looked away, feeling terrible. But something had shifted—tough-girl Janie was showing me a whole new side. She's as vulnerable as everyone else.

Without thinking, I put my arm around her. "What I did was stupid, Janie."

She wiped her face with her sleeve, then turned to me twitching her now-familiar Janie eyebrow. "Yer little trick made me face this thing, so maybe I owe you. But no more kissing, unnerstand?"

"Okay-I-won't! So, uh, how did you get rid of the guy?"

"I didn't. I was terrified of him. But after he did that, he ignored me and started making his moves on other women in the serving line. I was relieved, but also furious that he did what he did and then tossed me aside like garbage.

"But there was a reckoning. I had warned Louise about him, and sure enough, he made the same play on her. She knew some Russian but pretended she didn't, and eventually *they* wound up among the trees. She said that when he grabbed her, she locked onto his eyes and zapped him with that Hum-stare she learned from Roselin. We never saw him again."

I let out a long breath.

"I'm glad you're hearing me," she said. Then she relaxed and once again bumped her hip against mine. "And I probably still like you."

It felt good to breathe again.

*

I must have completely dozed off, because she had somehow moved me onto one of the bunks. I barely remembered her putting the blankets over me.

Fat snowflakes were still ticking against the little window. Deep sleep came fast.

Sunlight blazed through the same little window when I was awakened by rattling cookware. Janie had stoked the fire and was already serving some of Mrs. Kemp's eggs, oatmeal, and tea.

Still a little worried about my 'incident' last night, I sat down before my egg and only glanced at her.

With her hand on her hip, she said, "Good morning, yer welcome, and ya get to clean up."

I managed to mumble, "I will, and, uh, thanks for the egg…and letting me back in…and forgiving me."

Janie let out a hint of a smile.

"'Sall right."

As she packed, I cleaned up as promised, then swept the floor. Once we were outside, Janie secured the door with a fresh sprig of pine. "This is a token of appreciation."

I liked that.

The morning air was crisp without that windy bite. The snow was blindingly white, with animal tracks everywhere. I was loving it!

"We'll stay on the Isabel Path," said Janie in tour-guide mode. "The path descends almost 4,000 feet down to the eastern coast. We should be on the Great East Coast Path later today. It's me favorite one; It always takes me home!"

A twinge of envy…where is home?

"Sooo," I said, "These paths are for the Islanders, and the roads are for the Russians?"

"More or less. We've been buildin' our path system for generations. Then about forty years ago the Russians started tearing up our land to build their military roads. I wish they wouldn't make such a mess of our Island!"

"So, it's *your* island and not *their* island?"

"It's always been ours!" she said, as if it was obvious. Then she sighed. "At least we like to think that. We got here first, but I suppose we have to thank the Russians for keeping the British out of our hair."

She looked at my quizzical face and said, "Okay, Gordy. History lesson! Remember I said our ancestors were mostly shipwrecked female convicts bound for Australia? Well, within twenty years they had built a whole new way of living. They were organizing tribes, managing families, starting new religions! But down inside, they knew they were still convicts under British law, so if the British ever arrived, it would all be over.

"Our only defense was to watch for ships then do whatever we could. A Spanish gunboat showed up around 1803, I think, whose master, De Salazar, had colonial ambitions. He marched ashore with most of his crew and announced our Island now belonged to the king of Spain! We knew enough to act docile, but they were abusive anyway, to say the least! We waited until our 'defense committee', specially trained for such an incident, copied their costumes and stole a few of their hats. When the crew was drunker than usual, we used one of their rowboats, surprised the two guards on their ship, and burned it!"

"So what happened to the crew?"

"That's another story. Then we began to trade with some Japanese families who had settled on the northeastern coast. Somehow *they* arrived and built a string of villages without any of us noticing."

"Japanese families?"

"Yes, and that's *another* story," she said with a wink.

"Anyway, in 1820, a big ship was spotted flying a strange flag with a two-headed bird on it. It finally anchored at Old Bay, right near where you washed up. It turned out to be the *Vostok*, captained by a fellow named Bellingshausen. He was sailing the oceans around Antarctica to claim anything overlooked by the other European colonizers.

"Our Island was his first major find. One of the ship's officers spoke English, allowing conversation with our locals. When they first saw us, fair-skinned and half-naked, I'm sure we were like no one they'd ever seen before. They soon found out they were dealing with an intelligent and no-nonsense group of women, not loyal to England, but to their own tribes, and to our founder, Mother Cecelia."

She took a long breath. "See how well I remember my tenth-year history lessons?"

I nodded, duly impressed.

"So this Captain Bellingshausen declared our Island, and its inhabitants a possession of the czar of Russia. He was savvy, and promised us that Russia would prevent the British from giving us trouble. We had to trust 'im, and they've been 'ere ever since."

"So I've noticed," I said.

"They pretty much let us be, as promised, but they took great numbers of seals and whales, and nearly killed off our sea otters! Fortunately, few Russians wanted to settle here—too far from home I guess. But they've been awfully busy with their military business lately!"

Janie's lecture was interrupted when we emerged from the trees. A vast coastline revealed itself before us...

"Whoa!" she said. "This spot always gets to me, though I haven't walked this path in quite a while. That's Weddell Bay down there, and we'll head north once we get to the beach."

The little worm of doubt in my brain persisted—*Is all this real?*

After two more hours of brisk downhill hiking we approached a colorful village tucked among shore pines and thick shrubbery.

"This is the Greenfield tribe, an' I'm, gettin' ready fer lunch," said Jainie.

We were soon among houses painted in pale shades of pink, turquoise, yellow and green. The path widened into a street with shops, cafes, an inviting inn, all with little signs saying **WELCOME TRAVELERS**.

Janie stopped and said, "I been meanin' to tell ya—I have a friend here who I'd like to say Hullo to—is that all right with ya?"

"Uh, okay, sure."

"Good! His name is Bryan, and he lives right over there." She turned and headed toward a yellow stucco house facing the tribe's commons. I followed, amused and curious by Janie's new itinerary. She opened the door and called in, "'Aay, Bryan, are ya in here?"

"In the back," called a voice. "Is that *you*, Janie?"

"Yeh. Hope I'm not botherin' ya."

A tall, broad-chested fellow with a boyish face and curly blond hair emerged, eyes wide. "Heyyy, what a surprise!" He wrapped her up in a hug that looked suffocating. I was put off by his big grin. He looked like one of those guys who always gets what he wants.

When he glanced at me, Janie said, "This is Gordy. He's gonna stay with me family up at Gifford. He's had some memory problems, an' claims he sailed here on a raft from California."

I thought we weren't gonna mention that...

Bryan looked at me, eyes wide again. "Well now, that would be quite a voyage! You mean, California in America?"

"Yep, that's the one," I said, finally looking directly at him.

"Say Bryan, I've really enjoyed yer lovely letters, an' I didn't think I'd be coming by here until just the other day. So, um, would ya like to join us fer lunch? We're headin' over to th' Field Creek Inn. I'll even treat." She looked at me, and I nodded at the prospect of food.

"Ahh, I'd love to, Janes," he said, "but I have some, ah, work to do on the house."

At that moment, a tall woman appeared from a back room, a loose gown hanging off her shoulder. She smiled at us and put her hand around Bryan's waist.

"Oh, uh, this is Megan," said Bryan, suddenly red-faced. "Meggie, meet Janie, and uh, Jordy."

"Goodtameetcha," she said, grinning with her big white teeth.

Janie slowly looked her over, and then at Bryan. I felt for Janie, but I was weirdly glad that Bryan had this Megan person.

"Ah. Too bad yer so busy," Janie said. "I was hopin' we coulda chatted. By the way, me friend's name is Gordy."

"Sure, right," Bryan said, while Megan ran her hand up and down his back.

Janie turned to me, "Shall we get some lunch?"

"Sure!"

We were out the door without another word.

The inn was a short walk from Bryan's house, and by the time we arrived, Janie had already blown off a string of expletives, winding down with, "…and he deserves that twit!" She barely paused when a young waiter quickly dropped off some menus. He eventually returned to take our orders.

Janie continued, "I passed through here on my way to Covenmoor, and we met in this very café. He was a charmer, that Bryan. We, um, had quite a night of it, but I was young, just out o' the house, and bent on bein' a witch, so I didn't stay. I sure missed him for a while. In his letters he said he'd *loooove* for me to come visit again. What a plonker!"

This seemed a great time to just listen. Janie sipped some water, sighed, and looked at me. "I didn't tell ya about Bryan 'cause I wasn't sure I'd see 'im. He hasn't written me in quite a while, yet my hopes soared when he came out an' hugged me. I felt so good fer a minute there…"

Her eyes shined as she looked at my blank gaze. "Ahh, someday yer'll know what I mean."

"But I'm confused," I said. "I thought you were attracted to women, like Estelle."

Janie looked through the window into the distance. "Bryan made me feel I was special. But after Estelle happened, I *was* confused. Afterward I drifted on to Kronstadt, got the cafeteria job, and then *you* came along."

"Me? What did *I* do?"

She leaned toward me with a serious look. "You're the kind of friend I didn't know I needed, especially after yer little stunt last night pushed my buttons." She looked up with a twist of a smile. "I think that was good for me."

"So, ah, do you know which way you…?"

"I'm still figgerin' it out."
So much to take in…Janie, Russians, witches, Hum energy, my dream-journey.
And whooo is Roselin?

We had been staring out the window for some time when Janie suddenly froze. She slowly turned to me and whispered, "There's someone out there I recognize from the base, standing across the street."

Sure enough, a fellow dressed in a kind of leisure suit seemed to be studying the landscape, but he didn't seem alone. "Hey," I whispered back, "I see a woman up the street watching *him*."

Both of them looked entirely out of place.

Uh, oh.

We were still spooked when our sandwiches arrived, so we did our best to chomp them down without looking like anything was amiss. The thought of someone out there watching us made it hard to swallow. Janie casually looked for a back door as we finished up. She bumped my foot. "Get ready to move…"

But when we stole another quick glance at the street, the man and the woman were both gone.

Who *were* they?

Janie finally said, "Okay, that either happened or it didn't, but that guy rattled me, and I want to get into the bush as far and fast as we can. But we're gonna need more provisions for the trail, and we'll have to take a chance on the food shop here. I have a feeling Alaine had something to do with this!"

That blockhead feeling again…

'Sorry Janie."

"Aww, no worries. Ya didn't mean it. But no more chattin' away like that again, unnerstand?"

"Okay, fine, but you had to tell Bryan about my raft trip here, so it's not just me!"

She looked at me, then out the window. "Okay, fair call."

Janie paid and asked if we could go out through the kitchen. Outside she said, "Your turn with the backpack. We're going to head up the coast and then stop at Alison's Beach. Let's go."

The grocery-shop visit went without incident, and I was determined to not complain about the now fully-loaded backpack.

"So what is Alison's Beach?" I said.

"It's sort of a walkers' resort with a great body-surfing beach."

"Body surfing?" I immediately brightened.

"I thought you might like a swim break."

Janie led us down a little-used track through brambly scrub for about an hour before we returned to the main path. "I'm not too worried about Russians catching us out here—no roads and a lot of hiding places. I don't know if that guy was even watching *us!* He sure got to Greenfield in a hurry if he was."

As we continued walking around Weddell Bay, Janie began to relax. Also, the sunshine was getting too warm for our sweatshirts. Janie had stopped to pull hers off and gave me a jolt when her undershirt rode up to reveal her, um, chest. I quickly looked away to admire the landscape.

She saw my shyness. "I hope I didn't flash too much there, Mister Gordon."

I glanced at her, my face glowing.

"Ohthatsokay!"

"I should prob'ly warn ya—Islanders, when they get near a warm beach, tend to wear very little in the way of clothes. We call it sky-clad, get it?"

"Sort-of."

Is that what I saw in those Sunshine Health *magazines I found once, where whole families, were outside with no clothes on? But all that seemed like another world. No one I knew ever did that!*

She looked at me like she wanted me to say more, but all I could do was smile sheepishly.

The landscape was indeed stunning. Far above us, last night's snow was still visible on the upper slopes we had left earlier this morning. These mountains felt like a shield between us and the Russians, reminding me I never wanted to be in a room like that again!

*

We eventually arrived at a bluff overlooking a large sandy cove where good-size waves were rolling in. I could barely make out several tiny swimmers in the surf near a cluster of beach huts.

"That's it—that's Alison's Beach," said Janie.

"Wow, you're right, the waves look great!"

By the time we reached the hut-village, I was dragging under the heavy backpack. Janie bought us fresh bunberry-orange drinks at a juice-stand, then led us straight onto the beach. The waves crested and boomed invitingly, and I dumped off the pack with great relief.

Though the sun was warm, the breeze was chilly, but that didn't seem to bother anyone. Janie was right—the swimmers and sunbathers were nearly all "sky-clad." I felt weirdly embarrassed but also curious— what to make of all this?

Janie pulled out the one towel we shared, threw off her clothes, tossed them next to it, and ran into the water. "Gaaa! It's cold," she shouted."

I looked away—her nakedness was too much. I decided to wear my baggy undershorts, though they made me feel self-conscious and dumb. But while thrashing around trying to get used to the chill, a churning wave overtook me and snatched them off! Then a pleasant revelation—swimming with nothing on felt wonderful. Since everyone else was already this way, I gave up worrying. Janie was further out and luckily ignored me. Also, I caught a few good rides right along with the other swimmers.

Later, back in our clothes, we found two stools at a beach-bar called the Sandyfoot Cantina. Janie's thick hair was salty and wild.

"So, nature-boy, how was yer swim?"

I blushed and stared at my drink. "It was okay." Then I looked at her. "More than okay, I really liked it. Thanks."

"Thought ya might. You'll get used to this in no time."

Then she ordered fish-and-rice dishes for us. When they arrived, I gave my serving a skeptical look.

"You'll adore it," she said. "It's a sautéed dish we adopted from our Japanese neighbors. Those are chunks of South-Hebrides tuna and various veggies, stir-fried, then served over steamed rice. It's good! And uh, we're on a budget now, so I need yer to like it. Here, try this tamari."

I didn't 'adore' it, but I liked it enough. In fact, I was surprised about the food here. At home I didn't want anything but sugary cereal, hamburgers, bananas, and canned peaches.

Full and satisfied, Janie sat back and said, "I remember an inn outside Bentley where we can stay tonight. It's only about two miles from here. Tomorrow I want to show yer some more stuff, especially Wave Point."

"Wave Point?"

"Yeh…every January, during the highest tides, the Wave Festival is held there. People from all over camp there for a week or so, and at night everyone dances to drums and flutes. They also dance to the rhythm of the waves on an ancient stone platform, just above the surf. I hope yer getting all this, 'cause it's important."

"Uh, yeah. I saw it mentioned on a calendar in your uncle's office."

"Anyway, the dancers always got wet from the waves, so they began a tradition of almost-no-clothes. The energy can get pretty wild. When the Hum comes swirling through, as it always does, the dancing becomes a kind of fertility rite. Yer'll have to come back in January and check it out!"

"Okaaay," I said with a twitch of hesitation…*fertility rite?*

In the tiny settlement of Bentley, we found a trailside inn called the White Rose Retreat, run by an affable white-haired couple. The place was made up of roomy canvas tents, a shower-shed and a communal kitchen.

"I wanted to stay here the last time I came through," said Janie. "Let's give it a try."

"Fine with me." My feet were sore, and my body was bone-weary. Janie had carried the pack since our swim, and looked equally exhausted. This was one long day!

In our spacious tent, we were so tired we could barely spread our bedding on the cots. Janie crawled out of her clothes and straight into her sleeping bag, rolled over and said, "'Night."

"Mmf." I said.

Later in the night I heard her cry out, loud and clear, *But is it LOVE?*

*

"Dang!" Janie said, startling me awake. "I wanted to be on our way by now. We must've slept 12 hours."

I looked at her, still half asleep. "I'm hungry."

She tossed her pillow at my head. "Then arise and help me make breakfast!"

In the camp's kitchen, we put together two hefty servings of beans, eggs and some local pineapple. While packing up, she said, "Ya get to haul this for the first few hours today. Me back needs a rest!"

The path led us to the next village, hidden deep in the coastal hills. "We're coming into the Silverhill tribe," said Janie. "They make the most gorgeous silver jewelry, but it's all done in secret. They know that if the Russians ever find out, the tribe will be mining silver for the Soviet cause! They call themselves Hillians, and they only show their wares at short-notice trade fairs."

"That must be a hard secret to keep."

"Yeh, but it helps that the Russians don't really care what we do among ourselves, especially out here. But as a precaution, forget anything I ever said, or say, about silver mines!"

"Yes'm."

Janie was heating up again about the Russians. "The Soviets talk a lot about 'communal sharing', especially with our wheat and wool, but they're really a bunch of greedy bastids!"

"So the Russians, uh, rule the island and they can take whatever they want?

"Yeh, they *ruuuule* this Island." she said, her eyes blazing. But with a twinkle she added, "At least they like to think they do."

The subject was dropped.

*

At the Hillians' general store, Janie bought me a wide-brimmed bush hat. "Yer face an' neck are gettin' red, my man, even when yer not blushin'."

I tried it on in front of the little mirror by the hat display, and we both agreed—I looked good.

In a half-hidden glass case in the back of the shop, we found a display of exquisite silver pendants and earrings shaped into tiny leaves, sleek animal shapes and sinuous mermaids. I was amazed at the artistry "I've never seen designs like this."

Janie selected a necklace with a pendant featuring an acrobatic otter. She tried it on and said, "Yeh, they make wonderful things here. I'd let yer buy this for me if ya had any money..."

Her impish look and the lovely pendant provoked something.

"YouareincrediblybeautifulJanie!" I said it before I could stop myself.

Janie's face turned unexpectedly red. "Aww, that's nice o' yer."

I tipped my floppy new hat at her, thinking who knows what.

On the path again, the ocean remained to our right, the steep mountains to our left.

ZWOOP

After we walked some distance, Janie abruptly moved behind me and started digging into the pack, nearly throwing me off balance. She pulled out an apple for each of us and said, "Here, this is for now, and we'll have lunch at the ruins I wanna show ya."

"Ruins?"

"Yeh, ruins. A whole town. Wait'll ya see 'em."

About two hours later Janie led us on an overgrown side path to a substantial cluster of tumbled-down stone structures not far above the beach. Stunted trees and weeds grew everywhere, giving the place a haunted, very-long-abandoned look.

The walls were mostly single-story, but the stonework was impressive. Blocks as large as refrigerators were shaped and fitted tightly with no visible mortar. We followed an ancient street paved with equally massive stone slabs.

"This is *amaaazing*!" I said.

"We're coming into our Sacred Coast," said Janie. "We call this place the Freshwater Ruins."

"Sacred Coast?"

Janie's face softened. "Ah, certain places are the soul of our Island. Roger's Dreamland, The Coast of Nevermore, Mt. Hayes, and the Sacred Coast, to name a few. These ruins are one of our spiritual places."

"It sounds kind of religious. Is it a church or something?"

"Oh, much better than any church. Hum energy is very strong on this coast."

Ah..

"So, is the Hum some kind of religion?"

She gave me a quick look.

"That's been debated. Many Islanders all the way back to Mother Cecelia think the Hum delivers spiritual messages from the Goddesses or from the Universe itself. Roselin believes the Hum is purely in the realm of physics, coming from that place where energy and matter meet."

I mulled over this while we walked.

"I like the spiritual-message idea..."

"So, Gordy, I'm curious now—whaddaya do back home fer *your* spirituality?"

That was easy. "I go straight to the beach and look at the ocean for a while."

"Ah. I get that."

We sat down in the shade of an ancient wall featuring a weathered carving of an animal head – a lemur or a cat? We leaned back to rest our eyes.

I looked down a weed-littered street. "So, uh, who built this place?"

Janie gave me that here-comes-another-lesson look. "All we know is a culture we call the Old People built towns like this all over the Island, some dating back twelve thousand years. The College of Antiquities at Putney University is dedicated to your very question!"

"Why do you call them the 'Old People'?"

"It's the best way to describe 'em, I suppose. We don't know much about 'em, or even what they called themselves."

"Then they left?"

"We think they abandoned the entire Island about 900 years ago, but I sometimes wonder."

"You mean some of them might still be here?"

"Dunno."

I looked around as if I might spot an Old Person.

"So where did they go?"

"Dunno that either. Let's eat, I'm starving!"

The prospect of lunch overwhelmed my curiosity as Janie dug into our pack for more apples, a chunk of hard cheese, a tin of sardines, and a plum tart for dessert.

"I see you found some nice snacks back at the Silverhill store."

"Yeh, and the tart came from Greenfield. You can get quite a variety of edibles from the tribes who cater to travelers. And some of them let you work for an hour or so for food. Ya don't need much money on the paths."

My mouth was too full to reply.

As we ate, I stared at the ocean off in the distance. A meadowlark sang nearby, which took me back to quiet mornings at home, before things went crazy. Now I wonder if I'll ever go back there, and what I'll find if I do.

"Let's look around," said Janie.

*

Leaving our pack, we wandered through more ancient streets until we came upon a large open-air room with some of its walls still in place. A red-veined marble floor had been swept clean of debris and was surprisingly smooth. The room was empty except for a massive chair dominating one end. It seemed to have been carved out of a single block of white marble. A throne!

"Wow! This looks so, uh, new."

Janie stepped up to the chair and sat down as if she were ready for her audience of petitioners. "Hey, Gordy, this was carved to fit two rear-ends! Does that mean there were two leaders?—a king and queen, a prince and princess?"

I climbed up and sat next to her. The chair's arms were carved with faint markings, very worn, as if by centuries of human contact.

She nudged her rear-end against mine. "This double-seat makes things pretty cozy," she said with a wink.

Trying to ignore that, I observed how tidy the room was. "I wonder if someone comes by to maintain this place?"

"Dunno," said Janie.

We sat there taking in the open-air room, and the silence.

Then something began to vibrate the marble beneath us, a soft tingling sensation under my butt, and Janie's eyebrows went up. Soon a soft rumble, like distant thunder, approached from several directions.

"Ooh, this is wild!" said Janie. "I haven't heard the Hum this deep in a *looong* time."

The sound travelled through the room and right through my brain, leaving hints of messages and images, too fleeting to consciously remember.

The intense resonance lasted only about a minute before it drifted off toward the ocean.

We stared at each other in wonder. *That was awwwesome!*

"I've never heard it that loud and deep," I said.

She merely nudged my butt one more time and flashed a quick wink as she hopped off.

Is she testing me?

"What was that all about?" I said.

Janie went a little quiet. "I'm not sure, but this could be a place where Hum energy might be focused. Maybe that's why the Old People built this."

"Do you think it was trying to tell us something?"

"Danged if I know."

When we returned for our pack, Janie pointed out a small lake just beyond the ruins. "We call it Freshwater Pond, and it's fed by a warm spring. We can fill our canteens there, and maybe even swim."

"Uh…okay!"

At the pond, Janie wasted no time to strip down and wade into the water. She seemed to linger, showing off her backside. "Ooh, it's a bit bracing, Gordy!" she called back. I hesitated only a few seconds, stopped thinking altogether, and followed her lead. The water was chilly but tolerable, and the sun was warm. I swam toward Janie, not knowing how close to get, given the situation.

She gave me a funny look then dove, and a few seconds later something grabbed my ankle!

I jerked my leg, couldn't shake the grip, and I was helplessly thrashing. Then Janie surfaced and yelled "Gotcha!" I wrestled with her, trying to get an advantage, but she was strong. We kept at it until we both held on to each other almost like a hug, then she planted a hard wet kiss on my mouth and pushed away.

"Hey, no fair! You almost gave me frostbite when *I* tried that!"

"I'm just playin'…altogether different! You can blame that Hum we just heard."

I wonder what spiritual messages she *got?*

She grinned and splashed at me before swimming back to shore, leaving me with a buzzy-warm feeling, embarrassingly physical down there, and crazy emotional up here! The only word I could think of that described this weirdness was…*zwoop*.

I paddled around in the water until things settled down, then joined Janie to take my turn drying off with our single towel. While I quickly fumbled for my clothes, Janie simply went to the spring to fill the canteens. Coming back, she saw me look away and said, "Hey, it's okay if we see each other this way. Now just relax and look at me before I get insulted!"

I looked at her, full on.

She's beautiful!

With an embarrassed smile I said, "Okay, I'll try to get used to it."

Janie snorted and got dressed.

*

Refreshed after our lunch and swim, Janie set the pace for some serious walking. My still-wimpy legs could barely keep up!

After an hour or so, we reached the main path again, which led us to a rocky bluff. Janie said, "Let's stop a minute."

Below the bluff a small stone platform jutted into the surf. A family was camped not far from it, the first fellow travelers we'd seen all day. They had set up tents and a flapping canopy next to a fire pit. Two kids were digging in the wet sand while a tall fellow, probably their dad, stood nearby with a-fishing pole. On the platform, a woman wearing only a long flowing skirt had begun to dance. She moved slowly at first, then with a more rapid tempo. Her face seemed to glow as exploding waves bathed her in a fine spray.

Such graceful motion!

"That, Gordy, is the Wave Dance!"

The whole family—the kids playing, the dad fishing, and the woman's graceful movements made a lovely scene. She was at one with the ocean's energy, her hair flying as she danced with increasing abandon to the rhythm of the booming surf.

I was thoroughly enchanted.

"Hey Gordy, you can stop starin'," Janie said, though she seemed to be staring too. "Let's stay here a while to give 'em some room. She's in her own world and I don't wanna interrupt that."

The dad and the kids must have heard her and they looked up. They waved at us, and we waved back. Janie said, "I've danced to the waves a couple o' times meself. Sometimes alone like her, but usually in a crowd with crazy drumming. It felt like being blessed. It's hard to describe."

As we sat there, I began to feel a strange deep gratitude; I was glad to be here. I said to Janie, "Thanks for getting me out of that jail, or whatever it was, and for forgiving me."

Janie watched the dancer. "Yer welcome."

*

Janie broke the spell when she abruptly said, "Now we'll have to figure out how to get around Silent Bay."

Then I remembered. "Didn't Norbert say something about Russians there?

"Yeh, their navy is building a submarine base there, an' don't get me started about their stupid submarines! Let's just pretend we're taking a sightseeing detour up into the hills for a while."

I looked at her, curious to know more. "Uh, okay."

"We'll stop at the Bella Shore tribe to see if they know anything," Janie added. "The Bellas are nice people. They host the Wave Festival and maintain the beaches here. The festival would be chaos and the whole place a mess without them."

The Bella Shore post office consisted of a service window and about thirty post-boxes, which shared space with the village barber shop. By luck, the postal window was still open.

"They'll be able to tell us how to get around that Russian base," said Janie. "I've hiked through here before, but the situation keeps changing."

I began to feel a little nervous.

An older fellow wearing a green plastic visor sat behind the window, reading a newspaper. In the neighboring shop, a very skinny barber in a button-down shirt and shorts was trimming someone's beard. The guy in the visor looked up at us.

Janie said, "Hullo. We're wonderin' about the detour north o' here."

He folded the paper carefully and sat up. "On a walkabout are ya?"

"Yeh."

"So, ya know about the sub-base, right?"

"Yup."

"Well, to avoid it, follow the new path up toward Helen Peak, and then down Sixmile Creek to the Kowloon River. Then you'll see the main path again. The red arrows will point the way." Then he added, "The Otter Preserve is off limits now, and they patrol the whole peninsula day and night, just so ya know."

"Bloody Hell!" muttered Janie. "We'll miss it completely. I wanted to show it to ya, Gordy, but I don't wanna risk..." She remembered the clerk. "Oh, uh, thanks mate, fer the help."

"Welcome," he replied, and went back to his paper.

"All right, let's get some food here and we'll find the detour. We can walk a few more miles before dark."

"Janie, are you sure this is safe for us? What if a patrol spots us and brings us in? Asks questions? Calls their headquarters in Kronstadt?"

She steadied me with both her hands on my shoulders.

"Relax, Gordy. We're just two walkers tryin' to get home to Gifford, and ya lost your ID 'cause yer not quite in this world—how's that?"

Not in this world? That's definitely a possibility.

"Okay...I guess."

"Trust me, but just in case, keep that hat low over yer eyes."

*

The detour was well-marked with cut-out red arrows attached to wooden stakes. Following them, we hiked into more brush-covered hills until we spotted Silent Bay off in the distance. From here the bay looked more like a lake, but I could just make out a narrow channel to the ocean, mostly hidden between steep bluffs. At first the landscape appeared uninhabited, but then we spotted some trucks disappearing under a huge camouflage net. There were no submarines visible anywhere.

"That place looks creepy," I said. "They must be hiding their base under that huge tent-thing."

"Yeh. Now stay low, an' assume we're being watched. I don't want them to think we're at all interested by standing here gawking. And if they catch us out here, they will fer-shur assume yer a spy!"

She led us into us a wooded ravine well out of sight of any patrols, to camp for the night. "I think we'll be safe here, Gordy."

The evening grew chilly as an icy breeze wafted down from the nearby mountains. We put on our sweaters, set up our tent, and Janie made some soup on the little stove. No campfire tonight!

After supper, we settled into our sleeping bag and blankets, both letting out sighs of relief after another long day.

I was beginning to drift off when Janie said, "Now don't be shy, 'cause I'm cold and I want to cuddle with ya."

I didn't know what to say. I'd never been 'cuddled' before. Finally, gathering some courage, I turned to her and said, "Okay."

She seemed to take forever fussing with the sleeping bag and blankets to make up a larger bed while I tried *not* to think about what might happen next. She said softly, "Okay, lay down on yer side facing away from me."

She soon scootched up to my back, pulled the covers over us, and gently put an arm over my middle. At first I stiffened up and she said, "Just relax, I'm not gonna *do* anything."

As ordered, I relaxed, and it actually felt nice.

"I like it, Janie."

"Mmmmm," she said.

In the morning, Janie was facing the other way, her back snug against mine. I moved to look at her, in a kind of wonder.

Why does she even like me?

I must have awakened her, and she said over a yawn, "Do yer know why I like ya?"

My eyes went wide. *How did you know...?*

She wriggled onto her back and looked up at the tent ceiling. "When I saw ya in that jail room, there was somethin' in yer eyes that struck me, and it was more than the Hum thing! I don't think I felt anything like that with Estelle. This is different. It's hard to explain."

"Different than Bryan?"

"Yeh, different than him. I finally saw Bryan fer what he is—a fake! But yer just *you.* Ya don't act like yer anythin' other than who ya are, and ya have real courage to be trampin' around with someone ya don't know, on an island you've never heard of, not to mention yer family in California bein' in some kinda limbo. And besides all that, yer kinda cute."

Zwoop.

I gulped, and concentrated on a fly crawling on the tent ceiling.

"Now I have to pee," she said, "and we need to get going."

OTTERS AND RELATIONSHIPS

We quickly downed a breakfast of dried-fruit and smoked-salmon, and were on our way again. It was all uphill at first. Finally, from the top of the big hill Janie called Helen Peak, a long stretch of coast lay before us. "That's Otter Bay," she said. "And see the coastline toward the horizon? That's where I grew up, and that's where we're gonna stay a while. Whaddaya think?"

I gazed at the panorama in front of us and felt a little overwhelmed by all this *geography*.

"Uh, it's nice, Janie. I think I could stay here a while."

"Well, I hope ya can, 'cause I don't know where else I can take ya."

When I spotted a road in the distance, Janie said, "In case yer wondering about that road, the Russians were once planning a big hotel at Gifford Bay, but when the Great War hit them in 1940, it all stopped. No hotel."

"So the Russians no longer use that road?"

"They use it enough, so we'll stay shy of it!"

*

Our detour-path eventually joined Sixmile Creek, just as the postmaster had described. The water was clean and swift-flowing, so we stopped to wash the dust off and have lunch.

While we were sitting and eating, several lemurs, or monkeycats, approached and sat up to watch us. "I've never seen these guys so friendly before," said Janie. "They must like ya."

"Ummf," I tried to reply while chewing. "I dunno about that, but I like them a lot."

"They remind me of our sacred otters," she said. "That's why we call this place Otter Bay. The little guys, the otters I mean, have only come back during the last twenty years or so."

"So why are they sacred?"

She looked at me. "Okay, bear with me here because this might sound strange. Before the Russians showed up, our ancestors were strugglin' to survive. Getting enough to eat and not getting' sick were a big deal then. But there were a few bright days, like when someone got married.

"Now, here's the strange part. One day, near a settlement way west of here called Womby, there was a wedding. Everyone was walking through some woods on the way to the ceremony, and several people, including the bride and groom, met an otter leaning against a gum tree. The otter was the usual plain brown color but the trees around him were *glowing* in rainbow colors. This otter looked at each person, and somehow knowing their name said, 'Don't worry, Elsa, everything'll be all right.' We know this because this Elsa person, and several others, described the event in their diaries."

A prickling in the back of my neck. "An *otter* said this?"

"Yeh. Some people didn't see the otter at all, and they insisted the event never happened. It occurred more than once before the sightings stopped—sometime after the Russians arrived."

"Janie!" I said. "This happened to me in a dream! A few months ago I was having a terrible time at school, and one night I dreamed an otter was leaning against a tree, and it told me the exact same thing, that 'everything would be all right'. And the trees surrounding it were shimmering in radiant colors!"

Janie looked at me, and said with a catch in her throat, "Oooh, something is definitely going on here, another reason why you're here. This is way more than random coincidence!"

Not to mention mind-boggling!

*

After lunch, we finally rejoined the East Coast Path. We had to cross the road twice, but, like Janie said, there was no sign of Russian traffic. Now we were once again walking among the beach-dunes beyond the town of Otter.

"Ahh, it feels so good to be back on these beaches, *my* beaches," said Janie. "Now we should camp—I know a place up ahead."

She led us to a wooded campground just above some impressive surf. It was a popular overnight spot, complete with toilets and a water spigot. The familiar ocean breeze and the soothing roar of the waves were reassuringly like home. I put up the tent while Janie set out cheese and apple slices.

And we weren't alone.

As night fell, other campfires flickered-up in the woods around us. Our own fire felt nice against the damp sea air. "At least it's not so cold tonight," said Janie, looking at me, "but we can cuddle again if you want…"

"Sure," I said, trying to act cool while grinning inside.

Her steady breathing behind me felt like more than a blessing.

*

In the morning chill I was thankful for Janie's warmth.

Voices began muttering outside, causing her to stir behind me.

"Good-mornin'," she said, and leaned over to give me a smooch on the cheek.

Mmmm.

A male voice not far from our tent got Janie's full attention. "That guy sounds familiar!" And she was soon up and dressed. Once outside, she called, "Hey, Josh!"

I dressed in a hurry and joined them. Janie was talking excitedly with two young guys. "Gordy," she said, "This is me good friend Josh, an' his partner Colin, who are from Elsinore, right near Gifford."

"Uh, hi Josh, hi Colin…" I was about to say more when Josh pulled us all in for a group hug.

Whoa…this is a first!

Janie was grinning. "Meet Josh the hugger! He says they're on their way home from Putney, and they have a *real* truck with room in the back if we want a ride!"

Colin said, "We sold our entire load of berries at the Fantasia Market. It was a good run."

Josh added, "It's a long drive back, so we usually stop here to camp. So nice to run into ya, Janie."

"You too, Josh," Janie said, blushing a little, and I felt another brief pang of jealousy. *Is he another old boyfriend or something?*

The two men invited us to share their breakfast. Colin said, "Josh caught some perch in the surf this morning, and it's too much fish for just us."

"Ya gotta have some," said Josh. "We have some bunberries left, too."

"I have a tin o' milk we can serve with those berries," said Janie. "An' who's makin' coffee?"

Josh served up the grilled fillets as we sat around their inviting fire. Back home, Mom had given up trying to serve me fish, but somehow this was different. I picked out the bones and ate it all.

While Josh and Colin sat back with their coffee, chatting quietly, Janie said, "Hey, Gordy, let's walk out to the surf."

We were barefoot for the first time since Alison's Beach, and the sand felt wonderful. As the waves ran over our feet, Janie said, "Lemme tell ya about Josh. We grew up together, and I once had a big crush on him, but he was always, well, polite, and we just stayed friends. He loved farming, which is what they do in Elsinore, and after he finished school, he went at it full-time, like a calling. Then Colin showed up on his Long Walk, stopped at Elsinore, an' worked there alongside Josh. They got along, Colin stayed, and now they live together, like bein' married."

"Two *guys…married?*"

Janie gave me a where-have-you-been look. "It's an old custom here that began when many of the women partnered up together, those 'other marriages' I mentioned before. Quite a few of the men then followed suit. It took a while to overcome the old religious taboos, but it seems to work, an' lemme tell ya, some o' the back-country tribes are quite an education in creative togetherness!"

Just then Colin and Josh ran past us like racehorses into the surf, white butts flashing. While keeping an eye on their fine physiques, Janie asked me, "Didn't they say anythin' about that in yer school? We went through a three-week section called 'Relationships' in our Loving, Caring and Being class."

"That's amazing, Janie. I don't remember one word spoken about 'loving' at my school!"

*

When we returned to camp, Josh and Colin were back in their shirts and shorts and already loading their gear into the truck. Janie and I quickly packed our own gear and then climbed into the back. The covered cargo space was cramped with empty crates, camping gear, two old suitcases, and the powerful smell of ripe berries.

"Hang on," shouted Colin. "The road is only partly paved, and full 'a chuck-holes. If you need us to stop for anything, just bang on the cab."

And we were off, lurching and bumping as promised.

After about a half-hour of inhaling dust, Janie slapped the cab. When the truck stopped, she said, "I gotta pee, and my butt is sore as hell."

I coughed and said, "Mine too, and the dust is making it hard to breathe."

While Janie headed for the bushes, Josh and Colin climbed out and stretched their long arms. The road had become more like a meandering path.

"Hey," said Colin, "Let's pull off the tarp now that we're nearly home. No need to worry about prying eyes out here."

Underway again, the fresh air was wonderful, and we could see things! Though I still wondered about those two "observers" back in Greenfield, Janie seemed much more relaxed.

Beyond a point called Bob's Rocks, we passed through Ignatz, a town with one store, six houses and a small museum. "I stopped here on my way south last year," Janie said. "That museum is full of old newspaper comic strips, many from America, that someone collected. I heard they named the town after a cartoon mouse."

"Oh, yeah," I said. "Ignatz! He's always throwing that brick at Krazy Kat."

Janie looked skeptical. "Ya don't say."

"They have a special relationship, so I've heard."

*

After another bumpy, dusty hour, we approached a settlement of tiny houses around a rambling inn with a beach-side café. A hand-painted sign said *Julia's Paradise*. Josh parked and jumped out of the cab and said, "This is our favorite lunch stop—shall we dine?"

Leaving the truck by the road, we followed a narrow path down to the inn. "You'll love Julia's," Janie told me. "They have the best seafood and rum drinks, though I suppose yer a bit young fer the rum."

The breezy restaurant had few walls and no doors. A young fellow looking like he just came off the beach showed us to a table. Mid-day sunlight glistened on the waves just outside as men and women in swimshorts and not much else casually walked by.

"As you might have guessed, Julia's is a haven for the beach people," Janie said.

I looked at the chalkboard menu. "Hey, they serve hamburgers!"

When our lunches arrived, Janie peered at my plate and said, "That is a strange-looking sandwich, especially that thing of burned meat in there."

I shrugged, assembled everything with the proper condiments, and deliriously chewed on my first bite. Janie rolled her eyes.

Josh and Colin, clearly tired from their long trip, ate quietly. Finally Josh said, "We should move on. A lot to do back home."

Meet the MacEvoys

The road ended at the edge of a little town next to a wide sandy bay. When the truck's clattering motor finally stopped, the quiet was intense. "This is Hockney. Gifford and Elsinore are just a short walk further," said Janie.

After we all hopped off, she asked Josh, "So how did you get this truck?"

"This is officially a 'people's truck'," he said. "The Soviet Agricultural people rent it to us and the Hockney fishing co-op. We applied for it as the Elsinore Bay Commune, and they said okay. The Russians get part of our shipments in trade for the rent and gas coupons. It's fair enough."

They tossed their gear and several empty crates into the back of a dusty pedivan parked nearby. Josh said, "The truck stays here, so we use this 'van to get up to our farm. It's a lot of pedaling, but we love the quiet—no engines."

Almost in unison, they both said, "Good meetin' ya, Gordy!" And Josh added, "Take care, Janie!" and they ambled off.

The gentle slope ahead of us was covered with carefully-tended farms that likely included Josh and Colin's berry fields. The bay at the foot of the slope was busy with boats and fishermen, and with kids playing on the sandy shore. A paved bayshore path connected at least four distinct villages, busy with people walking, pushing carts or driving pedivans, while seagulls screeched overhead.

Janie followed my gaze. "Well, here we are," she said. "That's Elsinore Bay, an' beyond the sand spit is Gifford Bay. An' off in the distance that way begins the Coast of Nevermore."

Janie paused, let out a deep breath, then she said, "Our house is this way."

*

As we walked toward Gifford, Janie said, "It's Gifford Haven on the map, but everyone just calls it Gifford. The commons is over there, and our house is the sandy-brown one just up the hill."

She took another deep breath. "Now I need to say some things about me parents…"

Uh oh, here we go. They probably won't want me.

"Me mum and dad are, ah, kind of distant. They keep to themselves. Dad builds furniture, has his own shop in back of our house. He and a few other wood-masters have made Gifford well-known for its pencil-pine furniture."

I thought of the navy commander's solid-looking pine desk.

"Me mum isn't the huggy-cuddly sort. She says she needs alone-time to write her articles for the *Islander News,* and other stuff she won't show me. They're both like that—not wantin' to share much o' themselves. Also, when I was little they would sometimes stare at me like I was a space alien or something. That memory still feels a bit creepy.

"But you might be lucky, Gordy. Me dad lives in a house o' females, and since yer a boy, he might take to ya just fine."

Then Janie brought up something else. "*Annnd,* we need to keep quiet about yer run-in with the Russians, especially with me mum. They didn't like me working on that navy base in the first place. Me dad told me I was selling out."

"So, I guess you're not going back there."

"Nope…and don't tell 'em anything about Estelle, either."

*

A few minutes later we were approaching Janie's house. A brick path led us under a wooden archway nearly hidden by a bushy bougainvillea. A handmade sign at the top of the arch said…

MacEvoy.

"We always use the kitchen door, through the yard this way."

Janie's voice must have carried. A tall woman was leaning against the door frame as we approached.. Her strong jaw, long gray braids and heavy eyebrows were intimidating, yet oddly friendly.

"And who might this be?" the woman asked Janie, before saying hello.

"Hey Mum! This is a friend o' mine who needs a place to stay."

Her eyebrows shot up as she studied me. "Ahh, Janie, you've done it again! Bringing home some creature like that baby randall fox you found. And how are we going to afford to put him up?"

Creature?

Before Janie could answer, the woman said, "And where might you be from, young man?"

Janie intervened with a sigh, "Gordy, meet me mum, Sheryl. Mum, this is Gordy."

Her manner ruffled me, but I managed to explain. "I'm from California, in America. I, uh, came here in a kind of dream."

I looked at Janie.

"He was washed up on the beach at Old Bay, and Uncle Norbert and my friend Louise at work helped him get away from some Russian sailors…"

Oops!

I shot a surprised look at Janie just as Sheryl said, "You are an *American*? And how could you just 'wash up' on this Island? And what is this about the Russians? All I know is they have no use for Americans."

Janie's father, as I assumed from her description, also emerged from the house. "Hey, Janie, welcome home! And what is all this commotion?"

"Now don't interrupt, Alan," Sheryl said sharply. "Janie just showed up with this boy who says he's an American. I feel very uneasy about this."

Janie saw the panic in my eyes. "Mummy, he doesn't have any place else to go. Some Russian guys were harassing him just because he's an American, and he is definitely *not* a spy!"

Oops again!

I couldn't help but give Janie a now-we're-even look.

"A spy! Well, I should hope not. Now let me think about this while I finish my article. It's due tomorrow."

Sheryl gave me another sharp glance before going back inside.

Not a good start— just like I thought.

Janie took a deep breath and turned to her dad, who was quietly waiting.

"Gordy, this is me dad, Alan."

"Um, nice to meet you." I offered my hand.

Alan smiled, and gave me a warm handshake. "This is a tall tale I'm hearing, Gordy. Let's go out to my shop and you can both tell me everything. And by the way, Janie, a telegram from someone named Louise is waiting for you in the house."

Janie ran off without a word while I followed Alan to his workshop, shaded by a broad, wind-shaped evergreen. "That's a pencil pine," said Alan. "Planted it myself."

We passed by a stone-lined fire pit and several well-worn wooden chairs. Red geraniums bordering the brick paths reminded me of Mom's gardens (again) back home.

The memory stung, but I kept breathing.

Under the pencil pine, lush ferns and water plants surrounded a small cement-edged pond. Among the ferns I spotted two beady eyes staring back at us. As we approached, a sleek sea-otter popped out and sat up like a large cat, its eyes focused on mine.

The intelligent look in its eyes was startling. "Who's this?" I asked.

"Oh, this is Sebastian. Sebastian, meet Gordy."

The otter blinked, then bounded out of the yard and off toward the bay.

"Sebastian belongs to no one," said Alan. "One day he simply showed up sniffing about the yard, and I decided to build this pool for him. He splashes a while, lolls about, then he's off to the bay to get his fish or clams. He won't eat anything we feed him, but he loves his pool. He even brought a girlfriend with him for a while, and they were a joy to watch when they played together."

I'm beginning to like this guy...

"Is he like the sacred otter Janie told me about?"

"Well, he's the same *type*," Janie said, huffing up behind us, apparently having found Louise's note.

Alan said, "Come in, come in, both of ya." He looked at Janie. "I'm so happy to see you again, Janes. Been quiet here without you."

"I've missed ya, too, Da," and he allowed her a brief hug.

I tried to not be envious. *Maybe Janie's parents aren't perfect, but at least she has parents.*

We dusted off some chairs in the back of Alan's shop. He reached into a small cupboard, pulled out some glasses and a bottle, and poured. "Have a taste of our bunberry wine, an Elsinore specialty, Gordy."

I was getting used to this wine-all-the-time. *At least it doesn't seem to mess up these people like it did Mom.*

"Okay you two," said Alan. "Let's hear how Gordy came to be here."

I told him as much as I could about my dream, the raft trip, my capture on the beach and being questioned. Janie and I took turns talking about Louise, the napkin notes, and the pedivan ride with Norbert. It felt such a relief to let all this out and Alan seemed like someone I could trust.

He listened quietly through all of it, then said to me, "So, you're telling me Commander Zevnikov thinks you're a spy?"

"Yeah."

"And they kept you in a locked room until your friend 'did something' to their alarm system…?"

"Yeah!" we both replied.

"And this was about a week ago?"

"Yeah."

"Ahh. I did see on the telly about the air raid in Kronstadt. They said an American bomber was sighted over our northern coast, heading south. We were all pretty worried for a while, but then we heard nothing more about it."

Janie and I looked at each other, then she said, "My co-worker Louise triggered that alarm, I think with Hum energy."

"Whoa," said Alan. "Your friend used the Hum to mess with the *Soviet Navy*? I'd never heard of anyone 'using' the Hum before."

"I hadn't either," said Janie, "but she's had training, and I think that was the first time she put it to use."

"I'm astonished!" said Alan, trying not to grin. "Now I understand that wild story on the news—they were embarrassed!"

But his near-grin quickly vanished. "Now Janie, exactly *who* knows about this caper of yours?"

"Uh, well, Gordy *miiight* have let it slip back at the Bell Orchard tribe, but I think we're fine. A girl there was curious about how Gordy got here."

Alan took a sip of the wine. "Well, we can only trust this won't get back to the Kronstadt naval base."

Janie and I looked at each other. "Yeh," we both said.

Alan added, "Then we'll not mention the word 'Russian' or 'Soviet' again, to anyone! Also, we need to agree on a story."

Janie said, "How 'bout this: Gordy washed up on the beach near Kronstadt. He had nearly drowned and lost his memory. He didn't know where he was. In a daze, he wandered into town, right into the MacEvoy meat market. Uncle Norbert talked to him and suggested I bring him here."

Alan took another thoughtful sip of wine, "That sounds plausible enough, and that'll be Gordy's story from now on, got it?"

Did he wink at me?

"Got it!" I said.

"And how is brother Norbert?" Alan asked.

"Oh he's fine, quiet as usual. He says Hullo. An' by the way, can we set it up so Gordy can be a resident of Gifford and go to school here?"

I looked at Janie wide-eyed. *Resident? School?*

While Alan studied both of us, Janie said, "I assume ya'd like to stay here, Gordy. Right? And wait'll ya see our school—you'll love it!"

Alan sat back, wine glass in hand, thoughtful.

"Now Gordy," he said, "what about your family back home? From your tale, it sounds like you disappeared from them without a trace."

His words sent me right back there. Tears welled up and I looked at the floor—suddenly lost, confused, and nearly shutting down. Janie put her hand on my shoulder.

"I wish I knew what *did* happen," I said. "My brother is probably having a terrible time trying to sort it out."

"Perhaps you can write to him," said Alan gently. "I believe there might be a way to get a letter to California."

"You think so…?"

"Meanwhile, I can ask around about you staying here. I'll also check with your mum, Janie. I think she'll be okay if we build a *hoot* for Gordy, and he helps us out, perhaps for an allowance."

"Aww, thanks, Da!"

"A hoot?" I asked, feeling a little better already.

Alan said, "It's a little room, like a hut, that young people build for themselves when it gets crowded in the house—an extra bedroom."

"Oh."

"And don't thank me yet, Janes. I still have to talk to your mum."

*

As we followed Alan out of his shop, I felt like I'd been traveling forever, and in different realities! So many questions swam in my head…

What's going on back home?

What about Ricky? How is he feeling? And…Mom?

Will I ever see either one of them again?

Janie gave me a look and asked, "Are you all right?"

"I'm just wondering if I'll ever go home again."

She thought a moment, and then put her arm around my shoulders. "Ahh, I dunno Gordy. That's a tough one, given the way ya came here. This dream 'o yers seems pretty far-fetched. But I'm lookin' at ya now, so ya must *actually* be here."

She pinched my neck once again—hard.

"Ow!...Janie!"

"That's real, right?" She grinned and gently caressed the sting and the anger away.

Ahhh...just keep rubbing there.

She took my hand and led me outside to the old chairs by the fire ring. "Let's siddown."

She pulled out Louise's letter. "She sent it fastmail...lookit all the stamps! Listen to this..."

Janie,

I'm riding the train to Blindhaven, having left Kronstadt and the naval base behind. My friend Zorba, a groundskeepers at the base well versed in Russian and with sensitive ears, told me yesterday that Soviet Navy higher-ups likely invented the American bomber story, which you might have seen on the news. She said Zevnikov also didn't want to make matters worse by having to explain 'the boy', or his disappearance, so a discreet request came down to those involved: "forget he ever existed!"

"That means they won't be looking for me...right, Janie?"

"Shush! There's more."

I'm on my way to Covenmoor to meet Roselin. I'm sure she will have lots of questions about Gordy. Maybe she'll figure out why he's Hum-connected and why he's really here. You know what I mean?

After I see Roselin I'll come up to meet with you both, so stay put!

L.

"I have a feeling Louise and Roselin will have an interesting talk," said Janie.

I'm sure they will.

I was still elated about Zevnikov's "forget he ever existed" order when Alan returned and sat down with us. "I had a talk with your mother, Janie, and I think she'll be okay with having Gordy stay with us. And Gordy, you'll need to apply for residency in the Gifford tribe to be eligible to enroll at the Upper School in Elsinore."

Janie was looking very pleased.

"Here's how this works," he said. "Assuming you want to live here, Gordy…you do, right?"

If you guys really want me. "Um, if that's okay with everyone."

He eyed me. "I assume that means yes. We'll set up an interview with Bea Terwillegar, the Younger here in Gifford, and she will relay her opinion to Miss Oliphant, the Elder of the Elsinore Bay tribes. If Bea says you're in, you're in. Miss Oli will most likely accept her word.

"I see."

"It can be a slow process, but it works."

*

My curiosity about the interview overcame my dread of it. Two days later I met Bea the Younger at Gifford Hall, the tribe's community room. Janie had told me that a *Younger* is something like an elected office manager for the tribe. She asked a lot of questions, starting with the tough ones of how and why I came here. I related Janie's story, parts of which were not really that far from the truth. I dodged the 'why' parts as best I could.

Finally, Bea looked at me and took in a long breath.

"I'm not surprised you're unsure about where you want to live, given the circumstances of your getting here," she said, "but do you feel certain about settling in Gifford?"

I looked out the window at the settlements surrounding the bay, and at the people walking by. I thought of Janie and her parents, who have offered to take me in. *Where else would I go?*

"Yes," I said.

She raised an eyebrow, but went on. "Though I do have trouble believing your claim of amnesia…"

Uh, oh.

"…I'm pleased the MacEvoy family is willing to support you. I'll accept your request based on your openness and your Hum awareness. You are no ordinary foreign person! I'll recommend residency so you can enroll in Elsinore Upper School."

"Oh, okay—thanks!" I was breathing with deep relief.

"Don't thank me yet. This must be approved by Miss Oliphant, as I believe Mr. MacEvoy explained."

I nodded and tried to smile thorough my conflicted feelings.

Do I really want to stay here or go back home? Could I go back even if I wanted to?

*

As Janie had predicted, Alan seemed to like the idea of another 'man' around the place. He set up a cozy alcove in the back of his shop, complete with a bunk, some shelves, and little table with a kerosene reading lamp.

"This will be yours until we get your *hoot* built."

I cleaned the cobwebby window, which revealed a lovely view of the bay, while Alan brought in some bedding. Though I sometimes sneezed sawdust, I grew to like my alcove.

Sheryl eventually warmed up to me once she saw I wouldn't be underfoot. She also said that I'd likely be accepted into the tribe—she was a lot more confident than I was.

By the next week, when I still hadn't heard from Miss Oli, Janie could tell I was fretting with doubt. After supper one evening, she took me on a leisurely walk around Elsinore Bay, passing by the other villages along the way.

She said, "Yer gonna be all right. You know that, dontcha?"

I touched her hand, and she took hold of mine, and that was all I needed.

"Thanks, Janie."

Later that night I heard the workshop door squeak open. Janie silently slipped into my bunk and snuggled against my back, laying her hand flat against my belly. I briefly looked around at her, then fell asleep most blissfully.

*

The next afternoon I was sitting in the yard reading a brochure titled *Course Offerings, Elsinore Bay Schools* when Janie crept up within an inch of my ear and loudly whispered, "Anyone home?"

I nearly jumped off the chair. "Jeez, Janie!"

She set down an armload of books and papers. "Whatcha readin'?"

I read aloud the course offerings: "*Math, Science, Literature, History, Housebuilding, Depiction.* That's drawing, right? And here's the one you told me about, *Loving, Caring and Being.* It's hard to believe some of these are high school courses."

"Well, it's good yer readin' that because you've been accepted by the Gifford tribe *and* yer officially invited to attend Elsinore Upper School! Mum just told me that ya passed the requirements exam to get into tenth year. Yer supposed to start third term on Monday."

Yesss! I jumped up and wrapped my arms around her.

"Okay, okay, huggyboy."

When I let go, she said, "I dug out me old book bag, one o' my favorite fountain pens, and other stuff ya might need. They'll issue you a personal journal when ya get there."

She picked up the brochure. "And I think you'll enjoy the courses. I nearly flunked *Housebuilding*, and I thought the *Loving* class would help me get Mel Hastings to fall in love with me, but it didn't work out that way. The teacher said I was missing the point!"

She held up the books. "Ya might get something out o' these: *Origins of Islander Tribes, All We Know about the Old People* and some novels, all published in Putney."

"Wow, Janie. Thanks."

"Don't thank me, and quit saying 'Wow.' The books are from me dad's library. I'm not a big reader meself, except I remember finding *Islander Tribes* quite fascinating. Oh, and I had these old comic books in my closet. I don't read 'em anymore so you can have 'em."

I set down the books and quickly thumbed through the stack of comics. I didn't see a single familiar title, though they all looked interesting. "You're sure you won't miss these?"

"Nah. I'm done with 'em."

"Aw, Janie…thanks!"

*

My acceptance into this tribe, and the MacEvoy family, felt at once wonderful and strange.

Is this my new life?

What about my old life?

Has that ended?

And Janie is still a mystery.

A LETTER TO RICKY
AND A
STRANGE LAMP

After Janie left, my thoughts drifted to my 'old life'.

What happened back there?

Then I thought of Ricky.

When I carried Janie's books and comics into my alcove, I saw Alan at work and told him about my acceptance.

"Hey, that's great news, Gordy. Goodonya!"

I tried to be joyful about it, but he sensed a hesitation. "I'm wondering if you can help me send a letter to California?"

"Ah, yes," he said. "Here's what I can do. I sometimes write to my friend Robbie in Australia. Fortunately, he lives in Fremantle, where our freighter is allowed to drop off mail once a month. I'll tell ya what, Gordy. You write your letter, address it to your home in California, and I'll tuck it inside my own letter to Robbie. I'll ask 'im to send it on."

I lit up and wanted to hug him. "Thanks!"

I had the whole weekend before starting school, so I used some of Janie's notebook paper and the pen she gave me. Propped up on my bunk, it took hours of writing and rewriting until it sounded right.

Dear Ricky,   July 24, 1964

You're probably wondering what happened to me.
Well, I'm not dead! But I'm not sure where I am, either.

Here's what I remember...
After Mom yelled at you and you left, she went to her room really early. I watched TV for a long time, thinking she'd come back out. Then around midnight, I went to check on her. When I saw her there on her bed, I could tell something was wrong. I got really dizzy and went to my room.

I know this sounds crazy, but try to hear this. When I fell onto my bed, I blacked out. The next thing I knew I was out in front of our house looking at a big raft. Our neighbor Mr.

Barnes had built it and said I should get on it because a big tidal wave was coming. I knew I was dreaming, but Mr. Barnes seemed to really be there!

The raft saved me from the wave, then it took me all the way down to the end of South America, then across the Atlantic Ocean, past Africa into the Indian Ocean! For weeks I woke up day after day on the raft until it got wrecked by a storm, and I was washed up on this island. It's sort of near Australia and they call it New Island. (Not New Zealand, in case you're wondering).

I don't think you'll find it on any maps—but if you see Mr. Barnes, ask him about 'New Island', and about my dream!

You'll probably never believe me, but that's what ~~happened~~ I remember. And the weird thing is I don't know if the dream has ended!

What I'm wondering is, <u>did I actually leave, or is someone named Gordy still there</u>?

And was there really a tidal wave that night?

Since then, I've been waking up every morning here, and it all seems real. It looks real, it feels real, it even smells real, but no one has been able to tell me for sure, so I'm still wondering.

I put down Janie's pen and walked outside to look at the bay. The distant roar of the surf on the outer beaches helped calm me down.

Maybe I am meant to be here, on this 'other side'.

After a while I went back to my bunk and picked up the pen.

Now I'm living with a family named MacEvoy in a place called Gifford. It's a tribe, not a town (long story). My friend Janie brought me here after I was ~~caught by the Russians~~ found on the beach. I almost drowned, but when I woke up I saw lemurs!

Janie is your age. You might like her. She asked her parents if I could stay with them, and they said okay. Her dad is going to help me build my own room, like a hut, out in the backyard. They call it a 'hoot'.

And I'll be going to school here. They call it Upper School, like our high school. I'm in 10th year, and 11th year will be my last year, so I'll graduate when I'm seventeen!

I don't know how I'll ever get back home again, because they don't have any boats or planes going to California, or anywhere except sometimes to Australia. That's the nearest country. Janie's dad is going to mail this to a friend of his in Fremantle, Western Australia, and he will re-mail it to you. His name is Robbie in case you might wonder.

I feel really bad about what happened with you and Mom that night.
I hope she's okay.
I hope you're okay too!

Gordy

*

Elsinore Bay Upper School was an easy walk from the MacEvoy place. It felt strange to wear the uniform—blue shorts, a yellow button-down shirt, with the Elsinore school crest sewn on, and my tie, blazing with bright purple, blue and yellow stripes. Last week Sheryl must have purchased these and had left them on my bunk, plus a pair of sturdy sandals. The outfit, and Janie's well-worn school bag gave me the giddy sensation of being a real Islander.

At the last minute, Janie re-tied my tie for me, checked me over and pronounced me fit for tenth year.

I looked at her. "So, what are *you* gonna do now?"

"I dunno," she said. "I was thinkin' I might see if Roselin still wants to train me. I'm not sure if I'm ready fer that Hum-energy hocus-pocus, but I could enjoy learnin' more about herbal potions. I'm just not keen on going back to Covenmoor."

"Oh, right," I said.

As I left for school, Janie waved me off like I was her kid.

What a strange friendship we have.

On the path towards school, two other kids joined me.

"Hey," the girl said, "I've seen yer up at the MacEvoy place. Are yer buildin' a *boot* there?"

"Uh, yeah. They're letting me stay with them. I'm Gordy."

"Hi Gordy…I'm Annabelle, but call me Anna, and this is me twin brother Andrew. We're in Ninth Year, and ya sound funny."

"Well, um, I just arrived a few weeks ago—from California, in America."

Anna's eyes widened, "Whoa! I've heard of California—you have sea otters there, and they are nearly extinct, just like ours once were. I've read about our otters, and someday I want to be an Otter Specialist!"

I immediately thought of Sebastian. "I think I saw something about otters in the school catalog."

"Yeh, and there's much more," she said, "like the Otter Appearances, and the Otter's conversation with Roger Putney, an'…"

"Hey Anna, take 'er easy," said Andrew.

I liked her exuberance—she knew a lot more about sea otters than I did, and I wonder who this Roger Putney was—that name was everywhere—Putney the city, Putney University, Roger's Dreamland, roger coins…

I noticed Anna had a sun-weathered look, like most kids here, deeper than a seasonal tan. I liked her braided hair. We all had on the same uniform—the Elsinore colors. Only our footwear varied— sandals for me, Andrew in something like home-made flip-flops, Anna barefoot.

During my first week of classes, my science-and-math teacher, Mr. Roanhart, introduced me as 'the boy from California', then asked the class if anyone knew where that was. No one responded. He then pulled down a classroom-sized world map and asked me, "please illuminate everyone by showing the class where you are from."

I slowly walked up to the big map, where, to my surprise, I found New Island prominently featured in the southern Indian Ocean. The Soviet Union, Europe, and Asia shared center stage to the north, and North and South America were at the far left edge. The US had no state lines, and only a few cities were labeled. I also spotted a small red hammer-and-sickle stamped on the map's lower corner. Was this an *approved* map?

I used Mr. Roanhart's pointer to show the class where California was. I felt bold enough to slowly trace the route of my voyage, leaving out all the dream stuff. And feeling a bit cheeky I said, "If someone back home asked me where New Island was, I wouldn't have had a clue!" Some of the kids laughed, and a few stared in bewilderment.

Maybe I'll fit in…just maybe.

But a week later, two boys from Mr. Roanhart's class followed me home from school. I recognized their snickering voices, often heard in class, and I felt their aggression. And here it came, that same old fear of the brats and bullies who gave me so much grief back home. These two, both taller than me, soon caught up.

One of them shoved at my shoulder, and said, "We dunt like ya here, Capitalist."

"Yeh," the other one said, and pushed my other shoulder. "Ya talk funny, too."

But this time, something was different. I'd been through so much mind-bending weirdness in these last several weeks, I didn't care what these two goofballs might try to do to me. In a flash I spun around, ready to scream in their faces. But when I looked into their eyes, my rage vanished.

They stared back, and paused.

Then without thinking I almost shouted, "Hey! Do you guys like comic books?" Giddy and nervous, I set my pack down and quickly pulled out a pile of Janie's comics that I'd been carrying around. "I have a *Captain Planet* and two *Adventures of Kaiser Spinks*."

The bigger boy hauled back as if to send them flying, but the other boy stopped him, and without looking at me took my offering. He tugged at the bigger boy's sleeve, said nothing, and they walked off. I shuddered first with disbelief, than relief, and even a tiny thrill of victory with my bribery. I had already read those comics, and I still had more.

We did not become friends, but at least they left me alone. Whenever I finished a few older issues, I left them inside the smaller kid's desk. It was easy because the boys always arrived late for class.

*

By mid-October, with Alan's assistance, I had built a rather handsome shelter for myself. Alan provided the wood, some windows, a fine, slightly-weathered paneled-pine door, and shingles for both the roof and walls. I could read Alan's notes and drawings well enough to visualize the project, and I was glad Mr. Barnes had taught me how to use tools.

Alan was pleased. "You're doing some good work there, Gordy. You might as well finish this on your own, and just holler for me if you need help. How's that?"

"Sure. Thanks," I said, floating a bit.

When the *hoot* was nearly complete, I sat in one of the old chairs at the fire pit to admire its progress. *This is far beyond a kid's clubhouse. Did I actually help build this?*

Just then Sebastian waddled out of his pond, sat on his haunches and stared at me with his intense black eyes. When I asked him, "How's the fishing?" he turned and began licking his behind. But when I asked him, "What am I doing here?" his eyes locked onto mine, like he was seriously considering my question. Unlike my dream otter, he said nothing, but I could sense something going on inside there.

*

The next morning at breakfast Alan said, "Gordy, I'm building six large tables for the village library, and I'm going to need some help. What do you say about becoming my apprentice?"

I was surprised and pleased that Alan thought I could be a real carpenter!

"Yes, I'd like that. Thanks!"

"Sheryl and I appreciate the chores you already do, but working in my shop will help us even more. And I'll pay you—you're going to need a roger or two for more clothes, treats, and schoolbooks now and then."

Ah, those island coins. I remembered Nobert giving some to Janie.

I said to Alan, "I was beginning to wonder how I could earn money."

"Well, here's payment in advance," as he pulled two silver coins out of his pocket. "We used to trade only with Russian rubles, but their frequent scarcity forced us to create our own currency starting with these one-rogers. We still get gouged sometimes because we have to use their rubles and kopeks for change. One of these will go a long way—it's worth about a hundred rubles!"

"Nice!" I said, "They remind me of our fifty-cent pieces back home, but the lady is, um, way different."

*

Soon after my *hoot* was completed, Janie knocked at the open door with a bottle of wine and four glasses. "Housewarming present," she said cheerily.

We had just settled at my snug dining table when Sheryl swept in and said, "I have something here to light up this place." Sounding like a salesman, she held up an odd-looking glass lamp shaped like a leaping dolphin. "The Biganess tribe up in the Highlands developed this new light source that lasts almost forever! They've been making oil lamps for years, but we all know kerosene is expensive and hard to get. This lamp is still experimental according to my friend Isabella, who helped create it. She gave it to me to try out."

Sheryl handed it to me to set on the table. It was heavy, and appeared to be made of solid glass.

"Switch it on, you'll see!"

When I flipped the switch at the base, a tiny ember appeared in the dolphin's body, accompanied by a soft *mmmm* sound. After a few sputtering pulses, the entire dolphin lit up, and for a moment it emitted a bright steady warm light, until it startled us with a loud *fwap!* and went out.

A strange smell filled the room.

"Oh dear," said Sheryl. "This happened earlier today. I'll show it to Alan. Otherwise I'll send it back to Isabella. She said this might happen since they haven't quite, um, perfected the technology."

Janie asked, "Mum, how did they figure out how to make these lamps?"

"Isabella told me someone named Roselin Bell provided notes and drawings. I'll bring out an oil lamp."

Janie perked up. "Roselin! She had told me she was developing a lamp like this, so I'm not surprised."

I said, "Well, even though the lamp went out, it put out good light. Maybe Alan can fix it."

"Fix what?" Alan said as he walked by the door.

A few days later, Louise showed up.

Janie and I were sitting around the fire pit, finishing a late lunch. I was just thinking it might be chilly enough to start a fire, when Janie shrieked so loud I jumped.

"*Louise!* You're finally here! I was beginning to wonder if you'd fallen off a cliff."

Louise threw off her dusty backpack and grabbed Janie in a rough embrace.

"Ooh, ya smell so earthy, I love it!" said Janie. "Look at yer hair, and what a tan!"

"Oh, it's just me, Janie, my own sweet sweat most likely. And you look more than healthy yourself. I knew that job wasn't suited for you."

When Louise saw me she said, "Hey Gordy, stand up like a man and gimme a hug!" When I did, her squeezing me made me think of a python.

Janie said, "Would ya like some food or juice or wine? I got yer letter and now I wanna hear what ya been up to."

"I'd love a glass of wine, and maybe a sandwich…?"

"Got it!"

Janie soon returned with a fat sausage sandwich for Louise and a bottle of Highpeace Golden Moscato—so said the label. She poured a glass for each of us.

Whoa. I've never seen Janie so accommodating.

"Ooh, this is good," said Louise. She took a deep breath between bites. "So much walking—I'm glad I can finally rest a while. It's a long way up here from Covenmoor."

"Yeh," said Janie. "Done it meself a few times."

Louise put her feet up and worked on her sandwich. "Leaving that cafeteria job was the best thing for me! I loved the walk over the Wicklows from Blindhaven. The snow up there was magnificent. Nature never felt so good!"

I put my feet up too, and listened.

"My visit with Roselin took a lot out of me. She wanted to know *everything*! She was full of questions about the 'air raid'. She knew this was the first time I had utilized my Hum training, and she particularly wanted to know how that guard reacted to my interruption. Then she critiqued me about triggering the alarm system. In the end, she said I did pretty good work!"

After a few more bites of her sandwich she added, "And she had *more* questions once I mentioned Gordy here."

Janie began tapping her foot.

"And what I want to know is exactly how ya did it—both with that guard, *and* their air raid system."

"Ahh," Louise evaded. "I'm not sure how all this works, but Roselin trained me to tune in with my mind to specific levels of Hum energy and frequencies. She showed me how to *feel* the inner workings of sub-electrical energy, the elementary pulses, to get to that bridge between matter and energy. She says it's inside all of us, but very few us are aware. The trick is to hit the right frequency *and* the right energy field. There are so many Hum fields!

"Then she taught me how to *transmit an interruption*. This means I channel the energy through a certain Hum field to someone's brain. Just by looking into their eyes I can temporarily scramble that person's thoughts and memory."

"Whoahh…" said Janie, as we both instinctively looked away from Louise.

Louise kept going. "It's similar to what our witchy ancestors would have called casting a spell. With this technique, the person usually recovers a few hours later, and hopefully forgets what had happened."

"But this sounds like you *are* casting a spell," said Janie. "You're a witch just like Roselin."

"I'm learning!" Louise beamed proudly. "I could just as easily have given that guard a seizure or blown out all the light bulbs in the building."

"So," I said, "who else can do this?"

"According to Roselin, only she…and I."

We both stared not-quite-directly at Louise, then Janie said, "So how did Roselin discover this? It sounds like major science."

Louise finished her sandwich and took a long sip of wine. "All right, I'll tell you what Roselin told me when I visited her just now, and I'm trusting you both to keep this to yourselves!"

"I promise," Janie and I both said at once.

She had our rapt attention.

*

"Roselin loves digging," Louise began, "and she loves science. As a girl, when she wasn't in witchcraft training, she spent her free time poking around some nearby ruins looking for interesting artifacts. When she was allowed to leave Covenmoor to attend Upper School, she excelled in science, always curious! Her teachers insisted she attend Putney University, which she did on a scholarship. She majored in archeology, minored in physics.

"Then for her senior dissertation, she chose to dig at a site inside a tower at Beatty Point, not far north of Putney. What she found there changed her life, and also added to our Island's history."

She's loving this. Louise must be crazy about Roselin!

Louise picked sandwich crumbs off her plate, licked off her fingers, then returned to her Moscato.

"I know all that," said Janie. "So, what did she find?"

"An entire library," Louise whispered.

"A *library?*"

"Roselin never mentioned this to me," said Janie. "Are ya sure this is cool…telling us?"

"Yes, it's cool. The plan was to only dig through the rubble to the tower floor, and record any artifacts they might have found. When they reached the floor, Roselin sensed a hollowness under a large paving slab, which they managed to pry up. They were amazed to find a narrow staircase that wound down to a sealed wall. When they finally punched a hole through the wall, there was the library!"

"Roselin *found* this?" Janie said. "I heard rumors of a big discovery back then."

Louise paused and took another long sip of her wine.

"Go on," Janie said.

"All right, here's what changed Roselin's life. Among the eighty-odd scrolls and 250 leather-bound books, a skinny single volume somehow attracted her." Louise paused.

"Okaaayy," said Janie. "So what was it about?"

"I'm not supposed to tell you."

"Oh," we both said.

"But I can tell you a few other things…"

She's teasing us.

Janie sat back, her arms crossed.

Louise's wandering eye was dancing. "Roselin and her team selected a few books and recorded everything in them in the time they had, including sketching every glyph and symbol. They logged in every book and scroll, then mapped the site before they had to return to Putney."

"Why couldn't they just take photos?" I said.

Louise and Janie both gave me a look.

"Not likely, Gords," said Janie. "The Soviets forbid cameras—serious penalties if yer caught with one."

Louise continued. "Roselin told me the professors were of course amazed at the find, and went out to Beatty Point themselves to check it out. When they returned they told Roselin and her team to say nothing about it, for fear the Russians might try to grab the library for themselves."

"So, what happened to the, uh, library?" Janie asked.

"According to Roselin, Peter Broadmoor and the other professors at the College of Antiquities transported the whole thing, every volume and scroll, to a 'secure room' next to his office. It has rarely been mentioned since."

*

Louise waved her empty glass at Janie. "Ya got any more of this?"

She seemed to be enjoying herself a little too much, and my trust in her was wavering.

What is she really up to?

After giving her the rest of the bottle, Janie said, "Louise, ya gotta tell us what changed Roselin's life."

"I can't. All I can say is, Roselin learned the Old People knew a *lot* about Hum energy."

"Well, I'm not surprised," said Janie. "They probably heard the Hum like we do."

"Ah, but Roselin discovered they had also deciphered the *physics behind the Hum*, and she became obsessed. She told me she had to find out what the Old People knew. She realized it had something to do with why she was a witch—something beyond casting spells.

"She told me she worked on this for years, putting her physics studies to use, learning the science. She had to be very low-key when she wanted information from the librarians or the physics professors at Putney U., so she acted like the witch she was—attempting to unravel the scientific mysteries behind certain spells. Some of the profs were amused enough to lend her theoretical papers and a few textbooks, but others refused, saying she was 'unqualified'."

Louise's face took on a dreamy look. "Then Roselin met a physics graduate student named Todd Clifford, who offered to get her the more esoteric stuff. His charm and credentials definitely helped. I met him when Roselin was training me. She wanted to study his reports, so she told us both to basically get lost. Todd and I, ah, had some nice talks…"

Janie smiled. "Looks like his charms worked on you, too."

Louise blinked, sat up, then said, "Ah, well, yes. Roselin told me that nothing made sense until Todd handed her a recently-published paper about something called quantum mechanics."

"*Quantum what?*" Janie and I said simultaneously.

"The physics of the extremely small."

"Oh."

"So how does the Hum work?" I blurted.

"It's way over my head," said Louise. "You'll have to ask Roselin about that. I just know she has figured out a few things, including what I demonstrated back there at the navy base."

"Ah," we said.

Louise's wandering eye darted around more than usual, and her frizzy hair looked like an explosion.

This woman is intense!

*

"Which brings to mind the big reason I'm here," she continued. "Roselin wants to see you both. She wouldn't tell me why, but she was clear she wanted all three of us to be there."

"Does this mean we have to go to Covenmoor?" said Janie, not enthusiastically.

"Ah, no. She's moving up to the northern coast—to a tribe called Samantha's Wild North."

"*There?*" Janie said.

"They usually call it Wild North for short," said Louise, looking at me. "It's a ten-day walk from here, over the Highlands and along the Sheffield Desert coast."

"Is that one of those 'creative-togetherness' tribes?" I asked Janie.

Louise grinned, "You might say so, Gordy. Before she founded Wild North, Samantha was Roselin's mentor at Covenmoor. Roselin told me Samantha had given her a standing invitation to stay at Wild North, so Roselin is heading up there to do some 'deep thinking' as she calls it."

"So what kind of place is it?" I said.

"It's an invitation-only tribe for women, Gordy, but you'll be okay there as Roselin's guest."

Uh-oh.

"It's all women there?"

"Well, there may be some girls your age too. You'll probably learn a thing or two," Louise said with a wink.

I might have to hide somewhere.

Louise went on. "Okay, I wasn't going to say this, but Roselin was not her old confident self when I saw her. She mentioned something about 'stirring up' the Russians with my air raid, so she wanted to get as far away from them as possible. She also told me the Americans and the Russians are in a race to make more powerful bombs like the ones that destroyed those cities in Japan. She is afraid that if *any* government finds out what she has learned about Hum energy, there will be unfortunate consequences, to say the least."

"You mean they would make *bombs* from the *Hum*?" I asked.

"Yup, that's what worries her."

Jeez!

"This *does* sounds serious," said Janie, who for once looked serious.

"Roselin said we should start out for Wild North at the end of next week. Are you guys up for the trip?"

Janie didn't hesitate. "Sure!"

I looked over at my *hoot*, the new home I had completed only last month. I also thought of school and said, "Will I be coming back here sometime soon? I still have the school year to finish, and I promised to help Janie's dad."

Louise leveled her wiggly eye at me. "I'm sure you'll finish, Gordy, but it might be a little while. Roselin needs our help. Like I said, she's really worried."

"But I just met a couple of cool kids in my class, and…"

"We have over a week before we leave," said Louise rather abruptly, "so you can see them until then. Janie's dad will hopefully understand, but don't say anything about where you'll be going, or why. Got it?"

I slowly nodded as we all sipped some more wine.

Do I even have a choice?

"Hey, Louise," Janie said. "Let me show ya where you can clean up and sleep."

After they went into the house, I sat for a minute to absorb all this new information. *What could Roselin possibly want from* me?

I finally got up, a bit wobbly from the wine, fetched a sweatshirt out of my *hoot* and walked down to the bay.

The soft evening breeze and the shimmering moonlit water began to calm me down until…

"Boo!"

Janie had crept up behind me once again.

"You're really good at sneaking up on people, Janie."

"It's how I show my affection," she said with a grin. "I ran out here to see if ya really wanna go on this trip. I know Louise can be a bit pushy. She thinks Roselin is the cat's pajamas, as you've prob'ly noticed."

"I was just thinking about that, and also how much I like it here. I guess I'm ready for another trip—as long as I know I'll have a place to come back to."

"Ah, ya will, fer sure. Me mum and dad both like ya, and that's rare, especially for me mum. She came 'round when she saw how well you could put wood together. Yer *boot* really impressed her. I just checked with me dad and he told me he'll miss you but he'll definitely want ya back in his shop!"

"Well, that's good to hear," I said. "So yeah, I'm up for going. I get why Roselin would be worried, the bomb-making *does* sound scary. But I'm still not sure why she needs *me*. I've never even met her."

Janie grabbed my shoulders. "I don't know either, and this is for being brave!" She gave me a wet smooch on the cheek and abruptly walked back home.

I was floating again, just a little.

OFF TO MEET THE WITCH

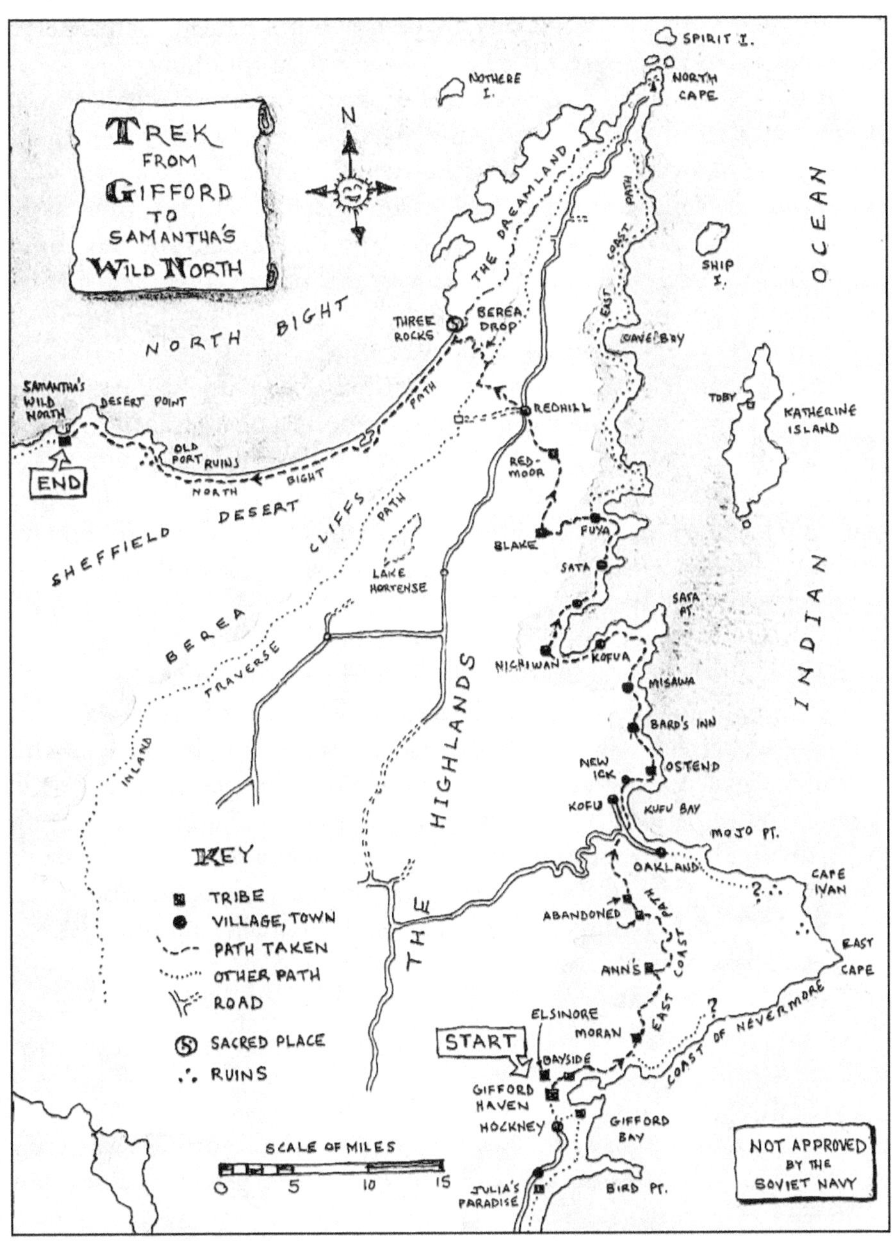
TREK FROM GIFFORD TO SAMANTHA'S WILD NORTH
N
SPIRIT I.
NOTHERE I.
NORTH CAPE
THE DREAMLAND
EAST COAST PATH
SHIP I.
NORTH BIGHT
THREE ROCKS
BEREA DROP
WAVE BAY
SAMANTHA'S WILD NORTH
DESERT POINT
REDHILL
TOBY
KATHERINE ISLAND
OLD PORT RUINS
PATH
RED-MOOR
END
NORTH BIGHT
SHEFFIELD DESERT
CLIFFS
PATH
BLAKE
FUYA
SATA
BEREA
LAKE HORTENSE
SATA PT.
TRAVERSE
NICHIWAN
KOFUA
MISAWA
INDIAN OCEAN
INLAND
BARD'S INN
NEW ICK
OSTEND
HIGHLANDS
KOFU
KUFU BAY
MOJO PT.
KEY
OAKLAND
CAPE IVAN
TRIBE
VILLAGE, TOWN
PATH TAKEN
OTHER PATH
ROAD
SACRED PLACE
RUINS
ABANDONED
ANN'S
EAST CAPE
THE
EAST COAST PATH
START
ELSINORE
MORAN
BAYSIDE
COAST OF NEVERMORE
GIFFORD HAVEN
HOCKNEY
GIFFORD BAY
SCALE OF MILES
0 5 10 15
JULIA'S PARADISE
BIRD PT.
NOT APPROVED BY THE SOVIET NAVY

Louise's estimate of a week had become a month.

Roselin had written to tell us of a delay. She offered no details, only her estimated date of arrival at Samantha's Wild North.

Louise was grumbling about it because she was camped out in Janie's bedroom, with Janie, and frequently butting heads with Sheryl. "I'm sure glad Louise isn't the boss of *everyone,*" I told Janie.

It was November, the ocean was warming up, and we had a mid-term break from school. Anna and Andrew, who were never apart, invited me to swim with them in the surf. I noticed they *did* wear very snug Speedo-style swimsuits, so I wore some old shorts. Anna wore the same outfit as Andrew, swimshorts only, and though she was about as boyish-looking as Andrew, I had a hard time not looking at her. If she noticed, she paid no attention.

It's just the way it is here. Get used to it!

Afterwards, they invited me to their house for lunch. Back in our clothes, they bombarded me with questions about California, my journey on the raft, and then more about California. This swim-and-lunch routine continued for several days, where they both asked questions while sharing very little about themselves. I finally told them, "I have to go on a trip with my, uh, cousin in a couple of days, and I'm not sure when I'll be back."

"Oh, wow, ya just got here. Where ya headed?" asked Anna.

"Umm, not sure about that either. Up the coast I think."

Also, Roselin's delay allowed me to finish most of tenth year. On my last day at school, I remembered the two would-be bullies, who seemed to have forgotten me. A little voice suggested a goodwill gesture before I left. As they were leaving the building, I caught up with them, my heart thumping, and handed them a few more of Janie's discarded comic books, of course keeping the best ones. The taller, scarier boy, who I think was named Scott, actually muttered *thanks* without looking at me, and they walked off.

And that was that.

*

We were finally ready to start our walk to Wild North. It was early December, almost summer, and the days were getting longer and hotter.

The night before we left, Louise had spread out a map on Janie's bed. I listened in as they chatted excitedly about our route while we all loaded our backpacks.

This trip was feeling more and more strange.

"Hey, um, Janie?" I said.

They both looked up. "What?" said Louise.

"I, um…nothing."

Louise sighed and started rolling socks.

As if she read my thoughts, Janie said, "Trust this, okay?"

Louise added, "Besides, how often do you get invited into the presence of an extraordinary enchantress like Roselin?"

"Okaaayy," I grumbled, flashing Janie a hopefully reassuring smile.

As we finished stuffing our packs, Janie and Louise each included a bottle of bunberry wine. Mine was too full of comic books I'd bought at the general store in Hockney.

*

The next morning we exchanged good-byes with Janie's parents. Alan said, "Take care now, and I want you back here soon. You've been a great help in the shop." Then he handed me another roger, saying, "A small bonus."

Sheryl grabbed both of my shoulders. "Safe journey, and if a letter from your brother arrives, we'll keep it here for you."

"Thanks, Sheryl," I said. "And thanks for having me. Building the *hoot* was really fun. I'm going to miss it."

Before I knew it, we were on our way, grunting under our gear.

"I'm planning on us staying at a place called Ann's tonight," said Louise. "The sun's gonna be hot, and we'll be climbing over some hills, so we'll stop and swim when we can, yes?"

"Fine with me," said Janie.

"Okay," I said warily, swimwear options coming to mind. *I feel almost okay about swimming with Janie, but now there's Louise…*

The Eastern Coast Path followed the beach beyond the last village of Bayside, then abruptly turned inland at the mouth of a creek. But a narrow trace continued along the coastal bluffs. A crude arrow-shaped sign that said NEVERMORE pointed toward the bluffs. I felt an overpowering urge to go that way. *'Follow me!'* it almost screamed.

Janie saw it too. "Someday I'm gonna hike out there," she said.

Louise nodded to the main path. "Okay, guys, fine. But today we're going this way."

"Aww, no fun," teased Janie.

I agreed.

About a mile inland, along the creek, we passed a crew of men and women wearing white headscarves and little else, building a house. While one mixed wet sand with a sprinkling of cement, another shoveled the mixture into a long-handled brick mold, then a third one worked the handle, making one brick at a time. On top of a finished section, two women were lashing long, slender gum-tree branches together to make a roof-frame. Only the doorway and window frames seemed to be made of sawn lumber, the rest was sand-blocks and those branches. Compared to the tract houses going up everywhere in California, this seemed like an exciting new way to build!

We walked on and by lunchtime we were hot and ready to stop.

At a traveler-supply shop in the village of Moran, Louise bought some juice drinks and sandwiches. As we sat under a shady tree eating, I tried to figure out what the Moran tribe did for a living. A big clue was that several shelves in the shop were filled with white porcelain dinnerware, all labeled, "Authentic Moran Irish Ware."

I pointed to the display. "Do they make this here?"

Janie said, "Yeh, this is the home of Moran-ware. They often haul crates of their stuff past our village. This is a pottery-tribe."

"And then they sell it for a living?"

"Yup. Moran ware keeps our Irish Islanders in touch with their roots. The Russians buy a lot of it, too."

"So, uh, the tribes all make just one thing?"

"Most of 'em," said Janie. "Way back it was agreed that other tribes wouldn't try to muscle in on a tribe's occupation. But if a tribe gets sloppy with quality or delivery, another tribe can take over the trade. It happens sometimes."

I wonder if this would ever work back home?

After our lunch, we followed the creek into a rocky gorge. The route was steep, the heat intense, and we were sweating.

Louise seemed to be slowing down and finally said, "Hey, let's stop for a swim. I know a beautiful place up ahead with a waterfall just above it—you'll love it, Gordy."

We soon found it—a shaded pool surrounded by moss and ferns misted by the splashing waterfall. We all dropped our packs and in no time Janie and Louise had stripped and were wading into the water. "Wow, it gets deep fast," said Louise.

I decided, once again, to go with local custom and shrugged everything off. Once I was in the water (and over the shock of the chill!), it felt like the best idea anyone had all day.

*

At dusk, we arrived in the settlement known as Ann's. Louise's destination was the Hyperion Inn, a two-story stone structure partly covered with a local pink-blossomed vine-rose.

"I stayed here once a few years ago," said Louise. "It's a fancy name for a very humble establishment. The beds are comfy, and the food is simple but good—my kind of place."

We were lucky to get in just before the kitchen closed, and there was only one room available, with two beds. Louise warned us she snores. "I kick, too, just so you know."

Janie looked at me with a straight face and one raised eyebrow and I couldn't help but answer her the same way. And so it was arranged, with no comment, except a quick look from Louise.

My strange new feelings about Janie persisted, much different now than that whole kissing-according-to-Ricky thing. I don't know how to describe it, but my heart was racing again with a strange longing.

That *zwoop* feeling again.

*

We all politely took turns using the bathroom down the hall to change into our sleepwear, then we collapsed in our beds.

Janie kept to her side and didn't say a word, but when Louise's loud snoring assured us some privacy, she whispered, "How ya doin?"

"Dunno…can't sleep."

"I had a feeling there might be somethin' goin' on…"

I turned to face her, her eyes barely visible in the darkness. "Well, um, something's happening in me. I really like it when you hold me when we're sleeping, and now I'm feeling like I want to hold you without anything on."

Janie was quiet for so long I felt I'd blown it and would be sleeping on the floor. She finally said, "Okaaay, I get what ya mean. I was wondering if this might happen. I know we see each other swimming an' all, and we *have* slept together…"

Oh, crap! I wish I hadn't started this.

"Janie, I'm being weird! Forget I said that. We'll just go to sleep, okay?"

"Hey, sailor, 's'all right," she whispered. "An' I'm glad yer brought it up. It's been on my mind too, and I'd love to do that, except fer two little details. One, I think yer *allllmost* old enough, but not quite. And two, I think I do prefer girls. Does that make sense?"

I hesitated. "Yeah…I guess. But what about that guy Bryan?"

Janie gave me a long, almost sad look and said, "He was probably just the right person to help me realize my, um, preference."

She then gave me a hug and a smooch right on the mouth. "Let's get some sleep, and yer definitely not bein' weird."

As she turned away I felt good but also a little lost. I lay awake wondering why Mom or Ricky didn't tell me more about this stuff. My high school in California definitely should have a *Loving* class. Janie was probably right—I'm too young because I don't *know* anything!

I finally turned on my side and reached around her. She took my hand and held it against her warm belly.

Stay calm. Breathe.

THE JAPANESE COAST

BREAKFAST
Bangers and Mash
Eggs
Toast or Porridge
Coffee, Tea, Juice

The words were hand-printed on a chalkboard at the Hyperion's dining-room doorway.

"What are bangers, mash, and porridge?"

Janie sighed. "Bangers are sausages, mash is potatoes, and porridge is oatmeal, silly!"

"Ooh, I'm hungry—I want all those, the eggs over medium!"

"Yeh, me too. Did ya hear that, Louise?"

Louise ordered for the three of us and then said, "Eat hearty troops, 'cause it's going to be another long day. Tonight I want us to be in Kofu. It's the first of several Japanese villages that we'll walk through. When we reach the last one, called Fuya, we can stay and rest for a day. From there I know of a back-path that will lead us to the Highlands."

Janie added in her friendlier mentor-voice, "Gordy, I've been up this way once. Those fishing villages were settled 150 years ago, and *nothing* has changed there. They grow rice, yams, and giant bamboo from seeds and shoots they brought with them. Because they practice Buddhism, they had to leave Japan in the early eighteen-hundreds to escape the Shogun."

"The who?"

Janie gave me her disappointed-teacher look. "Didn't you study Japanese history in school? Japan was once run by a powerful guy called the Shogun, who was backed by his own army of soldiers called samurai. But he felt threatened by the teachings of Buddhism, and declared the practice punishable by death! So, to survive and keep their faith, a group of fishing families left Japan on a huge raft. They secretly lashed all their fishing boats together, added planks and tiny pre-built huts, rigged up sails, and drifted off, all in one night. It took them three years hopping from one place to another, so the story goes, until they finally landed on this coast!"

"So they came on a raft too?"

"Yeh. I guess yer not the first one."

*

Happily full of breakfast, we hiked through a narrow valley with towering cliffs on our left and some lower hills to our right. Hundreds of birds circled above us, many darting into tiny holes in the soft stone. their sharp chirps echoing. I asked Louise, "Are those swallows?"

"Yes. We call 'em tweeters, similar to Australian swallows. The tweeter nearly became our national bird, but they were outvoted by the pelican lovers. We like tweeters 'cause they eat mosquitoes."

I took a deep breath of the fresh air. No trace of that old California smog! "This is such a dreamlike place, but it's not a dream, right, Janie?"

She rolled her eyes and ignored me.

After another mile, the mood changed. We had come upon an abandoned settlement. Empty ruined houses and yards full of weeds lined both sides of the path. It was clear no one had lived here for a while.

"What's this place?" I asked.

"Ah, a dark story here," said Louise. "I read about it in the *Putney Times* a few years ago. This is the first of two abandoned tribes. Apparently, a young man from one tribe allegedly abused a girl from the other tribe that's just up the path. Everyone pointed fingers. Then the tribal Elders got involved, taking turns accusing one another of worse crimes and evildoing. The lies and false rumors eventually led to vandalism, threats, and one night, a vicious attack, then a counterattack. There were several deaths, including two entire families massacred."

"Louise, that's incredible!" said Janie. "How can people be led to believe lies like that?"

"Apparently very easily."

I looked quickly around, trying to find traces of violence, but there were only a few crumbled walls and collapsed roofs half-hidden in the weeds.

"Most everyone left after that, though some characters remained, stupid and stubborn to the end. When I walked through here with some friends about five years ago, I saw a couple of them, watching us. I'm glad I wasn't alone!"

By the time we passed through the second ghost-settlement, equally ruined, a cloud of grief overcame me.

Janie finally said, "You look a little down, Gords."

I kicked a rock, then kicked it again. "Yeah. These two tribes remind me of my mom and dad."

Janie took my hand and gently squeezed it.

*

The valley widened and became patched with farms and fields and cows. We eventually spotted another settlement, definitely populated. A sign by the path said JERSEYLAND.

A dairy tribe, I'll bet.

We stopped for lunch at Jerseyland's only eating place, Plum's Dairy Café, and I immediately asked for a tall chocolate shake to add to a bacon-and-cheddar sandwich followed by apple pie with ice cream. The cheerful servers in this place helped ease the memory of those ruined villages.

"This is the best lunch ever—thanks, Louise!"

"Better to thank our benefactor. Roselin gave me a pile of rogers and rubles before I left, so we would be well-fed and lodged, and to arrive at Samantha's quicker. Our job is to keep walking, so are you two ready?"

"Yes, *ma'am!*" said Janie, giving me a wink.

The path followed the Oak River back to the coast, where we came upon a refreshing salty breeze. The sun was long over the hills when we reached a town called Oakland, where we found a fish and chips shop with tables on the seafront promenade. I was definitely ready for a rest.

"That's Kofu Bay out there," said Louise. "Only a few more miles to Ko-FOO. That's how you say it."

Janie winked at me again.

"How do you know about all these places, Louise?" I asked.

She kept her gaze on the path. "After Upper School, I wandered around the Island for a few years. And I love to learn things."

"Have you ever been to Samantha's Wild North?"

"No, but Roselin told me how to get there."

So we really don't know what we're getting into…

*

By dusk we were in Ko-*foo*. It felt like a different world! We slowed to a stroll as we entered a stone-paved street lined with small wooden houses and shopfronts, all built in the traditional Japanese style, according to Louise. Carefully-tended gardens and towering bamboo filled the few open spaces. The locals appeared to be dressed in workaday clothes, but with lively colors and patterns. A few of the women wore elegant *kimono* (no 's' for plural, says Louise), and gave us a slight bow as we walked by. Lanterns were being lit, and the two restaurants I saw looked busy. The signs were in Japanese, but most were subtitled in English.

At the far edge of town, we turned onto a lantern-lit path that led us into a forest of bamboo. We soon reached a secluded cluster of elegant wood-and-plaster structures. "This is a *ryokan*," Louise announced, "a traditional Japanese country inn."

An elderly woman in a brilliant floral-patterned kimono greeted us with a polite bow. She and Louise shared a few words, some in Japanese, and we were soon led to our room.

We were asked to leave our shoes on a large stone slab outside the door. As we entered, I marveled at the elegant sliding doors, or *shoji*, according to Louise. The unpainted plaster walls, dark timber beams and bamboo ceiling gave the place a very old look. An elegant flower arrangement on a low table brightened the dimly-lit room.

Our host opened a concealed closet door and showed us our *futon*, or bedding, and a kind of kimono-robe for each of us.

A smiling much-younger woman soon appeared with towels. While we were setting up our futon-beds, she filled a deep, wooden tub called a *furo* (says Louise) with hot water. The woman gestured to a bar of soap, a brush and a large bucket of more hot water, then the tub, to suggest how to do it.

This was all so fascinating!. After our hosts left, Janie looked at the big steaming tub and said, "They prob'ly want us to clean up before we go in to eat, right?"

"You got it," said Louise. "So, who wants to go first?"

This has *to be real...it's too different not to be.*

After our meal, the lights were extinguished early. I slept well.

*

After a hearty breakfast of fish, roasted yam slices, rice, and strong green tea, we started out. We hiked along a steep coastline dotted with beached fishing boats, small farmsteads, rice paddies, and Buddhist temples. Even Louise seemed impressed. Then the landscape opened to a broad sloping benchland below towering cliffs. We had reached a tiny European-looking settlement called Ostend.

Ostend felt like the end of the world. It's few scattered houses and produce fields gave it a rural English look. The surf was inviting, though, and Louise allowed us a quick swim. I couldn't get enough of the waves, which were perfect here for bodysurfing!

Ostend

Beyond Ostend, the terrain became steep, forcing us to hike on switchbacks from sandy beach to rocky headland then to sandy beach. On the way we met other hikers, pushcart-haulers, and a few Long-

Walk wanderers, who were inclined to stop and chat, though Louise's sense of urgency kept conversations brief.

After climbing over a particularly lofty stretch of bluffs called Seton Heads, we arrived at The Bard's Inn, a seemingly out-of-place Old-English-style tavern surrounded by a cluster of similarly-designed houses.

"This place celebrates Shakespeare!" Louise said. "It was built in the style of his day by a stage actor who still works in the Putney Repertory Theater."

But she made no sign of slowing down.

Janie and I both gave Louise a beseeching look. *Pleeeeze?*

"Okaaay," she sighed. "Let's have a quick lunch, but then we need to keep going."

The inn looked like the most authentic 'experience' of Old England outside of, well, England. We were served bowls of lamb stew and dark bread, plus a glass of plum wine. We barely had time to admire the beamy décor and finish up before Louise had us walking again.

Janie asked her why the big hurry and Louise said, "Hey guys, Roselin needs to see us, and she told me the sooner the better, so I'm just following orders."

I didn't mind moving on. The Bard's Inn was cool, but I really wanted to see more Japanese villages. I loved how they built their houses out of natural stuff like clay, straw, bamboo, rice paper, and unpainted wood.

That night we stayed at another *ryokan* in a village called Nichiwan. The next day we headed to Fuya, the northernmost of the villages. Louise promised us a two-night stay in Fuya at the Blessed Mountain Inn so we could rest up.

On our way, the usual sunny weather turned dark, and for much of the afternoon a heavy monsoon-like rain swept down on us. Waterfalls—long threads of white—sliced down from the misty cliffs.

Without proper rain gear, we arrived at the inn soaked, chilled, and exhausted. Louise spoke quietly with our host and then she announced, "Okay, we're all going to take a hot bath and then I've arranged for a massage for each of us, all before suppertime!"

A massage? Uh-oh.

"The massages will be in private rooms, and the bath will warm us up beforehand. Bathing together will save time. Sound okay, Gordy?"

My head was spinning. "So, um, how does the massage work?"

"You've never had one? Janie said, surprised.

"All you need to do," said Louise, "is lie down on a padded table and someone rubs oil over your muscles to work out the stiffness. The best way of course is don't wear anything, and afterward you'll feel like bliss warmed over! Do you think you can handle that?"

A tiny voice reminded me: *Just go with it. You might even enjoy it!*

"Okay, sure."

Louise and Janie both regarded me, smiling, and Janie said, "He's growin' fast."

We slept in the next morning—what a luxury!

Upon waking up, Louise and Janie began chatting about how wonderful their massages felt.

"So, how did it go for you?" Janie asked me.

"Uh, good," I said. "Thanks for telling the massager that it was my first time. She spoke English and explained what she was going to do, and why. That really helped."

Louise said with a grin, "I'm glad, Gordy. I chose her especially for you, instead of the hunky guys that worked *us* over."

We had slept through the breakfast served by the inn, so we had lunch in a dark café in 'downtown' Fuya. There were only three tables.

Afterwards I announced, without explanation, that I was taking a walk. Yesterday's rain had continued into the morning, but it seemed to be finally over. Once outside, It felt liberating to set off with no backpack and no direction in mind. I wandered the rain-washed streets of Fuya, bowing slightly to passing locals as they bowed to me. I also enjoyed the almost-ancient feel of the place.

A side street eventually led me to the beach, and I sat on a low seawall. I needed this—just mindlessly gazing out at the boats and the ocean.

TO THE HIGHLANDS

The next morning we made it to the dining room in time for breakfast. The Blessed Mountain Inn's house special was sauteed scrambled eggs, salmon, and chopped green onions over a pile of steamed rice.

Surprisingly not bad!

Louise, eating hastily as usual, said between mouthfuls, "We're going to need some extra snacks today, since we have to climb about 3500 feet and it's all wilderness. We're hiking up into a rocky canyon—a route I've used before. We'll find water and maybe a swimming hole along the creek. There are no villages until we reach Blake, a strange little tribe up on the Highlands.

"And Gordy, I challenge you to figure out what the Blake residents do for a living!"

"I accept." I was ready for a riddle.

"After Blake it will be an easy hike to Redmoor, where we'll stay the night at my friend Todd's place. He's that, uh, fellow I met back at Covenmoor, the guy that helps Roselin with her research."

She's blushing again!

"Any questions, troops?"

"Nope!"

*

Louise's canyon route began just beyond the inn's wooden gate. The path immediately became a steep climb—narrow and twisting with switchbacks. She was right about the rocks, the canyon was full of them, mostly huge ones. Luckily, the blue sky showed no sign of rain.

Will we even get up *this?*

But the path's ingeniously carved steps and switchbacks made the climb bearable. Wind-blown pines clung to the ledges above us, the rain-swollen creek rushed beside us, and after a morning of climbing, we heard waterfall sounds somewhere off the path.

Louise finally said, "Let's stop."

With sighs of relief, we dumped our packs and found our way to the splashing creek. We came upon a huge sunny rock that gently slanted toward a deep pool. Boots soon came off, and we propped up our tired feet.

Ahhh.

Janie said, somewhat listlessly, "I'll go in if you guys do."

No response.

Finally, Louise peeled off her clothes and said, "I'm feeling lazy" and she just rolled into the water.

"*Aaack!* It's *freezing!*" She shouted.

Janie followed, screamed, and with only a little hesitation, so did I. The water *was* biting cold but also refreshing, and it felt great to climb back onto the rock to warm up in the sun. It was hard to leave it.

Our path eventually left the creek and became more or less a staircase carved into the rocks. We sweated in the heat, stopping frequently for a drink and to catch our breath.

Suddenly there were no more steps—we had reached the top!

When we looked back down to the ocean, Janie said, "I can't believe we're up so *hiiiigh*!"

"Welcome to the Highlands!" said Louise.

"I've never seen anything like this," I said, "Not even in *National Geographic*! How come this island isn't known anywhere?"

"Long story." Said Louise. "Something to do with, ah, different planes of reality. I know about your Geographic Society, and yes, I've not seen any mention of our Island in any of their publications. This is troubling to some Islanders, though others think it's a blessing."

I looked at her, "So it's not just the Russians and their rules about maps? I mean, this place really is…unknown?"

Janie said, "Well, the *Russians* sure know about it, and some Australians, like me dad's friend Robbie."

"I'd never heard of it until I came here," I said. "And this is a big island. Mr. Barnes put a map of it on the raft, so somehow *he* knew about it."

Louise was incredulous. "You really sailed here on a raft all the way from California? That has to be over 10,000 miles!"

"My lit-up map said 16,144 miles just before it quit working."

"Ah, Gordy, you're telling some tall tales."

I shrugged, smiling sheepishly.

Louise rolled her eyes and said, "Okay, guys, maybe we should stop here and have a snack, since we probably won't find provisions in Blake."

Louise pulled something from her pack she called *sushi*—rolls of white rice and raw fish wrapped in seaweed, neatly boxed into three servings. "I ordered this from the inn to bring along."

After I examined it with some hesitation, it wasn't bad!

As we ate, the only sounds came from meadowlarks and the whistling wind. Then almost imperceptibly, a deeper resonance took over, and we were soon grinning. *The Hum!* The sound came in low at first, then rose an octave or two, gathered intensity, and seemed to sing to us in deep, echoing tones. Then it drifted off.

"Ummm. Feels like we're bein' welcomed," said Janie.

Refreshed, we set out again.

*

Wide expanses of prairie grass stretched to the horizon under ribbons of high clouds. The air was chilly and pungent with some kind of local sage, the sun intense—I was glad I had my Hillian hat!

About two miles down the path, we spotted a young woman sitting cross-legged on a massive rock. She wore a loose white outfit, her long dark hair floated on the breeze and her eyes were closed. She slowly twisted her torso while letting out soft alien-like moans. Then we saw more women and a few men sitting on other nearby rocks, humming deeply and chanting phrases, as if answering the woman's lead.

Are they all in a trance?

Janie whispered to Louise, "Is this the Blake tribe?"

"Must be. Roselin told me it's the first settlement we'll see up here."

"So, what do you think they do, Gordy?" Louise said.

"Uh, meditate?" I said.

"Close. Roselin told me they chant to the sound of *Om*. She says it's the universal sound at the core of Hindu and Buddhist traditions. The Hindus say it is the first sound uttered by God at the creation of the Universe, and it is the most profound concept of life-energy..."

"Whoa, slow down!" said Janie.

Louise took a long breath, then said, "And Roselin said this is another intense Hum-area on the Island, though she doesn't know why."

We looked again at the sitters, who gave no sign of noticing us as we passed by.

Louise added, "A woman named Cerise built this place with the help of her followers only a few years ago. I think that's her with the long hair. Roselin knew her back in their university days, and said that Cerise named the settlement after her pug-dog, Blake. Don't ask me why."

Janie said, "A pug, ya say. Well, o-kee-do-kee."

That Cerise person looks so young—or maybe she's ageless.

As we walked on, I took one more look at the blissful-looking meditators on their rocks. "They look happy." I said.

"Oh, I think they're beyond happy," Louise muttered.

*

We were dragging our tired feet when we finally reached the settlement of Redmoor. An orange sun was setting over the plains to the west, and the dry wind had turned chilly.

"There are seasons up here," Janie said. "3,500 feet makes a real difference. Brrrr!"

Louise led us up to the door of a tidy, whitewashed stone house she must have visited before, and knocked loudly. A boy about ten years old answered and she said, "Hey, Staniel, remember me? Is your father here?"

"*Daaaad*," the boy called into the house, then left us in the open doorway. A tall, freckled fellow in a dark green sweater soon appeared and grinned at Louise through his reddish whiskers.

"Heeeyy, Louise! Good to see ya! Welcome all of you! Stan and I were just sitting down to eat, so come on in and join us. I'll put more eggs and veggies in the pan—it's scrambled-egg night."

Louise dumped her pack, pulled Todd into a long hug while Janie rolled her eyes, then said, "These are my friends, Janie and Gordy."

He looked at us with a fetching smile. "Very nice to meet you both. I'm Todd and that's my son Stan in there." He gently grasped my hand in both of his.

I like the way people shake hands here.

He led us into a low-ceilinged dining-living area that adjoined a spacious kitchen, where a massive clay-and-iron cookstove heated the room. Stan was picking at his pile of eggs while reading a comic book, which immediately caught my eye.

"Do ya like comic books?" he asked between bites.

"Yeah." I sat next to him.

"I'm done with this pile," he said, and pushed it over to me.

These were comics I'd never seen before, except the *Kaiser Spinks* Janie had given me.

I said, "Do you have any *Superman* or *Uncle Scrooge*?"

"Uncle *who*?"

I wished I had some of those to show him. From my backpack I pulled out my mixed bundle of old and new comics and set them next to Stan's pile. His eyes went wide!

While we were busy reading, Todd offered wine or juice. He didn't seem surprised at our arrival, so he must have received word from Louise. She had moved up cozily beside him to help him chop onions and stir more eggs. They chattered about what they've been doing in the last year or so, as if it was an ongoing conversation.

Todd finally said, "Okay boys, clear the table!" He brought in a heaping plate to pass around and we ate quite ravenously, saying little.

Louise broke the silence. "We're heading up to Samantha's Wild North to see Roselin.

He looked at her. "Oh, is she staying there now?"

"She just moved there from Covenmoor. I didn't mention it in my letter—thought I'd tell you here. She's been worried about what the Russians might do if they ever learned about Hum energy."

Todd looked at her with concern. "Well, I'm glad you stopped by. I've been thinking about Roselin lately." He looked at Janie and me. "I assume you're all familiar with her research and discoveries over the years…"

"I gave them an overview," said Louise.

"Ah, good. Well, recently I learned some news about that ancient library Roselin discovered. I wrote an update for her, and I'm glad I didn't send it to Covenmoor!. I'll give it to you in the morning. She'll want to know about this, Louise, so I trust you'll get it to her."

"Oh, yes, of course."

*

After we ate, Janie volunteered me to wash the dishes, my least-favorite chore. "Come on, Gordy, it'll be quick. I'll dry, and Stan here can put 'em away, awright Stan?"

When we finished, Todd could see we were all about to fall asleep, even standing up, so he showed Janie and me his guest-alcove. He nodded to the smallish double bed piled with extra blankets and said, "This is what I have—hope it's okay."

Janie replied matter-of-factly, "It'll be fine. Thanks!"

Todd gave Staniel a hug before pointing him to his room, said good-night to us, then led suddenly-docile Louise through a beaded curtain. I heard some giggling.

After we were settled, I said to Janie, "Uh, you're okay about sharing the bed?"

She must have picked up my uncertainty. "Listen, Gords," she said yawning, "It's fine with me if we sleep together. I really like doing that with you, but just relax and sleep, okay?"

"Okay," I said with relief.

"And remember, I'm definitely *not* yer girlfriend!"

"Sure, I get it. I'll just sleep."

*

In the morning I made a beeline for the stack of comic books Staniel had left out the night before. His *Bob and Alex* comics were kind of funny. Bob, a not-too-bright weasel, was constantly getting tricked by Alex, a very smart raven, but that was practically all they did. I liked the *Kaiser Spinks* stories better—Kaiser was an old guy who went on crazy road-trip adventures with his cat Geronimo. I was so engrossed

I didn't notice the morning chill until Janie, full of purpose, came in and began stoking the big earthen cook stove.

Soon Louise walked in wearing what must be Todd's red flannel nightshirt, drooping to the floor. Her dreamy look, crazy-frizzy hair, and a slight aroma suggested more than I really wanted to know.

As Louise was filling Todd's tea kettle, Janie took one look at her and said, "Ya looked like yer slept more than well."

Louise grinned as she put the kettle on the cooktop, then almost floated back down the hall.

Janie took it upon herself to make breakfast, since there was no sign of Louise nor Todd. They finally appeared, both dressed and neatly combed and we ate without anyone saying much, partly because Stan and I were still absorbed in our reading.

I looked over at Stan.

It really is *more fun reading comics with someone else.*

When we were ready to go, Todd said he was glad we had stopped by, and held up a large envelope. "Here's the report for Roselin."

When Louise took it, he pulled her to his side and gave her a warm wet smooch on her neck, leaving me with a weird pang of envy.

No one ever smooched me *like that before.*

She winced and giggled and gave Todd a smooch back. Janie made a face while Stan and I looked away from all this nonsense.

Todd finally said, nodding at the envelope, "It's intended for Roselin, and I'd rather you didn't read it, but if you must, just don't advertise it. And by the way, give her a big hug for me!"

As we were leaving, Stan ran out with about a dozen well-read older comic books, some missing their covers, and said, "Here, Gordy. These were under my bed, and I already read them. You can have 'em."

"Uh, thanks!" I said. "Someday I'll get you some *Uncle Scrooge* comics if I ever find any."

"And *Superman*!" he said.

*

Back on the path, I felt a stab of envy for Stan's easy relationship with his dad. I could see Todd really cares for him.

Louise still had Todd's report in her hand, and, while raising an eyebrow, she opened the clasp. Reading the first page, both her eyebrows shot up. "This part is about Cerise and the Blake tribe," she said. "Todd says they are experimenting with, um, Hum energy and fertility."

"*What?*" Louise and I both asked.

Louise kept reading. "Well, apparently Roselin asked Todd to go out to Blake and talk to Cerise." She read on and said, "And it looks like Todd got some very frank answers about their practices."

Janie grabbed the report and read it as we walked.

"Whoa," she said, her face slightly red. "This is more than meditating, and I thought *I'd* seen some weird stuff."

"Can I read it?" I asked.

"No!" they both said.

Janie went to the next page, which was another report altogether. "Listen to this," she said. "There is talk at Putney University about the Old People library being shipped to Moscow!" Then she went quiet, looking worried.

"*Shite*…that's bad," said Louise. "Roselin'll go crazy when she hears that!"

On the path from Redmoor to Redhill

We stopped to let Janie tuck the envelope into Louise's pack, then said very little until we approached a larger town called Redhill. A few colorfully painted shops and houses were surrounded by open pastureland and a few sheep corrals, but no sheep. All was quiet except for the constant singing of tweeters and meadowlarks.

We saw no one, and the shops were closed. A ghost-town with chirping birds. Was it a holiday? Janie spotted a fountain in the dusty town square, so we could at least fill our canteens.

A few miles beyond Redhill Louise began to slow down. Janie said, "Ya look a little wrung out. Ready to stop fer a bit?"

"Oh, I'm all right, but, yeah."

*

The sun felt good as we lay back in the grass. Louise and Janie pulled their hats over their eyes. An occasional bee buzzed by.

I reached for a comic book.

Janie said to Louise, "So, are you and Todd an item?"

Louise took a long breath, leaving her hat in place. "It's been a puzzle. He's always been very welcoming on my visits, but he never initiates anything, if you get what I mean."

"Maybe he's protective of Staniel."

"Could be. He told me he moved out to Redmoor from Putney to deal with his grief after Stan's mum left both of them to 'find her own way'. He says the local school is good for Stan, and he likes the quiet there so he can write his research articles. We keep in touch."

"He seems like a nice guy," I said from behind my comic book.

"Yeh, Louise. You've kept him a big secret," said Janie.

"Aye. I have."

I could tell Janie wanted to know more.

Louise lay quiet for a while, then snorted awake, dislodging her hat.

I put down my comic and said, "So, um, where are we headed now?"

She slowly sat up. "The Berea Drop. It's a crazy-steep path that will take us back down to sea level. Wait'll you see it."

"Well…if yer up for it, Louise…" Janie teased.

Louise gave Janie a squinty look, then laughed when Janie squeezed her eyes shut. She then hopped to her feet. "Oh, I'm up for it, guys. Let's go!"

It must have been a little past noon when our trail met an intersection, beside which a painted stone obelisk read BEREA DROP with an arrow. "We should be on the beach in maybe three hours," said Louise.

The beach in three hours?

At first, I saw nothing but grassy flat land ahead. Then the horizon appeared oddly closer as the grass gave way to bare rock. Just as the land ended, a distant but familiar roar sent a chill down the back of my neck. Surf! We had again reached what looked like the edge of the world.

"*Whoooooo!*" said Janie. "This is *a-maaay-zing!*"

A salty wind washed over us as we reached the edge. Far below lay miles of coastline, the ocean shimmering beyond in pale colors under the sun.

This has *to be real.*

Unlike the canyon we ascended yesterday, the edge here was nearly a sheer cliff! We took a cautious look at thousands of feet of vertical drop. In the distance to our left, a crescent beach curved off for many miles. To our right, the shore ended at some rocks, beyond which everything was obscured by a dense fog.

A weathered board leaning against a rock shared these hand-painted words:

4,099 STEPS
Take thy time, not thy life!

At the cliff's edge, the path indeed descended in a series of steep twisting steps that disappeared around the first switchback.

"Now you see where the name came from," said Louise.

"Yeah," I said. "And what's with the fog down that way? It's so clear everywhere else."

Janie and Louise took a long look at it, and they said, nearly in unison, "Ahh, that'd be the Dreamland."

I looked at them, my face a question mark.

Louise paused, retreated a few steps from the edge, then dumped her pack. "Let's have some lunch."

*

We relaxed against a massive rock that blocked the wind, and Louise passed around some of Todd's home-made trail mix and tasty lamb jerky.

While chewing, Janie began, "Okay Gordy, you've probably noticed this Island has a few, er, oddities."

I nodded slowly.

"Well, behind that fog down there is a place we call Roger's Dreamland, discovered by Roger Putney, who I'm sure you've heard about. He stumbled into it while on his twenty-year Long Walk."

"Twenty *years?*"

Janie went on, "Did ya see those rocks in the surf at the edge o' the fog? That's the portal called Three Rocks where you can get in. Once ya step up into it, ya close yer eyes and imagine a place you'd like to be. The trick is to believe it's there, then, when ya open yer eyes again, it'll *be* there! All ya have to do is walk in. If ya don't do it right, you'll just see that fog, or nothin' at all. Does that sound about right, Louise?"

"Yup, so I've heard."

I stopped chewing. "So, uh, what do you do there once you get in?"

"Well, it kinda depends on what ya *wanna* do. It's mostly a place to escape into, but it's also a world you can make up or imagine as you walk through it. The place has been recorded on maps, but the Dreamers always come back with different stories about what they've seen there. Some Islanders don't believe in it at all, an' call it the Great Woo-Woo."

"Have either of you been there?"

"I haven't." said Louise.

"Not ever?" said Janie. "Some of me friends have told me the warm surf and the sandy beaches all act as kind of a turn-on, and lovers go there to, you know, do it. Some people also believe they grow younger if they stay there long enough, from drinking the water from the Pools of Selene, or swimming in the Bay of Songs, that sort of thing.

Pools of Selene? Now my mind was racing.

"Oh, I've heard those stories too," said Louise. "And I've also heard it can easily turn frightening, a dark place with weird sounds and strange creatures, and that people have had psychotic breakdowns there, and some have never been seen again. It looks to me like someone or something is messing with nature in that place, and I really don't want to go there."

I was wide-eyed. "Can we check it out?"

"No!" said Louise. "I don't want to risk you getting lost in there. My job is to get you both to Roselin, and soon. At least now you know where the Dreamland is, so maybe on another trip."

YET ANOTHER PLANE OF REALITY

Full of lunch, and with the Berea Drop still ahead of us, we were slow to get up. We had already hiked over ten miles from Todd's place, and Louise said we needed to cover several more before the end of the day.

The steps looked scary at first, but I noticed they were carefully carved into the cliff-face, with heavy iron hand-holds bolted into the rock at the steepest turns. The wind threatened to blow us off balance, so I was glad for those handles.

"Who made this path?" I asked Janie.

"Good question," she said. "What do you know, Louise?"

Louise went into her since-you-asked mode. "I read somewhere that our ancient predecessors built it. They had established a harbor-town down there that is said to date back 11,000 years, possibly the oldest ruins on the Island. We call it Old Port. We think this path connected the port with farms or settlements up here, but we really don't know."

"There ya go, Gords," said Janie.

After negotiating the seemingly endless steps and switchbacks we finally reached the soft sand of Twentymile Beach, the longest continuous beach on the Island, according to Louise. The air had become much warmer, and the damp saltiness reminded me again of home, which brought on all sorts of feelings.

The Berea Drop Path ended at another trail intersection, this time with a little stone obelisk labeled **NORTH BIGHT PATH** with arrows pointing in both directions.

"Hey," I said, "I can see those three rocks just up the beach. That's where you can go into the Dreamland, right?"

"That's where you can *visualize* going in," said Louise. "There is no guarantee you'll get in."

"So, we're not even going to try it?"

"No, Gordy. Didn't you hear what I said?"

"Okay, okay! But what if we just *looked* at it from those rocks. They're so close!"

"*Gordy!*" Louise said.

"Aw, Louise," Janie said. "It wouldn't take long to walk over there. I'm a little curious too, and like he says, we can just look in on the place."

Louise glared at both of us, her wandering eye twitching. Then she sighed and said, "Okay, just a *look*. I've wondered about it too after all the talk I've heard."

"Yay! Thanks!" I said.

We soon arrived at the three large rocks. Another obelisk nearby marked the end of the North Bight Path with the word END. There were no signs pointing to Roger's Dreamland, and the fog obscured everything beyond this point.

Beyond this point, the Dreamland.

As we approached the three rocks, we spotted some steps that disappeared among them. I dropped my pack and said, "So I go up there and close my eyes and imagine?"

"Yes, Gordy," said Louise, "And remember what I said, only take a look!"

I cautiously walked up the damp, mossy steps into a kind of tunnel. It opened to a small ledge, and beyond that, the same rolling surf splashed a few feet below. The fog-softened sun glared off the water, and there was nowhere to go from here.

Okay, here goes!

I shut my eyes and envisioned a more tropical soft-sand beach edged with palms and lush foliage. Beyond that stood a palm-thatched shack of a café whose sign said COLD JUICE DRINKS.

When I opened my eyes, it was there! Warm sand, palms, and the juice stand, just as I had envisioned it. I was now barefoot and wearing a bright green Hawaiian shirt adorned with red parrots.

Now I have to check this out.

I couldn't resist taking a few steps, just to feel the warm sand under my feet, to make sure the whole thing wasn't a mirage. And I really wanted the jumbo-sized pineapple-orange juice combo advertised on the sign!

I walked over and sat down on one of the tall stools stuck in the sand. I was the only customer. An older woman stepped out from the back who immediately reminded me of a neighbor-friend of Mom's named Virginia. Without a word, she served me the house special shown on the sign, as if she knew my wishes.

It was an exquisite combination of juices. *Perfect!*

Then Janie walked up!

"Well, look at you, hombre," she said.

"Hey, Janie, you made it in!"

She sidled onto an adjoining stool, ordered something she called a mai-tai, and said, "I can't believe this! Just a minute ago I was standing on that ledge and now I'm *here*."

Then she added, "Ya know, Gordy, yer were only supposed to *look* in. You really scared Louise."

I studied my drink. "I just couldn't help it," I said, "This place is so cool. Is she coming in too?"

"No."

"Oh."

"She saw you disappear and tried to come in after you, but something happened. She was yelling and gasping, and when I ran up to her, her face was white as a sheet! I helped her crawl back from the portal and told her to just sit and breathe. After a few minutes, she seemed to come back to normal.

"She told me she had shut her eyes, but she couldn't think of anything she wanted to visualize, so when she opened them again, there was nothing but a black void all around her, with no sound and no sense of up or down. She was terrified, Gordy!"

I felt awful. "Sorry, Janie."

"When she recovered enough I came in to look for you. When I stepped up to the gap in the rocks, I was irritated and frustrated, and I instinctively knew I had to let go of all that, take a deep breath, slow down. So I thought, *Awright, I see a nice restaurant on a beach serving mai-tais at the bar.* I shut my eyes.

"And boom! The crashing-surf noise was immediately replaced by Hawaiian-sounding ukulele music. When I opened my eyes again, a place called Charlie Wu's Tahitian Spa appeared just above the beach, with an open-air bar right on the sand. The only customer at the bar was you! A handsome young bartender in a tight black shirt appeared from nowhere, set down my mai-tai, then disappeared."

She raised her glass to me. "So cheers, Gords!"

To me, it was still a juice stand, yet definitely worth celebrating over. I raised my glass to Janie. "Cheers! Pretty wild, huh?"

Janie said, "Yeh, definitely wild enough. There's also a gal sittin' over there I wouldn't mind meeting."

"Huh, that's weird," I said. "All I see is this wooden counter next to a soda-pop cooler and a chalk-board menu hanging from a nail. An older lady in a green bandanna served me, and I think she's somewhere in the back."

Janie was thoughtful. "Ah, then we're lucky, Gordy, because we visualized *almost* the same thing. I'm completely amazed at how this is happening, and I'm gonna come back here someday!"

She finished her drink and ordered another while I worked on my juice.

*

Louise gasped with relief when she saw us step down from the portal.

"*Gordy,*" she said as sternly as she could muster, "I said only *look* in."

"Aw, Louise, he didn't go far," Janie said. "He was sitting at a juice bar, close enough to the lovely restaurant that I envisioned." She then handed Louise a present, ice cubes still tinkling. "Here, I brought ya somethin' from Charlie Wu's!"

Louise blinked, then accepted the drink and took a sip. "Is this a *mai-tai?* I can't believe this, Janie."

"I thought yer could use it," Janie said with a slightly bleary look, and then she sat down rather hard.

"I guess you must have had one or two yourself," Louise said, cracking a grin.

"Three," said Janie.

We all laughed. When Louise raised her glass for a toast, we laughed again, for no reason. Janie told me later she'd asked her cute bartender to add a little rum to my pineapple juice.

*

We eventually recovered enough to keep walking. Twentymile Beach was probably the most isolated place on the island, with not a single settlement anywhere. Finally, we laid our sleeping bags out under the evening sky. Louise put together a supper of nuts, seeds and raisins, and the last of Todd's jerky, and, warmed by our campfire, we watched the stars appear.

I was lured down to the surf by an enchanting sliver of a moon settling over the ocean. While watching the waves, I tried to figure out Roger's Dreamland. How can all those sights, sounds, smells, and even the taste of the pineapple juice, be 'real'? I promised myself I'd return.

As the night sky deepened, the waves flashed an eerie white glow when they crashed. Fascinating! I had seen it on the raft, and a *National Geographic* article explained it as phosphorescence from tiny plankton animals. Above the waves, the thin moon slowly disappeared into the ocean leaving billions of stars and a brilliant Milky Way. Then one, two, then more galaxies, tiny and colorful, became visible.

Why do those galaxies seem so close here?

And something was happening. A new sense of *belonging* was working its way into my consciousness. Was it because I was accepted here, or maybe even *valued?* Since settling in Gifford, and now on this trip to meet the mysterious Roselin, I felt *maybe* I belong on this Island, with these people.

I hope so…

Then I thought of Mr. Barnes. I wonder what he's doing now? And why did he send me here? I should write him a letter like I did to Ricky, except I don't know his address.

And Janie…

I love it when she smiles and says she likes me. *I just don't know what to do with that, uh, physical thing.*

"I'll bet yer thinkin' about me," Janie said.

Urk! I jumped and stared at her, my face turning red. She had snuck up behind me again. "Yeah," I said, "I was, but not only about you. Other things too."

"Like what?"

"Like why was I *brought* here, and why did I have that dream?"

"About the raft?"

"Yeah."

"Actually, Gordy, I still have a hard time believing yer raft story! Are ya sure yer just didn't come by boat from Australia or somethin'...and ya wanted to tell the Russians a tall tale?"

"Nooo! I really came... Okay, I *dreamed* I came on the raft, and this new, um, *existence* has continued, day after day, right up 'till now. I wish I could figure out how to say it so you'll believe me."

Janie smiled. "Okay, okay, I believe ya, but, ahh, maybe ya should talk to Roselin about it."

*

In the morning chill, we huddled around the campfire, waiting for the last of our water to warm up for tea. When Janie grumbled about how thirsty she was getting, Louise said, "Hey, trust me. Todd said there's a spring at the Old Port ruins, and we should be there in a few hours. The last of our water went into this porridge, and please thank Todd for the raisins and nuts," she said as she served it up.

"Not bad," I said, trying to smooth things over. "And thanks!"

Janie ate with no comment.

Twentymile Beach

We were soon packed and under way. We followed Twentymile Beach a to a place called Bryce Lagoon. It had gotten hot, so without a word, we all stopped for a swim in the salty sun-warmed lagoon. It was heavenly. And as usual, I couldn't help but gawk now and then, much to the amusement of both women, who always caught me at it.

Beyond Bryce Lagoon, the path followed the coastline just above the beach, mostly over sandy, scrubby hills. The sandy parts slowed us down, and it was getting hotter. It was no fun being thirsty in a desert!

Further along, we spotted another obelisk with an arrow pointing inland. The faded paint said SHEFFIELD PATH.

"That path heads south, through the Desert Wonder Tribes, as some people call them," said Louise. "We stay on this one, and Todd said we'll see the Old Port ruins shortly beyond this marker."

And sure enough, as soon as we spotted some crumbling stone walls in the hazy distance, Janie said, "Hey, I see green plants up there!" She ran up the barren hillside to a patch of lush grass and brush. We followed her to find clear water trickling out of an old pipe into a mossy stone basin.

Ahh, water!

We all dropped our gear and took a long redeeming drink, then filled our canteens.

"This tastes dee-vine," said Janie. "I was worried we might have to get out the bottle of wine I packed back at Gifford."

"Do you still have that?" asked Louise. "I, um, shared mine with Todd."

"Yup. I'm saving it as a gift to Roselin."

"Oh, she'll *looove* that," gushed Louise.

While we filled our canteens, I looked around at the ruins. There was no sign of a harbor. The 'port' must have been the large sand-filled basin partly surrounded by a stone one-time seawall.

We found some shade and sat down to rummage in our packs for anything edible. "I hope they have something better than nuts and seeds at this Wild North place," said Janie.

"Yeah," I added.

"Oh, I'm sure they are well stocked. Roselin told me they grow a lot of their own food, and the mail boat delivers fresh provisions every two weeks or so."

"The mail boat?"

"Yes, Gords," said Janie, patiently. Didn't you see that schooner anchored back home in Gifford Bay?"

"Oh, yeah, I saw it sitting there a couple of times. I just thought it was somebody's boat."

Louise said, "The mail boats are our own seagoing postal, freight, and passenger system, with no assistance from the Russians, thank you. Maybe someday you'll get to ride on one."

Ooh, that would be sooo cool.

The schooner Quandary *on its mail run.*

And speaking of mail, only last year we started printing our own postage stamps!" She dug into her pack and pulled out a letter Roselin had sent her. "See?"

"Ah!" I said, staring at it. The resemblance to Mr. Barnes left me slightly unnerved.

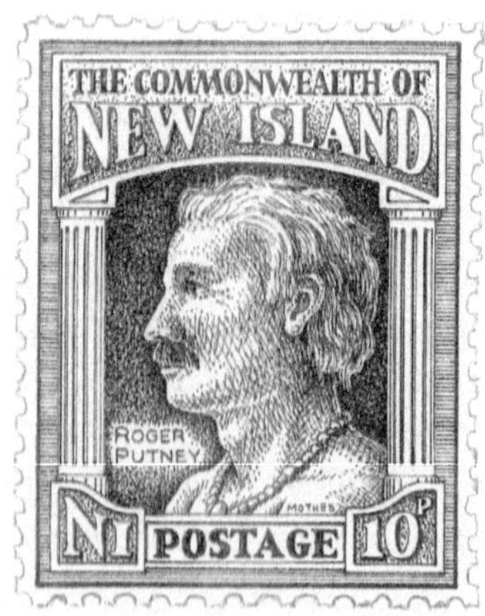

Louise said, "Okay, guys, ready for the final leg? If we start now, we'll arrive at Samantha's before dark!"

ROSELIN

We said little during the last few miles. I glanced at Janie and Louise, wondering what they were thinking. My own mind was full of questions about Roselin: *Is she really an enchantress, a spell-caster? Will she make me into a mind-slave?*

I couldn't say anything to Louise. I knew she'd laugh or cast her one good eye at me and say nothing. I've wondered about her ever since she zapped that guard. She's so *intense.*

Beyond the Old Port ruins, the path followed a series of rocky bluffs just above the crashing surf. The sun was still hot but the surf-spray helped cool us off. We paused to take in the view from a major promontory. "This is Desert Point," said Louise. "We're almost there!"

A short distance further we heard voices. Sitting near the bluff's edge were the first people we'd seen in two days, all women. They fell silent and watched us, with no sign of a greeting.

Okaaay…

The path soon descended toward a cluster of tile rooftops surrounding a lovely tree-shaded commons. Bright red and green parrots flashed in and out of the foliage. Beyond the trees, a short crescent beach opened to the ocean.

I said, "Hey, is this it?"

"Must be," said Janie.

Louise spread her arms, "Behold…Samantha's Wild North! Let's go say hello."

*

As we entered the plaza-like commons, a clear voice called out, *"Louise! Janie!"*

From a nearby house, a barefoot, dark-skinned woman in a flowing purple gown walked toward us. The low sun cast a golden halo around her frizzy head. Having met very few dark-skinned people, and none like her, I was already enchanted! Her face had lit up at the sight of us, eyes flashing with an astonishing brilliance. She wrapped Louise, then Janie, in long and enviably heartfelt hugs.

Then she looked at me. "And you must be Gordy."

"I, um…yes," I said, trying to act like I meet witches every day.

She took both my hands and held them in hers. "I'm so glad to meet you. I'm Roselin."

Her deep-brown eyes seized my complete attention. Her energy was warm and somehow familiar, like I felt around Mr. Barnes, but stronger!

I said breathlessly, "Louise and Janie have, uh, told me a lot about you."

Still smiling, Roselin arched an eyebrow ever so slightly, then turned to address all of us. "We have a lot to talk about, but right now, I want to get you settled, then feed you."

As we followed Roselin across the commons, she seemed to glide over the ground with an almost ethereal lightness and grace.

Then Janie's nose twitched, and she whispered loudly to Louise, "What's that stink?"

"Dunno," said Louise. "Something in the ground maybe?"

Roselin led us up a short path to an inviting cottage next to a slightly larger house. Red geraniums bloomed everywhere.

"Samantha isn't here, so I'm staying in her house. I fixed up the guest cottage for you all. I hope you'll like it."

She showed us into the cottage. A tidy sitting room featured a large window that overlooked the entire village. An archway opened to a small kitchen where Roselin gestured to a massive earthen brick wood-fired stove. "This will heat the rooms, and there is a separate little firebox here for the kettle, should you want tea or coffee. And just remember, firewood is scarce, but you can usually find enough along the beaches. Oh, and the loo is in the back—not enough water here for flush toilets."

A doorway led to a bedroom containing a double and a single bed, plus an alcove with a sink and a small tub. "I hope you are all fine with one bedroom," said Roselin. We looked at the beds and exchanged a quick look. "No problem," said Louise. "I'll take the single and move it to the sitting room."

"Ah, I remember your snoring," said Roselin.

*

After our tour, Roselin took us down to the tribe's lodge for a late supper. A pinewood-paneled hall opened into a sizable library lined with built-in bookshelves across from a massive stone fireplace. Dusty bound volumes filled the shelves, and an enormous tapestry dominated another wall. Several reading chairs were scattered about, each with its own tiny side table lit by a glowing oil lamp. Some of the chairs were occupied by residents who glanced up at us, then quickly resumed their reading.

I was beginning to wonder why this tribe was so notorious. So far, everything seemed almost stodgy.

I glanced back at the tapestry, which pictured a long-ago English-style countryside. As Janie wandered up beside me, I took a closer look.

Whoa! So much for stodgy.

Tiny, well-developed men and women, mostly naked, were romping and dancing among several animal-human creatures. Many more figures were half-hidden in the trees or cavorting in the stream. The needlework looked old and was expertly done.

As Janie and I gawked, Roselin and Louise chatted in the kitchen, beyond the spacious dining hall. I pulled myself away to join them. Roselin was heating up a potful of what she called mulligan stew, a tribe specialty. Louise was busily setting up the kitchen's work table with slices of fresh flaxseed bread, a tub of butter, and a bowl of grapes.

Roselin seems like a regular person so far. Maybe she won't make me a mind-slave after all…

*

Janie had disappeared, then returned with her bottle of wine. Presenting it to Roselin, she said, "I just wanted to bring ya something for havin' us here! This Elsinore bunberry red is one of our best vintages!"

I was surprised at Janie glowing face. She never blushes!

"Oh, this is wonderful, Janie. Thank you!" Roselin gently shut the kitchen door, then went to the cupboard for glasses and a corkscrew. She opened the bottle, took a long sniff, then slowly and solemnly poured the wine. Raising her glass to us and said, "I'm so glad you're all here!"

Feeling bold, I asked her, "I've been wondering what kind of tribe this is."

"Well, Gordy, in spite of the rumors, I think of this place as a sanctuary. Samantha the Seventh, as she calls herself, is an old friend of mine. She established Wild North about twenty years ago for women who need a safe place to figure out what's important in their lives. So in return for some help with the gardens and animals, women of all ages are given a place to stay, with no real time limit. Of course, there have been *other* activities initiated by certain residents, past and present, but it's pretty quiet here at the moment."

Roselin sipped her wine. "When I arrived last week, nobody was doing the dishes, so to speak. I was told Samantha had mysteriously left about a month before, and I was shocked to find the place in such disarray. I still needed a place to live and work, Samantha or no Samantha, so, once I got a handle on things, I told everyone she had sent me here to assume her responsibilities. They were happy to have some order for a change, and no one objected. So far, so good!"

"You just kind of…took over the tribe?" said Louise.

"I guess you could say that. I want Samantha to get back here, though—some of these residents are high-maintenance."

"I'll bet," muttered Janie.

"So, what do the, um, residents *do* here?" I asked.

"Well, I guess you could call it 'independent study'. At least that was Samantha's intention. I'm not sure what some of them are actually doing, but they seem more or less content at the moment. I really don't have time to delve into their business. As for me, they think I'm researching and writing about the Old People."

Louise said, "The place seems awfully quiet. Where is everyone?"

"Let's see…some are on the hill waiting for the sunset. You might have seen them when you arrived, and others are studying or reading, or just out walking. Oh, and Lane and Vermilion, who are both about your age, Gordy, are out looking for some goats that got loose. I've told everyone you were coming, and most of them will want to meet you. We don't get many guests here."

She checked the stew. "Okay, it's ready. Grab a bowl and serve yourself from the pot. We have more wine, too! And the tap water is from our spring—it's good for you even if it smells a little like sulfur."

"Ah," said Janie. "*That's* what I smelled."

Roselin sat down at the head of the spacious table. "Come, sit." she said, and we all settled around her with our bowls of mulligan stew.

Even though the kitchen door was closed, she lowered her voice to nearly a whisper. "There is so much I want to tell you all, and so much more I want to find out from each of you! First of all, I need to explain this tribe. The residents here are an inquisitive lot, and prone to gossip. So if they question you, please tell them you have come to stay as my guests. You, Gordy, are on vacation from school, and Janie and Louise are searching for their true purpose in life, which, for all concerned, isn't too far from the truth, yes?"

"Maybe," muttered Louise.

"I get it," I said. "This Hum stuff needs to be, um, secret, right?"

"Yes, Gordy."

Her eyes lit up. "And, I have learned something new about Hum energy…the very essence of the Hum is what we know of as love!"

Everyone paused, and Janie said, "The Hum is *love?*"

Roselin nodded. "Yes. According to what I've learned, it appears to be the actual energy source *behind* the sensations in our brain that we perceive as love."

She took another sip of her wine, seemingly pleased with herself, and we thoughtfully resumed our supper.

I had never thought much about 'love' until I started feeling all this stuff around Janie. Ever since I first saw her, I've felt waves of elation and joy, then longing, confusion, fear, and sometimes all of it at once. At home, I only dwelt in survival mode. When I was around Mom, Ricky, or especially Leon, the subject of love just never came up. I don't remember anyone ever saying 'I love you' to anyone else.

Were we all deformed or something?

*

We sat back with full stomachs, the wine long gone. Crickets chirped loudly outside.

"Say, I'll bet you'd all like to bathe in our hot-spring pool," said Roselin. "The effervescent sulfur-water is just the thing for soothing sore muscles after long walks!"

"Ooh," said Louise, "I'd love that, but I just want to sleep—we had quite a hike today. Ask me again in the morning!"

"Same here," added Janie.

I felt gritty and indeed sore, and also a bit brave, so I said, "Sure. Just tell me where to go."

"Oh, I'll take you there. It's not easy to find it in the dark. Besides, I need a good soak myself."

Oops—alarms again. Soaking in a probably small pool, in the dark, with this intense person who is also a witch?

Then came a tiny voice. *Trust Roselin like you do Janie. They're on your side. Just let it happen.*

After saying good night to Janie and Louise, who both indeed looked tired, I waited while Roselin fetched some towels and a lantern. By now, I wasn't surprised when bathing suits weren't mentioned, but

I did bring my long sleep shirt to wear afterwards. I quietly followed her through the warm night to a wooded ravine hidden behind the tribe's veggie gardens. The sulfur smell grew stronger as we came upon a secluded, steaming pool concealed among huge rocks. Roselin set the towels and the lamp on a nearby bench. No one else was there.

I was so busy admiring the shadowy beauty of the setting, that when I finally stepped into the water, Roselin was already up to her chin, looking discreetly at the sky. As I waded deeper, the heat of spring water welling up from fissures in the bottom created a perfect hot bath. I blissfully sank into it.

The Milky Way glowed in multiple colors, illuminating Roselin's upturned face.

"Do you see Andromeda?" she asked me. "It's that colorful ellipse just left of the Milky Way."

At first, I didn't see it, but then it was there, as if Roselin had *willed* it.

"Yup, now I see it. I didn't know you could see galaxies without a telescope."

"Oh yes, and much more. Multiple galaxies and sometimes huge nebulae appear very close. It depends on the time of year."

I looked at her.

Soooo much to take in—the long day, this marvelous pool, and Roselin.

Then, softly but clearly she said, "I felt your presence on the Island, Gordy, even before Louise told me about you."

Whoa! I was all attention now.

"And when she told me about your awareness of Hum energy, I knew I had to meet you. I have a strong feeling you are meant to be here. My question is *why?*"

"Mine, too." I whispered.

We both watched the sky for a while.

"Louise told me you're from California in the USA, right?"

I was jolted back. "Uh, yeah."

"So, tell me—when did you first hear the Hum? Did anyone else hear it there, and how does it make you feel?"

I searched for the right words. "Um, when I was six. My neighbor Mr. Barnes may have also heard it. And it makes me feel safe, especially when I'm upset."

Roselin lit up. "That is what I'm most interested in. The Universe *wants* us to feel safe, to feel loved, to feel good, and I believe the Hum is the messenger! It's what I was describing earlier this evening, and I know other Islanders feel this. I've seen it in their eyes when the Hum is around us."

"So, *love* is why the Hum feels good?"

"In a roundabout way," she said. Then she gave me a steady look, causing a shiver inside, but I held her gaze.

"Now, Gordy, I want to share something important with you. Can I trust you?"

In the dim glow of the lamp, her intensity went straight to my heart. "Yes."

She looked at me once more with the slightest hint of a smile, as if she had decided something. Then she closed her eyes and took a long breath. "An ancient people known as the *Ur* delved into secrets of the Hum which they probably should have left alone. I fear that their use of Hum energy might have caused their ultimate end."

"Ahhh," I said. "Janie told me a little about them—the Old People, right?."

"Yes. The Old People. You've probably noticed the ruins they have left behind. Anyway, they somehow determined that the Hum resides in that place where mass and energy meet within *every neutron in the Universe*. They had found, like I have, that the Hum *is the essence* of every material substance and form of energy we know, from a nerve synapse to star plasma."

Her gaze intensified. "Now, Gordy, here is the sticky part. The Ur also discovered a way to manipulate, or harness, Hum energy. It's a mystery how they did it, but I've realized that this *manipulation* can be extremely dangerous. I'm most fearful of what might happen if the Russian military, or any government for that matter, ever gets hold of the information."

"Is this what Louise used when she set off the alarm system?"

Roselin let out a barely audible sigh. "Yes, it's that and a few other things. Here's what I haven't told Louise nor anyone else—all this information is in a book I found. I call it the *Ur Codex*. Its original title is an intricate symbol meaning 'The First Sound of God' with a subtitle that says 'The Immutable Laws of Nature'. The original book is locked up at Putney University, but no one knows what it says, except me! I have only recently translated my hand-copied version."

"Ah, I remember Louise told us about this…"

Roselin shot a look. "Oh, she did, did she?"

"Uh, she said you learned some stuff from an ancient library you found under some ruins, and it's been bothering you…"

"She did, did she?"

Roselin went silent. The steaming water soon calmed to a wavy mirror, reflecting the dim lamplight.

"So, Louise told you about my Beatty Ruins discovery when I was an archeology student?"

I nodded.

She sighed again, quite audible this time.

"Well, I'd like to keep this quiet to protect the Ur library. I'll have to speak to Louise. I'm beginning to worry that she talks too much."

I kind of noticed.

"I'll tell you this, though: My crew and I were simply astonished at how well-preserved that library was. I was immediately drawn to this Codex, a perfectly preserved volume about the size of a slim novel. When I opened it I was instantly enchanted by the complex symbols as well as the beauty of the calligraphy.

"This was my first taste of the Ur language. I furiously began copying everything into my notes, though of course it meant nothing to me at the time. Then, after working through the first few pages, a folded sheet of vellum fell out of the Codex right onto my notebook. And Gordy, I confess—I left it where it landed and closed my notebook cover over it! That single sheet turned out to be the key to deciphering the entire Ur language into ancient Sumerian, which I'd studied in Antiquities school. It took three years, using that key, to translate my copy into Sumerian, and then into English.

"I discovered that the Codex deals with levels of physics that scientists are only now becoming aware of. It wasn't until I'd spent *more* years studying quantum mechanics that I was able to grasp what the thing was talking about. The more I learned, the more I was hooked! Putney University has the entire Ur library, but I'm the only one who has deciphered the language. Are you still with me?"

I nodded as I looked at her in complete awe. And it dawned on me: Roselin is carrying one heavy load! "So, um, is the Hum sometimes evil?"

"Oh, not at all. The Hum simply *is*. Just like uranium simply *is* until it's refined to create a bomb! You see, the Hum is not only everywhere out *there*, but it is also in *here*, deep inside everything, including the neurons in our brains."

Aahh! Approaching overload.

"But I couldn't stop, Gordy! The Codex also outlined a method of concentrating Hum energy into *light!* Lamp oil and candles are expensive here, and I wanted to create something useful from all my research. So from the physics described in the Codex, I wrote a paper, with diagrams, on how to build a lamp powered by Hum energy. I gave a copy of the paper to my friends at the Biganess Tribe, who make lamps. I wanted to see if it was actually possible to create a Hum-energy light source, and it was! I have seen their prototype, and they say the technology appears safe, but I've recently had misgivings about it all, not to mention unsettling dreams."

"Oh, wow," I said. "Janie's mum gave me one to light my room…she said she got it from a friend of hers at Biganess. It didn't work very well though."

"Ah, so you've seen one, and it didn't work?" Roselin's eyes turned dark with worry, but after a few minutes, her face lit up.

"Now, enough about me," she said. "I want to know more about you, Gordy. First of all, just *how* did you get here?"

I was surprised at her shift in conversation, but I didn't hesitate. I told her about my last terrible evening at home, the dream about Mr. Barnes, the self-navigating raft, and then waking up on the beach. I quickly added, "And Janie thinks you might know whether it was a dream or something else."

Roselin stared up at the sky. "From all the dream-stories I've ever heard, Gordy, yours is unique."

I waited for more.

"It sounds to me when you saw your mum that night, you had a shock, and you went into what the Tibetan Buddhists call a bardo state."

"Bardo state?"

"Just a theory. My training back in Covenmoor included Tibetan Buddhist spiritual practices, taught by a visiting teacher. I found the Tibetans' point of view fascinating. They say the *bardo* is a place between death and rebirth, and there are many levels of bardo. You might have slipped into a dream-bardo that lasted the length of your journey. When you woke up on that beach, you were in a sense, reborn!"

"Reborn? Does that mean I, um, died?"

"Well, your body survived, but your mind had a nasty shock, and to deal with it, you kind of checked out. So you might have experienced something similar to death. I think your friend Mr. Barnes had appeared right then to help you."

"Yeah, he was there all right."

"I mean *actually* there. From your description of his role in your dream, I have a hunch he hears the Hum like you do, and you two have a connection you might not be aware of. I think he used his Hum-awareness to send you here."

Mind overload!

She looked at me with a kind of knowing smile, her eyes shining again in that dim light. "Again, Gordy, just a theory. I think this Mr. Barnes cared a lot about you back there in California, and he wanted you to be safe. I can tell he must love you."

Love me?

We were both quiet for a while.

Feeling very bold, I said, "Louise says you're a witch, but you don't seem like a witch to me. Do you have, uh, special powers, like spell-casting?"

Gazing at the sky with a hint of a smile, she said, "A real witch never tells. You'll just have to find out."

"Oh."

We stared at the stars long after the lamp went out.

PART III

HOLY MOTHER OF GOD

LANE

"Hey Gords, wake up!" Janie said. "Roselin wants us at the lodge fer breakfast."

I couldn't remember coming to bed. The long day yesterday plus the mind-warp evening must have literally put me out. Did I fall asleep in that magical pool, and did Roselin bring me back? It was all like…a dream.

"Missster Gordeee," she sang.

"Okaaay, I'm getting up!"

I crawled out of bed wearing the sleepshirt I had brought to the pool. Someone must have put it on me.

Once Janie and Louise left, I tossed it off and got into my last clean shirt and shorts, quite wrinkled. I tried to comb my wild hair, failed, and marched out.

On my way to the lodge I heard parrots screeching, then saw flocks of them flashing among the tree branches. When I entered the dining hall, the din of voices and the warm smell of breakfast hit me all at once. About forty women and a few younger girls sat around four big tables, all chattering at once. When they noticed me, the room suddenly went quiet.

I froze.

"Mr. Gordon Love," Roselin called out, "Please meet the noble and dedicated members of the Wild North Tribe."

There was scattered laughter and a few waved to me, and I waved back, grinning shyly.

"Uh, I don't know what to say, so I'll just eat, okay?"

After more laughter and cheers, I heard Janie call out, "Gordy! Over here!" I sat down next to her and gazed at all these people. I was 'the new boy' once again, this time in an isolated village with no roads, phones, TV or even electricity.

When the food dishes were passed around, I immediately began devouring the customary Islander fare of bangers, mash, eggs, and sauteed greens. I never thought I'd eat fried vegetables all mushed together! I asked for more bunberry juice.

Everyone was noisily chatting with everyone else—except a girl sitting across from me who was intently leaning over her breakfast.

Thick wavy auburn hair covered most of her face, as if she was trying her best to say *please don't notice me.*

Next to the girl sat a tanned woman in a faded plaid shirt, her dark graying hair cut quite short. She looked up at me and said, "Hello. I'm Meredith."

"Uh, hi. I'm Gordy."

"So, um, Gordy," she started right in, "I'm curious. What brings you all the way to this place?"

I tried to remember my spiel. "Well, I'm on break from school and wanted to see some different places. Roselin invited my friends and me to stay here a while, and, uh, here I am!"

One eyebrow rose slightly as she continued eating. "Are you on a…spiritual quest?"

I looked at my plate, not sure how to answer that kind of question. I said, "I dunno. I just came along with them. No real plans."

"So, you might be staying a while?"

"I think so, for a while."

"Well then," her smile brightened as she nodded to her right, "my daughter here would…"

"Mu-uum!" The girl growled in a deep voice.

"…or I myself would be happy to show you around our village and acquaint you with what we do here." She turned to her daughter. "What do you think, Lane?"

The girl blinked hard, then shut her eyes in a grimace. I could easily sense her discomfort, remembering my mom doing things like this.

"That's all right," I said, "I'll be fine."

Meredith kept her smile. "As you wish. But if you ever feel lost, we live in the turquoise house toward the beach, and you're welcome to stop by any time. I'm a writer and I usually work in the back room, so knock loudly."

"Okay," I said. Then I thought of the wall of books I'd seen the night before. "I'm just wondering—is that the, uh, village library in the other room?"

Lane snorted while drinking her juice, winning a stern look from her mother.

Meredith sighed. "Yes, that's it, I'm afraid. The books are mostly donated by previous residents—obscure reference manuals, some actually ancient, a few English and Russian novels, and plenty of local stories published in Putney."

"Oh," I said, "I actually like comic books, and *National Geographic* magazines."

The girl looked up. "Comic books?"

"Yeah." I turned to her. "Do you have any?"

"Only some old ones, but I know where you can get new comic books." she said. "It's a place called Hopp's Store! It's in the desert, not too far from here."

"Really?" This was getting interesting.

"Yeah. Mr. Hopp has *tons* of comics. He gets them from all over the world somehow. I've never seen so many—and they're all different. Mum took me there once."

"Do you think he has *Uncle Scrooge* or *Superman*?"

"I dunno, you'll have to ask him. Do *you* have any comics?"

"Yeah, a few. You wanna trade?"

"Sure." Her face brightened with the hint of a grin.

She's pretty, she seems cool, and she's smiling at <u>me</u>!

Meredith was smiling at her plate. She said, "Well, I'll leave you two. I need to get to work."

As we finished our breakfast, Lane said, "Sorry about my mum. She gets a little pushy sometimes, like she has this agenda for me. Since my school lessons ended last week, she's been trying to get me interested in something, anything, so I don't pester her. And I *am* doing stuff, like helping feed Samantha's chickens and milk goats. Did you know Samantha, the tribe's leader, disappeared? And this week I'm on kitchen duty, so I need your plate."

I gave her my plate. "When you're finished with your, uh, job, can I bring my comics over to your house?"

"Okay. How about in an hour?"

I couldn't help but grin a little.

Maybe this place isn't so weird after all.

*

At a table in her shaded back yard, Lane and I spent a couple of hours devouring each other's comics. Then she said, "Do ya want that tour my mum offered?"

"Sure."

She was up and walking before I knew what was happening. She first showed me around the tribe's compound, then the veggie gardens, the chickens, the goat pasture, and finally the beach.

We barely said a word, but she gave me a *lot* of quick looks, which of course made me think about Ricky and The Look.

Don't panic…she's just being friendly.

I soon gathered that Lane had been craving companionship. On those mornings when she was free, she showed up just after sunrise calling me out of bed. She either wanted to check out the beach at low tide, help her feed the chickens, or some similar project. If they were awake, Janie and Louise would sing out, *"Gordeee, wake uuuup! Your giiirlfriend is here."*

I began to like Lane. She was someone I could talk to without dwelling on the fact that she's-a-girl. I found her presence comforting and felt I could trust her. She told me about her growing up with just her mom in a neighborhood called West Putney.

She patiently listened to my rambling stories about Mom and Ricky, Mr. Barnes, and growing up in California. She seemed fascinated by my raft-dream, and about all that has happened since I arrived here, and she didn't doubt any of it! Her frequent intelligent questions both challenged and elated me—a whole new level of friendship.

But sometimes her exuberance has been overwhelming, and I've had to ask her if we could just read or something. It's been fun going along with her projects, but just not all the time. Occasionally I've tried to evade her, but in this small village she's treated it like a game, and she always finds me. One thing I've noticed when we've gone swimming is she always wears something, so I do too; both of us not wanting to show off too much.

Being with Lane has felt a lot different than being with Janie—more relaxed, but with a deep feeling of something beginning. When Lane smiles at me, there is a beauty in her face and a growing intensity in her eyes I can't begin to describe.

Is this *The Look?*

*

When Lane was on kitchen duty, I often wandered the paths into the hills, or poked along the headlands and beaches. I occasionally met other residents, who, as Louise had said, were all women. Some were friendly and stopped to talk, while others turned away.

"Why do some of them not like me?" I asked Roselin later.

"A lot of the women here have had unfortunate experiences with men," she said, "and your presence may be triggering old traumas. And some of them don't like *anyone*, so don't take it personally."

This brought up memories of my own trauma from my dad's tirades, so I could gather what she meant.

I saw little of my one-time travel companions. Louise spent much of her time with Roselin up in Roselin's study, and Janie has been busy with that Vermilion girl lately, tending and milking the goats. Janie has also been more distant. She sleeps on the far side of our shared bed, nudging me away if I move too close. "It's just me, not you, Gordy, and you know where I'm at. We're still friends, okay?"

"Uh, sure."

But I really wasn't sure. *What is going on with her?*

*

A few days later Lane said, "Hey Gordy, wanna go on a trip? We've read these comics so many times that I'm just dripping with boredom. Let's go to Hopp's Store! We can hike along the coast to Fillmore, only eight miles from here, and they rent pedicabs there. We can ride one to Hopp's, buy our comic books, and ride back to Fillmore all in one day. And we can stay at the Fillmore Inn. Mum and I have stayed there before."

I was impressed that she would come up with something like that, and I was awed by her planning—rent a room at an inn together? But I was also bored, and a hike to somewhere, anywhere, sounded like fun.

"I think my mum will let us go," she said. "I just have to convince her how much good it will do both of us to be out of her hair for a couple of days."

The Fillmore Inn and Bernard Hopp's comic-book shop both filled me with an intense curiosity, to say the least.

"Sure, let's do it!"

*

"No, Lane, I will *not* let you go!" said Meredith. "First of all, you want to stay at an *inn,* for two nights, with a *boy*? No offense, Gordy, but how can I trust you in this situation with my daughter? Also, there are Russian soldiers stationed not far from that area, all nervous about the Americans out at Capricorn Lagoon. I've heard stories of what can happen to young girls who wander too close to soldiers."

I felt Lane's fury rising like heat from a stove.

"I have an idea," I said. "How about if Lane dresses like a boy? I could lend her some of my clothes and my wide bush hat. We'd also keep an eye out for any soldiers and stay away from them."

Lane latched on to the idea. "I'll even cut my hair." And then, wild-eyed, she said, "And, if I don't get out of here soon, Mum, I'm gonna go *craaazzy!*"

Meredith studied her daughter. "Well, let me check with Roselin. She might know more about what's going on over there…and don't you dare cut your hair!"

"'Kay, Mum."

Meredith looked at me. "As for your staying at the inn, I can only trust Lane's judgement, Gordy. If *anything* untoward happens on this little trip, I will have you drawn and quartered!"

Lane looked at the floor, grinning.

"But this all depends on what Roselin says," Meredith added, "so leave me alone until I find out."

Lane rolled her eyes, and we wandered over to the lodge to pass the time.

That afternoon, Meredith found us and said, "I had a talk with Roselin over lunch. She says you won't likely be bothered. The Russians have been very civil to the locals, since they need our help watching the Americans. I read about the American CIA invasion in the newspaper a while ago, so what she says makes sense.

"And you look rather boyish already, Lane. If you keep the hat on, wear Gordy's baggy shirt, and use common sense, I'll feel okay about your little trip."

"Eeee-yes!" Lane squealed as she lunged at her mom with an energetic hug. "We'll pack snacks and food and sun-lotion. We'll need money, too, to buy comic books and rent the pedicab. Can I have my allowance, Mum? Maybe a couple of weeks ahead too?"

"I still have a whole roger, so I'll bring that," I said.

"Okay, okay! Slow down!" said Meredith. "And don't forget to take *plenty* of water."

Meredith gave me one more look. "Roselin also assured me I could trust you, but what I said still goes, Mr. Gordon."

"I promise I'll be good to her," I said, grinning at Lane.

Lane grinned at me with that light in her eyes—this time more powerful than ever.

It was Lane's turn to serve breakfast and then clean up afterwards, so we couldn't start out until mid-morning. I was nervous and flustered, trying hard not to think about the trip, nor of my growing feelings for Lane.

She finally came out with her pack on, and we set off.

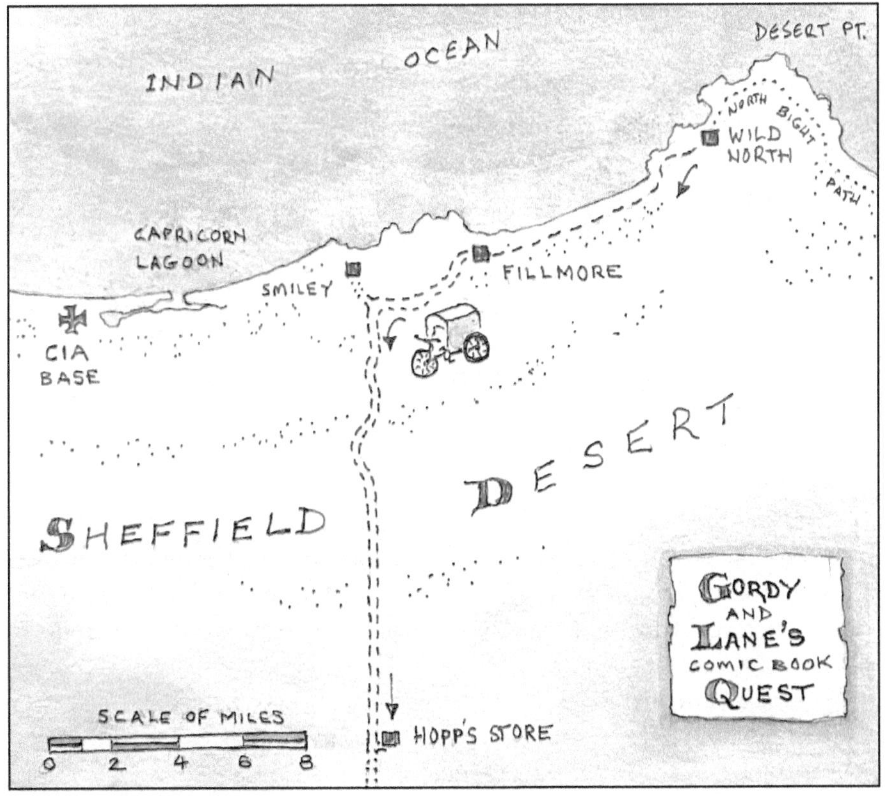

The well-marked path took us west over more hills and headlands and finally along a sandy beach toward Fillmore. Looking inland, sand dunes and dry hills stretched to the horizon. I could see how isolated Lane must feel here, especially since there was no school nearby. She told me that 'school' was her mom giving lessons in the lodge to a varying number of transient kids.

"And I don't have any friends," she said, "because they always seem to leave about the time I get to know them."

"Sounds rough," I said. "How long have you lived at Wild North?"

"Too long! Well, actually about a year. Me mum likes it here 'cause she can write without anyone bothering her. Did I tell you we once lived in West Putney? Mum taught a freshman physics class at Putney U., and for some reason, left her job. She brought a ton of books with us, mostly about physics and all kinds of weird religions, and she's been researching and writing about all that."

"The physics writing sounds like what Roselin is, uh…oops!"

"What?"

"I wasn't supposed to say anything about Roselin, so forget I said that, okay?"

"Oh, you mean Roselin's thing with Hum energy? I know all about that, 'cause she and Mum talk about it *all* the time."

"Oh."

So much for big secrets.

After walking maybe two miles, we agreed it was snack time. We dropped our backpacks and sat down with some nuts and raisins. The beach was untouched and wild, the offshore breakers roared. Feeling delightfully light-footed without my heavy pack, I walked down to the surf to look for any exotic junk that might have washed up.

Lane joined me. We didn't talk.

When we began to stroll along the shoreline, she quietly took my hand.

An unexpected jolt! But I didn't let go, and after a minute her firm grip felt just plain good. She continued looking ahead, saying nothing.

This felt different than when Janie held my hand. Lane's grip was tingley-yet-comforting. I tried, with little success, to shift my attention to the waves or the beach.

"Dibs on the shell!" She suddenly said, and ran ahead to pick up a brilliant abalone. She returned to show me its mother-of-pearl interior.

"Wow," I said. "That's really pretty." And I meant it.

"I'll give it to Mum for letting us take this trip," she said.

Afterward, we munched a few more nuts and raisins, but once we were on our way, I felt hungry again. "I hope we're getting near Fillmore. I'm ready for supper!"

"Yeah, me too."

This time we (mostly) kept our hands to ourselves, but I think we both enjoyed the *potential* of holding hands.

We walked what felt like another ten miles, but it was probably more like two. Finally, Lane spotted some whitewashed buildings and green trees huddled among the barren hills. A sign beside the path read

STAY AT THE FILLMORE INN
Your Home - Just Ahead.

At last!

"We'll be there in ten minutes," she said. "We can have supper, then look for a pedicab to rent. The inn served really good fish dinners when Mum and I were there."

At the check-in desk, Lane asked about a room with two beds. The clerk, a thin severe-looking woman, looked us over then told us, "Our rooms are all booked, but we have some beds in the bunkhouse, if that'll do."

"Oh, okay…we'll need two nights," said Lane.

The woman looked in her book, and said, "If you'd like, I'll have a room with two beds available tomorrow night."

"We'll take it!" Lane said.

"Awl-right," she said. She quickly flicked the beads on an abacus—a process I'd never seen before. "For the two of yer that'll be 480 pence. 160 for tonight, 320 for tomorrow night. Towels are extra, payment in advance. Shall I put your meals on a tab?"

"Yes, please," said Lane. "And add the towels—I need a bath!"

Lane turned to me. "Me mum did this same routine with the meals-tab. Cool, huh? Now, can we pay for this with that roger you have? Then I'll have enough to rent the 'cab and buy comics."

I handed over my roger, feeling quite grown-up on this venture with Lane. I was glad for the towels and was also relieved the innkeeper didn't ask any questions about us reserving the room.

For supper we chose the special on the chalkboard:

Local flounder caught this morning,
grilled and served with fish-dip sauce.
Holyoke chowder.

"Holyoke?"
"Those are little local clams," said Lane. "Very tasty!"

*

The bunkhouse was a large, screened, breezy room that let in the sound of the ocean. We were sharing it with two guys and two women, all of them muscled-up and sunburned. They said they had walked overland across the desert all the way from Merritt. They were about our age, maybe a little older. A tall blond fellow named Terence seemed to be in charge. He invited us to walk out to the beach and look at the sunset with them. I thought I'd walked enough today, but Lane looked at me with raised eyebrows and her fetching grin.

Well…okay.

On our way out she took my hand, which now seemed almost natural.

At the beach, Terence asked us where we were from, and I only said "Gifford," not mentioning Wild North. I was learning to keep quiet! He told us they were headed for Roger's Dreamland and asked if we'd been there.

"I have," I said, "but only for a few minutes."

Lane and the hikers were all ears when I described my brief visit to the juice shack with Janie, and Louise's scary incident.

Then they all asked questions at once, like I was an authority. "Was it easy to get in? Did it feel different there? Did you see any other people?"

"We gotta go there some time!" said Lane.

That night, the bunkhouse air felt stuffy, and our fellow-travelers all snored, especially Terence. Facing each other in our neighboring bunks, Lane and I rolled our eyes at the snorting and wheezing. She reached a hand across and we finally fell asleep.

At breakfast, Terence and his friends grabbed all the food they could carry from the buffet table, and waved goodbye. On their way out they talked about Wild North as a water stop, and one of the girls said she dreaded meeting any of those crazy women she'd heard about there. Lane looked at me. "I should tell that twit that one of those crazy women is my mum."

We skipped the plundered buffet table and ordered breakfast in the dining room. "These fat waffles are lovely! We never get them at Samantha's," said Lane as she piled on fresh berries, whipped cream and honey.

No argument here!

*

Next door, the Fillmore Mercantile rented a variety of handcarts, bicycles, and two canvas-covered kayaks. They had a single two-rider pedicab with nearly-flat tires. While Lane was pinching them, the proprietor said, "Someone talked me into buying this to rent, but who uses pedicabs around here? Yer lucky I have the one! I'll fill up the tires."

When he finished, he dusted off the seats with a flourish. We stowed our box lunches, provided by the inn, and several jugs of water. Lane wrote down our destination and estimated return time in the rental logbook. "People have gotten lost in the desert," the owner informed us. Waving to him, we eagerly set off, each pushing on our own set of pedals. I was glad for the optional fringed canvas roof since the sun was already ferocious.

The straight single-lane dirt road was boring, and it was getting hot. The sand also slowed us down, despite the 'cab's wide tires.

We had to get off the road once to let some military trucks go by, probably on their way to Capricorn Lagoon. Young, wide-eyed soldiers sitting on benches in the back gave us a hearty wave.

Seeing any Russians still gives me the creeps. I just hope Zevnikov's order was a real thing.

There was no other traffic.

Finally, Lane spotted a boxy stone building on the next rise. Sure enough, the sign on it said HOPP'S.

As soon as we pulled up, Lane climbed out and made a beeline for the door. The thick stone walls made the inside refreshingly cool.

We were the only customers. The store held a meager, slightly dusty display of snack foods, canned goods, wine, and soft drinks, plus some random tools, hardware, camping gear, and, in a corner, a hand-operated pump over a sink for filling canteens.

But no comic books.

A voice in the back said, "Yes?"

"Halloo," said Lane. "We, uh, thought you had comic books here."

"Oh, I do, I do," the voice became clearer as the shopkeeper, who looked surprisingly young, emerged from a back room. "I am Bernard Hopp, at your service," he said with a slight bow. "I recently moved my comic collection to the second floor. Some are for sale, and others are not. Shall I escort you?"

With a flourish he gestured toward a staircase along the wall, partly hidden by a bush-hat display.

Upstairs, Lane and I both gasped at the sight of row after row of shelves displaying thousands of comics, none of which looked familiar. Their covers were neatly arranged facing out, all softly lit by a big overhead skylight.

Lane had already spotted some of her favorites. "Wow, you have *Crimson Comet*, and *Dan Dare*, some old *Bunty*, and, oh, some *Captain Planet* comics. I'll take this one, this one, these two over here, and…"

"I've never seen these," I said to her. "They must be from other countries."

"Yeah, mostly from England and Australia, I think. Oh, look, here's a *Kaiser Spinks* double-issue!"

Mr. Hopp added, "I acquire most of these from Europe, through Australia. The Russians don't officially care to see American publications here, but without fail, their soldiers passing through often ask for *Superman*, *Spider-Man* or *Batman*."

"Say, Mr. Hopp," I said, "Do you have any Disney comics, like *Donald Duck* or *Uncle Scrooge*?"

"Well, as I said, the Russians…" Then he looked at me. "Hmmm, as a matter of fact, young man, I received a rather large shipment of Walt Disney titles late last week, and some I will sell. Come this way."

He led us to a table in the back of the room, and on it were stacks of copies of *The Adventures* of *Uncle Scrooge* and *Walt Disney's Comics and Stories featuring Donald Duck*. Some were as recent as last month, and others dated back to the early 'fifties. All of them looked new!

Lane peered over my shoulder as I flipped through the multitude of titles. "Look at these, Lane! I've never seen these issues before. Um, how much are you asking for these, Mr. Hopp?"

He paused and studied me more closely. "Hmmm…might I ask your name?"

"Uh, sure…Gordy Love."

"Ah. Well. It appears, Mr. Love, that this shipment came from a benefactor." He rummaged in the packing material and pulled out a folded sheet of note-paper. "Please read this."

I opened the neatly typed note.

Dear Mr. Hopp,

These titles are for your admirable collection, with one request: If a young man named Gordon Love should inquire about any of them, please allow him to choose, free of charge, a copy of any issue for his reading pleasure.

Sincerely,

Edward C. Barnes

Lane was reading it too, then she watched the expression on my face turn from startled surprise to an 'ear to ear grin' as she described it later.

I finally blurted out, "How—how did he know where to send these?"

Mr. Hopp said, "I, too, entertained that question. But now I see this fellow must know you, and also knew of your approximate time of arrival."

Lane looked at me, wide-eyed, "Jeez, Gordy, who *is* this guy?"

Mr. Hopp added, "I have occasionally received shipments of donated comics someone may have found, say, buried in a closet, but I have never received anything like this, and I must say it will add a new level of variety to my inventory. Please express my hearty gratitude to your friend."

A wave of joy, longing, sadness, and a hundred questions swelled up inside me.

I can't believe this.

Blinking back tears, I looked at Lane and said, "This is the first time someone was this *nice* to me. Mr. Barnes was, *is*, my only real friend back home in California. First, he helped get me here in my dream, and now this!"

Lane's expression looked as perplexed as I felt.

I finally selected twenty-six different *Donald Duck* and *Uncle Scrooge* comics, and a few others I purchased from Mr. Hopp's collection. I then gave my comic-book money to Lane, who had a field day selecting thirty-seven different issues from the shelves.

My mind was still reeling. *What is Mr. Barnes up to?*

Then I recalled Roselin's simple yet powerful words from that first night…

He must love…me.

*

Outside, we sat down in the narrow shade of the building and started reading while eating delightful egg-salad sandwiches from our Fillmore Inn box-lunches.

"This is the best lunch I've *ever* had," Lane said, her mouth full. She glanced over at me, "Hey, Earth to Gordy!"
I tore myself out of my comic book. "Oh…yeah, mine's good too. And thanks for your idea to come here."

She gave me a long, level look. "I'm not so sure this was all *my* idea."

We spent the afternoon pedaling back to Fillmore. A rising ocean breeze was slowing us down, but its coolness knocked back the stifling heat. No traffic this time.

When we returned to the inn, our private room was waiting for us, but it had only *one* double bed, not two! The room and the bed both looked exceedingly small.

Lane looked at me. "Whadaya think? Should we complain? I think it *might* be okay. I've never slept…um…is this okay with *you*?"

My thoughts went straight to sharing beds with Janie, but that was no help here.

I don't want to be rude and say "no," but if I say "yes," will she want something? Lane is giving me all these new feelings, and I don't know what to do with them. And worse, maybe I'll do something stupid and she won't like me. Oh, crap!

I took in a deep beath, then said as casually as I could, "Yeah, I guess I'm okay with it."

She flashed me a serious look—hopeful trust?

*

The Inn was busy that night, the dining room nearly full. Lane looked tired, and seemed deep in her own thoughts as we ate another seafood dish—this time it was seasoned chunks of sautéed salmon served over steamed rice.

"Not bad for life in the desert," I said between bites. "I don't think I've ever been this hungry."

"Yeh, not bad at all," said Lane with a sleepy-eyed smile.

I realized I was tired too. "Wanna turn in early?"

"Okay, but I'll need a bath first."

"Ohyeahmetoo," I said a little too quickly.

She looked up. "Are you okay?"

I hope so…

"Uhm, yeah…well, mostly okay, I think."

"Yeah, me too, mostly," she said.

Back in our room, I was suddenly shy about what I should wear to bed. It felt too warm for my long sleep-shirt.

I said, "Would it be all right if I sleep in my t-shirt and undershorts? It's, um, pretty warm in here."

"That's fine," she said from behind the door of the tiny bath. A bit later, she emerged steamy and glowing in a pair of baggy pajama shorts and an oversized sleeveless undershirt, with WEST PUTNEY SURF CLUB printed across the chest.

She was more beautiful than ever, and my heart was pounding.

How could someone like you *want to be with* me?

"I hope this is okay," she said.

"Uh, yeah, and cool shirt, by the way." Then I blushed, wishing I hadn't said that. *Now she'll think I'm ogling her chest.*

I took my time soaking in the bath, trying not to think about how Lane looked just then. After I put on my shorts and t-shirt, I still felt shy.

Okay, now I'm squeaky clean, teeth brushed, and trying very hard not to dwell on the fact we are about to share a bed.

When I came out of the bathroom, Lane was all tucked in, looking at the ceiling.

I climbed in and settled at a respectable distance, almost hanging off the edge, and also looked at the ceiling.

"So," I asked her, "where is West Putney?"

She quickly turned to face me. "It's just west of Putney, silly, though I forget—you've never been there. We lived in an apartment right near the ocean, and surf-riding was starting to catch on then. When we left,

Mum was learning how to surf on one of those new lightweight surfboards, and I wanted to learn too. I really miss that place."

Though my mind was still racing, I finally said, "Yeah, I miss my old hometown too. I liked where I lived in California." Still looking up, I went on. "But I was lonely a lot. I had some friends, but they didn't always want to be with me." I glanced at her. "One kid told me to my face I was *boring*. And whenever I mentioned hearing the Hum, they all made fun of me. And no one was at home at my house. My mom worked a lot, and my brother Ricky was usually out with his friends."

"No dad?"

"No dad."

"Same here, just Mum and me."

When I looked at her again, her eyes were tearing up.

"Hey, Lane, what's wrong?"

She shifted to face me, took a deep breath, and said, "I-I'm not sure. Maybe it's because I've been lonely too. Also, me mum told me we might be moving again. She says she wants to be closer to the big library in Putney, so we might go back there."

"But didn't you say you missed living there? In West Putney?"

"I did, and I'll probably like it there again, but, um, there's something else going on…I've never had a friend like you, Gordy. You like doing the same stuff I like to do, and you don't make fun of me, and you're definitely *not* boring. So if we move away, I'll be back where I was."

I rolled on my side to face her, my heart thumping. "Aw, Lane, you mean that?"

"Yes. I was going crazy there at Wild North with no one to talk to. Samantha was kind of like a dictator, and that tribe is full of some pretty weird people. Then she just left one day, and the place fell apart fast—no rules, people arguing, food running out, the lodge a mess. Mum was ready to move us out, and then Roselin showed up."

"Wow! Well I'm sure glad you guys stayed!"

Lane smiled and looked back at the ceiling. "I've been sort-of friends with Vermilion, who's a little older than me. She's nice, but she never really talks about anything except the goats and her own problems. She's the one with that wild red hair."

"Yeah, I've seen her. What about your mum—do you do things with her?"

"Well, sometimes, but she's my *mum*!"

"Yeah, I know what you mean."

"Mum had been a lot more fun and cheerful when we lived in West P. But then something came over her about a month before we moved here. She got worried and distracted and kept looking out the windows. She also shut herself in her room for hours to 'be alone with her writing'. She's writing here too, except now she sits with Roselin every evening and they talk and drink wine. I like Roselin, and Mum seems happier, so I guess that's a good thing."

I'd closed my eyes and I must have been smiling, because she said, "What're you grinning at?"

"I like to hear you talk, even when you're sniffling!" I looked over as she grinned through her tears, and my heart melted a little more.

We both lay quiet, my heart and brain seemed to be settling down. I looked at her. "I feel peaceful here with you."

"Me too—with you."

"Should I turn the out the lamp?"

"Okay."

*

In the dark I lay there on my back with a strange, almost physical twitchiness lurking somewhere behind my random thoughts. No sounds except the distant surf through the open window. Finally, the noises in my head began to blissfully fade until...

Lane turned and pressed her lips gently but firmly to the side of my neck.

Ooh.

It tickled, but I didn't move, and neither did her lips for a long time. When they did, they slowly drifted, with the help of her tongue, toward my ear, then to my shoulder. I lay there in a time-freeze.

Oooooh...

This was so weird and strange and good—I had no idea what to do. I briefly thought of Janie holding me during our nights together, but this felt *waaaay* different.

Lane stopped and gave me a questioning look.

No more thinking...

"Um, you can do that again if you want."

She smiled. "Maybe later. Now close your eyes."

I soon felt her arm move over me, her body scooch closer as she kissed my forehead, my eyelids, nose, chin, both cheeks and finally my mouth.

Gleeeep!

She stopped and said, "Is it nice?"

I nodded.

"Now kiss me back. Just make your lips go slack. It'll feel better."

I did and it did…and out of nowhere some kind of floodgate burst open and we grappled with each other like two lost souls. Lane climbed on top of me, and we kissed every inch of each other's faces. She did things with her tongue that just about sent me through the roof!

Zwooooop!

With her on me, I suddenly realized what was happening beneath my shorts. I tried *not* to imagine what might exist under hers! When she pressed down on my, um, bulge, she gave out a soft moan that thrilled and worried me all at once. *Is she okay?* Breathing hard, we stopped to look at each other, both wide-eyed.

What are we DOING?

She slowly moved off beside me and rested her cheek on my chest. When I began to stroke her back, she tugged at her shirt and said, "Could you reach under and scratch?"

"Sure." I was able to reach her entire back while her cheek stayed where it was—that felt so nice.

"Yeah, there, ooh…up there, and there. *Yesss!*" We were breathing slower as I gently scratched and tickled, but my heart was still thumping. I was pretty sure she felt it.

What a mind-boggling new world…in so many ways.

"How did you learn how to kiss like that?" I finally said.

"Vermilion taught me. I saw her kissing Janie once, and I was curious, so I just went up and asked her."

"Vermilion was kissing *Janie?*"

"Yeah, hadn't you noticed?"

"Uh, no."

"Anyway, Vermilion looked at me kind of funny, then she smiled. I wasn't sure what kind of lesson I wanted, so I waited until she held my face and started in."

"That must have been strange."

"I just pretended she was you."

Ahhh.

It had been a long day and we were both feeling it.

Finally Lane yawned and said, "This time it's goodnight for real," and within minutes she was snoring.

I lay awake, weary yet still buzzing, but not for long.

*

It was nearly noon when the innkeeper rapped on our door, jolting us awake. "Time to move on in there unless you want the room another night," she said.

We looked at each other, and Lane softly crooned, *"Morrrniiing!"*

Soon we were dressed, packed, and out of the room in time to have lunch downstairs. At our table, we didn't do much except grin at our food and eat. Finally I said, "I'm glad we'll get back today, I'm almost out of money!"

"Yeah, me too. I'll have enough to pay the tab, I think."

Our return to Wild North was slow going, especially with the added weight of our comic book trove. Lane walked sluggishly in the heat, and I was happy to slow down to her plodding pace. The afternoon sun was intense, as usual, with hardly a breeze off the ocean. Finally, Lane said, "Let's stop and go swimming!"

After last night, I still wasn't sure how to 'be' with Lane, so I decided to swim in my undershorts, and she was in her surf-club shirt and sleep-shorts. We ran into the surf, which was surprisingly cold compared to the sultry air. "Oh, now this feels good!" I said. I waded out toward a big swell, attempting to body-surf it, but the wave threw me over and yanked off my flimsy shorts!

"Don't look!" I said as I scrambled to find them.

Lane not only looked, but laughed. Then a bigger wave hit her from behind, tumbling her mercilessly until she came up with no shirt!

Hah! I pointed, and we both laughed until the next wave knocked both of us over. I was giddy with this new excitement I still couldn't describe. I caught several waves, enjoying the clothes-free exhilaration. Lane swam out and rode a few bigger swells, showing me up with her skill. She yelled with delight as the waves carried her in, one after another.

Exhausted, we stumbled out and eventually found our lost 'swimwear'. We tried not to look at each other, but we didn't put anything back on, either. Lane pulled a large bath towel from her pack, which I recognized was from the inn.

She spread it on the sand and said, "Here, let's lie down and warm up for a few minutes." Neither of us made any moves, but we couldn't help occasionally gawking and grinning.

By late afternoon, tired and raw with sunburn, we finally reached the bluffs that told us we would soon arrive at Wild North. We decided to stop and watch the sun settle into the ocean.

"Gordy," she said. "This has been such an amazing trip. I'm so glad we...

The flash came from behind us—a blinding blue-white light that erased all the color from Lane's face and from everything else.

HOLY MOTHER

We both turned to see a thin, fading, bluish line shooting straight into deep space—originating from somewhere inland. We had barely absorbed this when the ground jerked violently beneath our feet, forcing us to sit down hard on our backpacks. Without a word we grabbed each other as the land rocked back and forth. A few rocks tumbled, dust rose, and flocks of shrieking birds erupted from their roosts.

We held each other until the movement stopped, but it didn't seem over yet.

The birds were still agitated when a deep thunder-like BOOM hit us from the direction of the flash. This was followed by a howling roar and the most agonizing in-your-belly screeching hum-sound I'd ever heard. It eventually exhausted itself, slowly receding into distant echoes, then finally, silence.

"*Holy…Mother…of…God,*" whispered Lane.

We sat there a long time holding on to each other. At some point we must have gotten up and began to walk, but I really don't remember.

*

We soon stumbled into Wild North to find the place clouded in dust and smoke. An eerie glow from a few small fires and several lanterns lit up the commons. Walls had crumbled, and injured residents were being attended to. Above the agitated human sounds, the local parrots were still squawking in the trees. Some of them had learned to talk, and I distinctly heard one screeching, *Armageddon! Armageddon!*

Meredith saw us and yelled, "Lane!" and she rushed to embrace her mother. Janie, Vermilion and Louise were huddling with Roselin, who was sitting very still on a bench.

Janie shouted "Gordy!" I ran to them and dumped my pack as she stood up to hug me. We both said, "Are you guys all right?"

"Yeah," I said. "Lane and I were watching the sunset when it happened."

Janie nodded toward Roselin who looked absolutely stricken. Her eyes were red as she slowly said, "My belly feels like it was ripped open—that terrible, anguished sound. My god, what has happened?"

Louise had wrapped her arm around Roselin's shoulders. "I wish I knew," she said.

For a long moment we all stared at each other, stunned.

Then Roselin seemed to wake up. She shrugged off Louise's arm and slowly stood up.

She looked around at the crowd.

"I need everyone to listen up!" she said.

The chatter continued.

"HEY! LISTEN UP!" shouted Louise.

Silence, except for the parrots.

Roselin spoke to the crowd. "First of all, we must get to higher ground as quickly as possible—that earthquake may have generated a tidal wave. Second, stay out of your houses until morning. If you must go inside, don't touch any beams or walls. Just grab what you need for the night, and then get up to the headland—the sunset meadow should be high enough."

The fires were almost out, and the people on the ground were all able to get up with some assistance. Everyone began to gather blankets and move toward the headland.

Lane ran over to me, gave me a quick hug, and said, "Me mum says thanks!"

"Thanks?"

"Yeah, for bringing me back safely." She smooched my cheek then said, "See you up on the meadow?"

"Okay."

Janie was looking at us with that raised eyebrow of hers, and I told her, "We got our comic books."

"And maybe more than comic books..." she said with a wink.

Janie's still Janie, even now.

We had gathered up bedding, water, and snack-foods for our night on the bluff. Louise helped Roselin up the hill, and none of us said much. Soon the entire tribe was spreading out blankets, tents and even folding chairs on the moonlit meadow. Someone had brought up driftwood and lit a fire in the stone-ringed fire pit. Several tribe-members huddled around it, staring at the flames, trying to process what had happened.

What in bloody hell was that?

Was it a nuclear bomb?

But that light was so thin, like a rocket going up.
Its speed was incredible!
And that noise! *My ears are still ringing.*
Yes, that awful screechy-humming at the end.
It couldn't have been the Hum. It sounded so...angry!

During the long night, Roselin, Janie, Louise and I shared stories about growing up—their childhood adventures on the Island, and mine in California, highlighting more details than we might have otherwise. I only saw Lane briefly. She ran over and squeezed my hand, gave me a memorable smooch, then quickly returned to her mom.

Not that much later we heard a louder-than-usual roar of a wave breaking, and at daybreak we saw the little beach had been swept clean. Roselin's prediction was right—a tidal surge had indeed washed over it, but thankfully it stopped short of the village.

"I'm glad it came no further," said Louise. "We'll have enough to clean up."

*

In the morning we slowly returned. I walked into the lodge and found Lane staring at the wreckage in the kitchen. Seeing her distress, I stayed to help her.

In the lodge library, Meredith cranked the generator-handle to run the radio. She tuned in to the official Russian-sponsored (and only) news station, broadcast from Putney. She quietly replaced fallen books while we all listened.

...again, Soviet Naval Command has determined that last evening's explosion was an attack by American imperialists, an attack which fortunately failed, as it missed our major installations. The force of the blast, however, damaged buildings in a large area of the eastern Highlands, and we have reports of destruction over much of the island from the tremor caused by the blast.

We have also received reports of injuries, but so far, only four deaths, though we have not yet heard from many isolated settlements. We also have reports of harbors and boats damaged by tidal surges in both Putney and Skegness.

All military posts are on heightened alert, and all roads island-wide are closed until further notice. All Islanders please remain at home and remain tuned in to this station until Soviet Naval Command has given an all-clear.

Meredith said, "That's going to mean trouble. I'll bet the Russians are swarming all around that American outpost at Capricorn Lagoon. That's only about fifteen miles from here."

Just then Janie walked in, curious about breakfast.

"Hey Janie," I said, "Could you give us a hand in here?"

"Yes, *sir*," she said, and then her face fell when she saw the mess. The floor was littered with broken crockery, shattered glass, pools of spilled food, plus a sink full of unwashed supper dishes left behind when everyone fled the building.

"*Shite*," she muttered loudly. Janie did not like cleaning up messes.

"I have my house to clean up," Meredith said brightly. "I'm glad you can help, Janie."

We washed, swept, mopped and finally got the place ready for Molly the breakfast cook, who was patiently waiting in the dining room, listening to the ongoing news. ("I only cook, I don't clean!")

Lane and I couldn't help making passes at each other while we worked, which confirmed Janie's suspicions. She maneuvered near me to whisper, "*Yooo* and *I* need to talk soon."

When the breakfast bell finally rang about three hours late, the weary tribe poured in and eagerly sat down. It might have been the quietest breakfast ever served at Wild North.

Near the end of the meal, Roselin stood up to her full height, put on her best leadership face, and dinged a glass.

A silent pause…

"How is everyone doing?"

Fine.

All right.

It could have been worse.

I have a headache.

I didn't sleep at all.

"Yes," said Roselin, "we all have had quite a night! Now, I assume you've all heard the news on the radio."

After another pause she continued. "The Russians are saying the Americans are responsible for the explosion, and I believe there might be some kind of showdown at Capricorn Lagoon. Early this morning, I asked for two volunteers to hike over to Fillmore and Smiley and tell the residents they would be welcome to stay here should there be trouble. We're not that far away either, but the surrounding hills might give us some protection. So I'm letting you know we might have some guests for a few days, and I'd like everyone to be as welcoming as we can."

A few people grumbled, but there were no shouts of dissent.

Toward evening, residents of Fillmore and Smiley indeed began wandering into the compound. Some said they were hesitant to come because they had heard stories about 'those wild women'. We heard that others had retreated elsewhere, but most, like the steadfast proprietor of the Fillmore Inn, had decided to stay put.

The newcomers were graciously welcomed by (most of) the Wild North tribe. Some residents shared what extra rooms they had, but most could only offer tent-space in their yards. All were welcomed to join in for meals at the lodge.

That evening, there was a raucous supper with about thirty extra guests, mostly women, but also several men, kids, and a young, scared Russian sailor who had gone AWOL. A wary young woman sat close to him, with a reassuring hand on his arm. Overall, the exiles seemed to visibly relax.

I could definitely feel a buzzing of warm energy around the room. Maybe this disaster will soften a few misconceptions about this place.

*

The next evening, we were finishing supper in the still-crowded dining hall when Roselin quietly said, "Janie, Gordy, Louise—I need you to come up to my house."

When we arrived, she had already put out some chairs on the terrace. She gestured us to sit, and brought out something she called peach-dessert wine. "Let me fill your glass, Gordy. You're one of us now." Then Roselin raised her glass and said in a strange deep voice, "To love and health!"

The sweet wine helped us relax, though we remained alert with curiosity.

Roselin had closed her eyes, and seemed to be far away. Then she said, "I think I know what *actually* caused that blast. Louise, do you remember those two young engineers from the Biganess tribe who came to Covenmoor wanting to learn about Hum energy? To possibly use it to make lamps?."

Louise nodded.

"I must say their timing was, ah, auspicious. I had recently learned from the Codex a method to convert *photonic* Hum energy to visible light. I had just deciphered the relevant physics and was so excited by their request that I hastily wrote a how-to-build-it instruction guide and sent it with them to Biganess. They later surprised me with a working prototype, and I must say I was impressed.

"They demonstrated the 'switch' they had developed using my notes. It was a matter of simply sliding a tiny magnet toward a microscopic 'entanglement of quantum foam' to turn it on and off. The lamp was rather dim, yet I was surprised they were able to create the 'entanglement' at all. That is very unstable stuff."

Her face turned sad as she took a long sip of wine. "I believe they were working on a more powerful 'entanglement' when the explosion occurred."

Silence.

"So," said Janie, "Ya think they, um, blew themselves up?"

"Well, according to the news reports, that blast came from the tribe's location, and when it happened, I had a bad feeling that was Hum energy let loose. The noise at the end was a definite clue."

More silence.

My heart again went out to Roselin. She was suffering. The burden of her knowledge had been clearly bearing down on her, and now this. Then I remembered Todd's report, which I assumed Louise had given to her when we arrived. I said, "So that Codex will be even more dangerous once the Russians send the library to Moscow to translate it, right?"

"What?" Roselin flashed at me. "Where did you hear *that?*"

"Uh…didn't Louise give you Todd's report?"

Roselin's eyes went dark with rage as she turned her attention to Louise, who was suddenly looking at the floor.

Uh, oh…

Roselin furiously waved Janie and me off the terrace as she bore down on Louise with a blast of questions. Once we were down on the commons, the last words I heard from Roselin were, *"Bring it to me NOW!"*

As we quickly walked away I said to Janie, "What's going on? Why didn't Louise hand over that report?"

"Ah, Gordy. Louise told me the other day she was afraid Roselin was already too 'distraught' to see the thing. Louise is such a know-it-all, and she'd just bully me if I pestered her. I shoulda told ya what was going on, but I didn't know what to do about it meself. You prob'bly did the right thing, lettin' the cat out, so to speak."

I looked at her, relieved. "Thanks. I'm just glad I'm not Louise right now."

"Hey, ya wanna walk up to the headland with me?"

"What? Uh, sure."

Janie's sudden request heightened my wariness. On our way uphill, I glanced at her. I felt we had drifted even further apart since my comic-book adventure with Lane. Though we still shared the bed in the guest house, we had become more like roommates—no more late-night talks or cuddling. During the day I saw little of Janie *or* Louise.

While we walked up the hill, Janie said, all mock-cheerful, "So, Gords, howyadoin'?"

"Okay. How 'bout you?"

"Ah, fine. I've been wantin' to talk to yer about Lane."

Ah yes, so you had said.

She led us to a slab of rock near the edge of the bluff, where we sat. The wide ocean shimmered under brilliant stars and at least five galaxies dazzled us with their multi-colored brilliance. *Wow, those galaxies again, and different ones every night. This is all too much.*

"Hey, Earth to Gordy!"

"Oh! Uh, what?"

"I'm wonderin' where you and Lane are headed. I see ya together a lot, and I hope ya know what happens when sperm meets egg."

"Jeez, Janie, I'm not an idiot! Yeah, I know about that…from school anyway."

"Okay, okay, calm down loverboy," she said with a smile. "I'm glad ya have her as a friend, especially with all the recent craziness around here."

"I'm glad too. I hope you don't think I'm ignoring you."

"Not at all. I just care about ya is all, and I wouldn't want to see ya get roped into somethin' with her."

"Jay-nee!"

She persisted. "I can see you and Lane have been acting like star-crossed rabbits since ya came back from yer little trip. *That's* why I was getting a little worried about, um, whether you were *doing* it or not."

"Well, actually…"

"Ya don't have to tell me! I don't need the details."

"Well, *actually*," I repeated, frustrated, "we haven't been doing anything lately because Lane's been busy in the kitchen and I'm helping fix houses. And besides, Lane's mom is doing her best to keep me away from her, especially at night."

Janie looked surprised.

"Okay, Janie, try to hear me out. Our trip was really magical, and the Fillmore Inn was really cool. And at Hopp's Store, we discovered my friend Mr. Barnes had shipped a box of my favorite comics to Mr. Hopp, all the way from California—I couldn't believe it! Lane was there with me, and she was as touched about it as I was."

"How…what?"

"I don't know, Janie! He somehow knew about Hopp's comic collection and that I would show up at his store. Then Lane and I had this wonderful time reading our piles of new comics, talking a lot, and, um, enjoying each other's company." (My face grew hot remembering that part.) "And after we got back here, Meredith saw her looking at me kind of dreamily, and I think she went *Uh-oh.*"

"Yeh, I can unnerstand that." said Janie. "Me mum did the same thing when she heard about me kissing Mel Hastings in ninth year."

"Hey," I said, "I see you and Vermilion together a lot. What's up with *that?*"

Janie looked startled, then she paused and let out a little smile. "Ahh. I think we both needed someone. And I didn't know it until I wandered over to the goat pens one day and saw her feeding a newborn with a baby bottle. Her tenderness touched somethin' in me, so I started chatting. But she had assumed you and I were more-than-friends, and she thought I was messin' with her. When she made a cute remark about how young you are, I was ready to smack her! Then out of the blue she said, 'Aww, I wasn't meanin' to rile you. Ya wanna go bodysurfin'? The waves are good today!' Since then a lot has happened. I probably shoudda told ya."

Then I remembered Lane's mention of them kissing, and I grinned at her. "So, are you two in *looove?*"

Janie bopped my shoulder, and I rolled sideways off the rock, clutching myself in mock pain. "I *thought* something was going on," I said, lying on my back. "Now I get why I haven't seen you."

"Well, sez *yooo!*" She hopped off the rock and roughly pinned me down. "I just want ya to know I'm keepin' an eye on ya, big boy." She began to tickle me mercilessly.

"Aaaak! Are you *jealous*, Janie?"

Then I counter-attacked, and we rolled and wrestled in the grass, letting off weeks of pent-up tension.

PART IV
GET THE CODEX

ROSELIN'S PLAN

Two weeks later, the schooner *Meridian* was anchored offshore, having delivered the mail and supplies that afternoon. That evening, Roselin asked me up to her place. When I arrived, recent newspapers were spread out on the living room table, and Roselin again looked pale, her face drawn and creased with worry. Louise was still with her, so her transgression was apparently not fatal. Janie was nowhere to be found.

Roselin brought out glasses and a fancy-looking bottle labelled Highpeace Monastery Rosé. "I brought out my best vintage," she said, "because there is something I must do."

We waited as she poured wine for us, then raised her glass. "I'm glad you two are here, and I wish it was a happier occasion." She gestured to the newspapers. "I've looked over these newspapers, and I'm convinced that if the Russians discover the Hum energy formulas in the Codex, we'll likely all be annihilated!"

She had our attention.

"From what I've read, that blast probably killed everyone working on those lamps, plus at least ninety other people in the area, and several more are missing. It erased every building in Biganess and left a narrow hole over a thousand feet deep!"

"Ninety people?"

Louise was wide-eyed. "A *thousand* feet?"

"Yes, and probably much deeper, but only a foot in diameter. Here's an artist's sketch of it. They said it was lined with glass created by the intense heat! That hole verified my theory of the two-dimensional property of Hum energy. If the blast was *three*-dimensional, it probably would have blown away our entire Island, leaving a crater in the ocean!"

I shuddered at the thought.

"So," I said, "it wasn't an American bomb?"

"No, but I heard that Russian KGB agents are all over Biganess asking questions. Some locals told them there was a 'lamp factory' at the site of the blast, but again, I think we're lucky all the evidence was vaporized."

All this left me not only worried, but sad. "I thought the Hum was just this feel-good sound everyone loves to hear."

Roselin gave me a kind of bittersweet smile. "I wish it *was* only that. I had no idea the Hum had a dark side, Gordy. The Codex said nothing about the dangers of Hum energy, and I had to go and use all my wonderful quantum physics research, straight from the theories in that book, to basically *write a recipe for our destruction!*"

She threw her glass at the wall.

Louise flinched and looked at the floor.

Then Roselin's eyes flashed with a sudden ferocity that felt electric.

"I see only one solution," she said. "I must retrieve the Codex! I'm quite sure the rest of the Ur library is harmless. From reviewing my fellow students' notebooks, I found out the other books were all about Ur customs and history, their sagas and stories."

"But you are the only one who knows the Ur language." said Louise.

"Yes, but I know that won't last forever."

Roselin went on. "My friend Kate was one of my fellow students at that dig, and now she works in the College of Antiquities office. She of course saw that library, and has followed all the hush-hush afterward.

"When I was translating my copybook version of the Codex, and had realized what it was about, I asked her once if she ever had access to the library, and if she did, to look for a thin book with a special mark on the spine. She wrote to me a while back, and told me, sure enough, the book with the mark was there. She said that Broadmoor very proudly showed her the entire library, all set up nice and pretty in a locked room next to his office. I remember he was never very good at keeping secrets!"

Roselin fetched a notebook from her desk and opened it to reveal a strange drawing. "This is the mark I sent to her, that 'First Sound of God' symbol I told you about…"

Louise and I studied it closely. "Fascinating!" she whispered.

I couldn't help but glance at some of the other symbols in Roselin's notes—what a strange, weird language!

"Louise and Gordy, I must ask you now—I'll need your help to get the Codex. There will be risks, and we could get into some real trouble. Are you in?"

Oh, wow...I guess she's saying it like it is.

If I help, I suppose I'll be a spy after all.

But do I even have a choice?

Louise was nearly bouncing in her chair trying to get me to say yes. I finally nodded, and she almost shouted, "We're in!"

Roselin let out a grin I hadn't seen in a while, and the whole room changed.

"Louise, I'll need you to use your, ah, procedure to distract anyone who might try to stop us."

"Right!"

"Gordy, I'll need you to be a promising upper-schooler who wants to study ancient languages at the College of Antiquities at Putney University."

"Uh...okay."

Louise looked at me thoughtfully. "I can borrow my brother Steffen's school uniform if we can stop by my old neighborhood. What do you think Gordy?"

"Uh, sure, I kinda like wearing those uniforms."

"But first," Roselin said, "We'll need to create a fake Codex. Then we'll need to figure out a way to switch it with the real one, assuming Broadmoor will let us in that room."

"Oh, we'll figure out a way!" Louise said, in her cheerleader voice.

Roselin waved her notebook. "Lucky for us, I still have my scaled renderings of the front and back covers of the Codex. I was hoping Janie could help me make the fake copy, but apparently she's taken off somewhere. So Gordy, do you think you could re-create this book from my diagrams? I will need the cover, and that symbol, reproduced exactly from my layout. There are some old leather-bound textbooks in the lodge library that might be the right size and thickness. You'll have my permission to take one."

"Sure, um, yeah!" I said.

"Great!"

Once I said that, I nearly fell apart. *How can I actually make this book look real enough to fool a professor of ancient languages?*

*

With renewed excitement still in her voice, Roselin said, "We need to get to Putney, and the fastest way there is to take the other mail boat, the *Quandary,* which will be stopping here in eight days if it's on time. We'll have to be ready by sunrise, because it never waits long. The *Meridian* goes the other way around the island, and it would take much longer. Now, Gordy, you've never been to Putney, right?"

"No. Are there Russians there?"

"Yes, though you don't see them very often—nothing like in Kronstadt."

Some assurance, but not much.

Roselin was on a roll. "I remember Saturdays were always Open-House days at Putney U., when prospective students are invited to tour the Colleges with their parents. So how about if Louise and I take, um, 'Nickolas' here, to see Professor Broadmoor on a Saturday tour. Perhaps he will show the library to this promising scholar, just like he showed it to my friend Kate."

"Nickolas?" I said.

"Or how about Nick?" said Louise.

"Okay, 'Nick'," said Roselin. "And I'll be Eleanor, your history teacher, And Louise, you'll be my cousin Alice."

"*Alice?*"

"Yes, Alice. Now don't be difficult."

"Fine. *Alice* it is."

"Great! I'll try to make an appointment when we get to Putney. Hopefully, Broadmoor will be there, and he'll buy the idea."

"Then what?" asked Louise.

"Humm, I'll have to think on that. Just do the best you can with that fake book, Gordy."

"Will do!" I said.

We were quiet a moment until Roselin said, "You don't know how much I appreciate both of you willing to help me, especially now that we understand each other, right, Louise?"

Louise had shut her eyes. "Yes, Roselin. I only wanted to…"

"Enough! I already knew the Russians would want to translate that library eventually, so Todd's report only verified my hunch."

Roselin seems more wary of Louise—good!

Louise stood up, motioned Roselin out of her chair, and gave her a vigorous hug. "Would you like a massage to calm you down?"

"Don't be ridiculous," Roselin muttered. "We have to plan our expedition, get that book and then do something with all my notes—destroy them most likely. I hope those diagrams I gave the Biganess tribe were destroyed, and come to think of it, I haven't heard the Hum since the blast…"

Louise held her tighter. "Take a breath, Roselin. You're as stiff as a board," she said softly. "Let's get a fire going and I'll set up a table."

Roselin took a long breath. "Oh, why not?"

When I saw how this was proceeding, I said, "If it's okay with you guys, I'll head over to the lodge."

*

I found Lane in the kitchen, still putting things away. Everyone else had left for the night.

"Hiya, Lane," I said, trying to ignore the wobbly effects of Roselin's wine.

"Whoa, Gordy, you look tired. Were you up at Roselin's again?"

"Yeah. She's still terribly upset about the blast."

"Ah." Lane also looked tired as she closed the last cupboard door. "Say," she said, "can you sit with me a minute?"

"Sure." I followed her into the darkened library, and we scrunched together in one of the big armchairs.

"Ooh, this feels gooood," she sighed. "I feel like it's been forever since we've talked."

"Yeah," I said. "It has. After we got back I had the feeling you didn't like me for some reason—or that your mom was keeping you away."

"Ahh. She's been worried that you and I 'did it' during our trip, even though I said we didn't. I feel like she hasn't trusted me since then."

"So you *do* still like me?"

"Of course I like you, you doofus! I was beginning to wonder if you still liked *me*."

I stared at her. That look, that sudden spark in her tired eyes flooded me with wonder, longing and confusion once again.

She narrowed her gaze. "Are you okay?"

"Yeah, I think so, and yeah, I still like you."

She waited for more.

I sighed. "Roselin wants to go to Putney University to switch that Codex book with a fake. I promised I'd help her."

"You mean *steal* it?"

"*Sshhh*. I probably wasn't supposed to tell you."

"That sounds *dangerous*, Gordy. What if they catch you? The University and probably the Russians will give you hell if they do!"

Her concern nearly frightened me. "Maybe I should have said 'no', but what else could I do, Lane? Roselin says the information in that book is *terribly* dangerous."

"So when is this going to happen?"

"We leave for Putney on the *Quandary* next Wednesday, and don't tell anyone I said that!"

"That's only a week away! I'm so worried they might catch you; I don't even want to think about it!"

Her eyes were red and tears were coming, and my resolve to go began to falter.

Is this is our first argument?

"Well, somehow this feels right, Lane. I've been thinking about it, and I realize I've only been *tolerated* throughout my life, not *valued*. For whatever her reasons, Roselin values my help. And I trust her."

"I'll still worry about you, 'cause *I* value you too!"

"So you really actually still like me?"

"You are continuing to show major symptoms of doofitis, Gordy, but I'll probably always like you."

I soaked that in as we sat wedged together. Then my nose twitched. A salty, slightly musky, distinctly-Lane scent brought me back to that night at the inn, triggering completely different feelings.

Then out of the blue she said, "Hey, did you know Janie took off with Vermilion?"

Before I could answer, she pulled a note out of her shirt pocket and handed it to me.

Dear Lane,

You probably noticed I haven't been around much lately. Well, here's why: Janie and I have become really, really good friends! We decided to go on a walkabout together—not sure where yet, maybe to a farm tribe or to Putney. She wants to see the big city, though I prefer the back country. We both need to get away from the stress here.
Sorry I didn't say goodbye. It was a sudden decision.

Warm hugs,

Vermilion

I handed it back to her.

Lane said, "I had a feeling they were becoming more than friends, especially after I saw them kissing and stuff."

Then she looked steadily at me with her big eyes.

"And you'd better not *ever* leave me with only a stupid note!"

I bravely looked into those intense eyes of hers. "Don't worry, Lane. I won't!"

We sat, our minds drifting, and soon my eyes fell shut. Later, Meredith came in looking for Lane and found us in the big chair. I awoke enough to wave to her. She smiled a little, and let out a big sigh. A few minutes later she returned and put a blanket over us.

I think we climbed out of that chair around sunrise, and I slept in my bed well into the morning. At least now I knew why Janie wasn't there. I hoped I'd find a note from her somewhere, and sure enough, it was on the floor, tiny and tightly folded, probably tossed there when I pulled back the covers.

Dear Gordy,

I know I've been kind of 'distant' to you lately, and I wish I could think of the right words to tell you...
Vermilion and I have decided to go on a walkabout together. We're not sure where-to yet. We just need to get away from all the stress here.
You've been a big part of my life, ya know, and we'll see each other again, just don't know when.
Write to me when you can c/o MacEvoy, Gifford P.O., Elsinore Bay.

I'll write to you too when I know where you'll be.

Love,

Your Janie

PS: Please tell Roselin I'm sorry for bailing out.

*

At breakfast, Roselin looked resurrected, or at least well-rested. I sat down across from her as Louise joined us. "Thanks again for the massage," she said to Louise, "and for putting me to bed!"

"You're very welcome, Roselin," said Louise, beaming.

Now what's Louise up to?

When I finished eating, I left them and wandered out to the sandy cove, still pondering Janie's news. I was glad they had taken off. Maybe Vermilion will help Janie figure out what she wants.

Then I remembered last night, and how good it felt when Lane's mom brought the blanket.

As if my mind had conjured her, there was Lane up ahead, sitting on the beach. She didn't move when I quietly sat next to her and stared out at the waves. When I glanced at her, she glanced back with a twitch of a smile.

"I found Janie's note," I said. "It's pretty much like yours from Vermilion."

Lane tried to sound not-jealous. "Ah, well, I suppose you'll miss her."

"Yeah, I suppose."

She turned to me, her smile gone. "Remember I told you we might be leaving here? Well, Mum said this morning we *are* moving in a few weeks."

We looked at each other.

"Will you write to me?" I said. "I'll want to know where you'll be. I'll give you my address in Gifford."

"I suppose that will have to do," she said with a sigh. "But until then…" She pressed her hands firmly on my cheeks and gave me a blissfully long smooch right there in front of the ocean.

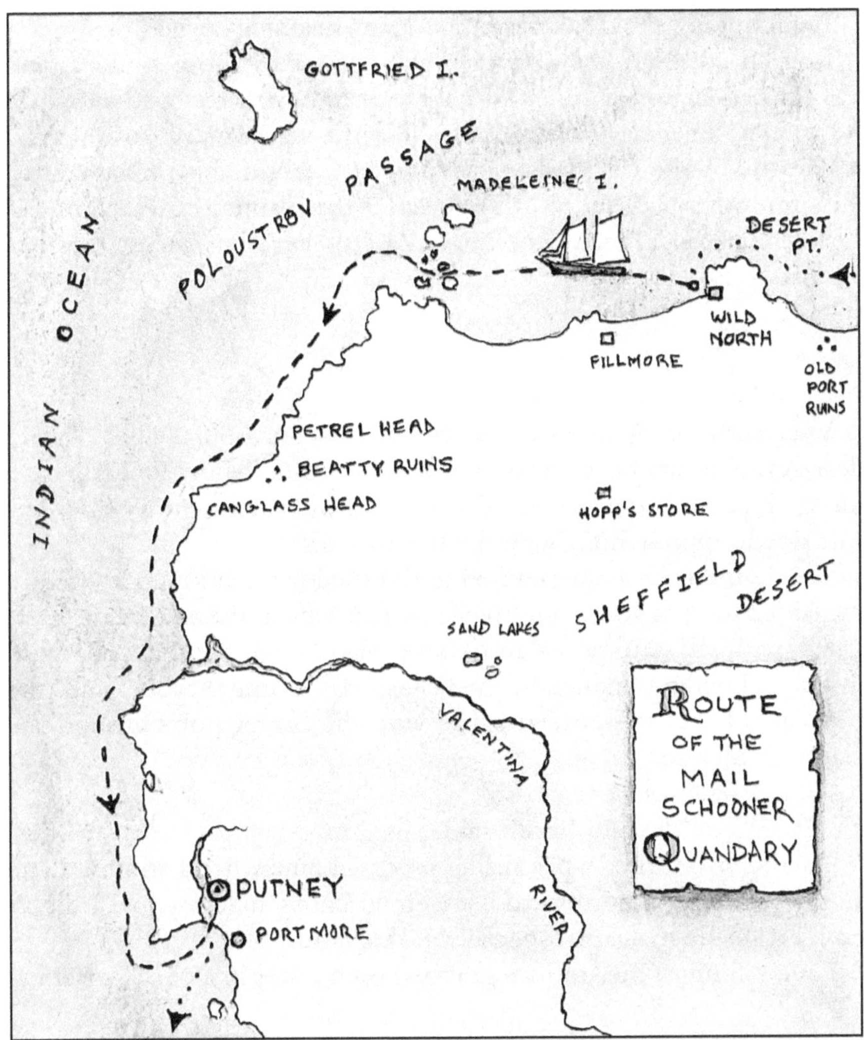

On the mail boat to Putney

$\mathbb{A}$ week later, we were ready to leave Wild North.

It took me a few days to create the fake Codex, complete with that strange symbol. At first I felt almost dizzy with doubt about this, but in the lodge library I found a dusty leather-bound volume printed in England in 1885. It was exactly the right size according to Roselin's notes. After many hours of trial and error, especially getting that design right, my cover looked quite authentic. Roselin found some lacquer that gave it the certain shiny finish she remembered.

She turned it over in her hand. "Yes, this should do the trick. Thanks, Gordy!"

I was hoping she'd say more, but I was beaming anyway.

Roselin added, "The *Quandary* will anchor offshore tonight, and pick up passengers at sunrise tomorrow. Meredith received word via the wireless telegraph in the lodge. It's the way we talk to our mail boats. And by the way, I also just received a message from Samantha. She's returning to Wild North right after the Flame Festival. I'm glad she's coming back," said Roselin. "I can't believe how many disputes I've had to listen to."

*

Very early on Wednesday morning, Roselin, Louise and I stood bleary-eyed on the beach, waiting for what would be my first trip on a sailing ship! The stars were still out when we watched the *Quandary's* skiff slowly approach through the mushy surf.

Louise-the-tour-guide pointed to the shadowy schooner, lit up by a few lanterns. "She's a proud boat—74 feet long at the water line, gaff-rigged, with six staterooms and a hold big enough for the mail, fresh produce, building materials, pedicabs, you name it. She and the *Meridian* connect the coastal tribes with the bigger ports around the Island. Cool, huh?"

Louise loves doing this!

"Cool," Roselin and I both said.

The sky had turned a promising predawn pink when I spotted Lane and Meredith walking toward us. I could barely hide my joy! I didn't think I'd see them again, especially at this hour.

Lane ran up to me, and we grabbed each other in a cheek-mashing hug.

I said into her ear, "I'll leave a letter at the Putney post office for you, if you're still heading there."

"Ah. Well, now I'm not sure where we're going." She pulled away to look at me. "Last night Mum said she might check out some smaller towns."

"Then write to me as soon as you guys have settled, okay? I know I'll be back in Gifford eventually. Just send your letter to me, care-of MacEvoy, Gifford P.O."

"Got it. And I'll expect you to be there soon, Gordy. I'm sure gonna miss you!"

I didn't know what to say to that, so I just hugged her again.

Then Meredith surprised me by putting her arms around both of us. "Gordy, you've been good for Lane," she said, "And I'll have to eat my suspicion that you were one of 'those' boys."

"Thanks," I told her. "She's been good for me too."

*

Lane and Meredith become tiny specks on the dusky beach as we were rowed out through the surf, (which was exciting in itself!). A painful ache in my chest made me realize how much Lane has meant to me.

This whole book-switch thing better work!

Once we boarded the *Quandary*, a steward gave us a tour of the lounge, the head, the snack bar, the baggage hold, and the lifeboats. "The head is the toilet, in case you wondered," he said.

The captain, dressed in pressed whites and a cap adorned with the Maritime Postal Services insignia, met us and got right to business.

"Hello, I'm Alma Mason." She glanced up at a little flag atop the mast. "We'll have a headwind this morning, but once we pass the Narrows, it should be an easy trip down to Putney. I expect to dock around six or seven tonight. Welcome aboard."

In the growing daylight, the sails were set, the anchor pulled up and the big schooner picked up speed. Passengers emerged from their staterooms looking for their morning coffee. Eventually Louise pointed out a string of small islands ahead. "We're heading into the Sparrow Narrows, between those little Islands." Glued to the railing, I stared at their surf-lashed shores and bushy terrain—those islands were that close! I felt a weird yearning to jump ship and explore all of them.

As we cleared the Narrows, a larger island appeared far to the northwest. Louise and Roselin had wandered off, so I asked one of the overnight passengers about it, and the fellow replied, "Ah, that'd be Gottfried Island. Don't know much about it, though I hear it's haunted, even cursed."

I felt a tiny chill.

"That'd be Gottfried Island."

Now heading south, the *Quandary* hugged the dry coast. The wind had moved behind us, and the boat rode gracefully over the swells.

We were close enough to the shoreline to get a clear view of a cliff called Petrel Head, as announced by tour-guide Louise, who had quietly reappeared beside me. Roselin soon joined us with a brass telescope, focused it on another nearby bluff, then handed it to me. "The captain lent me this so I can show you something. Take a look just to the right of that rocky point."

The old telescope felt comfortably heavy. I fussed with the focus, then saw several broken stone walls and part of a tower above the bushy shoreline. "It looks like it was a fort or something."

"That's the Beatty site, Gordy, where I found the Codex! I can't believe that was twenty years ago already. To this day I wish I'd never seen the thing."

Louise said, "I'm still amazed by your discovery, Roselin. You had no idea there was anything below that tower?"

"No, but *something* told me to dig there."

"Well, your instinct was right-on!"

While Louise continued to butter up Roselin, I enjoying looking through the captain's telescope. Further along the shore, I spotted a large red tent just above the beach, out of which several naked people ran and splashed into the surf.

I hastily handed the telescope to Roselin and pointed. "What's that place?"

"Oh! Well! That's the Imbolc site, one of my favorite places. Every February, Islanders who follow pagan traditions gather there for the festival of St. Brigid. I see they are busy already, though the festival is several weeks off."

"*Pagan* traditions?"

"Yes, Gordy, *pagans,* otherwise referred to as heathens, idolaters, heretics, infidels, unbelievers, atheists, and so on. We Islanders have embraced paganism, along with anything else people want to believe in. Mother Cecelia and Roger Putney both had a lot to say about the intolerance behind most religions! It's been a long road."

*

Someone from the galley announced, "Lunch is on."

On the deck we gathered at a large buffet-style table loaded with build-it-yourself sandwich-makings and fruit. The steward who had welcomed us aboard stood by to pour soda, juice or wine. Roselin said, "I suggest eating out here, Gordy. If you go below, the boat's heaving will likely take away your appetite."

I remembered that unpleasant sensation during my raft journey. "Good idea!"

After lunch, Louise and Roselin settled into some canvas deck chairs. The boat's graceful motion over the swells soon had them napping. Curious, I took a walk to see the workings of this ship. I stopped to watch the wheelman, and later a wiry older woman in blue shorts and a cheerful yellow shirt who was adjusting one of the sails. Neither seemed interested in conversation, which I could understand. Finally I found my own weathered deck chair, set it to "recline" and was soon dozing off to the rhythm of the swells.

I could really enjoy riding on boats like this.

After a while, a hard wave slapped the hull and jerked me awake. I looked toward shore and noticed the high bluffs had receded to a low, sandy coastline. I spotted a broad inlet in the distance and wandered over to the wheelman to ask about it.

"Ah, that'd be the Valentina River," he said. "A wide channel, but too shallow to sail into." He gave me a closer look. "Where might ye be from? I dunt catch yer accent."

I sensed a challenging tone.

"Uh, other side of the Island. I need to get going now." I edged away from him—no more chatting about *where-I'm-from!*

I soon found Roselin and Louise again, quite awake now. "Come join us for a glass of bunberry wine," said Louise. "We stole a bottle from the lunch table."

Roselin leaned back in her chair, looking refreshed. "I love the rhythm of the swells out here. Once this is over, I want to ride the mail boat all around the Island—the full tour!"

"This coast is beginning to look familiar, and greener," said Louise. "We're not far from Putney."

The hills indeed appeared greener with some scattered bushy trees. I spotted an isolated house, then more houses. The shoreline became dense with neighborhoods, roads and eventually what looked like a commuter railway.

Louise said, "Hey, there's Sunset Beach…and Little Bay…and my hometown, Boomer Beach! And soon we'll come 'round Putney Head."

I was happy that Roselin and Louise were in familiar territory, like they were returning home.

Home-home-home…where is *that?*

As we neared Putney Head, Roselin pointed to an older red-brick building just above the crashing surf, and said, "Say, let's stay at the Hotel Westend. See it there? It's a stodgy old place, but the rooms have incredible ocean views!"

Just then the boat swung gracefully around the Head. Louise said, "Ah, there's Putney Harbor, and Mt. Hayes."

I was again impressed by the massive volcano, far to the south this time, and by how *big* this island is.

Louise said, "Yes, let's stay at the Westend. I need a bath!"

As soon as we had tied up at the Ferry Street dock, Roselin found a pay phone and dialed the hotel. A few minutes later she returned and said, "We're booked for two rooms. Lucky for us it's a slow week. We can take the train and pedicabs from the dock—shouldn't take but twenty minutes. *Aaaand,* we must have supper at Shimizu, a great Japanese restaurant in town—are you all up for that?"

I was impressed. "Wow, Roselin, you really know Putney!"

"When I was at Putney University, I lived in Seville, which is just north of downtown." she said. "The rent was cheap, and the neighbors were weird, but mostly harmless. I saw more witchery there than I ever did in Covenmoor."

"Witchery?" I asked.

"I, ah, had some unusual friends."

The pedicab dropped us off at the Seville train station, where we found lockers for our bags. Across the street, the Café Shimizu was all dark wood, dim lighting, and low tables in tiny alcoves, each lit with an oil lamp. "This place opened in 1902, and it kind of looks it," said Roselin. "It's a landmark now."

After supper and a few train and pedicab rides, we checked into the Westend Hotel. Roselin and Louise took one room, mine was next door.

West Putney. The Westend Hotel is around the corner on the oceanfront.

"I think I'll take a walk along the seawall," I said, and Louise asked, "Didn't you get enough of the ocean today? Plus, it's already dark."

I grinned. "I can hear the waves booming out there. I just gotta check out the surf."

Roselin said, "Just make sure you meet us in the dining room at eight in the morning—we have planning to do!"

*

At breakfast on Thursday we sat by one of the ocean-facing windows in the Westend's spacious dining room. Roselin and Louise were enjoying an egg dish called 'quiche', and strong Indonesian coffee, while I had bangers and Irish pancakes with bilberry (different than bunberry) juice. Not bad!

When we finished, Roselin began a planning session. I was trying hard to not stare out at the waves crashing over the seawall.

"First," said Roselin, "I'll telephone Professor Broadmoor to see if we can visit him on Saturday. Then I'll try to talk him into showing us the library. Remember, Louise, you are my younger cousin Alice, and Gordy, you're my student Nick... *Yoo-hoo*, Gordy, pay attention!"

"*Oh!...*I'm here!"

"Remember, *Nick*, we are visiting campus because you've heard about Professor Broadmoor's fabulous library of Old People texts, and you are hoping you can see them. And make sure you call them 'The Old People' and not 'Ur'."

"Got it. I'm 'Nick', and it's 'Old People' only."

She gave me a look. "Okay, assuming he shows us the library, I'll point out the Codex volume to you, and we'll somehow switch it with the fake book, then exit as graciously and quickly as we can. That's my scenario. What do you think?"

Louise said, "Isn't there a chance Broadmoor might recognize you as his old student?"

"I doubt it. He could never remember me even when I attended his classes."

"Well, I just hope you know what you're doing."

"I don't," said Roselin, "so we'll just have to trust it will work out, okay?"

"I'm feeling weird about this," I said. "Am I supposed to just walk up and pick up the Codex book and put the fake one in its place, and no one will notice?"

"Well, that's the basic idea," said Roselin, hesitating. "I'll start up a chat with Broadmoor to distract him enough for you to make the switch. He's a pompous old guy, and immensely proud of 'his' discovery out there at the Beatty ruins. He might rattle on all morning about it if I encourage him."

Louise said, "But what if...?"

"Louise, if we have a *what if*, then you'll need to step in and do an intervention. You might also be able to help me distract the professor. Just watch things and be aware."

Louise looked doubtful, and I didn't feel very assured either.

Roselin turned rigid.

"Guys! We have to take a chance here, because I've heard more recent developments, good *and* bad. Last night I telephoned my friend Kate. The good news, she said, is they are still giving the tours on Saturday mornings, and Broadmoor will likely be there."

"And the bad news...?" I asked.

"And the bad news is the same as in Todd's report. Kate told me a woman named Adeline Brewer from the Ministry of Antiquities has been pestering Broadmoor. She wants to allow a Russian linguistics team to ship the entire library to the Soviet Union! The university is dead set against it and has taken the Antiquities Ministry to court. At best, this will delay the shipment only for a while. I fear we will never see our Ur library again, and, worse, they *will* succeed in translating the Codex!"

I shivered. *What if I goof, and drop the book, or someone sees me switch it, or…?*

I looked out the window again. The waves constantly crashing over the seawall seemed to reflect our feelings.

Roselin took a breath, then continued. "I have a friend named Esau who is willing to help us hide out after we get the book. I telephoned him as well, and explained our situation. He said we could stay at his home in the Maybeck Tribe, in South Putney."

Tribes in Putney?

Louise said, "I've heard that South Putney is notorious for dead-end streets and no-tell secrecy."

"Yes, that will help," said Roselin. "And from there we can decide where to go, because I really don't want to stay in Putney."

"Then I have a problem," said Louise.

We looked at her.

"I'm not too keen on hiding. Do you think there might be a way we can sneak into Broadmoor's library and switch the books without anyone seeing us? It might take them a while to notice, and if no one sees us, they won't even know who to look for."

A waiter came by with a cart to offer us more coffee and tea, then silently took our plates.

Roselin gave him a quick glance, then pulled her legs up, hugged her knees, and closed her eyes a moment. "Okay," she whispered, "what if we don't contact Broadmoor, and anonymously take the Antiquities School tour? We can just see what we can see. Then, if nothing else, we'll know how secure the library might be."

"I like that idea better," said Louise.

"But we really need Broadmoor," said Roselin. "Kate says there is no other way into that library and he alone has the keys!"

Louise turned to look out the window, brooding and quiet.

Roselin sighed, then looked at me and said, "Say, Gordy, how about if you come with me to the Putney Main Library today. It's huge! I practically lived there during my research years, and I need to do a little digging in the astrophysics section."

"Sounds good to me," I said.

Louise, having apparently given in, let out a long sigh and said, "I suppose we can also stop at my mum's house and see about my brother's uniform."

"Good idea," said Roselin. Then she added, "Also, Louise, we need to shop for some 'city-girl' outfits."

*

The streetcar ride to Boomer Beach, Louise's home-town, took only ten minutes. Her mom's house was on a narrow side street that ended at the beach, which reminded me a little of home. Louise briskly walked us to a one-story sand-block cottage lushly adorned with bougainvillea. As she opened the little gate, she said, "When this blooms, it becomes an intense purple cloud!"

She walked right in the front door and introduced us to her surprised mum, Lynanne, who automatically asked us if we wanted tea. As we all chatted in the kitchen, Louise quietly edged away. She soon returned, happily patting her bag, and sat with us just as Lynanne began to pour. Louise took one sip, then explained we had chores to do in town, but to keep her tea warm and she'll return for lunch. Lynanne sighed, then gave Louise a piercing glance, as if asking, *what are you up to now?*

We hugged Lynanne goodbye and took another train to the Newtown district, near downtown Putney. Louise marched us into the Solid Gold store, run by a recycling tribe. "This place was my favorite haunt while I was growing up," she said.

In the 'ladies wear' aisle Roselin laughed as they both held up dresses from the 1940s. They finally settled on two dull brown below-the-knee outfits to wear on our campus tour.

Louise then led us to the entrance of her favorite lunch counter on Hurd Street. "This place has the best cheap lunch in town. I'll leave you here since me mum doesn't like waiting. Meet you at the hotel this evening, yes?"

She abruptly left.

"Whew! Louise can be intense," said Roselin. I nodded in full agreement.

When we sat down, menus in hand, Roselin told me, "Louise has been a little crazy since the explosion. I'm still bothered by her not giving me those notes from Todd, and I'm beginning to wonder what she's thinking."

Me too.

After lunch we caught another streetcar to the Putney Main Library. Inside, beyond the huge lobby, I counted seven levels of shelved books, all facing into an atrium lit by a huge skylight.

Roselin led me to her favorite haunts—the periodicals section and the study carrels in the back. "The Russians have been pretty easy on us about foreign literature," she said. "They don't really care *what* we read, as long as it doesn't 'incite rebellion'."

She settled at a small desk. "This is where I'll be. Have fun!"

We were back at the Westend by suppertime.

*

The following morning, Friday, I was free—no plans! I quietly let myself out of my room and down the stairs. Passing by the hotel breakfast buffet, I pocketed two bananas and a warm muffin.

I remembered which trains to take and reached the Putney Library just as it was opening for the day. I admired its cavernous lobby, again, and headed straight for the study carrels Roselin had shown me. I wanted a quiet place to think, and to write.

My first letter, on borrowed Westend Hotel stationery, was to my brother.

Dear Ricky,   Feb. 5, '65

I'm still ok!

I'm in a city called Putney, sitting in the biggest library I've ever seen! I was staying in Gifford when I wrote last, but I have been traveling since then.

There is something going on here I should tell you about. They call it the Hum. It's a sound I used to hear at home, but I never said anything because I knew I would get laughed at. It sounds sometimes like bees or voices in a choir—in stereo. It feels like it's all around you, makes you feel good and then it goes away.

I'm telling you about it because <u>everyone</u> on this island can hear it. It's almost like a religion. And a couple of my friends here can do things, like affect people's minds, with what they call 'Hum energy'. I saw it done once!

A few weeks ago there was a weird explosion that caused an earthquake! My friends think it was an accident with Hum energy. They are worried, and that's why we are here in Putney.

I hope you are doing okay. I'm still afraid to ask about Mom.

PS: I have new comic books! Mr. Barnes—the guy who fixed our back steps—sent a whole box of them to a comic-book store here on the Island. If you see him, could you tell him thanks? And maybe ask him if he knows someone named Bernard Hopp?

Okay, I'd better mail this letter. The post office here told me they could probably get it to you. Say Hi to Mr. Barnes and show him the stamps—the one of Roger Putney looks like him.

Gordy

I moved down my short list.

Dear Janie,

How are you?

Roselin, Louise and I are staying at the Hotel Westend. It's right on the ocean in West Putney. Louise grew up only about two miles from here. She has been acting weird and I wish you were here with us!

Today I'm at the Putney Library. I took the trains to get here. I think this is the first day I've spent by myself in a long time. It's kind of fun just sitting around and watching people.

We will be visiting Putney University tomorrow. The College of Antiquities is giving tours for upper-schoolers, and we're going to try to see those books Roselin is interested in. That's all I should say about that.

I hope you and Vermilion are having a good time wherever you are.

I'm going to mail this to your house in Gifford. I'll try to get back there again soon, but I don't know when yet.

Say Hi to your mum and dad for me!

I miss you all!

Gordy

And finally…

Dear Lane,

We are staying at the Westend Hotel right on the ocean in West Putney. You probably know it! The surf is crazy—big waves were crashing on the rocks just outside the hotel windows this morning. They made me think of us bodysurfing.

Tomorrow we are going to go to an open-house day at Putney University. Maybe we'll get to see those ancient books, and please don't worry, we'll be careful!

So far I like Putney, but I don't think I'll be here for long, especially after tomorrow.

Like I told you, I'll eventually return to Gifford to stay with the MacEvoys. If you and your mum ever pass through, you'll (hopefully) find this letter at the Gifford P.O.

Know this: I will look for you—just tell me where you'll be.

Sincerely, and I mean it,

Gordy

(C/O MacEvoy, Gifford Haven)

I was still afraid to write to Mom. A creepy feeling inside kept me from even starting a letter. I couldn't do it.

THE SWITCH

"Where have *you* been?" said Louise.

The late afternoon sun was again blazing in the hotel windows as I walked into the Westend's dining room. Louise and Roselin had just sat down at our usual table for supper.

I took an empty chair. "I went back to the Putney Library to write some letters, then wandered around the city. I wanted to see if I could find my way on the trains, and I did!"

"Well, stick around from now on. Tomorrow will be a long day."

"*OkayIwill.* Can I still order something to eat?"

"Do I detect an *attitude?*" said Louise, as Roselin smiled and handed me a menu.

*

On Saturday morning we were ready.

Louise and Roselin were having fun in their matronly outfits, curtsying to each other with their long skirts. They looked so strange in them, since Louise always wore shorts and button-down shirts and Roselin her elegant all-purpose gowns. Steffen's Boomer Beach school uniform felt a little tight, but Roselin said I looked fine. She even trimmed and combed my wild hair to basic Upper School standards. Just before leaving, she also carefully stuffed the fake Codex in the back of my shorts and tucked my shirt neatly over it. We didn't say a word.

As we walked from University Station to the campus, Roselin said, "I was able to talk to Broadmoor on the phone, but I couldn't get him to agree on a meeting time, so we'll just have to see what happens." She looked at me. "Are you feeling okay about this, Gordy?"

"Yeah."

I did feel good. Roselin's mix of smartness, self-confidence, and humility drew me to her like a moth to a warm, steady light. I could see why Louise looks up to her.

Maybe Roselin's wisdom will somehow rub off...

*

Putney University was tucked in a grove of stately pines and pinoaks just beyond the massive Putney Main Library. I was awed by the impressive gothic-stone architecture, the spacious landscaping, the whole civilized *feel* of the place.

At ten a.m. sharp, we approached the College of Antiquities. A clean-cut young woman stood near the big double-door entrance. Her name-tag said 'Janelle'. She brightened with a broad smile as we approached.

"Hello," Roselin said, "We're here for the tour. I'm Eleanor, this is my cousin Alice, and my brilliant student Nickolas. Nick is *very* interested in studying ancient languages and wants to specialize in the U- er, Old People texts."

"Oh, how exciting," said Janelle. "There has been a lot of interest lately in those texts. No one has ever been able to translate them, you know."

"So I understand," said Roselin, with a quick glance at us. "Do you know if the texts might possibly be on display so Nick can see them?"

Louise discreetly poked me with her elbow.

"Oh, um, yes!" I said. "I would *love* to see the original markings. I've, ah, been wanting to study them for years and years."

Janelle paused. "Well…I'm not sure," she said thoughtfully. "This is an unusual request, but I could speak to Professor Broadmoor to see if you can have a look. He is almost always in his office."

Roselin was trying to keep a straight face. "That would be nice if you could ask."

Nudge.

Ow!

"I would be most honored," I said.

Since no other tour-goers had shown up, Janelle led us through the heavy doors. "The faculty offices are this way."

Roselin looked down the long echoing hall. "The smells in here bring me right back to when I was an undergrad—floor wax and old books!"

As we walked, Janelle went on about how rich this Island is in 'opportunities of ancient study', as she called them. "Putney University has the only archeology and ancient languages program on our Island," she said. "The Soviet Union has been generously funding new additions to our buildings, as well as providing us with the latest research materials on everything from archeology to quantum mechanics."

Quantum mechanics? I looked at Roselin, who shot a worried look back.

"And they are helping our ancient languages department as well," added Janelle. "Just this week, Professor Broadmoor has been discussing plans with our Antiquities Minister, Miss Brewer, to finally decipher the Old People texts. She has told us that a team of Russian experts will soon make photographs of the texts, fly those to Moscow, and insert them into a special computing machine they have developed. Their machine, I understand, has been designed to translate ancient languages, including pictographs, to modern Russian, and I suppose English! It just may crack the mystery of the Old Peoples' writing."

Roselin whispered to my ear, *"My friend Kate said this is the official story, and I shouldn't believe a word of it!"*

"And here we are!"

Janelle rapped firmly on Professor Broadmoor's office door. We stood there looking at each other for some time before the door slowly opened.

"Yes?"

"My apologies for interrupting you, professor. I have a promising student here who wishes to major in Ancient Languages. He says he would like to study the Old People texts, and he, uh, asked me if your collection might be available for a viewing."

Roselin and I could both see that Janelle was testing her limits.

The old professor blinked. His face had a just-awakened look, and his wrinkled shirt and longish white hair looked as confused as he did.

"And who are you, may I ask?"

"Oh, I'm Janelle Gavin—in your prehistoric architecture seminar," she said, slightly put off. "I'm giving tours today."

"Tours…"

"Yes, just as we do every Saturday, sir," she said brightly.

"Ah, I see. And these are…"

Roselin smiled broadly and offered her hand, "I'm Eleanor, this is my cousin Alice, and this is Nickolas, my straight-A history student. I had called you earlier and we talked about a possible look at your wonderful ancient library. It's okay if you don't remember, we just hope we're not intruding."

He stared at us for a moment, as if trying to recall something, then he huffed and fretted and finally said, "Oh, do come in. I would be happy to show you the texts."

I could sense Roselin's huge sigh of relief. She gave me a quick wink as we filed in.

Broadmoor led us through the clutter in his dimly-lit office. Books, papers and thick folders filled the shelves and covered most of the furniture. A model of the Parthenon, several globes, and a dusty stuffed penguin sat randomly here and there in the room. His desk was barely visible under more piles of papers and manuscripts.

He continued to a narrow closet-like door beside a rumpled couch. We carefully watched as he put on his eyeglasses, then fumbled in his pocket for the key. He found it, unlocked the door, switched on the lights, and ushered us into a well-kept windowless room.

Roselin gasped at the rows of leather-bound books lining one wall, and the scrolls in leather cases arranged in their own compartments on another wall. A large spotless marble table filled the center of the room. Everything was set up as she remembered it—Broadmoor apparently recreated the library exactly as it was arranged under the ancient tower.

She marveled (again) at the hand-tooled covers still in unbelievably excellent condition, with no sign of bug-damage or mold. Mysterious symbols in gold leaf almost sparkled on the spines, teasing us all with their riddles. It wasn't long before I spotted *The First Sound of God* symbol—the Codex!

Roselin's attention was already fixed on it.

I moved next to her as she resumed breathing.

Louise followed our gaze to the same book.

Now what?

Janelle was overwhelmed. "Oh, Professor Broadmoor, I never imagined these books to be so, um, ornamental, with all those marks and symbols on them!"

Her interest tickled Broadmoor's vanity. "Ah, yes, so they are. Shall I show you a particularly lovely volume?" As we watched, he pulled out the very book we had spotted.

Roselin shut her eyes.

"Now this one excites me the most," he said. He reverently opened it to a bookmarked page. "See these arrangements of symbols here? I have a feeling this particular book is trying to say something scientific or mathematical. That is why we want to, er, we *must*, decipher this language."

"*Oh, my ancient Goddesses,*" Roselin softly muttered.

Sensing Roselin's distress, Louise stepped toward the table, pointed to the scrolls and said, "These look intriguing!" Janelle noticed them too and joined Louise with more admiring comments. They soon distracted the professor from his talk about the 'lovely volume'.

Without thinking, I somehow found the courage to say, "Professor Broadmoor, that little book is absolutely stunning! May I have a look at it?"

Broadmoor was so taken by Janelle and Louise's wide-eyed exuberance, he simply handed the book over to me as he reached for one of the larger scrolls. "You *must* see this illuminated map of our Island as they perceived it in their day."

As Broadmoor unrolled the scroll on the table, I slowly eased myself next to Roselin while staring raptly at the pages of the Codex, a beautiful work of completely alien marks and glyphs. The layout of the marks *did* have an eerie similarity to complex mathematical equations.

Roselin let out a tiny *eeee* as she looked at the pages with me, likely remembering them from so many years ago. As we huddled, I deftly pulled the fake book out from the back of my pants, and smoothly laid it on top of the Codex, pretending to study the opening page.

Roselin whispered, *"Okay, what next?"*

"Just stay as you are!" I whispered, and I slowly slipped the Codex out from under the fake book and into her hands, and nodded to my backside.

"Ah."

Without interrupting her admiration of the now-fake book, she stuffed the Codex into my pants, and neatly arranged my shirt to cover it up, all while Broadmoor held court with Janelle and Louise.

That map must have been fascinating.

I had closed the fake book and was about to slide it into its place when a tight-sounding voice called out, *"Broadmoor—are you in there?"* A severe-looking middle-aged woman marched in, black bangs bouncing on her forehead. She stopped short at the sight of everyone in the library.

"Professor Broadmoor," she said, startling everyone. "I believe that we had agreed no one was to be allowed in here without my permission. She then spotted me holding the fake Codex and glared at me. "Please hand that over."

Roselin and I had both gone rigid, and, trying hard not to panic, I slowly gave the woman the volume. She saw the gap in the row of books and roughly shoved my little work of art into its place. Then, arms folded, she watched Professor Broadmoor as he returned the scroll into its case.

"And may I ask what is the occasion for this?"

The professor, flustered and confused by the sudden intrusion, said to her, "This young man is a possible student who wishes to study these texts, madam. I didn't think there would be any harm..."

"Student?" said the woman. "Ah, yes. Frankly, I'm surprised the University still allows you to teach."

She continued. "And you must know I am expecting to meet my associates here momentarily to plan our translation project. I had made an appointment with you last Monday, but I suppose you've forgotten."

Janelle whispered to Louise, *"That's Adeline Brewer. I've never seen her this bitch-, I mean upset, before."*

Just then two large men in business suits walked in. One looked about thirty and the other closer to fifty, both clean-cut with athletic builds, and they acted like they were in a hurry.

In a clipped English accent the younger one said, "My apologies for our lateness, Miss Brewer."

"Ah," said the woman. "It is fine. Gregor and Wassily, you know Professor Broadmoor."

Broadmoor nodded to the men and then he sat down, breathing hard. "I do not understand these sudden rules, Miss Brewer. I have shown these books to interested students and associates for years, and, as you can see, the library is still complete."

Roselin gave me the quickest glance that might have been a wink.

"Then may I remind you about the 'incident' a few weeks ago? Our Soviet associates in the Ministry believe there is a connection between that explosion and a certain kind of energy we have only recently heard about. As you once suggested, these books may tell us something about this. Gregor and Wassily are here to help me keep this library safe!"

Then she turned to us, looking first at Roselin. "And who might you be?"

"I am Eleanor," she said, standing tall and trying to sound as calm as possible. "And this is my cousin Alice. We are accompanying my history scholar Nickolas here. He is in his final year of Upper School and is interested in attending the College next term."

"Ah," Adeline said, relaxing a bit. "I noticed your Boomer Beach colors. I'm from Ramside, and I remember the football matches against your school—a good team! A pleasure to meet you, Nickolas. I apologize for my brusqueness, but we must get on with our meeting. I hope you continue to have a delightful tour."

We assumed (correctly) we were getting the rush.

Louise and Janelle led the way out. Roselin made it a point to walk close behind me, knowing those two guys were watching us. We nearly fell over each other trying to get out of Broadmoor's office.

Outside the building, we all took a long, deep breath. Even Janelle was shaken by the noisy entrance of Miss Brewer. "I must apologize," she said. "I had no idea the Ministry of Antiquities was so protective of that library. I feel bad for Professor Broadmoor."

"That's okay, Janelle," Roselin said, trying not to grin. "You didn't know."

I was ready to hug Janelle. *If only you knew how much you helped us!*

We were all trying not to look at each other, which would definitely have caused major grinning.

Janelle said, "Now is there any other part of the University I can show you? We have our new science complex, plus a wonderful student center, dining hall, and indoor racquetball courts, all in the same building…"

We almost all spoke at once. "We, uh, probably should be on our way."

Then Roselin said, "And we really appreciate your asking the professor to let us see that library. I do hope he won't chastise you later."

Janelle was back to her cheerful self. "Oh, I'll be fine. He and I get along pretty well when he remembers me. You have a nice rest of the day, and feel free to contact the admissions office for a catalog. You'll *love* Putney University, Nick!"

*

We didn't say a word as we nearly ran back to University Station. Roselin kept patting my backside to make sure the book was still there. Back at the hotel, we went straight to Roselin and Louise's room, slammed the door behind us and flopped onto the bed. I held up the Codex and we all let out a whoop!

I sat up and laid the book solemnly in Roselin's hands. She was quiet for a moment, then she said, "Gordy! I can't believe how smoothly you got Broadmoor to simply hand it over to you. Brilliant work!"

She smooched my cheek in a most loving-witch manner.

Louise said, "You hid the book in your *pants*? I was wondering where it was."

"Yeah. I couldn't just carry it under my arm."

"And the timing!" said Roselin. "If that scary woman had come in one minute sooner..."

"Yeah, I think my heart stopped when she took the fake book. I was so afraid she would open it!"

Roselin asked, "So, what was in that book?"

"Well," I said, "If Adeline had opened the cover she would have seen that same 'First sound of God' symbol on the front page. But if she turned *that* page she would have seen, in plain English, *An Introduction to the Proper Conduct of Horses and Hounds, by R.J. Chester, Esquire.* I, uh, hope it wasn't a valuable book."

"Ahh, Gordy, I *love* you!" said Roselin as she grabbed my shoulders and gave me another smooch on each of my blushing cheeks.

RUN !

On Sunday morning, we were in a cheerful mood eating eggs, bangers and toast with English marmalade at our usual table in the Westend's dining room. While looking out the window I said, "I suppose they could add an outdoor terrace, but then the surf-spray would probably get everyone wet."

"Ummf," said Louise, her mouth full.

Just then our now-familiar waiter walked by and quietly dropped off the Sunday morning *Putney Times*.

"Well, that was nice of him," said Roselin.

Then she spotted a small headline just below the fold.

RARE BOOK TAKEN FROM UNIVERSITY ARCHIVES

"*Uh, oh*," said Roselin.

"What?" Louise said, alarmed.

"Oh, *shite!*" Roselin hissed.

We huddled over the article.

An extremely valuable and irreplaceable book was taken yesterday from a collection of manuscripts belonging to Putney University. Two women and a young man allegedly conspired to remove the book while visiting the faculty offices of the College of Antiquities shortly before noon. They had replaced the missing book with a fake.

Undergraduate student Janelle Gavin, a volunteer tour guide, had escorted the three to ancient languages professor Peter Broadmoor's office. "They specifically wanted to see those old books," said Miss Gavin. After rigorous questioning, apparently neither Miss Gavin nor Professor Broadmoor knew the three individuals before the theft.

Ministry of Antiquities director Adeline Brewer is offering a reward for anyone who might have information as to the whereabouts of these persons. "The return of this book is of utmost importance," she said.

"We have to get out of here *now!*" said Louise. "It's still early enough, and maybe we can get to your friends in South Putney before too many people have seen this. They live near East End Station, right?"

"Yes," said Roselin. "Act casual, eat up, and let's pack!"

We were soon dressed in our usual outfits. We slid out of a side door into a narrow alley. Louise tossed yesterday's city-girl dresses and Steffen's uniform into a waste bin, but kept the school tie—she said her brother would be furious if she lost it.

At the West Putney station, Roselin said, "We'll have to separate. I'll meet you two at East End station. Try to act like you're carefree backpackers on a Sunday outing."

Louise and I had to change streetcars in Putney's Main Station, which is also the terminus for the overland express railways. When we found seats in our East End streetcar, a four-car overland train was slowly moving out under a sign, in Russian and English, that read **Putney-Kronstadt Express**. Once the train left, Louise noticed the two guys in their now-familiar business suits sitting at a bakery kiosk, occasionally glancing over their newspapers. "Uh, oh," she said. "I think those are the two men we saw yesterday."

As our streetcar pulled out, I felt one of them recognize us. They were too late to jump aboard, so they swiftly walked out of the station.

"Oh, crap!" said Louise. "But where are they going?"

As our streetcar picked up speed, the men climbed into a dark green jeep-like truck parked on the street. "Looks like military to me," said Louise. "I remember those little trucks when I worked down in Kronstadt."

"Well, let's hope they're just going home." I said.

Several minutes later we stepped off at East End station, the streetcar's last stop. Roselin was waiting near some parked pedicabs.

"Hey, Roselin…" I said.

"…We might have been spotted!" said Louise.

Roselin's expression quickly turned grim as she gave a pedicab driver the address. We threw our gear behind the seats and hopped in. The passenger seat was narrow, so I climbed on the other bike seat where I could help pedal. The driver, a lean, weathered, long-legged chap, was getting a slow start even with my help. No sooner had we gotten up to speed when I heard the growling of an engine behind us.

It was the two men.

"Crap again!" said Louise. "They *did* spot us!"

Roselin looked back, then shouted toward the driver, "We have a problem…see that truck behind us in your mirror?"

The fellow nodded.

"I think they want to try to steal something from us. Could you maybe find an alleyway or some narrow street to get away from them?"

He quickly glanced back at Roselin, wide-eyed. "I'll do what I can, mum."

"There's a big tip for you if you can do it!"

He looked back again, taking us in, "Say, yer not the book thieves, are ya?"

"Of course not!" Roselin said, looking away.

He grinned. "Hey, what's this all about? Are you in deep shite? I've never been chased before, but I've always wanted to see how fast I can go! By the way, the name's Ray!"

He was clearly getting into the adventure.

Once we crossed Banshee Road the streets became narrow, winding, and unpredictable. With my help pedaling, Ray managed to handle the corners without tipping over. The jeep-truck was gaining slightly, it's wide wheelbase giving it more stability.

Roselin spotted the Y intersection she was looking for—a landmark she remembered from earlier visits. She shouted, "Turn right!" But the pedicab was going too fast and it careened against the unyielding stone corner of someone's house.

Ray and Louise tumbled off. Roselin had held on, but she looked stunned by the impact. I saw her bag, with the Codex inside, flop to the ground. The cab's front wheel was hopelessly bent.

The truck stopped, and both men hastily approached us, each aiming a pistol, and shouting *"Stoyat!"* I remembered what it meant, and I froze.

I was afraid this would happen. Stupid! Stupid! Stupid!

The younger one said in clear English, "Give us the book."

Ray said, "Hey, I don't know anything about this. My passengers told me you were going to rob them, and I was just trying to get away from…"

"Molchat!" shouted the other guy.

Ah, yes, "Shut up!"

Roselin climbed off and tried to nudge her bag under the 'cab, but one of the men spotted her, and motioned her with his pistol to move away from the bag. As he approached to pick it up, the other fellow nervously waved his pistol back and forth, slowly repeating *"Stoooyy…stoyaaat…"* as if he were talking to a pack of dogs.

Meanwhile, Louise had focused her gaze on the bag.

Soon, a thin humming sound began to fill the alleyway, coming from every direction. Then it grew more intense and strangely melodious, especially in the vicinity of the bag. The two men apparently heard nothing. We looked at each other, realizing this was the first time any of us had heard any Hum sounds since the blast!

I couldn't believe what happened next.

Just as the man put his hand on Roselin's bag, he yanked it back as if shocked by a live wire. Then Louise gave out a sharp whistle, and when the men made the mistake of looking at her, she quickly focused straight into the eyes of one man, then the other, and they both simply stopped. Their arms fell to their sides, pistols clattering on the ground.

Everyone froze.

Finally, the hum sound drifted off, the alley became quiet, and Louise slumped against the wall, exhausted.

The two men remained stunned, staring into space. Louise, barely conscious, whispered to me, "You and Ray help them back to their truck. They, uh, probably don't know where they are."

Feeling very unsure about this, I put my hands on the younger man's arm, who, like a docile child, allowed me to guide him to the passenger seat. Ray, who at first seemed as stunned as the two men, came around and helped the older fellow slide behind the wheel. The men continued staring while Ray shut off the motor and removed the key.

Then he picked up the pistols and shoved them into his pockets.

Roselin seemed to have recovered and turned to Louise. "How are you doing in there?" she whispered softly.

Louise sat staring into space, but she eventually focused back on Roselin.

"I-I'm just really tired," she said.

Roselin turned to Ray, "Thanks for your help, and I apologize about your 'cab. We're not far from our destination, so we can walk from here." She stared directly into Ray's eyes as she pulled a small pouch from her bag. "Here are four rogers—for your promise to forget what happened here."

"Uh, sure. I…know…nothing."

"And you will toss those pistols into the harbor as soon as you can."

"Yes'um."

As we left Ray pondering what to do about his wrecked pedicab, Roselin said, "He can buy two new 'cabs for that amount, but he deserves it."

*

When Louise and Roselin were strong enough to walk, we started down a curving lane of walls interrupted by narrow, discreet doors. Roselin soon pointed to a certain blue-painted door, pulled a string which rang a bell, and the door immediately opened.

A voice whispered, "Ah, Roselin! I heard the commotion down the alley, are you all right?"

"Yes, and thanks for watching for us, Esau. I, uh, think we're okay now."

I looked at this small slightly-stooped man with his long blond ponytail. His confident smile was reassuring.

We just might get through this.

Esau quietly closed and locked the door and turned first to Roselin. "It's so wonderful to see you again!"

"You too, Esau! This is Gordy, and you might remember Louise."

"My pleasure. *Namaste*." He bowed to us with his hands pressed together. "Let's go where we can talk."

He led us through the tribe's workshops. Crooked hallways connected a mind-boggling rabbit-warren of rooms connected to more rooms, all quiet on this Sunday. Esau pointed out a massive machine that looked similar to a printing press. He led us past more rooms devoted, he said, to the production of writing-paper: trimming, box-making, envelope-making, packing and shipping.

"We specialize in fine paper," said Esau. We own probably the smallest paper-making machine in this part of the world, acquired from Sweden by way of Australia. Maybeck writing paper is known for its quality as far away as Eastern Europe."

"Nice speech," said Roselin, smiling.

"Thanks. It's my school-tour spiel."

We laughed, feeling more relaxed.

Roselin said, "I met Esau when we were both freshmen at Putney U. He insisted I stayed here at times to get away from my witchy roommates. His tribe has always welcomed me."

"We're about twenty members now, including six kids," Esau said. "After you called me, Roselin, I had no trouble getting an okay to help you get out of Putney. Everyone here heard that blast, and after you told me your situation, we were all in."

"You heard it too?"

"Oh yes! That was an *awful* noise."

The tribe-family commons included a large library-gathering room connected to a lovely shaded courtyard. Some people were reading, while a young girl played at a white baby grand piano. They nodded and seemed friendly. "We have a guest room for each of you, down this hallway. Take your time to freshen up, then we can meet in my study for refreshments, yes?"

*

That evening, we felt safe enough to truly relax. Once we were settled in his study, Esau shut the doors and brought out a large bottle of Seven Islands sparkling rosé. "Shall I assume we can drink to success?"

Roselin patted her bag to feel the *Codex* inside. "Well, we made it this far, so yes!"

"So, what happened to those two guys back there?" I said.

"You tell us, Louise." Said Roselin. "Esau is all ears as well."

Louise looked quite revived after her first glass of wine. "I, *ahem*, needed to stop them. My wonderful teacher here, Roselin, taught me how to erase memory, and I must say it took forever to follow the paths to both of their memory centers at once, but I think I was close enough!"

"If she did it right," said Roselin, "They won't remember a thing. It may be a while before they find their way back to what's-her-name, Adeline."

"Cheers, then!" said Esau, as if he heard this story all the time. We all raised a glass.

*

After sharing a quiet supper with Esau's family, Roselin led Louise and me into the courtyard for a private meeting. "We need to decide what we're going to do," she told us.

Louise looked agitated, her good eye darting at both of us. In a rush she said, "Roselin…would it be okay if I *didn't* come with you?"

We looked at her. *What now?*

"I've been thinking about this. Like I said, I don't want to hide. I just want to go someplace that's quiet, maybe visit Todd again for a while."

Roselin gave Louise a long look, her eyes intense. "I suppose you know what's best for you."

What is Louise up to? She gushes over Roselin, and now she wants to take off. I put on a bright smile. "Fine with me."

"Okay, uh…thanks, guys." She looked at Roselin. "Hug?"

Roselin graciously stood up and allowed a seemingly endless goodnight hug (*Ew, enough!*).

Louise disappeared into the dark hallway.

Roselin sat down again, her brow creased.

I waited, my glass in hand.

"That *snake!*" How can she sit there and tell me so casually she might 'visit Todd again for a while' when she *knows* that Todd is practically my only friend in the world." I just wonder how many *visits* there have been?"

I couldn't help but recall the goings-on between them back in Redmoor.

Better not say anything.

Finally, Roselin let out a deep sigh. "We can talk more about this in the morning."

*

Esau had invited us to an informal private breakfast after his family had eaten.

When we sat down, Louise didn't appear, and Roselin and I both knew she never slept late. Esau said, "Shall we wait a little longer for her?"

Roselin's eyes suddenly went wide with alarm before she bolted toward the bedrooms.

Shivers of sudden dread shot through me.

A strange cry immediately brought us to our feet and down the hall. We found Roselin sitting on her bed, stunned, her bag lying open beside her.

"Louise isn't in her room, and the Codex is gone!" she said. "I - I just can't believe she could have done what I think she's done."

Are you sure Louise took it?" I said.

Her expression changed into a fierce look. "Yes! As soon as I saw her empty bed, it hit me—Louise wants it all! I've been too trusting, eating up her constant praise, overlooking her 'slip-up' with Todd's notes. She must have taken it while I was sleeping—I should never have left the Codex where she could find it. *Shite!*"

Esau put a hand on her shoulder and said, "If this helps, I remember hearing someone leaving about four a.m. this morning. That outer door has squeaky hinges."

"But why would she *do* that," I said, "Especially if she can't read it?"

Roselin looked at me, "I don't know, Gordy. I think her Hum-skills have gotten to her head. I'm sooo thankful my notes and the translation key are still in my *other* bag!"

I sat down next to her, and we both tried to breathe.

Esau, with a deep sympathetic smile, offered his hand to Roselin, and we slowly returned to the dining room. She let him help her into her chair. I sat close beside her, and we quietly resumed eating.

Codex or no Codex, we still need to get out of Putney!

*

We slowly finished our breakfast, now clouded with sadness. Roselin said, "Esau, I'd like to leave Putney as soon as possible. Do you know how I could discreetly arrange a trip to Gottfried Island?"

Ooh—that spooky island I saw from the boat.

Esau raised an eyebrow, and said, "I'll have to ponder that one, Roselin. I'm needed in the shops now, so give me a few hours, okay?" With that, he offered her a hug, which she gladly accepted. He then picked up his mug of coffee and left. I Leaned toward her and said, "I remember Gottfried. I saw it from the *Quandary* on our way here. Some guy on the boat said it was cursed."

"Did he now? As a student, I was there on an archeology dig once, and I'm thinking it would be a good place to disappear. That curse tends to keep people away, people who might ask questions, and that's one reason I'd feel safe there. Of course I can't compel you to join me, but I think we should stick together."

I sensed a look of near-desperation behind her thin smile.

So is this why I'm here?

If not, why else?

"Okay," I finally said. "I'll go with you, but what about the Codex?"

Roselin almost smiled. "My witch's intuition tells me it will return to me, sooner or later."

"Whoa! Now that's *some* intuition."

Grinning now, she simply said, "There are some things I never taught Louise, and for many good reasons!"

I gazed at her in total wonder.

Then she took a long breath and said, "I hope you really *want* to do this."

"Yeah, I want to." I said. "Your, uh, *project* seems really important, so I feel good going along with it to help you. And maybe this is what

I'm supposed to be doing, right? Otherwise, I don't know why else I'm on this Island."

Roselin looked at me a long time and said, "That's a tough one, Gordy, especially when I think about what you've gone through. Now I'm curious, if you could do or have *anything*, what would you *want*?"

I was surprised she was suddenly interested in *my* desires, just after being so badly betrayed. I looked at her and finally said, "First I would want a place to *belong* to. I never felt I was a part of anything back home, nor even that close to Ricky or Mom. I felt like I was always looking in from somewhere outside. But with you and Janie and Lane, I feel *wanted*, a part of something. And that's why I don't mind going with you. And if we have to hide, well, I'll still be with you, right?"

With a weak smile she said, "Yes. You will."

*

We sat finishing our coffee, me still feeling stunned by Louise's shocking stunt. The only sound was the soft rumbling from the paper-making machinery in the shops. It was another workday here.

Then Roselin said, "I'm going into town this morning. We'll need supplies for our journey, and I want to go alone so you won't be endangered by any more 'incidents'. I'll wear a babushka scarf and pull a cart, just like every other Putney resident out grocery-shopping. Now, is there anything special you need? And don't tell me more comic books!"

I smiled. "I have plenty."

"I also want you to stay put—no wandering off!"

"Fine with me."

After Roselin left, I was happy to spend the day watching paper being made, or reading one of the (somewhat spicy) locally-printed novels from the tribe's bookshelves.

Roselin returned late in the afternoon, looking tired. "The Fantasia Market had everything I needed." She said. "The stalls there are run by Islanders who tend not to ask questions. I filled two carts! I rented a pedicab to bring everything back here. Nothing happened, but I felt watched all the same."

The stress showed in Roselin's weary eyes.

"And by the way," she said, "The military truck was gone—someone must have rescued our boys."

Just then Esau walked in, smiling. "I made some inquiries today. I can get you both on a mail boat that will take you to Gottfried Island."

A big sigh of relief from Roselin.

He explained, "I know this fellow Randall who tows the mail-schooners through the harbor entrance. And you are in luck! The *Meridian* will take on its cargo and passengers this evening, then leave with the tide tomorrow morning at first light. Randall will take you to meet the schooner on his pilot boat, and he will talk to Mr. Hadley, the skipper. They arrange this kind of discreet transportation from time to time, for a fee, mind you. That woman you saw likely has people watching the docks as well as the bus and rail stations, as you have already discovered.

"The *Meridian*, by the way, travels clockwise around the island, so you'll arrive on Gottfried Island in one or two days, depending on the wind. Once you're under way, It should be a safe trip."

Roselin was looking almost tearful as she took his hands. "How can I ever thank you Esau?"

*

In the early-morning darkness, Putney Harbor was deathly quiet and heavy with mist. The chilly air and my own excitement had me shivering as we waited on the pilot-boat dock. Esau patiently stood by while Roselin stared off into the harbor, her jaw set. I could only guess what she might be thinking or feeling.

A faint glow in the eastern sky promised a clear day.

Randall puttered about the pilot boat with its fringed canvas awning, engine chugging at idle. He reminded me of Humphrey Bogart on *The African Queen*. At Randall's signal, we silently loaded our gear aboard.

I whispered to Esau, "Can we trust this Randall guy? He's really sticking his neck out for us."

"Randall and I go back a long way," Esau said, smiling to himself. "He owes me a couple of favors."

Randall finally turned to us with a grin. "Randall Smithson, at your service. Esau here tells me you need some, ah, transportation assistance, and I'm always glad to help Esau."

"Nice to meet you, Randall. I'm Roselin and this is Gordy, and thank you!"

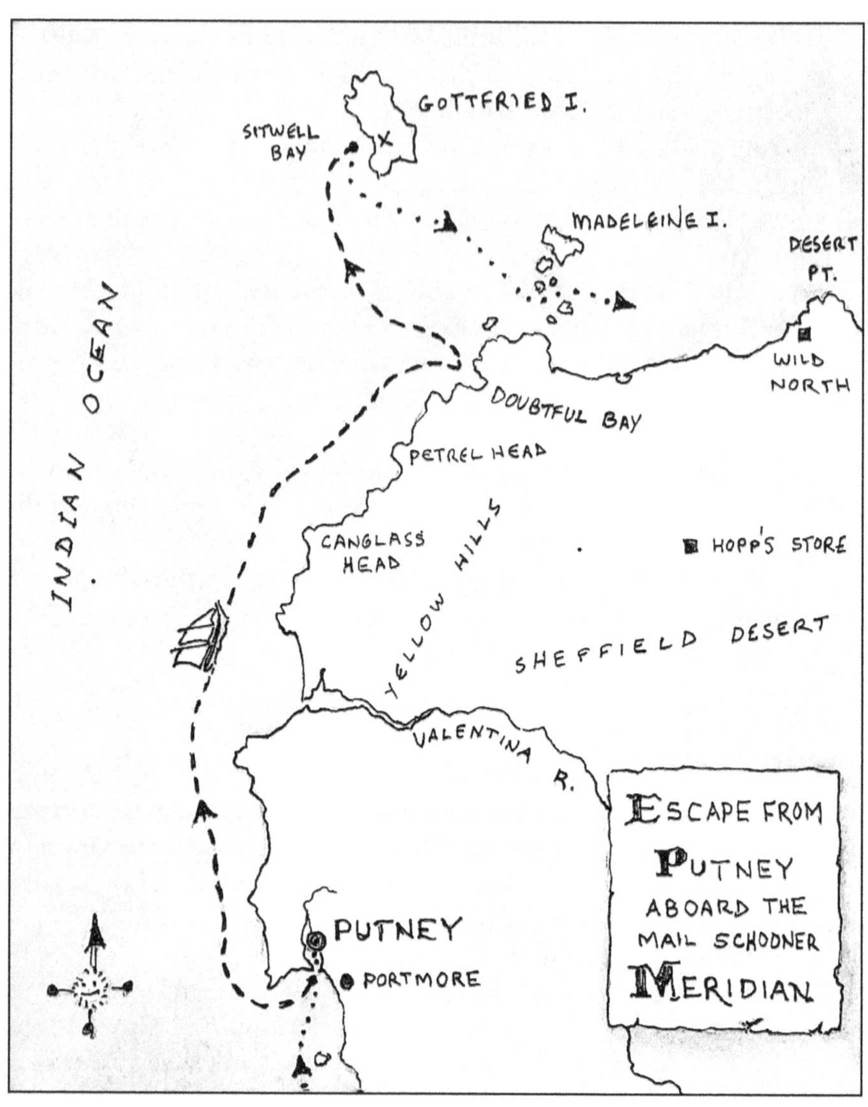

Two trains, a pedicab, a pilot boat and the schooner Meridian *got us out of Putney.*

Esau gave Roselin one more hug and a peck on both cheeks. "Safe journey, Roselin. And you take care of her, Gordon."

"I'll do my best!"

With a flourish, Randall gestured us aboard.

From the pilot boat we watched the *Meridian* slowly drift toward us on the outgoing tide. The eastern sky had become a bright yellow-pink as a busy crew bustled about the schooner's deck and rigging. Randall

228

brought us smoothly alongside, and a crew member dropped a rope ladder and hopped down, bearing a heavy tow-line.

While the sailor stood by, Randall attached the tow-line, then boarded the *Meridian* with the usual formality. He had quite a few words with Mr. Hadley while Roselin and I waited anxiously.

Randall hopped back down and whispered something into Roselin's ear, prompting a raised eyebrow and a witchy smile.

Finally, Mr. Hadley motioned down to the sailor to hoist our gear and help us climb aboard.

We stood at the *Meridian's* railing when Randall gave us a brief good-bye salute from his wheelhouse. The pilot-boat's engine suddenly roared, pulling the *Meridian* easily through the harbor entrance. Once we were well beyond the jetties, Randall cast off the tow-line and we were free.

Remembering Roselin's smile, I said, "So what did Randall tell you?"

She grinned. "He said Louise might be on board."

I looked at her, wide eyed.

"He said he knew about the book heist, could tell she was up to something, and put two and two together."

The crew quickly raised the sails to catch a freshening wind. As the sky brightened to an intense blue, we lingered at the railing to watch West Putney, Boomer Beach, and the other shoreline towns slowly recede.

What a relief!

In a golden-white blaze, the sun rose over the hills.

*

I left Roselin and spent a long time walking the deck. I needed it.

I also tried to spot Louise, but no luck.

All morning the wind was steady and favorable, but then came a change. A white sheet of high clouds obscured the sun as a stiff dry wind swept down off the desert. The thrashing seas forced the *Meridian* to hug the coastline. The water was calmer, but the wind was highly erratic, and by nightfall the boat had made little headway. Mr. Hadley told us we will need to spend the night in Doubtful Bay.

At dusk we bought a supper of sandwiches and chowder from the galley. Still no sign of Louise. The ship's cabins were all full, so sleeping on the deck was our only option. Luckily, the wind had calmed to a soft breeze. Without saying much, we unrolled narrow futon-like mattresses provided by the *Meridian*. We found a quiet spot on the midship deck, under the stars. Our own blankets kept us warm enough.

Roselin reached over to grip my hand and said, "Thanks, Gordy, for sticking with me, especially now."

I smiled back at her. "Ahh, you're welcome."

I tried to sleep, but that fitful wind kept me awake. The boat's erratic creaking and groaning didn't help either. Maybe I was just too wired to sleep.

A sailor strolled by on his watch.

A while later a different rhythm of rapid footsteps became louder on the far side of the deck. Someone was moving along the far railing, barely visible in the starlight. Then I recognized that frizzy hair under a floppy hat...

Louise!

I shook Roselin's shoulder and whispered, *"Roselin, wake up…She is on the boat, right over there!"*

I couldn't believe how fast Roselin jumped up and pounced, like a cat on a mouse. Louise was so wide-eyed with surprise that Roselin was able to employ, as she described it later, her 'iron-zap-you-are-mine' stare. When I got up to see if I could help, Roselin had Louise where she wanted her—locked under her brain-drilling gaze. Without moving her eyes, she said to me,

"Please get Mr. Hadley."

After rousing the captain, I quickly returned and watched Roselin struggle with Louise, throwing everything she had at her to get her to talk. Louise fought back, battling Roselin with her own brain-wave moves. After about twenty minutes of this, Louise, exhausted and mesmerized, finally whispered the location of the Codex.

I was ordered to get it.

When I returned, Mr. Hadley, wearing a greatcoat draped over his night shirt, stood by with an amused look on his face. The sailor on watch had also appeared, but the captain waved him off. While I held up the Codex, hastily wrapped in a pillow case, he nodded and then said to Roselin, "I suppose there can be no charge of theft, since this book had already been stolen, am I right?"

"Well, let us say it was *exchanged*," said Roselin.

"Of course," said the captain. "And you and this young man have never been on my ship! Rest assured, I will make no statement as to your presence nor about this incident. I will, however, feel much relief after we put you both ashore tomorrow. Now, please allow my passenger to return to her stateroom."

He retired to his cabin.

Roselin turned back to Louise and hissed into her ear, "Don't you *ever* come near me again." Then she let Louise stumble off.

Once again, I handed the Codex to Roselin, still wrapped. She accepted it without a word, but looked at me with a mix of deep weariness, relief, and almost a smile.

It was a weird night.

*

Mr. Hadley met us at the schooner's dining table during breakfast. "I asked Mrs. Atherton to remain in her stateroom," he said, "until you go ashore, and she said she would do so."

Mrs. Atherton?

Roselin said, "I assume you mean Louise?"

"Ah…yes, your 'associate'. She is apparently using an alias."

"I was so surprised she was here," said Roselin. "I guess she didn't think *we* would be aboard. My apologies for getting you out of bed last night."

"I must say I was in awe as I watched you two battle each other."

GOTTFRIED ISLAND

Sailing under favorable winds, the *Meridian* soon approached the hilly, treeless island and anchored near a wide cove that Mr. Hadley called Sitwell Bay.

We were standing at the railing. "Looks a bit barren," I said.

"It will have to do," said Roselin, her chin high. "I remember a fresh water spring and an abandoned house near this bay. Also, I've arranged with Mr. Hadley to resupply us on the next run in about two weeks."

The crew loaded our gear, groceries and drinking water into a landing skiff, similar to the one that ferried us from the beach at Wild North. From the skiff, Roselin called out, "Mr. Hadley, remember to stop here next trip—you have my resupply list!" He nodded, but he was looking out at sea instead of at us.

The boatman raised the sail on the skiff, which soon took us straight through the shallow surf to the beach.

We found ourselves standing on the sand next to our pile of all we owned. Roselin thanked the young sailor with a generous tip, quickly looked him in the eye, and told him, "You will forget everything about us and our stopping here." He only froze for a moment, then shook his head, and, still a bit dazed, replied with a salute. We helped him push off into the surf.

Soon the skiff, then the schooner, were gone.

*

We took a long look at our new home. The landscape was shadowless under a pale sky—not exactly bleak, more like *austere*. The familiar sounds of roaring surf and sea birds were oddly subdued. It could have been the dry air, but it was a strange quietness.

Maybe the island <u>is</u> cursed. Will I even sleep at night?

Roselin studied the weathered stone hut sitting on a low rise above the beach. "Ah, yes, it's still the same."

As we walked toward it, she said, "There's a story about a family named Piedmont who lived here some fifty years ago."

"And?"

"Well, from what I've pieced together, they were not a happy lot. A mother and father with two daughters had settled here, and after a couple of years both parents for reasons unknown became severely depressed. The father simply disappeared one night, and the mother drowned herself a month later. Their girls were only about ten and twelve, and I'm amazed at how strong kids are. They found their mother washed up on the beach, buried her, then managed to survive on their own for several months until the food ran out. In desperation, they sailed their family skiff all the way to Petrel Bay, where they had managed to beach it. Close to starvation, they were found by a local beachcomber. Their story was in the *Putney Times*."

I felt a chill. *I can't imagine being stuck here—orphaned on this empty place.*

"That sounds creepy," I said, "but a happy ending for the girls, I guess."

"Yes, and I think they are still alive. One of them published a memoir titled *The Gottfried Curse*."

Then Roselin said, "I was hesitant to tell you that, Gordy, when I thought of your mum."

I took a deep breath. "Yeah, it's hard not knowing what happened with her…or with Ricky."

I sat down on a rickety bench in front of the hut, picked up a stick and mindlessly nudged an ant.

Roselin gently sat next to me and said, "I know this has been quite a time for you. You've been an immeasurable help to me, especially taking that chance switching those books, and then spotting Louise! We would not be here, and have the Codex in my bag, if you hadn't been with me."

I looked up, "I guess your intuition was right—the Codex came right back to you!" I continued nudging with my stick.

She looked at me for a moment, then around at the beach and the hills. "I think you'll like it here, and it won't be forever! This island is big. It took me weeks to explore it when I was on that dig for school. Who knows, you might even unravel some secrets. There are weird rock formations in the hills, and pot shards and other remains from an ancient village near here. And I'll bet you'll be able to body-surf every day. Janie told me you two did that a lot."

Roselin's attempts at enthusiasm were not helping. When she said *bodysurfing* all I could think of was Lane.

And when will I ever see her again?

"So, how long *are* we going to be here?"

Roselin sighed and said, "Until I get some kind of a sign that it's okay to return to the Island. That's the best I can do right now, Gordy."

When I didn't reply she let out another sigh and said, "Okay, let's set up our camp and have some lunch."

*

Pushing in the creaking door, we found a single largeish room furnished with a dusty wooden table, two chairs and a sturdier wooden bench. Along the rear wall stood a massive clay cook stove next to a counter with a sink and a single faucet. It squeaked loudly when I tried it, but no water came out. Dust and mouse poops were everywhere—the place needed a good cleaning.

I climbed some steep steps to a narrow loft, and asked Roselin if I could sleep there. "That's fine with me," she said. "I'd rather use my tent for a proper bedroom!" She helped me shake out the loft's straw mattress, and, with makeshift brooms, we both swept out the worst of the hut's dusty debris. Outside, I helped her attach our freshly-purchased tents end-to-end to allow enough room to sleep in and to store her clothes.

We were finally ready to ready to make lunch. Looking for cooking utensils, Roselin opened a large pantry-cupboard.

"Hey Gordy, there are *books* in here! Also, some bug-chewed writing paper and an old pencil. And some dishes and bowls, and down here are some pots and a frying pan. The stove looks useable too, we'll just need firewood. We have been blessed!"

I looked at Roselin's find, but I didn't feel like reading the books, or writing, or doing much of anything.

"All right, O silent one," she said. "Let's see if we can cook up something. We'll need to get this stove going, so will you collect some dry wood off the beach? I want to make my 'admixture soup' for lunch, and for the next few days."

I peered into the empty firebox. "Okay," I said and walked out.

While gathering firewood, I looked around at the dry hills and the curved beach, all untouched by humans for a long time.

Maybe this place will be okay—it's just so empty.

I came back with an armload of firewood, and tumbled it into the firebox.

"Is this good?"

"Sure. Thanks."

"Okay if I go back out and look around?"

"Fine by me. Are you feeling any better?"

"Yeah, a little."

I liked it that Roselin cares about me. *I guess I should just get over being stuck here. She has enough oh her mind as it is.*

And what about those Piedmont parents—did a curse really get them?

*

I followed the sandy beach to the far end of the bay. Seagulls, terns, and sandpipers continuously trotted ahead of me or flew off with a squawk or two, their mealtime interrupted. Around a rocky point I found another sandy shore, then more rocks and more beaches. Tidepools brimmed with starfish, creeping crabs, tiny fish, mussels and varieties of seaweed I'd never seen before.

Gottfried was a strange place to call home.

On an impulse I turned inland. On the hillsides, chunks of rock lurked in the thin grass, a real toe-stubbing hazard in my sandals. I also had to watch for bird nests, which were merely smooth spots scooped out of the ground. A few were occupied, so I gave them a wide berth lest I be attacked by an angry mama.

Roselin was right—there were caves and dark crannies among the rocky outcrops. I poked a stick into one or two, wary of some creature that might leap out at me. Nothing did.

From the highest hilltop, the land fell away to the island's hazy far shore. The ocean beyond flickered under the pale sunlight. It *was* a pleasing sight, but it still felt strangely off in some way. I couldn't understand why my throat was tightening up—powerful feelings and questions were trying to get out, like, *what am I supposed to do now?*

When I returned, Roselin was sitting outside the door in one of the old dining chairs, quite still. Before she noticed me she looked a little lost, reminding me I wasn't the only one feeling weird.

She sat up with a start when I approached. "Ah," she said. "I was wondering where you were. Soup is ready!"

She had set the table with bowls and spoons. I wasn't sure of Roselin's cooking, and I couldn't help looking into her bubbling pot like it was, well, a witch's brew.

Roselin had brought her chair back in, filled our bowls, and looked at me as she sat down. "Gordy, it's just veggie soup. You'll like it!"

I took a cautious sip, and it was wonderful. This was something more than just the delightful flavor and the just-right warmth. In two minutes my bowl was empty.

"I've never had soup like this…may I have some more?"

Over my second helping, I said, "You looked kind of sad when I walked up. Are *you* okay?"

She took a spoonful and slowly swallowed. "I've been putting on a cheerful front, Gordy, but you know this has been hard for me. I feel that I'm slipping into broken-witch, a place I haven't been in a long time."

"Broken-witch?"

"Yes. I've grappled with this for years. The witches at Covenmoor were not patient with children who dug up pottery instead of bringing in newts and grubs. I was called retarded, useless and broken, and often laughed at by my fellow apprentices. The word 'broken' stuck like pine pitch. I finally realized it was up to me to survive, almost like those two Piedmont girls."

Some of this sounds familiar.

"I felt better once I started at Putney University. The archeology program actually *assigned* me to dig up old stuff. I loved it and I was good at it. Eventually bringing the Ur language to light gave me a deep sense of purpose that boosted my 'loving witch'. When I later discovered the physics behind Hum energy, I felt I was flying! These were *my* discoveries, and no one else's. It was exciting!"

The glow in Roselin's eyes had once again become riveting. All I could do was listen.

"When the lamp-makers from Biganess came with their request, the idea of *applying* Hum energy was too much to resist. Wouldn't a lamp capable of generating free light forever be the diamond in my crown? I had a hunch that my research, based on formulas in the Codex, could make it happen. So I wrote that 'recipe' and gave it to them, without testing it myself."

She took a deep breath.

"Then came the blast, and now they're dead."

She shut her eyes and let out a hiss... *"broken witch!"*

This was hard to hear. I wanted to hug her, assure her she wasn't 'broken'. When she got up from her chair, I stood so quickly my own chair fell over. I think the clattering startled us both out of our gloom, and when I offered to hug her, she hugged *me* with a ferocious squeeze and whispered, "thanks for listening."

She brought our empty bowls to the sink and twiddled the faucet handle. "Say, you wanna help me get water out of this?"

I looked at the faucet, then at her.

"I think you are a very loving witch!"

*

I had trouble sleeping that first night. The crashing sound of the waves, which seemed subdued all day, now seemed annoyingly amplified. I finally got up, went outside, and looked at the sky. The Milky Way was as brilliant as I'd ever seen it—clusters of stars and wild nebulae alternated with vast shadowy places all the way down to the horizon. I counted six other galaxies.

There was no moon, but a pale glow on the eastern horizon promised a gibbous-waning moon would soon rise. Roselin had told me about moon phases, and I loved the term *gibbous*, the fat version of *crescent*. Besides the surf-noise, a faint chorus of yipping drifted down from the hills—randall foxes according to Roselin.

Over the next few days we settled into our new home. I was able to reconnect the kitchen faucet to the spring, and I continued tidying up around the place. Roselin had started going through her notebooks, but she soon put them away. "After the explosion, I haven't been much interested in them," she said. "But I enjoy paging through the original Codex." She brought it out and showed me a page. "Look at these intricate symbols and the gorgeous colored inks, Gordy. They still look so fresh. I'm glad the book hasn't been damaged, given what it's been through lately."

From among the bug-chewed books in the hut's pantry, I tried to read an English version of *Anna Karenina*, but it was slow going. A paperback with a yellow cover titled *A Night in a Moorish Harem*, printed in Putney, was far more interesting. At first, I wasn't sure what a harem was, but I quickly found out!

Sometimes I took all-day walks. I found I could cover the entire island's shoreline in about ten hours as long as I kept a steady pace and brought water and a lunch. The surf was often rough on the island's southwestern end, and fun to watch. The walks were also profitable. I brought back strange-shaped shells and barnacle-crusted bottles, a few containing notes in unreadable languages. I also found plenty of firewood.

On other days I enjoyed wandering over the grassy hills and ravines. I was fascinated by little quick-footed mouse-creatures with furry tails, big lizards sunning themselves on the rocky outcrops, and an extended family of plump spotted rabbits sitting near their den. I admired their short ears and generous fur, and was fascinated by their strange dark spots—and they had babies in pouches, like kangaroos!

*

Our resupply boat was late.

Luckily, the spring provided plenty of fresh water.

Roselin had brought enough food for three weeks, and now we were well into week four. "I should have conserved our food," she said. "We're going to be out of almost everything in a few more days."

I thought about that for a minute. Back home I'd seen surf fisherman catch perch right from the beach, and I once read about how to skin and roast a rabbit in Ricky's *Boy Scout Field Guide*.

"Is there anything to fish with here?" I asked.

"No. I looked."

"Humm, how about a trap or something to catch those weird rabbits?"

"Nope. Those are pope bunnies by the way."

"Pope bunnies?"

"Don't ask me why."

"Okay, I'll dig up some clams, then. I've seen a lot of clamshells washed up on the beach."

Roselin brightened, then looked away, as if distracted. "Yes, good idea! There might be holyoke clams out there. Sure, give it a try."

I sensed something was off again.

"Are you okay?"

"Of course," she said, smiling, and looked away again.

I found a bucket and a small shovel-blade with no handle. The tide was out and sure enough, the exposed bay-bottom was covered with telltale mounds, each with a little hole on top like a tiny volcano. They all seemed to say, 'dig here'. I remembered this from digging up clams back home, so I knew what to look for. The clams were fat with boldly striped shells, and I soon had a bucketful.

When I presented my harvest, Roselin looked at them, grinning ear-to-ear. "You did find holyokes! Now I'm getting hungry," she said. "If you stoke the fire and boil them in a pot of water, I'll go up to the spring for some wild onions I saw there. Too bad we're out of potatoes, but I do have one tin of condensed milk left."

The chowder was exceptional.

By the end of week four, we were rationing the last of the flour, sugar, spices and salt, and foraging for the rest. Roselin searched the island for herbs, roots and lettuce greens in the wet spots. She enlisted me to scrape up sea salt in a low spot behind the beach. I also practiced throwing rocks and finally nailed one of the rabbits. It made okay soup with the wild onions and herbs, but the meat was tough.

One day, about five weeks in, I realized we had not heard the Hum once since we had arrived. I thought of bringing it up with Roselin but figured she'd already noticed. In fact, we had more or less stopped talking, except about the weather, or about what to eat next. Roselin looked stressed and distracted one day, then all happy the next, then stressed again. She was glowing and dimming like a pulsing light—a scary resemblance to my mom.

And she doesn't want to talk about anything, just like Mom.

To distract my worrywart mind, I continued my long meandering walks, eventually exploring every hill and dry gully on the island. On a low bluff at the far end of the island I found the remains of an ancient round wall surrounding a space a bit larger than our hut. The stones in it were tightly fitted—an impressive job. Bits of painted clay were scattered around it—pottery? They were too small to tell.

Around our hut were more recent artifacts. My favorite finds were a tiny ceramic doll's head, a 1912 one-ruble coin picturing the Russian two-headed eagle, and an elegant silver tea spoon, green with tarnish.

*

The days seemed to blend together as we continued our foraging, clam-digging and wandering. Our resupply visit now seemed like a myth. I longed to ask Roselin again how long we were going to be here, but of course she didn't know any more than I did.

The more silent she became, the more I worried.

One day, a heavy surf began to pound on the eastern shore of Gottfried. The sound of it carried all the way to our hut. The sky had also changed—something was coming. That night, downpours and blustery winds drove Roselin in from her tent, obliging her to set up a makeshift bedroom under the loft. She told me it was likely a monsoon, having drifted further south than the usual course of these storms. "This can last a while," she said, and she was right. It rained for three days before it finally let up, though the wind continued to drive banks of dark clouds across the sky.

I was longing to get out of that hut, and offered to go down to the bay and dig some clams for supper.

"Yes, yes, more clams!" Roselin said. "Great idea Gordy." Her giddy cheerfulness was unnerving.

When I picked up the bucket, she made no move to go out to gather herbs like she usually did.

On my way to the beach, a prickly feeling crept up the back of my neck, and I stopped to rub it—something was wrong. It was the very same feeling that hit me when I opened Mom's bedroom door!

I dropped the bucket and ran back, lurching and tripping as fast as I could.

The hut door was tightly closed, and something prevented me from pushing it in. I shouldered into it as hard as he could, and the firewood box tumbled over, scattering wood everywhere. Carried by my momentum, I plunged into the room, just as Roselin was raising a cup to her mouth.

I smacked it out of her hands.

It crashed against the hot stove, the hissing liquid creating a stink you wouldn't believe. She was stunned at first, then everything slowed down as she looked at her empty hands. She sat heavily on the floor, staring at nothing. Then after a few minutes she began to cry, softly at first, and then came a flood of long gulping wails.

I sat down next to her and wrapped my arm around her. It's all I could think to do. After endless minutes, Roselin's sobs began to recede, but I could still feel her anguish.

I whispered, "It's okay now…it's okay." For a long time we sat in silence until I said softly, "Do you, ah, feel like you can get up now? Maybe sit in this chair?"

Without a word, she let me help her up and into the chair. I sat down across the table and gripped her hands.

"Do you want some water or something?"

"Water would be lovely."

When I poured it from the jug, I noticed the heat-blackened stain on the stove. She saw it too.

"What *was* that stuff?"

She looked at me with a wry twist of a smile. "Belladonna and red miandra. The miandra berries will put you to sleep, then the belladonna will stop your heart. It's a painless way to go."

"Oh…"

"A real witch's brew."

That's not funny!

Eventually Roselin sat up a little straighter, staring out the open door, and slowly said, "I feel that all the research I've done has been a complete waste, and now I've made a complete mess of it all."

She kept staring.

"My problem, Gordy, is that I'm *stuck*! I can't let this information get into the hands of any governments, and I can't destroy this wonderful, priceless, beautiful book. The Ur, whoever they were, took great care to share their understanding of how the Universe works, and it's all in there! The book is a message in itself, an incredibly wonderful revelation."

Her words, and the crushing weight she has been dealing with, went straight to my heart. This could drive anyone over the edge!

"Maybe you can, um, hide it somewhere?"

"I could, but then I'd worry about being captured, and forced to reveal its location under torture. Or Louise might try to steal it again. Who knows?"

Roselin tortured? Nonononono.

"Also, my life has been all about the Ur, their language, the Hum, and this book I'm holding. I have no family, no home, just this. If I hide it, then I'd have to hide with it."

She hesitated, then pushed a folded note across the table. My stinging tears made it hard to read, but I saw enough.

"You wanted me to bury the book with your…body?"

I shoved the note aside. I couldn't look at her.

How could she do this?

I wanted to ask if she was inspired by the Piedmont woman who left her daughters here, but I didn't.

Then, in a flash, I saw Mom's pain in Roselin's eyes, and once again I realized…

I took her hands in both of mine and said, "Roselin, I really didn't know it was this hard for you. You are the most special person I've ever met—you mean more to me than…anyone!. Will you promise, promise, *promise* never to try this again?"

"No."

I felt like she'd punched me.

"But," she continued, "I promise I won't abandon you here. And now I feel even more terrible, since I *would* have left you here alone. I know this can't be pleasant for you, stuck here with me—a suicidal broken witch."

I looked at her, then glanced outside the door.

"This should all be over soon, Gordy. If you want, you can leave here if our resupply boat ever arrives. I won't keep you."

I gripped her hands a little tighter and stared at her with more conviction than I've ever felt before.

"I don't want to lose you."

She breathed in, then out, several times while looking straight at me. "You won't."

I smelled the reeking pot still simmering on the cookstove. "Now, can I get rid of the rest of that…*stuff?*"

"Be my guest."

I threw the remains of Roselin's smelly mix as far as I could behind the hut, cleaned up the shattered cup, then scrubbed the old cookpot thoroughly in the sink, shivering all the while.

Gottfried curse or not, she's still alive!

I said, "Umm, can we make some tea? I'm feeling kind of cold."

"Sure," she said. "Let's stoke up the fire and I'll make us some *normal* tea."

I smiled.

I think she's coming back.

*

While I gathered up the tumbled firewood, Roselin carefully prepared the tea with her hand-gathered herbs. She set it out in a pot with the two least-chipped cups from the cupboard. She also pulled out a small bottle of apricot brandy.

While the tea steeped, we sat down again, face-to-face, and she unstoppered the bottle. "I'm glad I had set this aside. It will go well with our tea. Want some?"

I nodded. She poured the tea and added the brandy.

Roselin then grasped both of my hands and looked at me intently. "Do you want to tell me anything more about your life back home?"

This is a twist…

I tried to dredge up something besides my lonely evenings burning hamburgers, reading comic books, watching stupid TV shows and not feeling much of anything.

She's triggering the things I've been trying <u>not</u> to think about.

Roselin's gaze was intense. "Just tell me what feels safe, okay? I feel I need to focus on *you* right now to take a break from *me*."

Ah.

I took a deep breath, sipped the loaded tea, and started in. "At home I felt like everything bad that happened was my fault—even my being *born*. I think my dad hated me even then because he had to give up his fishing business."

"And what about your mum?"

"I think she loved us as best she could, but she couldn't control my dad. When she was at work, Leon would sometimes let loose on me. I think I also had a temper when I was little, which would set off *his* temper. I remember only a few incidents, but I was afraid of him all the time. Then he left, and Mom made my brother Ricky take over babysitting. She was working two jobs sometimes to pay the bills. And in the last year or so she was yelling at Ricky a lot 'cause he was sneaking out with his girlfriend. And because Ricky was stuck with me, he liked to say things like, 'You're a *mistake*, Gordy. I heard Dad say it, so there!' I guess that sank in."

I paused, and looked at Roselin. She was completely focused listening to me; her caring gaze was almost too much to bear. *Is this what real love is like?*

Then something snapped. I got up fast, ran out the door and screamed as loud as I could…

"I'm NOT a mistake, DAD!"

"I'M NOT A MISTAKE!

"I'M – NOT – A – MISTAKE!

"I'M GORDYYY!"

Every bird on the beach flew off screeching.

*

My throat was sore and I was shaking when I sat down again. Roselin slowly broke into an ear-to-ear grin.

"What?" I asked.

"I think you know."

I looked down at my cup. *It must be this tea.*

"Then you came here," she said softly.

"Y-e-ahh. That bardo-dream makes a little more sense. I guess when I found Mom I really needed to get out of there. I'm so glad Mr. Barnes was there to help me."

"Ah, yes, your friend. I'm glad he was there too."

"Did I tell you he sent a box of comic books to Hopp's Store? It had arrived just before Lane and I showed up there. How did he *know* this, Roselin?"

Looking thoughtful, she poured more tea, adding more brandy. "Okay, bear with me here. The more I hear about Mr. Barnes, the more I believe you two are connected by Hum energy. The Codex says people who are Hum-connected can send and receive messages at subconscious levels."

Ah.

"So would you describe this Mr. Barnes for me? I'm getting a funny feeling about him."

"Oh, that's easy," I said. "He's a nice guy and he looks like Roger Putney on that ten-penny postage stamp."

Roselin slowly took a long, steady sip of tea. "Okay, good start. Tell me more."

"Well, when I met him, he was building his own house a few blocks from our house, and he took time to show me how to use some of his tools. He also has a kind look in his eyes, just like in, ah, your eyes. And whenever we talk, he *listens.*"

Roselin concentrated on her tea. "From what you told me back at Wild North, and now, I can see he really does care about you. You realize this, right?"

I nodded.

She gave me an amused smile.

The sun, finding a gap in the heavy clouds, blazed into the open doorway, right onto Roselin's face. "Wow," she said, blinking. "I'd almost forgotten sunlight!"

As I turned around to look outside, the brilliance had faded, but the weather was definitely changing.

"I'll go dig those clams," I said.

*

The next morning was sunny, the surf was quiet, and there was finally no wind. I lay in my bunk smiling for no real reason.

I heard Roselin stirring below. "Good morning up there," she said. "If you'd be willing to light a fire, I'll go pick some mint for tea."

"Sure!"

At least we'll always have tea.

"Then I'll need your help to move back into my tent again."

"Okay."

I was thrilled to see Roselin in better spirits. When she left, I jumped off the loft, fed the stove, lit it, and hopped back in my still-warm bed to luxuriate a moment.

Roselin soon returned with the mint. I heard some clattering, the pantry door squeaking, then silence.

"*Gordy!* How did all this *stuff* get here?"

"*What* stuff?"

I climbed down again and took a look. The pantry was full of cans and packets of milk, flour, fruit, beans, veggies, tuna, tea, rice, sugar, salt and seasonings all arranged in neat rows, and labeled with the distinctive Fantasia Market logo. Roselin reached in and hefted a few just to make sure they were real. She opened a tiny jar of fancy cinnamon, and sneezed. "It's real all right!" she said.

My skin prickled. "This…is…sooo…weird," I said. " It reminds me of the food locker on the raft—it was always restocked!"

Roselin quickly ran outside to see who might have done this. "No sign of anyone," she said.

As we stood there mystified, a low, vibrating hum, faint and distant, filled the air. We both went outside, and Roselin seemed to melt under its spellbinding sound, the first Hum we had heard in many weeks! As it intensified, it dropped to an unusually long and low *Om* sound, sending shivers right through us.

"I can't remember the last time I heard *that* kind of Hum," Roselin said, her eyes shining.

"Yeah, same here."

EDDIE

For the next two weeks, we took each day as it came. The restocked pantry remained a mystery. When I later shared my suspicion about Mr. Barnes, Roselin nodded thoughtfully, and then winked. "I think something's up," she said. "A witch's intuition."

She became more herself, relaxed but with a new kind of energy. She spent hours each day scouring the hills for every medicinal herb, seed, and root she could find. She often took me with her to explain their benefits. More than once she has said, "for such a sparse, windswept place, Gottfried certainly provides an impressive apothecary."

She also had that graceful walk again!

Is this what peace-of-mind feels like?

Then one day she asked me to make renderings of the plants she had discovered. I thought of the stubby pencil and the few yellowing sheets of paper we had left. When I went to the cupboard—surprise!— a new package, still sealed, of fine Maybeck art paper with six new pencils, an eraser and a complete watercolor set, all neatly arranged on top of five new *Uncle Scrooge* comic books!

Now I definitely knew who was behind this, and I was grinning like a lunatic.

This is just too crazy…

Roselin merely rolled her eyes and smiled.

Late the next afternoon I went to the cove to dig some more clams. A lower-than-usual tide led me further out, and just before digging I happened to glance up. On the horizon, a tiny reddish sail bobbed over the swells, slowly approaching.

I ran to the hut to find Roselin, who was just walking down the hillside, a loaded tote-bag slung on her shoulder.

"Roselin! There's a boat coming!"

She shaded her eyes with her hand and took a long look.

"Do you know who that might be?" I asked.

"Not yet."

Then the sail moved and the boat changed course, heading toward our cove. A man in a wide-brimmed bush hat sat at the tiller.

Roselin put down her bag and joined me as we watched him approach. I began to *feel* the guy before my brain registered who it was.

Then I knew.

"*Mr. Barnes! Mr. Barnes!*" I yelled.

The fellow wildly waved his hat at us.

Leaving Roselin gaping in astonishment, I ran into the shallow water and he threw me a rope, as if we did this all the time. I instinctively held it taught while he lowered and lashed the sail, then he hopped off the boat with another rope, or line, as he called it.

"If we pull together," he said, "I can tie 'er up here."

Roselin joined us and helped pull, and soon the boat was secure. For a moment we all stood there, then he nodded to Roselin with a smile and turned to me with his arms out.

I was fighting back tears when he gave me a long, vigorous guy-hug, my first ever. He smelled pleasantly of sea-salt and sweat.

Finally, we both let go and I said, "Uh, Roselin, this is Mr. Barnes. Mr. Barnes, this is Roselin."

"Hello Mr. Barnes. I've heard a lot about you."

"Hello Roselin," he said, looking right at her. The tone of his voice sounded like these two were somehow not strangers.

She offered her hand. He took it, and bowed his head to her slightly. "By the way, you may both call me Eddie."

I was still awestruck by his arrival out of nowhere. "You, ah, didn't sail that boat all the way from California, did you?"

"Nooo, no. I flew from Los Angeles to Melbourne, took the Trans-Australia Railway to Perth, and was able to get a ticket on a steamer from Fremantle to, ah…"

"Kronstadt?"

"Yes, that Russian navy-town. They were not too pleased to see me, but they had to allow my entry." He added with a wink, "They were obliged to honor a certain letter-of-passage I carried with my ticket."

His wink only mystified me more.

"I thoroughly enjoyed the train ride from Kronstadt to Putney. The next day I rented this sturdy little yacht out of Portmore. It's been a long trip."

"It must have been," said Roselin. "I can't conceive of such a journey."

Mr. Barnes—Eddie—was still holding Roselin's hand until he politely let it go. They continued to stand there trying not to smile at each other until I finally said, "Say, you wanna come up to our little house? I hope you can stay a while. We have, uh, *plenty* of food."

But we still needed a main course for supper, so I impatiently finished filling the bucket with clams.

*

I returned to find Eddie and Roselin sitting outside the hut chattering away like old friends. She had helped Eddie bring up fresh fruit and vegetables from his boat, along with his gear. When I brought the clams, we went to work. His onions and potatoes, along with the holyoke clams and our local wild celery soon made a fine chowder, filling the room with a hefty aroma.

Eddie had opened a bottle of Highpeace riesling he had bought in Portmore. "I've heard some of the best wines world-wide are made on this island, yes?"

"I wouldn't know about 'world-wide', but I'll take your word for it," said Roselin.

As we ate, the clinking of spoons made me aware of how quiet we, and the evening, had become. No sounds came through the open door—the surf was flat, the wind had died, and the birds were quiet. The room glowed with two tall candles Eddie had brought.

Finally, Eddie looked at me. "I'm sure you are wondering what may have happened back home, Gordy."

I looked down at my plate. I desperately wanted to know, but I also desperately didn't.

"Umm, yes?" I squeaked.

Roselin took my hand. I stopped breathing.

"I'm sorry to tell you your mother passed away. She never woke up at the hospital. The pills had done too much damage to her heart, and it failed her a few days later."

Eddie gripped my other hand while Roselin moved over to sit beside me on the bench. She pulled me toward her. I buried my face into her neck, finally sucking in air, sobbing.

"May I share more, Gordy?" Eddie said softly.

I felt like I was in a hole, but I nodded.

"Around midnight that night, I awoke with the strangest sensation—a distress signal—coming from you. Your shock felt so severe that I wanted to immediately offer you a safer place, so I sent you off in your dream. Then I thought of your brother and telephoned your number. He answered right away, heaving and gagging to the point where I could barely understand him! I was at your house within a few minutes."

Roselin and I were rigid with attention.

"When I arrived, he was walking in circles and hitting his head with his fists. It took me several minutes to calm him down enough to tell me what had happened. He said when he returned that evening, you were on your bed looking like you'd passed out. But by the time he had discovered your mom, and went back to wake you, you were gone! I can't imagine what the two events together must have done to him. Of course I feel responsible for part of that!"

This was almost too much to absorb.

"Over the next few weeks, I helped Ricky arrange a funeral, settle your mom's business affairs and all that. He would have been completely helpless, especially since your dad had disappeared and you boys apparently had no other close relatives. I came to check on him every evening after work, just to see if he was coping. It was the least I could do, especially since I couldn't fully explain to him your, uh, situation. He had a million questions I couldn't answer. I could only ask him to trust me that you would be all right."

I held on to Roselin feeling strangely guilty, and deeply sad for Ricky.

"Luckily," said Eddie, "we found your mom's will. She had appointed Ricky as executor of her bank accounts, and she had apparently salted away a considerable sum. The money has allowed Ricky to keep your house, and he is still living there, earning enough by waiting tables at that Greek restaurant on the highway. He has also gotten back into surfing again. I think he'll be all right."

"I should have called someone, an ambulance or something. I feel bad that I just passed out!"

"Gordy, there was nothing you could have done. It was out of your hands, as it had been for a long time before that night."

I finally looked at him, my face feeling blotchy and hot. I couldn't think of anything more to say.

Eddie continued. "When Ricky told me he had received your letters I was immensely relieved. By my Hum methods I knew you were okay, but Ricky needed proof. He said he'd replied to both letters, so they should be waiting for you at, uh, Gifford Haven. Is that right?"

I smiled, flooded with sudden relief. *Ricky is okay—and he wrote back to me!* "Yeah, Gifford is right. Thanks."

*

Eddie stayed on with us.

Except for telling me about Mom and Ricky, he said nothing more about why he had come all this way, though I was sure glad he did. I was delighted to have him around, just to feel his presence, and I didn't want to spook things by asking too many questions. I offered him the loft and used Roselin's now-abandoned sea-grass bed beneath it.

As Eddie adapted to our routines, Roselin seemed both calmed and alerted by his presence. She gave him looks now and then, but asked no questions. She was amused when Eddie tried to be helpful. With some rusted tools he found in the boat, he managed to repair the two old chairs, both of which were falling apart. He also tightened the door's hinges which were loosened when I bashed it in that day. Roselin's interest in Eddie, and his glances back at her, only heightened my curiosity. *What is up with them?*

It was strange at first to call him Eddie, though Roselin had no problem with it...

Oh, Eddie, would you like more coffee?

Oh, Eddie, would you come out and look at this bent tent pole?

Eddie, do you happen to know anything about the physics of a quantum entanglement?

In the mornings, he accompanied me on walks to my favorite places in the hills and along the beaches. He seemed pleased to poke around alongside me and find random artifacts. In a desolate ravine, I showed him a cat-sized skull I'd picked up. "Look at those *teeth.*"

"Maybe Roselin knows what animal this is," he said.

On our walks, Eddie asked me about my experiences since my 'departure' from home.

"Just tell me what you want to."

I nodded and sat down on a rock.

After drawing a long breath, I told him about my capture by the Soviet Navy, my escape, traveling with Janie, meeting Roselin, then Lane, the explosion, the book heist, everything.

He listened without saying a word.

*

Eddie's rented boat came with several fishing poles, and early one morning he announced he would show us what he knew about surf fishing. Roselin quietly nodded. We found some mussels and sand crabs for bait, and he led us to the point just beyond the inlet where his boat was beached. Roselin soon caught what she called a mulloway with crab bait, and then a small Australian salmon with an old rubber lure she found in his tackle box. Eddie and I both had our bait bitten off, but no catches.

"You have the magic touch, Roselin," Eddie humbly said.

Her face was glowing. "In my fifth year of school, limited as it was, we were taken out to a nearby beach where an old chap showed us how to bait a hook, cast out, and then 'feel the fish' when they came to nibble. I guess I never forgot that. How 'bout I show you next time?"

After the best salmon dinner ever, we were sitting around the little kitchen table with another bottle of Portmore wine.

Just as Eddie thanked Roselin, for catching *and* cooking that fish, I finally asked him, "So were you *really* there when I had that dream?"

Roselin was all attention.

He said, "Okay, Gordy, to answer that, I'll have to tell you that I knew you heard the Hum back home. I saw you listening to it once at my house. Your eyes were closed, and you were smiling and swaying. I was hearing it at the same time, so that's how I knew."

"Ah," I said.

"I nearly let on to you, but I like to think of the Hum as a kind of private spiritual place, like a refuge."

A rush of feelings. "Yeah, I think I know what you mean, especially after I got laughed at for talking about it," I said.

He glanced at Roselin, then back at me. "Roselin tells me the Hum is very real to the islanders here, but rarely heard elsewhere in the world."

"And," she said, "this man has somehow learned to 'read' Hum energy in someone else. This is something that took me *years* to learn! He read your energy back there, Gordy, your specific Hum signature."

This was starting to make sense. "Sooo, if you can feel my brain energy, can you read my thoughts too?"

"Not at all. I can only feel the energy."

"And it doesn't matter how far apart we are?" I asked.

"No. And what woke me up that night was your brain energy climbing to a frightful level. It felt like sparks were flying! That was probably when you looked in on your mom and then collapsed. I knew I couldn't get to your house in time, so I decided to try to 'be there' in your subconscious to help you get through what had just happened."

"Yeah," I said, "Roselin told me I probably went into a bardo-state."

Eddie thought a moment. "She's right. Your brain was so stressed out that it was shutting down, so I nudged a few neurons to help get your spirit out of there. I had to think fast. I knew you were fascinated by tidal waves, and you would trust me if I offered you the raft. This engaged your subconscious enough to construct the rest of your dream yourself. The things you saw on that long ocean journey were *your* doing. You have an imaginative dream-state, there, boy!"

"But how did you get me to the Island, send stuff, and then find us all the way out here?"

Eddie smiled, and looked at Roselin again. "Uhh, I can't tell you, at least not now, but I can say this much: Hum energy helped bring us both here. You might have noticed this region is on a slightly different plane of existence, a different reality, so to speak."

My mind was spinning. I remembered Louise and Roselin both mentioning a 'different plane of reality'.

Then I remembered that lit-up map. "So *you* made that glowing map with the blinking light?"

"Yes! What did you think of it? I'd never heard of this island until a few years ago, when I found an 'official' map of it at a junk shop. The coordinates on the map were accurate enough to help me program in your destination."

"Program?"

"It has to do with computers, but I needn't go into that."

"So the raft was guided by that oceans-map?"

"That's basically it, Gordy."

"So, it wasn't *all* a dream."

"Okay, maybe not," he smiled.

"So why did *you* come here?"

Roselin took a sip of her wine while staring off with a peculiar Cheshire-cat-like grin.

"I needed to be here," said Eddie. "Ever since I found that junk-store map, an inner voice said that someday I needed to see this place for myself. And there was more urgency when I became aware of your recent stress."

"And more will be revealed in time," added Roselin, still with that grin.

Ohh-kay.

Then I asked the scary question. "Could this Hum-force, or could *you,* ever send me back home, or somewhere else?"

Eddie took a sip of his wine. "I guarantee you'll never be sent anywhere ever again, except by your own choice! I don't see you having any more bardo-dreams."

"So I'm here for a reason?" I asked tentatively.

"You certainly must be," said Roselin. "And I'll remind you, Gordy, I'm deeply glad you're here, no matter how you accomplished the journey."

Blushing from Roselin's words, I had to ask Eddie, "Are you moving here, like, staying for good?"

Eddie shot a brief look at Roselin, then he turned to me. "I think so, Gordy. Before leaving California, I gave a lawyer-friend of mine the power to sell my house and make other arrangements in case I might not return. After you left, I had become more and more compelled to visit this place, especially knowing you were here!"

You came all this way because of _me_?

Roselin raised her glass. "Now, let's have a toast to getting this far."

PART V

HOME

Early the next morning, when I got up to pee, I didn't hear Eddie snoring as usual. But on my way to the outhouse, I heard low voices, then a giggle, from Roselin's tent.

Oh.

I'd never heard Roselin *giggle* before! I gave the tent a wide berth on my return to the hut.

Back in my sleeping bag, I could only speculate what the giggling meant! Too restless to sleep, I decided to get dressed, build up the fire, and make coffee. Roselin had shown me how to brew our dark-roast Fantasia coffee using her own special additives.

They soon walked in. "Ummm, thanks, Gordy—the coffee smells wonderful. Want some, Eddie?"

"Sure," said Eddie, "and how about breakfast? I suggest we have that mulloway, maybe with some eggs."

"Eggs?"

"Yes. I've been watching the petrel nests out there behind the beach, and I made a note of the ones that have new eggs in them. Feasting on some this once shouldn't hurt."

"I'd looove some eggs," said Roselin, and I nodded brightly in agreement.

As Eddie went out with a bowl, Roselin prepared the fish. "We eat this now or it goes to the crabs," she said, after giving it a good sniff.

*

Over breakfast and more coffee, Roselin looked at me with a kind of funny smile. She and Eddie were sitting close together on the little bench, holding hands. "Gordy, we have some plans to share with you," she said.

The giggling before and now this made me a bit wary. I slowly took another bite of the best scrambled eggs I'd had in ages.

"I'm listening."

"First of all, I've decided we've been on Gottfried long enough. Does that sound okay to you?"

"Yeah!" I smiled. No problem there.

Then Eddie said, "Remember what I told you about Hum-focused connection, no matter how far apart we are? Well, here is something else you should know. After you arrived on the raft, I continued to 'follow' your progress on the island. When you met Roselin, I could sense her very powerful Hum presence, though I didn't know who she was."

Whoa! I stared at him.

Roselin was looking off with that grin again.

Eddie continued. "Okay, fast-forward to my coming here. I knew where to find you, and, I must admit, I wanted to meet your friend. And I must say I'm glad I did!

"But before coming to Gottfried, I decided to spend some time in Putney to get to know what it's like here. In the train-station café near your Putney University, I overheard two students excitedly talking about an ancient library being allowed to stay in Putney. Apparently there had been a legal battle to prevent the library from being shipped to Moscow. Someone named Adeline Brewer had finally agreed to photograph the library on microfilm, and to accompany the film to Moscow for translation. One of the students said she was so relieved when Adeline had gone. This all came back to me once Roselin told me the story of why you two are here."

Whoa again!

I looked at both of them. "Does that mean we can go back?"

Roselin said, "Yes, Gordy, I believe it's safe enough now, especially with that Brewer woman off the Island."

"Ah."

"And as you might have discovered, Eddie and I have become, well, close."

I grinned while studying my plate. "Yeah, I noticed."

"And we have decided we want to spend some time together. I want to show Eddie my favorite places on the Island, and we want to help you get to where *you* would like to go."

"Ah…"

Then it sank in. I was not being invited along.

"So," Eddie said, "Where would you like to go? What would you like to do?"

I looked at both of them, dropped my fork and walked out.

*

On the windy beach, I walked fast, then ran, trying to shake off the pain and confusion.

It's happening again—rejected, shut out, alone. Crap!

At the far end of the cove, I stopped and flopped down on the sand, breathing hard. Flat on my belly, wrung out, angry, confused, I looked out at the mushy waves.

A lone gull walked on the sand a few feet away eyeing the piles of seaweed, ignoring me.

I stared at the horizon. The endless surf-sound began to soothe some of the pain.

Once my heart slowed down, my mind went strangely blank. My eyes closed and I was suddenly dreaming I was in a restaurant…

I'm in the noisy kitchen, full of busy cooks and waiters. I hear my mom's voice, but she is walking away from me through the crowd. She is saying something over her shoulder, but I can't understand her words through all the noise. I desperately want to hear what she is saying, but she only walks faster until I lose her. I panic at first, then I realize she is actually gone.

When it ended I woke right up. That gull was still there but I felt nothing, a void.

Then from far away, a faint new voice, almost singing, slowly brought me back to why I'd come out here.

Gorr-deeeee.

I refused to respond, but her lovely, teasing tone challenged my resistance. She approached and said softly, "May I join you?"

"I guess."

She lay down on the sand beside me, and looked at the ocean.

"Can I tell you something about me?"

I gave her the slightest nod, and continued watching the waves.

"I think we've both been looking for the same thing," she began. "For a long time, my research had been my 'home', the place I went to where I felt safe and whole. I was truly happy only when I was delving into something no one else knew about—and now we know where *that* got me."

I stared at the waves.

"What I'm trying to say, Gordy, is I think you and I are both looking for *love*, plain and simple. I realize that over the years I'd slowly given up loving or being loved until these last couple of weeks. And *you* helped me, do you know that?"

I turned toward her. Tears were running down her cheek.

"Do you know how *brave* you are? How, um, tenacious? You have earned my heart and trust, Gordy, and I can't say that for many people, except maybe Eddie…"

We both looked out at the surf for a while.

"But you guys want to leave me," I said.

She sighed.

"Look at me, Gordy. This is only a short trip—a kind of test for a couple of weeks to see if Eddie and I really like each other. Then afterward we, or maybe just I, want to meet up with you and talk about some things that have been on my mind, but I need to know where you'll be."

"I have no idea where I'll be 'cause I don't think anyone wants me!"

"Oh, stop it," she said. "I've seen you with Janie, and I think you are both very lucky she found you back there at the Soviet base. She told me how scared you were then, and how good a friend you've been to her."

"But she doesn't really want me…she likes girls!"

"Ahh, but she definitely wants you as a friend. Yes, she has an eye for women, and she's still trying to find her way, like you are. I saw her drama with Estelle back in Covenmoor, and I knew Janie would have challenges with her relationships. I wasn't surprised when she ran off with Vermilion. Perhaps that will work out. But *you*, in case you don't know it, are a reliable refuge for her to come back to…you'll see her again before long!"

A refuge?

I thought of Lane, and of the only place she would be able to find me.

I knew where I wanted to go.

*

When we returned to the hut, Eddie was waiting on the bench outside the door, a big sigh of relief on his face.

"Sorry I walked out," I said. "Can I still finish my eggs?"

We all sat down.

"I think the best place for me is Gifford," I told them. "I'll have my *boot* to stay in, and that's the address I gave Lane."

With that arch in her brow, she said, "Ah, yes, I noticed how close you two were getting."

I felt my ears warming up. "Yeah, she's a different friend than Janie."

"Okay, then Gifford it is," said Roselin. "And I want you to know you're part of us now, and don't forget it!"

I smiled at my eggs, then looked up at both of them.

"I won't!"

Then Eddie placed a small stack of coins on the table and said, "I don't know how long your journey to Gifford will be, so take these rogers for meals and lodging until you get there."

I was stunned. "Wow, thanks Eddie! I'll pay you back some time, I promise."

"And your letters from your brother should be there."

"Yeah, that's right! I can't wait to read them."

"Back in California, Ricky showed me *your* letters. He and I were both fascinated by your experiences here, and he was extremely glad to know you were all right."

This made me choke up. *I'm so glad I wrote to him.*

"Um, when will we be leaving?"

"After breakfast, if you'd like," said Eddie.

"As in now?"

"Start packing!"

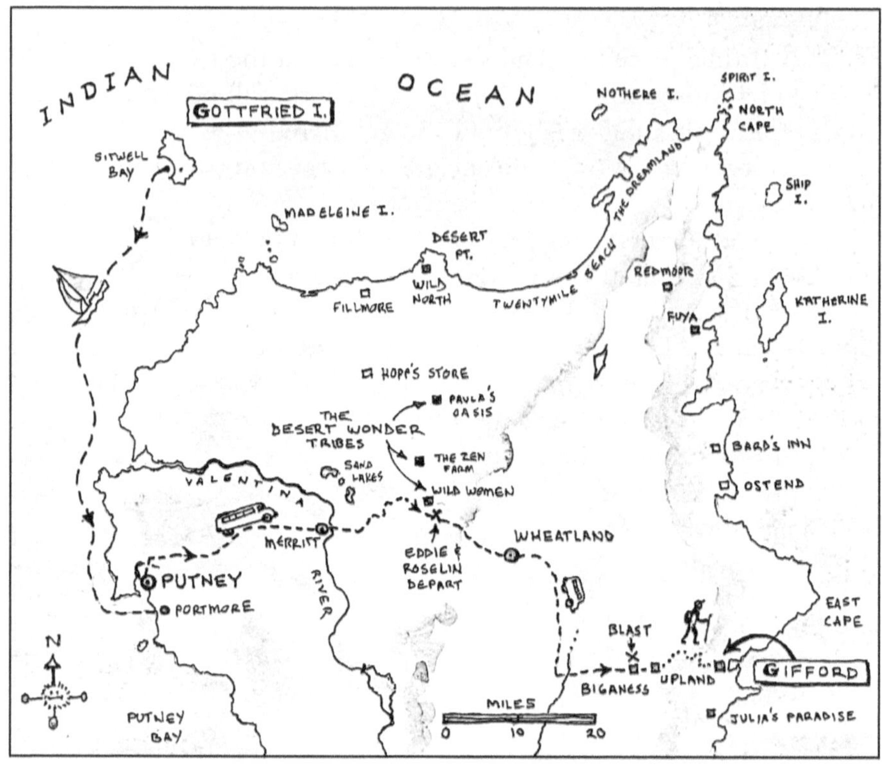

From Gottfried to Gifford—by sail, bus and on foot.

We had spent almost three months on Gottfried Island. I felt funny about leaving it, but I was more than ready to say goodbye to this strange, bleak and beautiful place.

I felt compelled to straighten up our hut by filling the wood-box, sweeping the floor, and putting everything, including some well-read comics, back in the cupboard. Pulling the front door firmly shut, I found a sprig (Janie's word) of fresh heather and stuck it in the crack between the door and the frame.

I took one more look around at this place of barren hills and pale sky, then picked up my dusty backpack.

Eddie and Roselin had already carried everything else to Eddie's sailboat. When I caught up to them, they were chuckling.

"What?" I asked.

"You'll make a good housewife." said Roselin.

"Well, I'm glad I did it, because I found this big bar of Fantasia dark chocolate in the back of the cupboard. I *might* share some if you're nice to me."

After we pushed the boat into the water and climbed in, Roselin said, "Okay, I'll be nice to you, Gordy. Now hand over some of that chocolate."

"I'll be nice, too," said Eddie.

"Okay, okay."

Once the wind had found us, Eddie handled the tiller and the sails with ease. "A frisky breeze and a following sea should get us to Portmore by this evening," he said. "That's where I rented the boat."

I watched Gottfried Island slowly fade into its own pale mist.

That place may or may not be cursed, but it must be haunted—I can think of no other way to explain its weirdness.

Gottfried was finally out of sight when Roselin said, "I've been studying the bus schedules Eddie so thoughtfully brought with him."

Giving Eddie a quick look, she continued. "From downtown Putney we can catch the overland Islebus and ride together to the Wild Women tribe, in the Dickle Hills. Eddie and I will get off there, and the bus will take you on to Wheatland, Gordy. There you'll catch a local jitney-bus to Outpost, the end of the line. From Outpost you'll have to walk the Outland Path to Gifford. Sound okay?"

"Uh, okay. I won't get lost, will I?"

"No. If you have doubts about directions out there, just ask someone. The Outland Path is the only way from Outpost to Gifford."

"So why are you going to stop at, um, Wild Women? And what *is* that?"

She took Eddie's hand. "I'm going to show Eddie the Desert Wonder Tribes. We'll stay a night at Wild Women. That place is more rumor than fact. It's a travelers' resort, but it's actually whatever you want to make of it. They are very accommodating," she said with a playful wink.

"From there we'll hike the Sheffield Path through the desert to The Zen Farm, a Buddhist organic-farming school, then to Pascal's, then all the way to Paula's Oasis, the loveliest hot springs spa there is, in my opinion. You'll love it, Eddie!"

Eddie rolled his eyes a little. "Roselin has been telling me a lot about these tribes."

"Then we'll continue on to meet up with you," said Roselin, "but only after we visit Roger's Dreamland."

"Oh, Eddie," I said, "You'll like that place! Janie, Louise and I stopped there on our way to meet Roselin."

"That's enough Gordy. I want that to be a surprise."

*

Just south of the Valentina River estuary we sailed along the coast as we headed for Putney. Eddie enjoyed skippering the little sloop. The breeze stayed fresh, the sky was no longer hazy, the temperature delightful. We enjoyed riding over the broad swells, and braving the occasional splash of salt-spray. Roselin let her hair fly in the wind, while I held on to my well-worn bush hat, which made me think of Janie.

Just before sunset, Eddie eased the boat alongside the rental dock in Portmore harbor, just south of Putney. We were windburned and hungry. The boat's owner, a round-bellied gent wearing a faded Imperial Russian captain's cap, helped us tie up.

"I see ya found yer castaways, Mr. Barnes."

"Yes I did! These are my friends Roselin and Gordy."

"Pleased to meetcha both." He said then added, "Say, after ya left, I pondered on how familiar yer looked. Then I realized, yer the very likeness of Mr. Putney on our ten-pence stamp!"

"Is that so?" Eddie said.

"Yup."

While we lugged our gear to a pedicab, Roselin said, "My friend Kate told me the Makepeace Hotel recently opened, and it's just across the street from the Fantasia Market, where we can resupply. She says the hotel was once a Russian bureaucrat's mansion that was gutted by a fire. Now it's fully restored, a lovely place. The staff is discreet, and I want a hotel *now*—I could really use a bath."

"And food!" I said.

"I think that settles it," said Eddie, visibly amused.

At the Makepeace reception desk, he checked us in as "Edward Barnes and family." Roselin was delighted when the breezy young woman at the counter merely smiled and readily gave us two adjoining rooms, payment in cash, no need for IDs.

The one-time mansion was indeed elegant. We were awed by the dramatic lighting in the lobby and hallways, while Eddie-the-carpenter admired the intricate pine woodwork. Near the stairs, a hearty roast-chicken aroma drifted in from the dining room.

After cleaning up, we quickly headed back down for supper. Candles in sconces illuminated the vaulted ceilings and cozy booths. Exhausted from the long day, we hardly said a word.

*

Breakfast was buffet-style, and what a delight after all those clams! I loaded up on eggs, bangers and mash, and even cereal with milk. At our table, we discussed what to buy for our (varying) overland trips.

Roselin said, "Whatever we don't want to carry, we should drop off at the Melville Charities shop next to the Fantasia Market. And if we split up, don't forget that our bus leaves at 1:30!"

At nine a.m. sharp we were at the Fantasia Market just as the huge doors opened. *Now I'll finally get to see this place I've been hearing about!* As we walked in, the main concourse seemed endless. Specialty shops lined both sides, filled with everything imaginable that one could need. Narrower side aisles led off to more, tinier, shops.

"Look at that ironwork!" Eddie said as he gazed at the high arched ceiling.

I enjoyed the rising murmur of voices echoing through the vast hall, such a change from our months of isolation.

So many people, so much going on!

"Okay boys," said Roselin, "It's time to get our start shopping—that is, Eddie, if you're willing to spring for it." She sidled up to his ear, "I'll make it up to you with massages and herbal remedies."

"Sure," said Eddie, grinning.

Just before noon we made it back to our hotel, stowed our purchases in our rooms, and immediately headed downstairs for an early lunch.

Sitting in a booth tucked in the corner, Roselin was quiet while Eddie and I chatted on. Finally, she said, "Something's been on my mind."

We both looked at her.

"I must do one more thing before we leave Putney. I need to deliver the original Ur translation sheet to my old professor."

"Professor Broadmoor?" I asked.

"Yes, I've always felt uncomfortable holding onto it in the first place, and I want to at least give him the means to translate the rest of the Ur library. What do you think, guys?"

"Um, why now?" said Eddie.

"Because I'm so relieved the library will remain in Putney! Perhaps if Broadmoor can translate it, he might redeem his stature."

Now I was worried. "Won't it be risky just marching in there and giving it to him?"

"And what if you were caught and then forced to hand over the Codex?" said Eddie. "Someone may still be watching that library."

Roselin looked down and muttered, "Yesss, you both have a point."

Our lunch arrived, and when the waiter left, she said, "But I have the sheet right here with me, and I want to do it anyway—it's important!"

We continued eating in silence.

"I know this is risky," she continued, "but I need you two to trust me. Eddie, would you please finish packing for me? And Gordy, I've already separated out my old clothes for the charities shop, so would you bundle those for me and donate them? I'm going to hire a 'cab to take me to the University, drop off the translation sheet, then head straight to the station. I promise I'll meet you two before 1:30."

And then she was gone.

We sat looking at each other, a bit stunned. "No arguing with a determined witch," he said.

We returned to our rooms to sort and pack. Though I was thrilled with all my new gear, I worried about Roselin.

Please don't get caught!

Ready to travel, we donated our old stuff, and Roselin's, to the Melville Charities shop, as instructed. From there we marched to the nearby bus terminal. Eddie and I traded off hauling Roselin's backpack—it weighed a lot more than mine! He and I both checked her inner storage pockets to make sure her notebooks and the Codex were there.

When we reached the station, I was nearly sick with worry about Roselin, and, like Eddie, I was straining my neck to catch sight of her. Above the entrance, a big sign read **OSTROVNYYE AVTOBUS**, and below it **ISLE-BUS**. The crowded terminal smelled of diesel exhaust and deep-fried fish from the cafeteria.

Eddie pointed to a small sign saying **BILETI-TICKETS**. "Let's just wait over there and hope Roselin finds us."

The big clock above the ticket windows already said 1:23. Eddie bought our tickets as we continued scanning the crowd for Roselin, with no luck. Then someone in a hooded monk's robe drifted up beside us and said, *"Boo!"*

Eddie and I both jumped. The hood came down and Roselin said, "Hi guys! It all went well! I'm running over to the ladies' loo to get this off. See you in a minute."

He and I looked at each other. *We can breathe again.*

At 1:28 she was back, wearing hiking shorts and a new shirt, sleeves rolled up. No gown this time. Eddie and I watched as she approached us with that confident-gliding walk of hers. She said to Eddie, "Have you bought our tickets yet?"

*

We boarded a Russian-built Zis-16 *avtobus* bound for Wheatland. I knew this from a picture featured on the timetable. The driver had already shut the luggage doors when we ran up. He gave us an annoyed look, and with a sigh pulled one of them open again, tossed in our backpacks and punched our tickets.

When we found our seats, Roselin said, "Compared to some of the buses I've ridden, this one is nice. The Soviets 'donate' old wrecks that barely run, but we Islanders fix them up and keep them going. They just started this ten years ago. There were no busses when I went to school here, only pedicabs. But there were no diesel fumes either—Putney smelled better then!"

Our bus finally rolled out of the downtown terminal, leaving a dense cloud of black smoke. "See?" Said Roselin.

As we stretched out on the surprisingly comfy seats, Eddie looked at her and said, "So, how did it go?"

"Fine!" she whispered. "I'll tell you more later."

I was happy to have a window seat, right behind Roselin and Eddie. Across the aisle sat a young woman holding a squirming toddler, who paused to look intently into my eyes. I smiled and he grinned back before playfully burying his face into his mother's neck. I turned to watch Putney's neighborhoods glide by.

Within a few minutes the bus stopped at Ramside station, where more passengers got on.

Ah, Adeline Brewer's old neighborhood.

When the last houses in Ramside receded from view, I felt a relief. We were safely out of Putney once again.

We rode over bone-dry hills, then descended into a hazy, flat, irrigated valley. The bus stopped at places called New Russ, Drain (*odd name*), and Scotia before reaching a bus-and-train depot in downtown Merritt. There we had a twenty-minute rest stop. The bus-station smells hit us once more as we walked in.

"I'm hungry again," Said Roselin.

Eddie bought fish-and-chips and fruit salads in the cafeteria. For drinks, we all looked over the variety of bottled sodas in a cooler, and I said, "What is *Kvass*?"

"Believe it or not," said Roselin, "It's a favorite Russian soda, made of fermented rye bread."

"Ewww."

"I'll try it," said Eddie, "and you can take a sip."

"You'd probably like the Leninade," said Roselin.

"*Leninade*? Is that like lemonade?"

"Sort-of. It's sweet and tastes like your American Seven-Up."

I brightened. "Okay, I'll try it. So, how do you know about Seven-Up?"

"Well, when I was a student at Putney U., a few cases marked 'Leninade' were mysteriously delivered to the dining hall, and the bottles inside were Seven-Up, bottled in Green Bay, Wisconsin! I think an alumnus living in Australia sent it. We all loved it, and those bottles are collectors' items now."

We spotted a table whose occupants were leaving. Once we were settled, Roselin leaned in toward Eddie and me.

"I apologize for bolting out on you at lunch, and I'll make this quick. I knew I needed to blend in on campus, and I found the robe for eighty pence at the Melville Charities shop. All the professors wear them, and no one paid a bit of attention to me.

"I then marched right into Broadmoor's office, and he was there, amidst his clutter, pouring some strong-looking tea. When he looked up, he asked, 'Would you like a cup?' as if he was expecting me! I said, 'Yes, thank you,' and we sat down together stirring in milk and sugar like we were old colleagues.

"Without another word, I handed over the single vellum sheet, and it was such a relief! As soon as he looked at it his mouth fell open, and I could tell he knew exactly what it was. Then I said, 'I owe you this. Now I must begone…enjoy your day!' and I left."

I looked at her, "You actually said 'begone'?" And Eddie said, "You did the right thing. I'm just glad you made it back in time. Are you sure no one recognized you?"

"No one did, and I'm glad I wore the robe, with the hood up, because Broadmoor's student, Janelle, passed me in the hallway."

Ah.

Our bus was called.

Before we got up to go, Roselin reached for my hands, and gave me an intense look I wouldn't soon forget. "I'm going to miss you Gordy. We'll be getting off soon, and you'll be on your own. Remember to change buses in Wheatland, and be sure to carry enough water when you start walking. There isn't much civilization out that way."

I didn't want to be reminded of our splitting apart, and I was very unsure about traveling alone across this Island.

What if they just go on their merry way and never try to find me? What if I get lost, or robbed?

What if… What if…

"I'm still feeling weird about this," I said. "Is it really okay to travel alone?"

Roselin said, "I assure you, it's safe. Islanders know the Rule of Payback."

"Payback?"

"Yes. 'Do unto the Universe (and other people) as you would have the Universe (and other people) do unto you.'"

"Oh."

"Nature is what you want to be aware of, Gordy, so carry that water, and try to stay out of nasty weather."

"That sounds easy enough."

"And it won't be long before we find you in Gifford, I promise," she added.

"And I'd like to see what you built there!" Eddie said.

"Yes, I'd like that too," I said. "Your carpentry lessons really helped."

A long, loud honk prompted us to board our bus. Again, we were the last ones on, and the driver gave us another look.

Leaving Merritt, the bus crossed an impressive stone-arch bridge over a sandy-bottomed river. People were swimming in the mid-day heat, and I wished I could join them (the bus was not air-conditioned). Roselin turned around in her seat, "That's the Valentina River, which flows out of the Highlands. You might see its headwaters later on."

Busses, Highlands, headwaters, long walks…

Just beyond the small town of Valentina, the road began to curve among some hills, and we stopped at a place called Davoo. Three young guys in wide-brimmed bush hats and very short shorts showing off their tanned legs passed our seats to get off. Roselin gave them an admiring look before informing me they would likely be trekking north to the Sand Lakes, a series of spring-fed ponds nestled among some giant sand dunes.

I felt a pull to join them, even to *be* one of them—they seemed so confident.

Then the road headed into a steep canyon. The driver shifted down to his lowest gear as the bus negotiated increasingly sharp curves and a brutal uphill grade. The road appeared to have no shoulder or guardrails. I tried not to look down. Then I remembered one thing Mom told me about riding on mountain roads: *just relax into the curves, don't fight 'em!* The cooler air coming in the open window helped, so I more or less enjoyed the ride. Roselin and Eddie, who often turned to check on me, were hanging on with varied expressions.

Deep in the upper part of the canyon, the bus came to a wheezing halt at a stone roadside shelter. Beyond it a narrow dirt trail twisted among some trees. There were no signs, and no words from the driver.

"This is where we get off," Roselin said. "I promise we'll see you in Gifford as *soon* as we can."

"Hold on," I said, and followed them outside. As the driver pulled their packs out from the hold, I hugged Eddie and Roselin and then Eddie again. It just felt right.

Seeing them walk away left a big hole in me.

Whoa—my first time here on my own.

*

Back in my seat, the bus lurched and careened with slow progress. We passed several stopped trucks and one old car with a hissing overheated engine, its occupants waiting nervously. Otherwise our ascent through the canyon was uneventful.

At the top of the grade, the bus stopped where a sign said…

THE OLD GLENEAGLES INN

…and everyone was allowed to get off for fifteen minutes. The inn sat on a rocky outcrop, and the view was like no other. Beyond the canyon lay the hazy green valley we had crossed. Beyond that lay more hills, then a bit of Putney, then the distant ocean. Squinting , I saw what might be Gottfried Island—a tiny pale silhouette on the horizon.

"Bus is leaving!"

The now-familiar Highlands stretched to infinity. Distant mesas spread out before us, reminding me of cowboy movies. What a change! The bus stopped briefly in Dundee, a quiet store-and-tavern settlement, where I only saw a few cats.

The bus finally arrived at its destination in Wheatland, just as the sun was setting. My connecting jitney-bus to Upland wouldn't be leaving until 7:15 the next morning! I knew this from the schedule, but I didn't want to face the idea of finding a place to stay for the night.

Now I had to.

I wish Janie were here—she knows how to find these places.

After retrieving my backpack, I wandered along the town's single commercial street, radiant in the deep orange glow of the setting sun.

Wheatland appeared to be aggressively supported by the Soviet Agriculture Union. Bright posters of happy, muscular men and women working in fields alongside eachother were tacked up everywhere. Several trucks and tractors were parked here and there, but no one was on the streets. The town looked as brown and dusty as the surrounding fields.

A restaurant fronted with tall, old-fashioned windows offered a welcoming glow in the growing darkness. As I entered, a hefty woman nodded a greeting and let me drop my pack just inside the door. She motioned me to a table, handed me a menu in both Russian and English, and waited. I pointed to the 'Hamburg and Chips' and the Leninade. While waiting I looked around at the faded floral wallpaper and the rough dining furniture, all dimly lit by oil-lamps. I felt I was in a different century.

For some reason, a deep sadness overwhelmed me. Was it this dining room? The tinny music on the Russian radio station? The smell of strange foods, or the two rough-looking men at that other table glancing at me?

All this traveling was wearing me down. I couldn't help but rest my head on my arms, feeling tired and…*dismantled.*

And maybe also feeling sorry for myself?

But then a plate was noisily dropped in front of my nose, and a fizzing bottle with a glass was set next to my ear, and the woman said, "*Kushat!* That means 'Eat'!"

I quickly sat up.

The 'hamburg' smelled delicious! Multiple layers of lettuce and tomato slices on top of a fat juicy beef patty on an open-faced toasted bun of dark bread with a load of mayonnaise—perfect! There was even ketchup on the side for the crispy brown potato-wedge 'chips'.

My meal was soon gone, and I felt a lot less *dismantled.* The place wasn't busy, so I opened up the maps and bus schedules Eddie had given me. To put off finding a place to sleep, I asked for another bottle of Leninade, which I was growing attached to.

When I paid the woman, who seemed to be the entire dining room staff, I asked her about lodging by pantomiming my head sleeping on my hands. She smiled, led me outside and pointed me to an inn on the next corner. "Soft beds! Good bath!" she said in a husky voice. I impulsively shook her hand and had left what I hoped was a good tip.

At first, I felt energized from supper, but when I walked into the grandly named Hotel Caledonia, I began feeling a shivery chill, and it wasn't from the evening coolness. When I dinged the bell, a thin girl of about twelve, with pale skin and frizzy dark hair, appeared through a once-pink curtain. While she took my money, a meaty-spicy aroma drifted in from behind her. "Your room is down that hall. The bath and toilet are a little further." Then she gave me a thin-lipped smile along with a key. The room number on the key tag said…

108

That's the street address of my house back home!

The chill intensified.

With every step I took down the hall, the floorboards creaked under a worn carpet runner, which for some reason added to my unease.

Something is very odd here.

At the door marked 108, I set down my pack and took a long, deep breath, turned the key in the lock, and slowly pushed open the door.

I fumbled for the light switch. When it came on, I froze.

My heart started pounding. I slowly glanced up at the frosted-glass ceiling light, then to the tan-painted walls, the brown furniture, the closet door, the wind-up alarm clock. They were identical to those in…*my old bedroom!*

All sense of reality disappeared. I was back where I was at that awful moment when I last saw Mom.

Am I having another bardo dream? Will it take me back home? Am I there already?

All my sirens were going off as I breathlessly took a step into the room and peeked around the door. Above the bed's headboard, the Hawaii poster with the giant wave *wasn't* there on the wall! In its place was a framed tourist poster titled, "The Putney-Kronstadt Express Passing Mount Hayes."

Oh!

Okaaay...

The Putney-Kronstadt Express Passing Mount Hayes

I needed some air.

I dropped my pack, locked the door, and marched out the front entrance as quickly as I could. I desperately needed to shake off this creepy déjà vu!

I walked and walked without thinking. The sun had long set, but a rising fat moon lit the way. I wandered past grain-storage towers and more farm equipment, beyond the end of the main street, which had now become a dirt path. I eventually stopped to look at a farm house, lit inside by a single lamp. In the yard a few scraggly gum trees rustled in the cold wind. This is so far from, well, *everything* I've known. How would it be to live here, in a farm-town run by the Soviet Agriculture

Union, on this Island in the Indian Ocean, and on a possibly different plane of reality?

This stuff could put me around the bend—but I'm not gonna let it!

When I returned, room 108 was just a hotel room, not very similar to my old bedroom at all. The spell had lifted! To soak off the lingering chill I took a long hot bath in the tub down the hall. Teeth brushed, sleepshirt on, I then got out one of my printed-in-Putney novels and went to bed.

I slept well enough.

*

The alarm clock worked! I was up and packed with plenty of time to have breakfast at that same tall-window café. The local jitney, whose sign above the windshield said UPLAND, was waiting nearby. The bus's age was disguised with a fresh coat of red and green paint on the outside and a warm cream inside. I could still smell the oil-based enamel. Behind the driver were school-bus style bench seats, plus a long seat across the back.

I was the only passenger until a dozen lower-school kids got on, accompanied by their teacher. They soon settled quietly into their seats, hardly making a sound. I guessed they weren't quite awake yet.

The driver hopped in, and the bus sputtered to life just as the early-morning sun blazed into the windows. We were soon rolling over the flat landscape.

The settlement of Edith consisted of three buildings, one of them a bookstore. I wanted to go in there, but the driver had only stopped to deliver and pick up the mail.

Next was the town of Highland Center, looking quite similar to Wheatland—more grain towers, farm machinery, dust and posters. "Change here for Eyremoor, Oakland and Kofu," announced the driver as he pulled up to a café and parked next to an even older-looking jitney. When no one responded, he stepped out to drop off and pick up more mail. Then with a grinding of gears, he took us south on a road that was thinly paved, and barely one lane wide.

Eucalyptus, er, gum trees were clustered in the distance to my left, and I suspected they might be growing beside a creek. I also noticed the tallest among them were flat-topped, as if they were somehow sheared off.

We reached a flag stop with only a sign that read **BESTWAY**, from which a dirt path led toward the distant trees. Two wild-haired young men with large backpacks were waiting by the sign. They got on, and walked by me to the back seat, trailed by a strong musky odor. All the school kids' eyes were on them. One child held her nose and said "Eww," winning a sharp glare from her teacher.

The bus soon crossed the suspected creek through a shady glen of more sheared-off trees. A little sign stated this was (once again) the Valentina River, though here it was barely a trickle.

The next village was Feltwell, and everything looked a little off—some of the buildings were damaged, and were now being rebuilt with those same compressed-sand blocks I'd seen over much of the Island. The surrounding trees looked like a giant mower had snapped off the foliage above fifteen feet.

While the bus was stopped, the teacher moved up and said, "I'm Lorna Babcock. Mind if I sit?"

"Ah, sure." I scooted over. "I'm Gordon Love."

She smiled and said, "We're on our way to see the Biganess blast site."

The blast! I forgot all about that.

I tried to sound nonchalant. "Oh…the blast. Is the bus going near there?"

"Yes," she said. "I'm bringing my earth-science class on a field trip to the site, where we'll try to decipher what caused the explosion. It's a kind of detective assignment where the kids will look at the evidence and then write reports."

Then she turned to her charges. "All of you, look at me and listen carefully. When we get to Biganess, we'll get off the bus and walk about a half-mile to the site of the explosion. Do NOT forget to bring your lunches, water and notebooks. There are no shops or facilities in Biganess. In fact, the tribe has suffered greatly, so I must remind you to be courteous to anyone you see there. Smile and wave if you wish, but do not gawk! Any questions?"

Would she believe me if I told her what caused it?

There were no questions from her students, and she turned back around.

"I'm curious," she said rather directly, "What brings *you* this way? I'm always interested to hear travelers' tales."

"I'm on my way to Gifford."

"Are you now?" I've never been down there. I hear it's quite a journey on foot from here. You know this bus only goes to Upland and then turns around, right?"

"Oh yes, I found that out in Putney when my friends and I bought tickets. They got off at a tribe called Wild Women."

Lorna Babcock lifted her eyebrows briefly, then she looked away with a hint of disapproval.

"Well," she said, "I hope they are prepared for the, uh, *activities* there, and I hope they're older than you seem to be."

"Oh yes, much older. They're just stopping there on their way to the Desert Wonder Tribes—a kind of walkabout."

"I see," she said.

I decided to drop the subject.

The bus started up again and turned left onto a one-track dirt road, leaving Feltwell behind. The trees and wheat fields gave way to rolling hills of wild grasses and millions of wildflowers. Scattered white dots in the distance turned out to be sheep. Alongside another creek a few white-barked gums had also been sheared off but were already sprouting new growth. I was glad to see these hills—better than that tedious flatness!

According to my Islebus map, we were approaching a flag-stop called Toseland. This place was nearly leveled, but many houses were already being rebuilt. Lorna's students had turned quiet as they looked out at the near-devastation. But then, standing along the edge of the dusty street, two toddlers waved wildly at the bus. Lorna's pupils waved back at them with equal energy, as if they were the first humans they'd seen in weeks. Once again, the driver hopped out to exchange mail bags.

*

A few bumpy, dusty miles later the bus stopped at what was once Biganess. We were all stunned. The village had been obliterated. Nothing was left but a few jagged tree stumps, cement floors with no walls, and rubble swept into piles. No one appeared to meet the bus, and there was no mail, but the driver wasn't surprised. "Haven't seen a soul in weeks," he said. "I stop here on every run anyway. Yer just never know."

One of the kids said, "There's nobody here at *all!* I thought I'd at least see people with bandaged heads and crutches."

"Jeffrey, that's enough!" said Lorna.

On an impulse, I got off with the school group to see the site for myself. When I asked the driver if I could take something out of my backpack, he said, "I'll not be able to take yer to Upland, then."

"That's okay, I'll walk there. I see it's only a couple of miles."

"Ah, yes, it's not that far. I'll drop yer pack there if you'd like."

"Oh, that would be great. Thanks!"

I needed a brisk walk just to stretch my legs, and it was a relief to carry only my little snack-and-water bag.

About ten minutes later I reached it—a shallow crater several hundred yards across, with a tiny hole in its center. The intense heat had fried the surrounding ground. There was no trace of plant life, and I was walking over what appeared to be solid glass! Roselin had said that the temperature of the 'event' was likely in the millions of degrees, enough to easily melt the sandy soil. Now I saw what she meant.

Surrounded by a chain-link fence, the hole was only about a foot wide. I Looked into it—weird spiral grooves along its edges disappeared into a darkness that left me shuddering. *This hole is more than creepy!*

I had to look away. It was not a pretty place.

Soon the excited chattering of Lorna Babcock's students drifted over the hill, and I moved away from the little enclosure. She was already warning them not to push against the fence, lest the blast-hole swallow them up! I pictured a small, thin child getting stuck in it. *Ooh, not good.*

I waved goodbye to Lorna and her class, and began picking my way around scattered blast debris and then east over some higher hills. As I made my way to Upland, thoughts about Roselin and Eddie flitted through my head like little butterflies.

I wonder how they are doing?

Did they really not know each other before?

And what will Roselin do with the Codex?

My mind wouldn't rest until I spotted some buildings ahead.

The village and the surrounding trees seemed to have escaped the blast, probably protected by these hills. Apparently this was Upland, and the bus was still there.

A few people were milling around the combination general-store, bus station, café and tavern that made up most of the town. The driver was punching tickets for another outdoorsy couple bearing towering backpacks much bigger than mine.

I waved to the driver, fetched my waiting pack, and kept walking right into the café. It was after lunch, but the fellow in the kitchen said he'd serve up a bowl of home-made lamb stew, if that would suit me.

I said it would, and then I asked him if there might be a room available for the night.

"Aye…in a sense." the man said. "Miss Renwalt rents rooms, breakfast included, but supper is extra. Her place is on the path toward the coast. It's the only house out by the radio tower, about four-miles from here, and I'd recommend her supper! O'course I'm assuming yer heading that way, to the coast I mean."

"Oh yes, I'm definitely heading to the coast."

The stew was accompanied by a chunk of fresh home-made bread, and was more than satisfying. I paid the cook for my meal and a Leninade I had pulled out of the cooler.

A full-stomach lethargy led me to a bench outside the café, where I sat beside my pack and finished my now-preferred drink. The street was empty, the jitney-bus gone. I barely noticed the lowering sun or the returning evening chill. Something inside me was going on, again. Something that felt *not finished*.

I left the bottle on the bench for a kid to cash in—ten-penny deposits here! I hefted my heavy pack once again, and walked east out of Upland. At the edge of the settlement a hand-lettered sign read…

This is the OUTLAND PATH
to Uva Glen, Elsinore, Gifford, and So On

…all under a fat red arrow pointing straight up.

I was glad to see 'Gifford' on the sign, and I liked the 'and So On'.

Beyond the sign the scrubby land became flat and soon dark. A fat moon again rose in the eastern sky surrounded by a ghostly glow. The dry grass twitched in the chilly wind.

The *not finished* feeling returned and grew stronger, creepier and weird—I mean *weirdly* weird. Tiny worms seemed to be eating what was left of my consciousness.

Then I was overwhelmed by a helpless, terrifying feeling of falling into something like that blast-hole.

What is happening?

I stumbled off the path, the whole world tilting. *Is this what they mean by vertigo?* My pack seemed to slide off on its own, I found myself on the ground, curled up on my side, arms tight around my shoulders, breathing hard, random bits of thoughts flashing. With my face an inch from the dirt, I felt like I'd never get up again.

Out of nowhere a familiar cigarette-raspy voice said,

Get up.

What?

Get…UP!

I tried to look around, but still felt stubbornly paralyzed.

I see you there, so stop this groveling. Get up, and go to that place you're staying tonight.

Where was this coming from? It sounded so real.

You can't be doing this and I won't stand for it. Now listen to me!

I recognized a familiar disappointed sigh, then…

Gordy, this is the last time I'll say this: I loved you and your brother and I always will—you have to know that! You boys were everything to me, but I couldn't hang on. I was mad at the world—furious and grieving about so many things that didn't involve you or Ricky.

Another familiar sigh…

None of what happened was your fault, or Ricky's. All I know now is that certain things are meant to happen, and you are *meant to move on with your life, right <u>here</u>, right <u>now</u>. So goddammit, get* UP!

That tone of absolute authority did it. I had no choice. The worms quickly disappeared.

Okay, okay, I'm getting up now…Mom!

*

Feeling very stiff and slow at first, yet sensing a kind of lightness, I stood up, slapped off the dirt, hoisted my pack and set off. I floated along with wonder at what had just happened.

The rising moon lit the way.

Sometime later I reached a blocky, flat-roofed two-story stone house standing next to a tall steel tower. A muffled engine put-putted near the tower's base. No sign of any blast damage.

Well, here it is.

Under a long veranda roof, the big front window cast an inviting warm glow. A porch light illuminated two rocking chairs and a wide front door. By now I was getting more comfortable knocking on doors inquiring about rooms. I liked this wide-open Islander friendliness toward strangers.

When I rang a hand-crank bell, the door opened almost immediately.

"Uh, Miss Renwalt? I was told you might have a room available."

She briefly looked me over, then replied, "Yes I do," in that innkeeper-welcoming way. She stood tall and thin with slightly graying hair, and a relaxed smile on her tanned face. She gestured me through the door, "Come in, come in!"

Her living room was warmly lit with both electric and oil lamps. Classical music (Tchaikovsky?) was playing on her radio. "I serve breakfast at seven, and would you like some supper?" Before I could answer, she picked up an oil lamp and led me through more rooms and into a hallway. Colorful rag rugs in various sizes were spread out over the floors. Through one door I caught sight of a large loom surrounded by baskets of fabric scraps and old clothing. "Please don't mind all my rug-weaving claptrap. This is what I do."

I marveled at her work-in-progress, and the clutter that went with it. "It looks fascinating."

"First, I'll show you your room, and then I'll put out some supper. I hope you like toasted cheese-and-sausage sandwiches."

"Um, yes…that sounds good."

The stew I had eaten back in Upland had long worn off, so her sandwiches, though unusual-sounding, had my vote.

I followed her upstairs to a still-sun-warmed, pleasantly furnished bedroom. It smelled faintly of lavender and other herbs, similar to Miss Renwalt herself. I sensed a quiet elegance about her. She could have been fifty, but with her hint of aloofness, she did not seem the grandmotherly, nor even the motherly type.

Two large muscular cats with gorgeous striped coats wandered into the room, and allowed me to pet them as they twirled around my legs.

"You enjoy the presence of kitties, I hope?"

"Oh, yes, we had them back home."

"Well, don't be fooled by these two. This one is Bonnie, and that one is Butch. They are eigers, an indigenous species, distantly related to craig's tigers, and if you threaten them, or threaten me in any way, Bonnie will have her fangs in your neck before you know what hit you!"

My eyes went wide.

"But don't worry," she smiled. "Treat us nicely and you'll be fine. And may I assume you will be staying?"

Bonnie made me hesitate, but only for a second. "Yes."

She offered both hands, Islander style. "I'm Angela Renwalt, and I'm pleased to meet you."

I took her hands. "I'm Gordon Love, er, Gordy."

"Ahh, I like 'Gordy'."

Then she tilted her head at me. "I've noticed your accent. So where might your home be, young man?"

That question again.

This time I decided to simplify things. "Well, home used to be in California, but now I live in Gifford. Long story."

"Ah," she said as she nodded with a tilted eyebrow, then shooed the cats out of the room. "In case you're wondering, that noise outside is the transmitter generator. I turn it off at nine, and let the battery take over."

Ah, that explains the electric lights.

Back in the kitchen, she offered me a chair as she prepared the promised sandwich, which she served with a bowl of miso soup and seasoned rice crackers. The soup brought me right back to the Japanese fishing villages.

Angela sat down with her own bowl of soup to join me. "I get my miso ingredients and these crackers from my friends down in Nichiwan, north of Gifford. I'm glad you like it."

I nodded while I kept an eye on the 'kitties' who crouched nearby, paws tucked in, eyes only slits, but ears alert.

"I've had a fair number of travelers stop by here," she continued, "but none from California, USA! I know our Russian friends don't take kindly to Americans these days."

"Yeah, the Soviet Navy asked me a lot of questions."

She smiled, and raised both eyebrows this time "So may I ask how you came to be here?"

I let out a sigh.

"I came here…uh, I was *sent* here, I think, by a friend of mine back in California."

Something in the way she was looking at me made me want to keep going. "I wish I knew just *how* I got here! At first it seemed like I was dreaming, yet maybe not. I do know that I woke up on a beach near Kronstadt and a navy shore patrol found me."

"Well," she said softly, "you must have had quite a journey."

Her quiet acceptance calmed me. Maybe I could trust her.

She took the bowls and my plate and soon brought out a dessert of warm apple cobbler and a pot of strong-smelling green tea.

"Do you want to hear more?" I asked.

She nodded while serving us tea and cobbler with ice cream.

I launched into my mom's breakdown back home, explained the bardo dream (as if I knew what 'bardo' meant), the raft voyage ending in a storm, my stay with the Soviet Navy, then meeting Janie, Louise and eventually Roselin. Then I asked, "Do *you* think I arrived into a different plane of reality?"

Angela's eyes were so wide they were spooky. She took a long breath, calmly poured herself some more tea and said, "I think you did, Gordy. And I too may have traveled here in a similar way."

What? I immediately tuned in.

She slowly got up and returned with a bottle of Highpeace Monastery brandy and two tiny snifters—that's what Mom called those glasses back home.

"Care for some?"

Jeez, wine and brandy are quite the custom here.

"Sure."

She gave me a hesitant smile as we toasted to each other's health. She took a deep breath.

"I grew up on a farm in Madagascar with my English parents. I was their only child."

Oh, yeah, Madagascar—it was on that oceans map.

"From my earliest memory they fought with each other. It was usually about money, each other's habits and their unfulfilled dreams because of *the child*, meaning me! The walls were thin in that house, and I heard things I don't think were meant for my ears."

This is sounding familiar—again.

"Over time," she continued, "I became miserable with shame—I was convinced I was 'the problem'. I felt they would likely be happier if I wasn't around, so I contemplated running away more than once.

"Their fighting was usually a lot of barking and hurtful words. Then came the night of my father yelling, glass shattering, my mother screaming, a heavy thud. I remember grabbing a blanket, running outside and crawling under our back porch, on the cold dirt with the cobwebs. I was in a black place, numb, and all I wanted to do was somehow disappear forever! It was a sensation I don't ever want to feel again.

"Then, from I don't know where, a soothing sound I'd never heard before started up. Ever so faint at first, I felt it more than heard it. It grew to a deep melodic humming that ran all through me, surrounding me with a kind of warmth, and growing louder until it overwhelmed all my senses and I blacked out. I was nine years old."

I stared at her in awe. "The Hum!"

"Yes, Gordy! Once the sound faded, I 'dreamed' I had become an albatross or maybe a frigate bird. I was still conscious as Angela, but no longer human. I found myself rising and gliding over Madagascar, already far from our farm, and from them. I flew effortlessly for days and nights, somehow knowing the right direction to follow. The sun rose ahead of me and set behind me. I saw gorgeous clouds by day and beautiful constellations at night, and I never felt lost.

"On about the fifth day, dark clouds quickly moved in from the south, then powerful wind gusts and battering rain began to throw me about, terrifying me. I was completely exhausted when, flying low, I spotted a grassy bluff above windblown crashing waves. I landed hard, then huddled in the tall grass and finally fell asleep. I still remember tucking my feathered head under my big wing!

"The next morning was clear and warm when I awoke on the grassy hillside. I was human-Angela again, still nine, still wrapped in my dirty blanket. But something had changed. I felt like a new person, and when I looked around, the air and landscape and smells were also new. I was definitely no longer in Madagascar. This is similar to your experience, yes?"

"Yes!" I said. "I too felt different when I woke up, though I was also terribly thirsty and full of sand."

She refilled our glasses.

"I must have looked a mess," she continued. "Fortunately, I had landed near a well-used path on the Island's southwestern coast. A woman on her morning walk stopped, took one look, and without a word, gently helped me stand. She asked, 'Are you all right?' and we somehow understood each other through our different accents. I could only tell her that I didn't know where I was—nothing else made any sense.

"She led me to her house about a mile away, and just like that, I was accepted into her family—it seemed natural.

"The woman's name was Sabrina, and she and her partner Janet adored their three kids and were happy to add a fourth. Sabrina had patiently listened to my albatross-dream story, and we kept that between just the two of us. When no one with my description was reported missing, I stayed with them and began a new life. At first I couldn't believe that they actually *wanted* me, that I would be *loved!*"

"Wow," I said. "So, you've been on the Island ever since?"

"Yep, I've had no desire to go back to Madagascar, and it's been thirty-nine years!"

"So, um, do you think you're still on another plane of reality?"

She looked at me thoughtfully. "After reading all I could find about the phenomenon, and there is very little actually, it is the best way I can describe my journey, and this Island. You know it is not easy to get here from the outside world—no planes except Russian military, and no boats except the steamer that sails to Western Australia every few weeks. To get here on that boat, I'm told you have to first find the ticket office in Fremantle—and then get by the Soviet military gatekeepers when you arrive. Only a few have done that, I've heard."

Somehow Mr. Barnes did it with his mysterious letter-of-passage.

"Do you, ah, think the Hum might have brought you here?"

"Well, I believe it helped," she said, "though I think other forces were at work too—I just don't know what they were. You don't know either, do you?"

"No. I think my friend Mr. Barnes had something to do with it, but he hasn't told me much."

"Is he the one who sent you here?"

"Yes, and now he's here too. He and my friend Roselin are on a tour of some desert tribes. I call him Eddie now."

Angela paused. "Your story only convinces me of the mysteries that swirl around us. I've been content to live here with my cats, weave my rugs, and rent my spare room to travelers. You are the first person I've met with a story similar to mine!"

I looked at her and shrugged. "Yeah, it's crazy."

Angela stood up and beckoned me to do the same. She held out her arms and said, "May I?" I nodded. When she put them around me I melted a little, and she seemed to as well. We finally let go, neither of us saying anything as she returned to her chair.

*

Too rattled to go to bed, I pulled on my windbreaker. She smiled knowingly when I told her I needed a head-clearing walk.

Under the now-high moon, I picked up the path that will take me to Gifford tomorrow. It wasn't long before the land simply ended, dropping off into a huge pale vastness. Far below I could barely make out a few dim lights that must be the Elsinore Tribes.

The distance *down* was incredible.

As I stared out at the distant glittering ocean, I thought of that weird vertigo episode earlier this evening. It felt like Mom was really there, knocking me down so I could finally hear her—her pain *and* her love for Ricky and me. Angela's story was also a revelation…

I don't need to feel alone!

Walking back in a kind of trance, I nearly missed Angela's house. The generator had been turned off, leaving only the sound of crickets. When I approached her porch again, I found her bundled up in one of the rocking chairs. She gestured to the other one.

"Nice walk?"

"I think I saw some lights in Gifford *faaar* below. What a view!"

"Ah, yes. It's almost too much to take in at times."

Then her expression shifted to an almost mischievous half-smile that made me pause. "This might seem inappropriate," she said, "but I would like to ask you something…"

Wary now, I nodded, waited and rocked.

"Would you like to share my bed with me?"

Zwoop!

"We don't have to *do* anything, mind you. It would just be so lovely to hold you. It's been a long time for me."

My first impulse was to panic, say no and leave. My second impulse was to panic, then decline as politely as I could so I could still stay here.

Will she throw me out if I say no?…maybe she won't. This is so weird, but maybe it's just the way people do things here.

But when I looked at her, I saw something in her eyes that told me she was speaking from a place deep in her heart.

When I finally calmed down all I could say was…

"Okay."

*

I couldn't sleep. We were on our sides, spooning, I think is the word. Angela had draped her arm loosely over my middle. Her deep breathing told me she was probably asleep, while I was working myself into a mental stew.

Aren't I supposed to do something? Should I kiss her? (Eww, that feels weird—she's almost fifty!) Or should I do some other thing I'm supposed to know about? At least Janie was clear in what she wanted, 'just hold me and I'll hold you', nothing more! Even Lane and I stopped after all that kissing at the Fillmore Inn. This just feels strange.

Her sleeping hand was resting an inch from my belly.

I was also feeling hot in my t-shirt and undershorts, and wondered if she was too, in her long nightgown. *Okay, I'll think about other things… who will I see in Gifford tomorrow? Will Janie be there…or Sebastian?*

But my heart was pounding, and everything went right back to that hand.

Then my own hand, seemingly without the aid of my mind, pulled up my t-shirt then gently pressed her hand onto my bare belly. Warm and slack at first, the hand twitched, and then slowly began to move on its own! What was I *thinking*? Gliding over my skin in a slow circular motion, her fingers and palm caressed my chest, returned to my middle, then drifted a little lower… I was aroused and frightened at the same time. I had no idea where this was going, even though I had started it. But then *she* started it by asking me to join her!

Her hand stopped over my navel, and her soothing, sleepy voice arose from behind me.

"How are you feeling, young Gordy?"

I couldn't find words, and only gulped while I squeezed her hand with my own, trying to signal *I'm okay.* Eventually I said, "I—I'm not sure what I want, or what *you* want. You're being really nice, but I don't know what to do."

An achingly long silence, then her voice at my ear, "Perhaps listen to your heart, and not so much your mind. Your heart will tell you what to do, and when to do it. But it *is* hard to listen, I know!" She moved her hand up to my chest, over my heart, and held it there.

I hardly knew her, yet I felt an incredibly soothing energy from Angela flowing right through that hand.

She then gently tugged at my shoulder, and I turned over to face her. We looked at each other a moment, then she said, "Long after I arrived here, I remained the wretched creature who hid under the porch with the spiders. My parents' fighting back in Madagascar had shattered my belief that anyone could truly love someone else, much less love *me.*

"So in spite of my adoptive parents' patience and caring, I was not very cuddly, especially as a teenager. I finally left home for a boy whose indifference matched that of my birth parents. Being around him felt strangely comforting at first, because it was familiar, but when he began to treat me like an unpaid servant, I left him. I think my heart had finally told me I deserved better."

She took a deep breath.

"I *wanted* to open up to others, including my well-meaning husband, who I met a few years later. He tried to push through my walls, to 'fix' me. But I still would not, or could not, change to his liking. He was generous though. When he left he gave me this house.

"Then about five years ago, while I was taking a walk and the Hum was flowing around me, I realized being loved is *my* choice, not anyone else's! It seemed almost too simple. And since then I haven't felt isolated nor unlovable. I have my kitties, a few dear friends, and the occasional interesting boarder, like you."

Then she motioned me to face away from her, and she once again reached her arm around me. Her sudden enveloping warmth was heavenly. Big knots slipped apart inside my chest.

"Also," she added, "I can feel *your* loving energy, right through my hand." She rested it firmly over my heart again.

"Really?"

"Yes. And to answer your question of what *I* want…"

Uh, oh, here it comes…

"Just this."

*

Long after seven a.m., I woke up alone with my ankles pinned under Butch and Bonnie, who were surprisingly heavy. Last night was all a blur until, with a smile, I remembered everything. I also remembered Angela's meal schedule and that I'd likely missed breakfast! Scattering the cats, I hurriedly fumbled into my clothes and trotted down to the kitchen. She was in her robe brewing tea, clearly looking like she had just gotten up herself.

"Am I too late for breakfast?"

"Oh, not at all, Gordy. I overslept as well. It was worth staying up just to share our stories!"

She held up a cup. "Jasmine tea?"

"Ah, yes. Thanks!"

She showed me my chair and we both sat a minute with our tea, perhaps waiting for something to happen.

I finally asked, "Could you tell me how long it might take to walk to Gifford from here? I'm returning to this family who took me in a while back."

"Oh, it's not long—about six hours I would gauge. You'll want to be mindful of that steep trail—one mis-step and you're over the cliff! Too many walkers have done that while looking at the view instead of the path in front of them. Bangers and Eggs?"

Six more hours! I grinned at the idea that by mid-afternoon I would likely be walking into Janie's yard! "Oh, yes, eggs and, uh, whatever else you said would be great!"

Feeling like we were genuine old friends now, we chatted quietly over breakfast. Angela's calm, low-register voice was a pleasure to listen to. After we cleared the dishes, she glanced at my shaggy head, left the room and came back with a bedsheet, brush, comb and a pair of scissors.

"You could use a haircut, especially since you're heading for a reunion—no extra charge!"

We didn't say much as she snipped and combed, and neither of us mentioned our 'cuddling'. She looked me over, smiled approvingly, and handed me a mirror. "Now you look a little more civilized."

She removed the sheet and stood behind me as we both looked at the mirror. Then she gave me a very wet smooch on the side of my neck.

Whoa!

"Oh-kaay," she said in a kind of singsong. "Before I get other ideas, you'd better be on your way."

We hugged rather awkwardly on her porch and I started off, only to turn back to pay for my lodging.

"Don't even think about it!" she said. "See that radio tower? The Soviet Ministry of Information compensates me monthly to maintain it and the generator, keep the critters from chewing the wiring, and other sundry chores. My husband taught me the basics, and convinced the Ministry I could do it just as well as he could."

She said a lot more with her eyes, which left me with a deep sense of gratitude. I dropped my pack and we hugged each other much longer this time. "Thank you," she said.

I didn't know what to say.

*

The abrupt edge of this part of the Highlands was even more stunning in daylight. I once again stood open-mouthed at the magnificence of the view. Bright puffy clouds billowed above me and also below. Among them lay the hazy outline of roundish Elsinore Bay, and the much broader crescent of Gifford Bay beyond.

I sat down near the cliff's edge. The wind pushed at me, and my thoughts tumbled one over another. *What just happened back there? Was that okay? Angela even thanked me!*

As I vigorously rubbed my freshly-shorn head, I realized there were probably a hundred possible answers.

The path was steep and very old-looking, with the same iron handholds as at the Berea Drop. A familiar strong updraft tried to blow me backwards. The narrow course of steps and switchbacks must have taken years for someone to shape and carve. Swallows, er, tweeters, darted around me in swarms. There must be a thousand nests in these cliffs.

About half-way down the cliff-face, a thick fog forced me to slow down. I had actually walked into the lower cloudbank. I took off my pack and layered up with my new sweater *and* my windbreaker.

Bless Eddie for buying this stuff!

After descending for another hour, my view opened up again. I was now close enough to clearly make out the Elsinore Bay settlements and—Gifford!

Back in the full sun again, the path opened up into a steep ravine, lush with tall gum trees and wind-sculpted pines. Off went my layers. In a pine-shaded valley among the lower cliffs, I spotted what must be Uva Glen. I stopped at the only shop there, bought a couple of chocolate bars, and refilled my canteen. My path then followed rocky, tumbling Uva Creek until it joined Gifford Creek. There the land spread out into the familiar berry fields surrounding Gifford. I soon spotted Janie's house, and I couldn't get there fast enough.

Along Uva Creek, almost to Gifford.

ARRIVAL

I had imagined everyone coming outside shouting, *Gordy, Gordy, you've returned!* Alan and Sheryl would most likely be there, and maybe Janie herself. Then Eddie and Roselin later on, and maybe even Lane someday…

But when I walked into the MacEvoy's backyard and called out *Halloo,* nothing happened.

Silence…not even a chirping bird.

I walked into the house, knowing they never locked their door.

"Anyone home?"

A clock's ticking was the only response. The kitchen smelled promising, as if a pot of soup was waiting, but everything was put away, cleaned up, tidy.

I dropped my backpack and sat down heavily at the kitchen table.

Well, I'm here!

I rested a few minutes, then filled a tall glass with water at the sink and sat back down.

Where is everyone?

*

I went back outside to my *hoot.* It looked about the same, but with an unfamiliar curtain blocking the window. I knocked on the door, but no one answered so I peeked in. I was immediately confronted with an array of female clothing pinned to clotheslines above the compact woodstove. Washed dishes and mugs were piled on the tiny counter. Sketches done in watercolor and pencil were mounted on the walls. The faces looked familiar, and wow, what poses…

Janie and Vermilion!

Then I saw that glass dolphin-shaped lamp sitting on a high shelf, covered with dust. I assumed Alan hadn't been able to fix it, and I was definitely *not* going to turn it on to find out!

This thing cannot stay here; it should not even exist.

I found a long-handled spade in Allan's shop, bundled the heavy lamp in a burlap sack, and hiked more than a mile into the bushy hillside, well away from any houses. Having made sure no one was looking, I buried the lamp as deeply as the shovel could reach.

When I returned, I realized how thirsty I was. Back in the kitchen, I refilled my water glass and sat down heavily (again) in one of the chairs.

Then on an impulse, I walked back toward the bedrooms and peeked into Janie's room. It was nearly bare except for her desk, her dresser and her neatly made bed. On the bedspread a folded note with my name on it stood like a tent on a short stack of letters. I sat down on the bed, took a deep breath, and picked up the note .

Gordy,   18 May

Janie told us you would be arriving 'sooner or later', to use her words, so we made this room available to you. She and Vermilion have moved into your hoot to have a little privacy, as our Janie put it.

We are all leaving today to relax for a while at Wave Point, where the Wave Festival is held. It's quiet there now, not so hot. Janie said you two passed by there on your way up here, and she had told you about the Wave Dance. You would love the energy of that event, Gordy, even if you might not care for the dancing. You <u>must</u> come with us next January!

Your brother's letters await you, plus another from your friend Lane, which she delivered herself. I'm not supposed to say anything, except to read hers <u>last</u>.

We hope we'll see you upon our return. Meanwhile, enjoy your new room!

Love and hugs,

Sheryl, Alan, Janie & Vermilion

PS: There are groceries in the pantry. You know where the cookery things are, so help yourself!

Also, Sebastian still comes and goes when he feels like it. Would you mind filling his pool for him? Thanks.

S.

I closed my eyes and sighed deeply with relief.
All is well!

Eying the small pile of letters with giddy anticipation, I pulled off my dusty shoes and grimy socks and propped myself up with Janie's pillows against the headboard.

On top were Ricky's two letters. I looked at the first one a long time before opening it.

I'll just have to bear this...

Dear Gordy,   Sept. 24, '64

This is probably the hardest letter I've ever written. I can barely write it now, never mind back in May when all this happened.

First, I'm glad YOU are all right, even though you're gone. I didn't know what to do when I found you missing.

Okay—Mom never woke up. She died on June 2 in the hospital in Santa Ana, where the ambulance took her.

I stopped.

Even though Eddie had told me already, I felt like I was being gut-punched all over again to see it in writing.

Mom...is...gone.

I slumped down into the pillows, breathing heavily. I was eventually able to read on.

I'm glad your friend Mr. Barnes came to our house when he did. I was really a mess from what happened to Mom (and you). He tried to tell me you were all right, but I couldn't believe him until your letter came. He knows some scary stuff!

He has since been helping me with Mom's business and banking papers, and guess what! She had enough money in the bank so I can keep the house and pay the bills—even the telephone. So when you come back, your room will be waiting for you.

I'm working at Sam's Greek Restaurant as a waiter now, promoted from bus-boy when they heard what had happened.

I'm still surfing when I can. *And* you should have been here last week when we had a high tide and a MASSIVE ten-foot south swell. All the streets got flooded, and the waves were too crazy to even surf on. I don't remember that happening since '58.

By the way, on that night you left, there was no tidal wave—you must have dreamed it. And you were (and still are) definitely gone.

I see you've found some friends where you are. I hope Janie is being nice to you, and you're being polite to her and her parents. It's hard to believe—you were washed up on a beach???

Then you scratched out something about Russians. What was that all about?

Okay, I need to fix my car (flat tire) and then go to work, so I'll put this in the mail.

Rick

Wow! Ricky, er, *Rick*, seems so grown-up now. Mr. Barnes was right; he had been through so much. I'm sure glad he got to keep our house.

But the thought of going back to my old bedroom gave me a chill, especially after that weird incident at the Hotel Caledonia. But it touched me that Ricky wants me to come back.

Next Ricky letter…

Dear Gordy,   March 4, '65

I'm glad you are still okay.

Where is Putney, and where is the island you're on? You were right, even our encyclopedia couldn't tell me anything. I asked Mr. Barnes if he knew, and he said the same thing you did— it's somewhere west of Australia. He later gave me a road map of it he had found somewhere.

I showed Mr. Barnes the letters you had sent to me, and he said you are right, there is a humming noise you and he hear sometimes. I saw you acting spazzy in the backyard once— were you listening to it then?

He says hello to you too, by the way. He's glad the comic books made it there okay. I didn't know he had sent them, and I haven't seen him in a while either.

Where are you living now? You sounded like you were traveling when you wrote me.

Are you going to stay on that island? I need to know because my friend Dwayne asked me if he could use your room for a while. Mom's room is still full of her stuff from that gift shop she had.

My friend Larry just came to the door and we're going to the Bluffs to surf! I'll take this to the post office on the way, and hey, I sure had to buy a lot of weird stamps to send your last letter. (They think your island is part of Australia.)

Stay out of trouble and write again soon!

Rick

I looked again at the envelope, and sure enough, it was half-covered in stamps and *Par Avion* stickers, including some extra stamps that were added in Fremantle. I also looked at the dates on his letters, then at a calendar on Janie's bedroom door… *Wow, it's the end of May and he last wrote in early March—time to write back!*

Now my letter from Lane.

When I looked closer at her envelope, I saw that the 'stamp' was a cleverly hand-drawn portrait of Scrooge McDuck, with a value of 1,000 rogers. I forgot I'd given her some of my Disney comics.

I could only grin.

I opened the envelope, which contained one sheet of note paper.

Dearest Gordy,

If you are reading this now, that means YOU'RE HERE!

And GUESS WHAT! Mum and I live in HOCKNEY, just over a mile from you. We are in the little yellow house, 17 Brewster Street, next to the East-Coast Path.

Get over here as fast as you can!

Love Youuuuu,

L.

YES!!

I jumped off the bed, pulled my sweaty socks back on, then threw them off and got out my sandals—I was done with hiking boots for now—and I was out the door.

I remembered Hockney was the only actual town among the tribes surrounding Elsinore Bay. I'd gone there with Sheryl once or twice to help her buy groceries. To find Brewster Street, I asked a girl of about ten, and she pointed toward the bay. "Head to the last street before the Path," she said, "then turn right."

I ran the rest of the way, rounded the corner, and, breathless, saw Lane sitting on a bench in front of their cottage, eating from a big blue bowl on her lap (Nut-Flakes cereal, she said later).

I stopped to study her face for a moment. She looked thoughtful and serious as she gazed out at the bay. Then she spotted me, went wide-eyed, and almost spilled her cereal.

Gordeeee!

She had her arms around me in an instant. "Hey, you're taller, and what a tan! Nice haircut, too."

Ooh, I hope she doesn't ask me where I got it.

We hugged and smooched right there in Lane's front yard as several hikers on the nearby path cheered us on like we had just won the World Cup.

She whispered in my ear, "Want some Nut-Flakes?"

She pulled me into her kitchen where she poured me a large bowlful, added milk and banana slices, and a minute later we were scrunched together on the bench. I had forgotten how hungry I was!

Finally satisfied, we simply sat there, watching the passing travelers.

"I'm glad I stayed around today," she said. "I had a hoping-feeling you might arrive—and here you are!"

"Yeah, I'm glad you stayed around too! Your note changed my whole day. I love the Uncle Scrooge stamp."

"I got the idea from the stamps me mum brings home. She works at the post office now."

"The post office?"

"Okay, I'll back up here. Remember that day at Wild North when I said we might *not* be heading to Putney? Well, just before she took off with Vermilion, Janie had a talk with my mum. Seems that Janie convinced her to take a look at Gifford or Hockney. So after you left, Mum said to me, 'Let's take the other mail boat over North Cape and get off at Gifford Bay.' And that was fine with me since you said you'd eventually be coming this way."

Now I was glowing.

"And I was worried silly ever since you told me about your 'project' with Roselin. Did you guys get that book?"

"Oh, yeah," I said, "We got the book, but we had to run for it. We were nearly caught by two Russian guys who pulled guns on us, and Louise did something to them, and they froze. It was scary!"

Lane's eyes went wide. "What did she do to them? I mean, I'm glad she saved you guys, but something about Louise gives me the creeps. I could feel it whenever I ran into her at Wild North."

"Well, I think you read her right. After we were safe, she stole the book from Roselin and ran off, and Roselin was devastated. But by luck we caught her with it on the mail boat! I don't think she planned on us being on board. I saw Roselin do some serious witchery to force Louise to give it back. Then she forgave Louise!"

"Louise stole it, then Roselin *forgave* her?"

"Yeah! It was weird. Roselin could have fried Louise's brains with her own Hum-powers, but she just warned Louise to stay away from her instead."

Lane looked at me as she took this in, then planted a smooch on my cheek. "Now lemme tell you more about *me*."

"Okay," I said, grinning.

"When we arrived here about two months ago, we met Janie's mum who knows the lady who owns this house. I think Janie sent a telegram or something 'cause Janie's mum seemed to already know us! Then Janie's dad told my mum he'd heard of a job opening at the Hockney P.O. Janie and her parents were soooo helpful!"

"Aww, that's great," I said. "Sheryl and Alan are good people. They've treated me like family."

"Mum had to practice lifting weights to get the job. She loads mail bags and packages on a skiff, sails it to the mail boat and returns with the incoming mail. She also had to learn to sail the skiff! The mail for Gifford and the other Elsinore tribes all comes through Hockney, which she also helps sort. She's hoping she might teach again sometime soon, but so far no jobs have opened up."

"So, your mum is okay with not being in Putney?"

"I think so. She likes the relaxed feel of this place. Plus, she's okay with the physical stuff at work—it's new for her and she looks great 'cause of it!"

Then I asked, "How do *you* like it here?"

"Well, okay so far. I missed you something crazy, but I've met some friends at school, and I think you'll like them. And I'm glad to be back in a real school. My eleventh year begins soon at Hockney Upper School."

"Oh, that's right!" I said, suddenly remembering school. "I need to see about *my* eleventh year. I missed a lot of tenth year!"

"So that means you'll be staying here, I hope I hope?"

I sighed. "I think so, but I just read some letters from my brother Ricky back in California. He says my room is there waiting for me…"

"Ah." Her smiled faded. "And, ah, your mum?"

"She died."

"Ahh, Gordy."

"I was always hoping she would have some way, somehow, made it. Mr. Barnes, er, Eddie, told me what happened even before I read Ricky's letters."

"Your friend who sent the comic books? You *saw* him?"

"Yes! I meant to tell you this. He came to Gottfried Island in a sailboat he had rented."

"Wait, where's Gottfried Island?"

"It's way out on the edge of everything, in the ocean north of Wild North. Roselin decided we should hide there, and we were there for several weeks before he showed up."

"So, it was just you two?"

"Yeah, just us. No one else lives there. It was okay at first, but I missed you a lot and Roselin got into a terrible mood about being a 'broken witch' and she tried to commit suicide by drinking some poison."

"Poison…*Roselin*?"

"Yeah, and I stopped her! I was outside but I was lucky to get to her in time."

Lane looked at me thoughtfully, put her hands on my cheeks and said softly, "Oh, I believe it was *way* more than luck, Gordy. You were meant to save her, and probably for a lot of reasons." She smooched me on the lips—a long wet one this time. "Where is Roselin now, by the way?"

A bit addled, I fumbled on, "Well, um, after Eddie arrived, they became *really* close friends. They acted like they already knew each other as soon as they met. It was kind of fun to watch them. Eddie had also learned that it was probably safe to return to Putney, so we sailed back with him. Just before we left, Roselin said she wanted to show Eddie the Desert Wonder Tribes, but not with me along."

"Ouch," said Lane. That must have stung a little.

"Yeah, it did, but I was okay with that after Roselin told me how she felt about me. From Putney we all rode together on an Islebus, and they got off at a place called Wild Women. I missed them immediately, especially since this was my first trip alone on the Island. I rode a couple of busses all the way to Upland, and then I walked the Outland Path down here."

"Wow, Gordy. Sooo, they're on a kind of honeymoon then?"

"I suppose you could put it that way," I said, rolling my eyes.

"Hey," she said, "let's go to the P.O. and say hi to Mum!"

*

That evening, back at Janie's, I realized I smelled a little ripe. I took a towel out to the solar shower, a tiny open-to-the-sky enclosure next to Alan's workshop. Once I stripped down and got in, I discovered the water came from a black-painted tank on the roof and was still quite warm—a blessing from the day's sunshine.

I was in my own world rinsing off when something wet slithered around my legs.

Aaak!

I jumped and banged my head on the shower head. The shape darted out and splashed into what water there was in Sebastian's pool.

Sebastian!

After I calmed down and dried myself off, I reached for the garden hose and started filling the pool as Sheryl had asked. Sebastian was delighted at this, swimming in circles more like an eel than an otter. When he stopped to preen himself, I watched him a while, then asked him, "So, how's fishin'?"

No response.

Then I remembered a long-ago conversation with him, and asked, "How do you know where *home* is, Sebastian? Is it some comfortable place you've been all your life, or is it a place, maybe even a strange place, where there are people who love you?"

Sebastian looked up at me as if I was finally asking him an intelligent question. He briefly regarded me with his tongue sticking out, then resumed licking himself.

Goofy otter.

When the pool was full, I finally realized I still had no clothes on! I must be getting used to this sky-clad thing.

I went back into the house for a bathrobe I had spotted hanging in Janie's room. The quiet house felt strange since it was usually filled with Janie's family—and Janie.

It felt good to be here, though.

*

The long day of hiking and last night's, um, events with Angela were catching up with me. I found just enough energy to put some wood in MacEvoy's cookstove and heat a potful of Sheryl's seven-bean soup.

Once I was in bed I thought I'd fall asleep right away, but instead my head churned. Ricky's letters made me feel sad yet relieved at the same time. I was glad he was okay after everything he went through.

Again I tried to imagine what it might be like if I returned. Ricky and his friends would probably be playing cards and drinking beer in our living room, just like they did on those nights when Mom was working. His friends sometimes acted like jerks, making stupid comments whenever I walked by.

Or there would be no one home at all.

Also, I'd be taking the same school bus every morning for at least two more years of high school. I'd see the same kids I didn't really like anyway.

And I'd lose everyone here.

*

The next morning, I applied for eleventh year at Elsinore Upper School. I'd missed almost half of my tenth year, so I had to do some intense studying and take a 'hardship exam' in order to avoid retaking the whole year. On May 29th they said I had passed the exam, and on Monday, June 1st, 1965, I was back for eleventh year. The routine and the new classes both felt good! Thankfully, and I wasn't surprised, a new (larger) school uniform was pressed and hung in Janie's closet.

The MacEvoy household remained quiet, so Meredith offered me an open invitation to come over for supper, which I gratefully accepted. She seemed to trust me now, and she actually said she was glad to have me around. She also said she was glad for Lane too. "From her, that's a big one!" Lane said.

Lane often walked with me back to Gifford after supper, or we'd walk along the bayshore, sometimes stopping to smooch. At other times, we would actually try to do our homework together.

*

In the afternoon a few days after school had started, I was walking up to the MacEvoys' gate when a familiar voice cried out...

"Heeeey, Gords!"

I looked around to see Janie and Vermilion, dark-skinned and sun-bleached, walking up the path, grinning. They were followed by Sheryl and Alan, both pushing one of those bicycle-wheeled carts.

"Well, the long-lost traveler has returned," said Sheryl. "I didn't know if we'd see you again."

Janie seized me in a vigorous hug, and stepped back. "Yer taller-leaner look agrees with ya," she said. "Nice haircut, too."

"Well, you're looking good too, Janie!" And I meant it.

Vermilion said, "Thanks for lettin' us stay in your *hoot*, Gordy, even though you probably didn't know it."

"Oh, I kinda figured it out once I looked inside. Nice drawings, by the way."

Alan said, "We were all speculating on whether you'd be here when we got back. Looks like you made it just fine."

"Oh, yes. And I found your note right away, Sheryl. Thanks for, ah, making me feel so welcome!"

I can't believe how good it feels to see them all again!

At the gate Sheryl said, "Hey, I need some help over here unloading this stuff."

*

The next morning, a Saturday, Janie said to all of us, "I think we should invite Lane and Meredith over for lunch."

Sheryl and Alan liked the idea immediately, and as soon as I offered to walk over to invite them, Janie said, "I'll come with ya!"

"Ah, sure...okay."

We hadn't walked five steps past the gate when Janie said, "So how're things with you and Lane?"

"Fine."

"Ah, good. So, how do ya like being back in Gifford?"

Is this an interrogation?

"Uh, fine so far, and thanks for letting me use your room."

"Not at all, Gords. I hope ya don't mind Vermilion and me taking over yer *hoot*."

"Nah, I like your bedroom. It's comfy!"

"Well, stay as long as ya want. Vee and I aren't sure what we're gonna do, and it's nice that we can have a little, ah, distance from the house."

I glanced at her. "I'm not sure what I'm gonna do either. Ricky's wondering when I'm coming back to California, and I don't know if I can live in our old house without our mom there. Or if that's even *home* anymore. What do you think?"

She looked at me. "That's a tough one. I guess it boils down to where yer people are."

I thought for a minute, looked at her, then away. "Yeah…"

"Yeh…what?"

"I dunno Janie. I suppose this place wins, especially the people, but I'm still not sure if it's *real* or not."

A sudden wild-eyed look…

Whap!

After smacking my head, she locked her arms around me and had me on the ground in no time. Flat on my back, in shock, my ear ringing, she straddled me. "Okay, is *this* real?" She slapped my face a few times, hard enough to prove her point. She stopped, looked down at me like a disappointed teacher, then planted a very wet and definitely passionate kiss on my lips.

"Janieeee!"

"That's to convince you that every time ya say that, Gordy, ya make me feel like *I'm* not real!"

We were in the grass next to the main path to Hockney. A couple walking by had stopped and the woman said, "Everythin' okay over there?"

Janie looked up and said, "Yeh, we're fine—just havin' a little talk."

I smiled and waggled my fingers to show them I hadn't (yet) come to severe harm. They nodded and moved on.

"Okay, okay," I said, breathing hard. "I'm convinced. This is all real, and you are *definitely* real"

She was breathing hard, too. "Yes I *am*, you blindman!"

She moved off, offered a hand to pull me up, then brushed the grass off my back.

We walked a while in silence.

"Okay, so where were we?" She said, like nothing had happened just then.

"Uh…where-is-home?"

"Yeh, exactly. You'll just have to figure that one out yerself."

I wasn't really surprised she had jumped me like that—I'd been spewing this *I don't know* stuff at her long enough. Then I remembered some news. "Hey, Janie, I got accepted into eleventh year by taking a special test. And I meant to show this to you earlier." I pulled out a laminated Gifford Tribe ID card with a tiny and rather appealing pencil sketch of my face on it. "I'm an official Gifforder!"

Janie stopped to look at it. "Ah, yer a *Giffidian*, not a 'Gifforder.' Welcome aboard, sailor!" She shook my hand and grinned. "And maybe it being official like this might put yer mind to rest about what-is-real."

We found Lane and Meredith sitting in front of their cottage, right where I found Lane that first day. When they saw us, they both gave Janie a long group hug. Meredith said they would be delighted to come back with us for a get-together. I left Janie chatting with (mostly questioning) Lane while I went inside with Meredith to help her make a fruit salad.

On the way back to MacEvoy's, Meredith walked with Janie, sharing stories about her job, the mail boats, and a certain captain on the *Quandary* she wouldn't mind seeing again. This generated more probing questions from Janie, to which Meredith seemed happy to respond.

Lane and I walked a few steps behind, holding hands, sort-of listening, sort-of not.

*

The next day I tried to write a letter to Ricky to answer his question about coming home, but I couldn't finish it.

I still didn't know.

A TRIP TO NEVERMORE

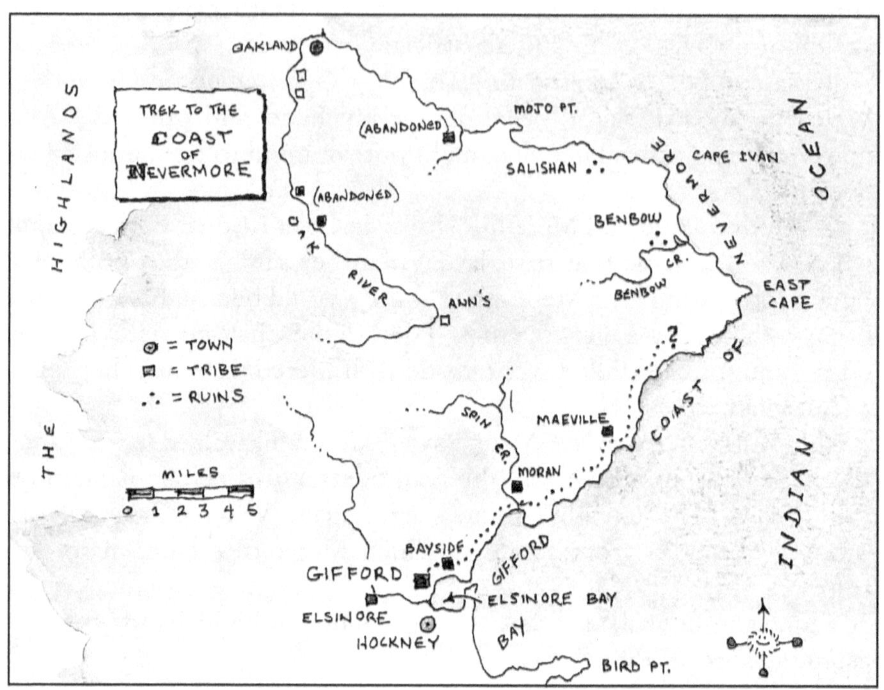

On another Saturday morning a few weeks later, Lane and I were once again sitting on the bench in front of her house with bowls of Nut-flakes on our laps. Since we went to different schools, we usually saw each other only on the weekends—quite a change from our days at Wild North.

"I've really been missing you," she said. "Our school holidays will be starting soon, and I want to *do* something."

"Sure," I said with a mouthful of cereal. "What are ya thinkin'?"

"Let's hike out to East Cape, in that part of the coast they call Nevermore." She lowered her eyes with a shy-smile look.

"Yeah, I'd like that," I said, as innocently as I could.

When I mentioned her idea to Janie later, she said, "Ooh, nice choice there, Romeo! Vee and I hiked out there a while ago, and it was fan-*tas*-tic! Ya gotta see Cape Ivan and Mojo Point with those stone towers. You'll feel real magic out there, and a week'll go fast!"

I was easily convinced.

By now my friendship with Lane had only deepened. We talked for hours or read together or simply watched the passing hikers from her front-door bench. She loved walking around Elsinore Bay on the busy promenade, or out on the ocean beaches, always curious (like me) about what might have washed up.

On the morning of our hike, I met Lane at her house. Meredith not only gave us permission, but wrapped us up in multiple hugs and a *you be careful* sendoff. We stopped back at Janie's house where we got the same treatment (though fewer hugs) from Sheryl and Alan. Alan said he'd miss me, but I had a feeling both Meredith and Sheryl were happy to have us out of their hair for a while. Janie gave me one of her mixed-message smiles, then hugged each of us.

*

We had planned on seven days and six nights of trekking. I tried *not* to think too much about the nights.

From Gifford, we walked through the last village of Bayside and soon left Elsinore Bay behind. At the fork where the East Coast Path turned inland, we paused at that same crude **NEVERMORE** sign-and-arrow that I saw with Janie and Louise so long ago.

This time we're going in!

I looked at Lane. "Is there an actual place called Nevermore?"

She looked thoughtful. "It seems to be more of a myth than a place. I asked my science teacher about it, and he told me that the name comes from a legend about a tribe who tried to settle out there, then disappeared, 'back in the time of nevermore'—a possible Old People story. It's supposed to be a benign place—no evil spirits. It's also not reality-bending, like Roger's Dreamland. Me mum even decided it was safe after she asked around, so that says something."

At the end of that first day, we set up camp on a low grassy bluff and hungrily ate up the last of Meredith's hefty sandwiches. The weather showed no sign of rain, so we unrolled our sleeping bags under the galaxies already flooding the sky. I counted *nine* this time, including the vast spiral wheel of Andromeda. We were both so exhausted from all our trekking and frequent bodysurfing stops that we barely said "goodnight", and we were out.

The next morning we passed the settlement of Maeville, a cluster of huts and a few abandoned houses. "I heard this place was once a farm tribe," said Lane, "but it didn't make it. Something about a mysterious energy that wilted their crops, which were then quickly overgrown by the local wild plants."

One of the houses was still inhabited. It had a freshly painted front door, in front of which sat an elderly fellow holding a steaming mug and looking at us. Lane waved and he waved back, then looked away. He didn't seem interested in chatting. We walked on.

After Maeville, the headlands grew higher, the hills more rugged, the beaches and rocky coves more inviting. Soon we found ourselves hiking along what was likely the most isolated stretch of the Island's eastern coast. Nobody lived out here, and we passed only two other hikers, a shaggy-haired young couple walking hand-in-hand. They grinned and waved at us but didn't slow down.

The Coast of Nevermore.

On the second night, we found a little meadow tucked among some huge rocks. Over our campfire supper, Lane gave me a shy look and said, "Let's put up the tent."

Zwoopy feelings once again pulsed through me. "Uhh, sure."

We had managed to sunburn our butts during our frequent stops to swim, and as we unrolled our sleeping bags, Lane said, "Fair warning…I'm pulling my sleepshirt off so you can put some sunburn lotion on my backside."

"Um, okaaay."

She gave me that same shy-smile along with a bottle of oil, pulled off her nightshirt, and lay on her belly. The moonlight enhanced her beauty to a disorienting level.

With my faltering motor control, I jerkily rubbed the slippery stuff onto her back, stopping short of her back*side*.

"How's that?"

"You missed something—my bum is *burning!* Rub me there."

She was right—it actually was quite red, her skin hot. I started rubbing perhaps too vigorously when she said, "*Ow!* It's tender. Slow down, use more oil, and do it gently—we have the whole night."

I took a deep breath and found a slower rhythm, remembering that massage I got at the Japanese inn. I added more of the oily lotion, tried long, deeper strokes, and continued almost mindlessly. She muttered softly, "Ahhh, betterrrr." Her approving grunts helped calm me down, but only a little. Then she wiggled her legs slightly apart and raised her butt almost imperceptibly. She said, "Now, a little lower..."

I hesitated, took a deep breath, then proceeded into places I knew nothing about.

"Still lower, yes, and to the left...*Ooohh.* Now lower yet...*Yessss.* More oil... *Ooh*...right there. *Ahhh,* don't stop..."

Jeeeez!

My mind was completely elsewhere, my body tumbling into a whirlwind of physical sensations. Lane tensed up and finally let out a tiny squeal, then another, and another.

After a while she lay there, quiet, and I settled beside her. She very slowly turned to look at me with a dreamlike grin and simply said,

"*Wow!*"

My frantic heart had only begun to slow down when she tugged at my shirt. "Okay Gordy, now it's my turn to do you. Take it all off and lie down!" While trading places, I was aware of my 'erection' (what a weird word) but I was thankful she pretended not to notice. Once I was on my stomach she straddled my legs and methodically rubbed the lotion into the skin on my back, my neck, my arms. Her touch felt caring, soothing, loving.

"Anything more?"

"Uh, my butt?"

"Ah, I *allllmost* forgot." (I knew she was grinning.) She moved over to my side, and gently rubbed the oil into my burned skin. *Oh, soooo soothing.* Then ever so gently, she slid her fingers down between my legs, nudging them gently apart, and did some other things until I was close to exploding.

How did she know *this stuff?*

She must have read my mind, because she bent down to my ear and whispered, "Remember I told you how I learned kissing from Vermilion? Well, I learned some other stuff from my older cousin Sukey. She always came along when me mum's sister visited us in West

Putney, and she always slept in my bed. Sukey was crazy about making out, especially with girls, and she knew I was curious."

Still addled by Lane's 'treatment', I muttered into the pillow, "Yeah, she must have been a very thorough teacher."

Lane laughed, then sprawled herself on top of me and applied her lips to my neck once again. Her weight and warmth and bare skin all felt more than caring. It was wonderful.

"Well," I croaked, trying to breathe, "I'm glad you know some things, 'cause I've been feeling like a klutzy zombie."

"Don't worry for a minute," she said. "You're learnin' fast and I love you 'cause you're you."

She moved off, then I rolled onto my side, and we just looked at each other. Then she snuggled up and gave me the longest kiss on record. Her smile, and her body, told me all was warm and well.

Ah…

Then she nudged me onto my back and started kissing my, ah, nipples. She lingered over one, then the other, licking and gently munching with her lips.

Ohhhhhh!

She straddled my middle again and leaned forward. "Now kiss mine!"

I stared at her a moment, befuddled with wonder.

I can't believe I'm doing this.

They tasted a little salty, but doing it was so…comforting! She moaned again, closed her eyes, then opened them again with a fierce, dark look. She wiggled around on my…on me, until I felt suddenly swallowed up, and I knew things were going beyond my control.

Ooohh, jeeeez.

Just as I sensed I was reaching that point of no return, she stopped, put a finger on my lips, and slowly lifted off to pull something out of her pack.

"You know how these work, right?"

I looked at the tiny foil envelope she was dangling.

"Yeah," I said. "I remember that lecture in our Loving class last year. I guess I didn't think about that when we were packing."

"Well, my mum sure thought of it."

After I got the thing on, we fumbled about, both of us asking, *Is this okay?* And, *How does this feel?* But we somehow found a rhythm, mixed with a lot of kissing, and we finally succumbed to nature's intentions. At least that's how Lane described it.

I couldn't begin to.

Later, I thought she might laugh at me, but I said it anyway, "What a cool mum you have."

"Yeah," she said with a giggle. "She gave me two dozen!"

*

In the next few days, we roamed the coast looking for isolated ruins and anything strange or beautiful on the beaches. Beachcombing and random wandering were two of Lane's favorite pastimes, as they were mine. We enjoyed poking around anything that looked old, abandoned, or both.

We found plenty.

The ruins called Benbow and Salishan might have once been small towns or outposts. Each had a distinctive round stone tower, partially crumbled but in better shape than the surrounding rubble-piles of one-time houses. I thought of mentioning these towers to Roselin but then decided maybe not for a while.

The beaches were rich with multicolored abalone, sea-snail, and pearly-white nautilus shells. The hills and headlands were blanketed with poppies, lupine and red miandra.

We ate snacks in front of watchful lemurs and swam in the surf whenever the urges occurred to us. We camped on different beaches or on grassy meadows out of the wind and under those brilliant stars.

On nights when we weren't preoccupied exploring each other, we talked until the sky got light, or listened to owls calling each other in the nearby canyons. We even brought a supply of comic books, and I read maybe one.

One night Lane described her dad. "He was always busy, it seemed, and he never had time for me. But one day when I was seven he took me out for lunch at a café—for the first time ever. Well, over lunch he told me his whole life story, then he said he was leaving."

"Whoa, sounds kind of familiar," I said.

"But I remembered his story, word-for-word."

"Do you miss him?"

"Not really. He was hardly home at all—had a job building roads for the Russians, at least according to his stories."

I told Lane about 'mad-dad Leon', as I called him, and about Ricky's surfing, and my mom's all-night parties when she was feeling good.

The talking was nice, but what I loved best was holding each other in blissful exhaustion until we fell asleep.

*

On Day Seven, we were dragging our feet back to Gifford, sunburned, muscles aching, sleep-deprived. Just as we passed the NEVERMORE sign at the path junction, the Hum swept over us—a full choir this time. It echoed off the hillsides, then swooped low and swirled around us in ever deepening tones. We had to sit down! I believe it visited at just the right time to recharge our batteries.

Maybe it was Hum energy or just an impulse, but right then Lane locked her eyes on mine with such an intense gaze of loving-kindness I nearly tumbled over.

But I held her gaze.

WHERE YER PEOPLE ARE

When Lane and I finally reached Janie's backyard, we could barely take another step—Hum-visits only revive one for so long. We shrugged off our packs and boots, and fell into the old wooden chairs around the fire pit. Sebastian's beady eyes watched us from his jungle-lined pool.

We put up our feet, releasing all that tension from hours of hiking. *Aaaahhh,* we both moaned.

Alan came out of his shop, his hair dusty from sanding. "I thought I heard voices. Welcome home, both of you! You look like you could use some refreshments, yes?"

Before we could reply, he brushed off his clothes, disappeared into the kitchen and soon returned with tall juice drinks and a platter of meats, cheeses and crackers.

He sat down. "Did you two hear the Hum earlier today? I was sitting out here with Sebastian, who usually ignores it. But this time he immediately stood on his haunches at full alert, as if listening to a secret code. There is a lot about him we don't know."

"Oh, I'm sure there is," said Lane, looking toward the otter's pool. "And I see you in there, Sebastian." The otter slowly blinked his eyes, like an approving cat.

"And, yes," I added, "the Hum was powerful out there. We had to sit a minute."

Alan assembled a cracker. "So, you look like you both had a quite a walk..."

We glanced at eachother, took a drink of juice, then sat back and relayed (some) of our adventures on the Nevermore coast.

When we paused he said, almost wistfully, "I've enjoyed a few walks out there myself, including a memorable trip with Sharyl, though that was a few years ago. Say, Janie and Vermilion will want to hear about your exploits too—they're around somewhere."

Just then the two emerged from the *hoot* looking wrinkled and sleepy.

"Hey guys, we heard the ruckus out here," said Janie. Vermilion only smiled.

Without hesitating, Alan returned to the kitchen and soon brought out more glasses and a pitcher of what he called his 'mystery juice'.

Janie settled in a chair next to Vermilion, studied Lane and me a moment and said, "So…how was it?"

"Fine."

She was about to fire off more questions when a voice called out, "Hey, travelers!"

"Mum!" said Lane.

Meredith and Sheryl, wearing wide-brimmed bush-hats, walked into the yard carrying string-bags of groceries. We pulled ourselves up to greet them with hugs.

All this hugging…I love it!

"Ooh, Lane, you could use a bath," said Meredith.

"Mu-uum!"

"You, too, Gordy," said Sheryl. "You reek of campfire smoke."

I rolled my eyes at Lane.

I'll want to hear *all* about your trip to Nevermore," Janie said.

*

Sheryl took the groceries inside, then came back with more glasses, a big bottle of Leninade and another of zinfandel. "Spritzers anyone?"

She and Meredith had just settled down with their drinks when Sheryl happened to look out towards the bay. "I wonder who that might be?"

We all took in the two bush-hatted figures wearing large backpacks walking up the path towards the gate.

"Looks like we'll need more chairs," said Alan.

Janie immediately recognized one of them. "Roselin!"

"And Eddie!" I shouted.

Everyone got up.

"Heeey, Janie," Roselin said, beaming a wide grin. "And Vermilion and Meredith and Gordy and Lane! We've hit the jackpot, Eddie!"

Alan then spotted the tall-masted schooner anchored in Gifford Bay. "Ah," he said, "They must have arrived on the mail boat."

Meredith added, "I'm glad it's my day off today or I'd be out there unloading mail…"

We all stood up as Janie announced, "Family! This is Roselin, and Roselin, meet me dad, Alan, and me mum, Sheryl.

Roselin dropped her gear, greeted Sheryl and Alan with her gracious smile, gave me a quick grin, then wrapped Janie and Vermilion in long hugs. She said quietly to Vermilion, "I'm glad you and Janie are safe. I think she really needed you back there."

Vermilion grinned. "I think I needed her too."

Eddie was doing his best to look dignified. He had slowly set his pack on the ground as all eyes fell upon him.

"Now," Roselin said, "I want all of you to meet a friend of Gordy's, and also of mine, Eddie Barnes."

A collective *Aahh*.

Eddie took off his hat and bowed, revealing a much shaggier thatch of hair than I remembered. Truly delighted, he reached out for everyone's hands in turn, giving mine a comforting squeeze. "I'm very pleased to meet you all."

He turned to Janie and said, "Roselin and Gordy have told me a lot about you."

"And Gordy hasn't told me near enough about *you*!" said Janie.

We laughed.

Alan, the perfect host, brought out more chairs from his shop, and more bottles and glasses from the kitchen. He then offered, juice, wine or spritzers to Roselin and Eddie, who, after a long sigh, both simply said, *"Yes, please!"*

*

Everyone had settled, glasses in hand when I happened to glance at Roselin. She exhaled a deep breath and gave us all a long look.

"I cannot keep this inside any longer. I must relay some news."

Everyone sat still.

"It's about Louise."

Uh oh...

"After Eddie and I visited the Desert Tribes and the Dreamland, I decided we should return to Wild North and catch the mail boat to come here. By then, Samantha had returned, and the place seemed as if she never left at all. It was a big relief that we could simply be guests there...but I digress.

"We had caught the *Meridian,* the same boat that took Gordy and I to Gottfried Island, and were sailing north when we ran into fog near the Sumbitch Islands," she said. "We had been drifting for several hours and I was leaning on the railing, staring at nothing when a shifty-eyed sailor joined me, who, I soon realized, loved to gossip. And you know how *everyone* on this Island gossips."

We raised our glasses, nervously agreeing.

"He and I shared a few helpings of honey-mead, or mostly he did, and we traded stories. Anyway, he began to rattle on about how, some several voyages back, a female passenger met a 'bad end'. Without too much prodding, the sailor described the woman, right down to her frizzy hair and wandering eye."

"Louise!" whispered Janie.

"Yes. According to the sailor, the captain was alerted by radio to look for 'three fugitives wanted for antiquities theft'. This must have happened right after you and I were put ashore, Gordy. Mr. Hadley apparently radioed back that he (correctly) had but one passenger fitting that description. I don't think he volunteered anything more."

"Whoa—he really covered for us," I said.

"Yes, he did. The chatty sailor told me that he, personally, was ordered to confine the 'waggle-eyed woman', as he called her, to her stateroom for the duration of the trip. She was brought all the way 'round to Putney—a twelve-day journey. At the dock, he and two other crew members were ordered to blindfold her, bind her hands, and march her off the boat.

"He told me that two large fellows in business suits and a spooky woman in a hooded coat were waiting there. I'm sure that was Adeline Brewer and the two guys that came after us. They must have remembered something after all."

Roselin took a deep breath. "Then that sleazeball sailor laughed as he told me that once she was off the boat, she tried to run and fell right off the dock. I could have smacked him, but I had to hear the end of it. He said, 'With her hands bound, she foundered in the water. One of the men shot at 'er several times'."

A thick silence. Eddie gripped Roselin's hand.

"Then the sailor added, and I quote, 'Dark as pitch it were. The woman on the pier yelled at the men to *get that book*, and made them dive after her, suits an' all. But they never found her, nor the book'."

A long silence.

Alan quietly said, "I listen to the news in my shop most every day, and I don't remember hearing any mention of a shooting in Putney Harbor."

"I'm sure it was hushed-up, Alan," said Sheryl, "just like so many other 'unconfirmed rumors' involving those Russians."

Janie looked around at everyone, her eyes shining. "I worked with Louise for six months at the Soviet navy base cafeteria down in Kronstadt. I liked her and admired her for standing up to the occasional creep we had to serve there. Did you know she freed Gordy from his cell? She took the chance because she immediately saw his Hum awareness—in an American, no less."

Roselin added, "And when Louise later told me about Gordy, I knew I had to meet him myself."

"Ah," Lane said to me, squeezing my hand. "So *that's* how you met Roselin."

*

The sun had set, leaving a pinkish dusk over the bay. We sat in a thoughtful hush for a while as we watched tiny lights blinking on as lamps were being lit on the *Meridian*.

Roselin set her glass down. "Okay, I'll say one more thing about this whole affair. That sailor must have had good ears because he told me that the woman, Adeline, later boasted to her associates that they had 'finally neutralized the witch.' I have a feeling Adeline assumed that Louise was *me*."

More silence.

"Apparently, Mr. Hadley never told anyone about us. After the incident on the dock, I could understand why he dared not return to Gottfried Island to resupply us. One day, I'll go out to his ship and thank him!"

"Do ya think, they, ah, closed the case then?" said Janie.

Roselin thought a moment. "They will always want the Codex. The sailor said that afterwards, they nearly tore the boat apart looking for it."

"But now we know that Adeline is in Moscow happily trying to translate the Ur library," said Eddie. "I have a feeling she'll be staring at microfilm for a long time."

"Then here's to Mr. Hadley!" Janie said.

We raised a silent toast to the *Meridian's* captain. Roselin looked more at peace than I'd seen in her for quite a while.

I asked her, "So, uh, do you still have the Codex?"

She took a long sip of her wine, smiled, and glanced at Eddie. "When we were in the Dreamland, we found a way to solve my problem not only with the Codex, but also my translated notes. It was the hardest thing to do, to put all that research away."

"So, what'd ya do with them?" Janie asked.

"Can't tell you. Not that I *won't* tell you, I really *can't* tell you. All I can say is that being a witch inside Roger's Dreamland has certain advantages."

"A toast to Roger's Dreamland!" said Eddie.

*

"I think we could use a bit of supper," Sheryl said. "Anyone want to help?" Alan, Janie, Vermilion and Meredith all nodded, slowly got up and followed her while carrying glasses and bottles.

Eddie and Roselin stayed with Lane and me, and the backyard suddenly grew quiet.

"Gordy," Roselin said, "Eddie and I want to share some ideas with you."

Eddie added, "Maybe we can talk a little later, yes?"

I paused as Lane gave me a quizzical look.

"Okay," I said.

I hope they're not running off again soon.

We all sat quietly while I speculated on what they might have in mind. Finally Sheryl called out, "Supper's ready!"

After a very chatty meal in the crowded kitchen, we all wandered back to the yard with mugs of hot tea in hand. Dusk had brought that familiar evening chill off the ocean, prompting Alan to build a fire in the pit.

We sat with our tea as a few stars began to appear.

Then Sheryl said, "I've only heard snippets about you, Roselin, and I'm curious about your whole Gottfried Island expedition."

Alan added, "Gottfried…I've heard stories of a curse."

"An' I wanna hear more about you and Eddie!" said Janie.

Roselin looked thoughtfully at the fire, then at the stars, sipping from her mug.

"Well," she began, "the haunted-island stories probably made Gottfried a very good hiding place. I didn't believe in the curse at first, but we *did* experience some strange things there." Her voice momentarily faltered. "It was a hard time for me, and for Gordy too. I finally had the Codex, but I had also realized how dangerous its contents were. After years of translating it, then after studying the physics, I found out it was surprisingly easy to harness the Hum as an energy source."

She took a long sip of her tea. "And you know what happened at Biganess."

"Oh, yes," said Alan. "We felt an earthquake and then that awful howling sound. I hope I never hear that again."

"Well, that explosion was *my* fault. I had foolishly allowed the Biganess tribe to develop a lamp using Hum energy. The Codex contained a formula that I *thought* would work, but it was evidently faulty, a disastrous failure."

"Ah, like that lamp that Isabella gave me…" Sheryl whispered to me. "Is it still in…?" I shook my head.

Roselin's face turned dark with that same anguish I saw back on Gottfried.

Don't go back there, Roselin. Please!

She let out a deep breath as if shaking something off. "After a few weeks on the island, the weight of it was eating me up. Gordy, bless his heart, was a wonderful companion through a very dark time."

She looked at me with a deep, soulful gaze, then nodded toward Eddie. "Then this guy showed up in a sailboat two weeks later, and rescued Gordy and me from Gottfried. I still don't exactly know how he found us, but I'm so glad he did!

"When we decided it was safe to return, we made plans to travel over our main Island. I wanted to show Eddie the Desert Wonder Tribes and Roger's Dreamland. Gordy rode with us on the bus as far as the Wild Women tribe, where we left him to continue on to Gifford."

Janie said, "I get this weird feeling you and Eddie knew each other from some other time."

"I've had that feeling too, Janie. But Eddie says he doesn't think so. He claims he only traveled here to see Gordy, and check out the Island."

Eddie looked suddenly shy, while Roselin looked up at the stars with that Cheshire-cat grin.

Janie didn't miss a thing.

*

The fire had reduced itself to glowing embers, the tea was gone, and we were all nodding off.

Then on some unspoken cue we all roused ourselves and slowly got up. Janie and Vermilion mumbled good-night and returned to the *hoot*. Lane gave me a sleepy long hug and a smooch before she and Meredith started their walk home. Sheryl and Alan decided to take an evening stroll along Elsinore Bay.

All was quiet, though I felt a tingle that something was up.

Eddie looked at Roselin, then they both looked at me. Eddie said, "Can we talk?"

"Sure!" We all sat down again.

"You first, Mister Barnes," said Roselin.

Eddie took a breath. "While we were in the desert, Roselin and I had many long talks about a lot of subjects, and one of them was you."

"Me?"

"Yes, you. Now I've known you since you were, what, eleven? I've come to admire you, Gordy, and I'll be *forever* thankful to you for saving Roselin's life out there on Gottfried."

I stared straight ahead, smiling. *Okayyy.*

"I think you and I have always had a special kind of connection. I could sense something when you first came to my house to watch me build—an energy that I hadn't felt from anyone so young before. And when I met Roselin, there it was again, although different in certain ways, of course…"

His words felt wonderful, but my eyes kept wanting to close.

Such a long day.

Roselin gave me a nudge. "Hey Gordy, he's leading up to something."

I nodded, eyes still closed.

Eddie continued, "Roselin and I are planning to marry sometime later this year…"

Marry?

"…and, you don't have to decide right now, but we would like you to come live with us—as our adopted son."

My eyes snapped open. "You want to *adopt* me?"

"Yes!"

Tears welled up as I tried to take this in. "I-uh, wow you guys, that would be wonderful, and also you being married!"

Then I thought about Ricky. "Uhh, there's this one thing. Ricky is wondering when I'm coming back to California, and I haven't said anything yet. I'm afraid I might hurt his feelings if I stay here instead."

Without hesitation Eddie said, "I'm sure Ricky will be fine. The important thing is to ask yourself what *you* need."

Roselin added, "It will be a while before we even have a place to live. We'd like to build a house, and we're going to look for a building site. Though we've only been here a few hours, I have a very good feeling about Gifford.

"We even took a walk around town on our way up from the boat," said Eddie.

Gifford? My mind raced with possibilities—*Lane and Janie will both be close by, and no more wandering!*

Then Eddie said, "Wanna help us build the house?"

"Yeah, wow, absolutely!"

Eddie switched chairs so they could hold each of my hands, and we all huddled under a blanket Roselin had found. The embers were still warm.

What an evening.

We were still staring at the brilliant sky when Alan and Sheryl returned. "You all look like you're up to something." said Sheryl.

Though half-asleep, I said, "Roselin and Eddie want to adopt me."

Sheryl's eyebrows went straight up. "Alan, didn't I say something like this might happen?"

"Yes you did. Now let's make up a bed for our travelers."

*

After a very late breakfast, I ran almost all the way to Lane's house to tell her the news. I found her inside doing her homework. "Hey Lane, Roselin and Eddie are getting married, and they want to adopt me!"

Lane's eyes went wide with alarm. "So you're going off to live with them?"

"Yes, but here's the best part. They want to build a house in Gifford! Roselin told me they are going to book a room at the Pleiades Inn, not far from MacEvoy's and will stay there until they find a site to build on."

Lane was speechless, then...

"*Eeee!* Gordy, that's *wonderful!*" She jumped up and grabbed me in a hug. "And I want to help! I've always liked to watch houses being built, and have wanted to try it. Maybe Eddie will teach me carpentry in trade for bringing lunches."

I grinned at her eagerness. "Great idea! I'm sure he'll be happy to teach you."

*

Later that day I was finally ready to finish the letter to Ricky that I had tried to write several weeks ago.

Dear Ricky,   Aug 1 , '65

I found your letters! Thanks for writing and telling me what happened. It must have been awfully hard for you! I'm glad Mr. Barnes was there to help you get through it.

You'll never believe this, but Mr. Barnes is HERE! He first traveled to Australia, then somehow found me and my friend Roselin on a way-out-there island called Gottfried. That was lucky because we were stuck there! He then brought us back to the main Island on a little sailboat.

Eddie told me about Mom before I found your letters. I was terribly sad for weeks until I had this strange experience where Mom sort-of talked to me. In her own way, she told me she was actually mad at the world, not you or me. She said she loved us, and you and I should carry on and be happy!

Roselin, by the way, is a real witch, and she's nice. She makes medicines from plants and also studies archeology and something called quantum mechanics.

Okay, here is the real news: Roselin and Mr. Barnes just told me they are getting married. and they want to <u>adopt</u> me.

I hope this doesn't sound too weird. Roselin really isn't the kind of witch you might think of. And I'm really happy being here with them. And this Island is kind of like California was, or maybe could have been, a long time ago. You'd probably like it (and the surf) if you ever come to visit.

So I want to stay here, and I guess I will be staying anyway because I don't know how I'd ever get home, even if I wanted to.

I'm glad you're okay, and you can have my room.

And 'Rick' sounds cool, but I'll still call you Ricky if that's okay.

Love,

Gordy

TWO MONTHS LATER

We were enjoying a weekend break during the house construction. Alan had encouraged Eddie to build with stone, and recommended a local mason, Elaine Darby, who knew her business. She has been quite the taskmaster, and our working lives have been entirely in her service—selecting, hauling, even shaping the stones with chisels, then placing the finished blocks within her reach. Lane, Roselin and I were all beginning to look like weightlifters! Eddie has been carefully watching the mason's methods, wanting to learn the process while hauling stone with the rest of us.

Glad for our break, I slept until noon. The smell of sausage-and-leek soup finally roused me enough to join Sheryl, Vermilion and Janie for lunch in the kitchen.

Janie glanced up. "Wow, Gords, yer lookin' good! All that haulin' and heftin' stone seems to agree with yer."

I smiled, basking in her approval.

Sheryl said, "I'm glad Eddie and Roselin found a building site so close by. Alan and I were able to sponsor them for their tribe membership, and they walked all over the village while consulting land records. They were lucky to find a site with no previous claim to it."

"The tribe *gave* them a lot to build on?" I said.

"Well, almost," said Sheryl. "Building sites in the villages are held in common by the tribes, and any tribe member can apply for a site, as long as they intend to live on it. There are, of course, the fees for the deed and plat-mapping."

Maybe someday *we* could build a house, Janes," said Vermilion.

Then Alan walked in from his daily trip to the post office, waving a folded newspaper. "This copy of the *Island Socialist Review* just arrived off the mail boat." He sat with us, opened the paper and said, "I never buy this Soviet rag, but I had to when I saw this article."

We read it twice before Janie said, "Roselin will definitely want to see this!"

A RADIO DISTURBANCE

The loyal workers at radio station KSOV reported several on-air disruptions last week. On at least four occasions, normal broadcasting was replaced by a curious humming sound.

Workers reported that the sound rang through the broadcasting rooms as well.

Soviet naval sources also reported 'suspicious malfunctions' in their telephone system at about the same time. Soviet Central Intelligence has informed us that American radar and tracking stations in the Indian Ocean were similarly interrupted.

Authorities are working around the clock to determine the source of these interruptions. Many radio listeners called in to say that they found the melodious humming to be quite pleasant, and hoped to hear more of these 'concerts'.

However, such disruptions are being taken most seriously. If anyone has any information regarding a suspected perpetrator, please contact the Naval Communications Office in Kronstadt, telephone number 7667.

When Roselin later saw the article, all she said was, *"Louise?"* "That's just who I was thinking of," said Janie.

*

That afternoon, Lane and I walked out to the beach with Janie and Vermilion. Our mission was to first body-surf and then to bring back firewood—a potluck dinner was planned for tonight at MacEvoys.

It was our first gathering in about a month. The four of us, plus Roselin, Eddie, Alan and Sheryl, all sat around the backyard fire with supper on our laps. We chatted mostly about house-building progress, especially about keeping up with 'typhoon' Darby, the hired mason. Eddie added that he and Alan will be installing the doors and windows soon.

We'd all seen the Radio Disturbance story and the conversation soon shifted to Louise. In spite of all her shenanigans, we were glad to think she might still be alive.

After supper, all the elders had retired. Vermilion, Janie, Lane and I had scootched our chairs together, and rested our bare feet on the firepit stones. They were kept warm by the still- glowing embers as we began to doze off.

The telltale squeak of a bicycle-wheeled cart slowly penetrated my half-asleep brain. Still in a fog, I looked down the path to see a rather tall fellow slowly approaching from the bay. He was pushing a felix-hauler loaded with a large travel bag and a surfboard.

Janie squinted toward the fellow and said, "Who's that?"

"Dunno," said Lane and Vermilion.

He walked into the dim light of our lantern and paused.

I looked at him and began to grin with growing recognition. He had longer hair and more freckles than ever.

When he saw me, he broke into his own familiar grin.

"Hey, twerp!"

MEANWHILE, ON ANDROMEDA

Hum energy released by the 'incident' at Biganess had just passed through the Andromeda Galaxy, 2.537 million light years away. The initial blue bolt of pure Hum, originally 0.23 inches in diameter, had expanded to over twelve light years across by the time it reached the galaxy's outer arms. This was a wide-enough swath to gently penetrate the atmospheres of 2.2 *billion* potentially life-supporting planets—those solid, wet, Earth-sized ones that aren't too hot nor too cold. Though Roselin knew that Hum energy travels far faster than the speed of light, she was nevertheless impressed.

Roselin also learned, some years later, that the Hum's highly energized wave-particles struck certain proteins floating in the warm oceans and watery muck of 7,164 of those planets, triggering mutations that would eventually alter their surfaces for a very long time.

New life.

Or maybe it was closer to 8,000 planets. Roselin needed to check her updates.

Ommmmmmmm.

And the sage said,
"You were here once, you just don't remember."

APPRECIATION

I've always wanted to write a book about the plausible impossible, and this is it! I humbly thank my family and my many readers and friends who encouraged me to keep working on this story, which began to take shape in 2018—seven years before its first publication! I also thank the Kaukauna Write Club and the Kaukauna Public Library for their support. Thanks also to Betsy Krizenesky for her assistance with Russian translation, and Owen Duescher for proofreading the novel.

Lee (Rusty) Mothes

ABOUT THE AUTHOR

Lee Mothes has always been fascinated with new ways of experiencing the world. His avid interest in alternative lifestyles, imaginary geography, and Tolkien's worlds have inspired him to create The Commonwealth of New Island, the location of *The Hum*. Lee lives in Wisconsin, USA, and frequently visits the coasts of California and Oregon, his inspirational homeland.

If you would like to visit New Island, explore

The New Island Guidebook
available on Amazon/Lee Mothes

or go to

www.newisland.net
www.oceansanddreams.com
Instagram: @leemothes

The Hum is available on Amazon.com
and IngramSpark.com.